PHILIPPA GREGORY

THE BOLEYN
INHERITANCE

HARPER

Harper
An imprint of HarperCollins*Publishers*
77–85 Fulham Palace Road,
Hammersmith, London W6 8JB

www.harpercollins.co.uk

This production 2011

First published by in Great Britain
by HarperCollins*Publishers* 2006

A catalogue record for this book
is available from the British Library

ISBN 978 0 00 791525 5

Set in Minion by Palimpsest Book Production Limited,
Grangemouth, Stirlingshire

Printed and bound in Great Britain by
Clays Ltd, St Ives plc

For Anthony

Jane Boleyn, Blickling Hall, Norfolk, July 1539

It is hot today, the wind blows over the flat fields and marshes with the stink of the plague. In weather like this, if my husband were still with me, we would not be trapped in one place, watching a leaden dawn and a sunset of dull red; we would be travelling with the king's court, on progress through the weald and downland of Hampshire and Sussex, the richest and most beautiful countryside in all of England, riding high on the hilly roads and looking out for the first sight of the sea. We would be out hunting every morning, dining under the thick canopy of the trees at midday and dancing in the great hall of some country house at night in the yellow light of flickering torches. We were friends with the greatest families in the land, we were the favourites of the king, kin to the queen. We were beloved; we were the Boleyns, the most beautiful, sophisticated family at the court. Nobody knew George without desiring him, nobody could resist Anne, everyone courted me as a passport to their attention. George was dazzling, dark-haired, dark-eyed and handsome, always mounted on the finest horses, always at the side of the queen. Anne was at the peak of her beauty and her wits, as alluring as dark honey. And I went everywhere with them.

The two of them used to ride together, racing, neck and neck like lovers, and I could hear their laughter over the thudding of the hooves as they went flying by. Sometimes, when I saw them

1

together, so rich, so young, so beautiful, I couldn't tell which of them I loved more.

All the court was besotted with the two of them, those dark Boleyn flirtatious looks, their high living: such gamblers, such lovers of risk; both so fervent for their reform of the church, so quick and clever in argument, so daring in their reading and thoughts. From the king to the kitchenmaid there was not one person who was not dazzled by the pair of them. Even now, three years on, I cannot believe that we will never see them again. Surely, a couple so young, so radiant with life, cannot simply die? In my mind, in my heart, they are still riding out together, still young, still beautiful. And why would I not passionately long for this to be true? It has only been three years since I last saw them; three years, two months and nine days since his careless fingers brushed against mine, and he smiled and said 'Good day, wife, I must go, I have everything to do today,' and it was a May Day morning and we were preparing for the tournament. I knew he and his sister were in trouble, but I did not know how much.

Every day in this new life of mine I walk to the crossroads in the village, where there is a dirty milestone to the London road. Picked out in mud and lichen, the carving says 'London, 120 miles'. It is such a long way, such a long way away. Every day I bend down and touch it, like a talisman, and then I turn back again to my father's house, which is now so small to me, who has lived in the king's greatest palaces. I live on my brother's charity, on the goodwill of his wife who cares nothing for me, on a pension from Thomas Cromwell the upstart moneylender, who is the king's new great friend. I am a poor neighbour living in the shadow of the great house that was once my own, a Boleyn house, one of our many houses. I live quietly, cheaply, like a widow with no house of my own that no man wants.

And this is because I am a widow with no house of my own that no man wants. A woman of nearly thirty years old, with a face scored by disappointment, mother to an absent son, a widow without prospect of re-marriage, the sole survivor of an unlucky family, heiress to scandal.

My dream is that one day this luck will change. I will see a messenger in Howard livery riding down this very road, bringing a letter for me, a letter from the Duke of Norfolk, to summon me back to court, to tell me that there is work for me to do again: a queen to serve, secrets to whisper, plots to hatch, the unending double-dealing life of a courtier, at which he is so expert, and I am his greatest pupil. My dream is that the world will change again, swing topsy-turvy until we are uppermost once more, and I am restored. I saved the duke once, when we were in the worst danger, and in return he saved me. Our great sorrow was that we could not save the two of them, the two who now ride and laugh and dance only in my dreams. I touch the milestone once more, and imagine that tomorrow the messenger will come. He will hold out a paper, sealed with the Howard crest deep and shiny in the red wax. 'A message for Jane Boleyn, the Viscountess Rochford?' he will ask, looking at my plain kirtle and the dust on the hem of my gown, my hand stained with dirt from the London milestone.

'I will take it,' I shall say. 'I am her. I have been waiting for ever.' And I shall take it in my dirty hand: my inheritance.

Anne, Duchess of Cleves, Duren, Cleves, July 1539

I hardly dare to breathe. I am as still as a block, a smile stuck on my face, my eyes wide open, looking boldly at the artist, appearing, I hope, trustworthy, my frank stare indicating honesty but not immodesty. My borrowed jewels are the best that my mother could lay her hands on, designed to show to a critical viewer that we are not quite paupers, even though my brother will offer no dowry to pay a husband. The king will have to choose me for my pleasant appearance and political connections. I have nothing else to offer. But he must choose me. I am absolutely determined that he will choose me. It is everything to me to get away from here.

On the other side of the room, carefully not observing my portrait forming under the painter's quick, sweeping strokes of the crayon, is my sister, awaiting her turn. God forgive me, but I pray that the king does not choose her. She is eager as me for the chance to leave Cleves, and to leap to such greatness as the throne of England; but she does not need it as I do. No girl in the world can need it as I do.

Not that I will speak so much as one word against my brother, nothing now, and nothing in the years to come. I will never say anything against him. He is a model son to my mother, and a worthy successor to the dukedom of Cleves. During the last months of my poor father's life, when he was clearly as mad as any fool, it was my brother who wrestled him into his chamber, locked the door from the outside and publicly gave out that he had a fever. It was my brother who forbade my mother to summon physicians or even preachers to expel the devils that occupied my poor father's wandering brains. It was my brother, cunning – like an ox is cunning, in a slow mean way – who said that we must claim my father was a drunkard rather than allow the taint of madness to diminish our family reputation. We will not make our way in the world if there is suspicion against our blood. But if we slander our own father, call him a sot, having denied him the help that he so desperately needed, then we may yet rise. This way I will make a good marriage. This way my sister will make a good marriage. This way my brother can make a good marriage and the future of our house is assured, even though my father fought his demons alone, and without help.

Hearing my father whimper at the door of his chamber that he was a good boy now, and would we let him out? Hearing my brother answer so steadily and so firmly that he could not come out, I wondered then if actually we had it all wrong, and my brother was already as mad as my father, my mother too, and the only sane one in this household was me, since I alone was dumb with horror at what we were doing. But I didn't tell anyone that thought, either.

Since my earliest childhood I have served under my brother's discipline. He was always to be duke of these lands sheltered between the rivers of the Meuse and the Rhine. A small enough patrimony; but one so well-placed that every power of Europe seeks our friendship: France, the Hapsburg Spanish and Austrians, the Holy Roman Emperor, the Pope himself, and now Henry of England. Cleves is the keyhole to the heart of Europe, and the Duke of Cleves is the key. No wonder that my brother values himself so highly, he is right to value himself so highly; it is only I who sometimes wonder if he is not, in truth, a petty princeling seated below the salt at the grand banquet which is Christendom. But I tell no-one I think this, not even my sister Amelia. I do not trust anyone very readily.

He commands my mother by right of the greatness of his position in the world and she is his Lord Chamberlain, his Major Domo, his Pope. With her blessing, my brother commands my sister and myself because he is the son and the heir and we are burdens. He is a young man with a future of power and opportunity and we are young women destined to be either wives and mothers at the very best; or spinster-parasites at the worst. My older sister Sybilla has already escaped; she left home as soon as she could, as soon as her marriage could be arranged, she is now free of the tyranny of fraternal attention. I have to go next. It has to be me next. I must be freed. They cannot be so pointlessly cruel to me to send Amelia in my place. Her chance will come, her time will come. But I am the next sister in line, it has to be me. I cannot imagine why they even offered Amelia, unless it was to frighten me into greater subservience. If so, it has worked. I am terrified that I will be overlooked for a younger girl, and my brother has let this come about. In truth, he ignores his own best interests to torment me.

My brother is a petty duke, in every sense of the word. When my father died, still whispering for someone to open the door, my brother stepped into his shoes but can never fill them. My father was a man in the wider world, he attended the courts of France and Spain, he travelled in Europe. My brother, staying at home as he has done, thinks that the world can show him nothing greater than his own duchy. He thinks there is no greater book than the Bible, no better church than one with bare walls, no better guide than his own conscience. With only a small household to rule, his command falls very heavily on very few servants. With only a small inheritance, he is alert to the needs of his own dignity, and I, who lack dignity, feel the full weight of his. When he is drunk or happy he calls me the most rebellious of his subjects and pets me with a heavy hand. When he is sober or irritated he says that I am a girl who does not know her place and threatens to lock me in my room.

This is no empty threat in Cleves today. This is a man who locked up his own father. I think he is quite capable of imprisoning me. And if I cried at the door, would anyone let me out?

Master Holbein indicates to me with one curt nod of his head that I can leave my seat and my sister can take my place. I am not allowed to look at my portrait. None of us may see what he sends to the king in England. He is not here to flatter us, nor paint us as beauties. He is here to sketch as accurate a representation as his genius can produce, so that the King of England can see which of us he would like, as if we were Flanders mares coming to the English stallion at stud.

Master Holbein, who leans back as my sister bustles forwards, takes a fresh sheet of paper, examines the point of his pastel crayon. Master Holbein has seen us all, all of the candidates for the post of Queen of England. He has painted Christina of Milan and Louise of Guise, Marie of Vendôme and Anne of Guise. So I am not the first young woman whose nose he has measured with his crayon held at arm's length and one eye squinting. For all I know, there will be another girl after my sister Amelia. He may stop off in France on his way home to England to scowl at another simpering girl and capture her likeness and delineate her faults. There is no point in my feeling demeaned, like a piece of fustian laid out for the pattern, by this process.

'Do you not like being painted? Are you shy?' he asked me gruffly as my smile faded when he looked at me like a piece of meat on the cook's draining slab.

I did not tell him what I felt. There is no sense in offering information to a spy. 'I want to marry him,' was all I said. He raised an eyebrow.

'I just paint the pictures,' he remarked. 'You had better tell your desire to his envoys, Ambassadors Nicholas Wotton and Richard Beard. No point telling me.'

I sit in the window-seat, hot in my best clothes, constricted by a stomacher pulled so tight that it took two maids hauling on the laces to get it knotted, and I will have to be cut free when the picture is finished. I watch Amelia put her head on one side and preen and smile flirtatiously at Master Holbein. I hope to God that he does not like her. I hope to God that he does not paint her as she is, plumper, prettier than me. It does not really matter to her whether or not she goes to England. Oh! It would be a triumph for her, a leap from being the youngest daughter of a poor duchy to Queen of England, a flight that would lift her and our family and the whole nation of Cleves. But she does not need to get away as I need to get away. It is not a matter of need for her, as it is for me. I might almost say: desperation.

I have agreed not to look at Master Holbein's painting and so I do not look. One thing is true of me: if I give my word on something I keep it, although I am only a girl. Instead, I look out of the window, into the courtyard of our castle. The hunting horns sound in the forest outside, the great barred gate swings open, the huntsmen come in, my brother at their head. He glances up to the window and sees me before I can duck back. At once I know that I have irritated him. He will feel that I should not be at the window, where I can be seen by anyone in the castle yard. Although I moved too fast for him to see me in any detail, I feel certain that he knows that I am tightly laced and that the square neckline of my gown is low cut, though a muslin neckpiece covers me to my very chin. I flinch from the scowl that he shoots up to the window. Now he is displeased with me, but he will not say so. He will not complain of the gown that I could explain, he will complain of something else, but I cannot yet know what it will be. All I can be sure of is that sometime today or tomorrow, my mother will call me to her room, and he will be standing behind her chair, or turned away, or just entering the door, as if it were nothing to do with him at all, as if he were quite indifferent, and she will say to me, in tones of deep disapproval: 'Anne, I hear that you have . . .' and it will be something which happened days ago, which I have quite forgotten, but which he will have known and saved up until now, so that I am in the wrong, and perhaps even punished, and he will not say a word about seeing me, sitting in the window, looking pretty, which is my real offence against him.

When I was a little girl, my father used to call me his *falke*, his white falcon, his gyrfalcon, a hunting bird of the cold northern snows. When he saw me at my books or at my sewing he would laugh and say, 'Oh, my little falcon, mewed up? Come away and I shall set you free!' and not even my mother could stop me running from the school room to be with him.

I wish now, I so wish now, that he could call me away again.

I know that my mother thinks that I am a foolish girl, and my brother thinks worse; but if I were Queen of England the king could trust me with my position, I would not break into French fashions or Italian dances. They could trust me, the king could trust his honour to me. I know how important is a man's honour, and I have no desire to be anything but a good girl, a good queen. But I also believe that however strict the King of England, I would be allowed to sit in the window of my own castle. Whatever they say of Henry of England, I think he would tell me honestly if I offended him, and not order my mother to beat me for something else.

Katherine, Norfolk House, Lambeth, July 1539

Now let me see, what do I have?

I have a small gold chain from my long-dead mother that I keep in my special jewellery box, sadly empty but for this one chain; but I am certain to get more. I have three gowns, one of them new. I have a piece of French lace sent by my father from Calais. I have half a dozen ribbons of my own. And, more than anything else, I have me. I have me, glorious me! I am fourteen today, imagine that! Fourteen! Fourteen, young, nobly born though, tragically, not rich; but in love, wonderfully in love. My lady grandmother the duchess will give me a gift for my birthday, I know she will. I am her favourite and she likes me to look well. Perhaps some silk for a gown, perhaps a coin to buy lace. My friends in the maids' chamber will give me a feast tonight when we are supposed to be asleep; the young men will tap their secret signal on the door, and we will rush to let them in and I will cry, 'oh, no!' as if I wanted it to be just girls alone, as if I am not in love, madly in love, with Francis Dereham. As if I haven't spent all day just longing for tonight, when I shall see him. In five hours from now I will see him. No! I have just looked at my grandmother's precious French clock. Four hours and forty-eight minutes.

Forty-seven minutes.

Forty-six. I really am amazed at how devoted I am to him, that

I should actually watch a clock tick down the time until we are together. This must be a most passionate love, a most devoted love, and I must be a girl of really unusual sensitivity to feel this deeply.

Forty-five; but it's dreadfully boring, just waiting, now.

I haven't told him how I feel, of course. I should die of embarrassment if I had to tell him myself. I think I may die anyway, die for love of him. I have told no-one but my dearest friend Agnes Restwold, and sworn her to secrecy on pain of death, on pain of a traitor's death. She says she will be hanged and drawn and quartered before she tells anyone that I am in love. She says she will go to the block like my cousin Queen Anne before she betrays my secret. She says they will have to pull her apart on the rack before she tells. I have told Margaret Morton as well and she says that death itself would not make her tell, not if they were to fling her in the bear pit. She says they could burn her at the stake before she would tell. This is good because it means that one of them is certain to tell him before he comes to the chamber tonight, and so he will know that I like him.

I have known him for months now, half a lifetime. At first I only watched him but now he smiles and says hello to me. Once he called me by name. He comes with all the other young men of the household to visit us girls in our chamber, and he thinks he is in love with Joan Bulmer, who has eyes like a frog and if she were not so free with her favours, no man would ever look twice at her. But she is free, very free indeed; and so it is me that he does not look twice at. It isn't fair. It's so unfair. She is a good ten years older than me and married and so she knows how to attract a man, whereas I have much still to learn. Dereham is more than twenty as well. They all think of me as a child; but I am not a child, and I will show them. I am fourteen, I am ready for love. I am ready for a lover, and I am so in love with Francis Dereham that I will die if I don't see him at once. Four hours and forty minutes.

But now, from today, everything must be different. Now that I

11

am fourteen, everything is certain to change. It has to, I know it will. I shall put on my new French hood and I shall tell Francis Dereham that I am fourteen and he will see me as I truly am: a woman now, a woman of some experience, a woman grown; and then we shall see how long he stays with old froggy face when he could come across the room to lie in my bed instead.

He's not my first love, it is true; but I never felt anything like this for Henry Manox and if he says I did, then he is a liar. Henry Manox was well-enough for me when I was a girl just living in the country, a child really, learning to play the virginal and knowing nothing of kissing and touching. Why, when he first kissed me I didn't even like it very much, and begged him to stop, and when he put his hand up my skirt I was so shocked I screamed aloud and cried. I was only eleven years old, I couldn't be expected to know the pleasures of a woman. But I know all about that now. Three years in the maids' chamber has taught me every little wile and play that I need. I know what a man wants, and I know how to play him, and I know when to stop too.

My reputation is my dowry – my grandmother would point out that I have no other, sour old cat – and no-one will ever say that Katherine Howard does not know what is due to her and her family. I am a woman now, not a child. Henry Manox wanted to be my lover when I was a child in the country, when I knew next to nothing, when I had seen nobody, or at any rate nobody that mattered. I would have let him have me too, after he had bribed and bullied me for weeks to do the full deed, but in the end it was he that stopped short for fear of being caught. People would have thought badly of us since he was more than twenty and I was eleven. We were going to wait till I was thirteen. But now I live in Norfolk House in Lambeth, not buried in Sussex, and the king himself could ride past the door any day, the archbishop is our next-door neighbour, my own uncle Thomas Howard, the Duke of Norfolk, calls with all his great train, and he once remembered my name. I'm far beyond Henry Manox now. I'm not a country girl who can be bullied into giving him kisses and forced to do more, I am a good deal too high for that now. I know what's what in the bedroom, I am a Howard girl, I have a wonderful future before me.

Except – and this is such a tragedy that I really don't know how to bear it – although I am of an age to go to court, and as a Howard girl my natural place should be in the queen's chambers, there is no queen! It is a disaster for me. There is no queen at all, Queen Jane died after having her baby, which seems to me to be just laziness really, and so there are no places at court for maids in waiting. This is so terribly unlucky for me, I think no girl has ever been as unlucky as I have been: to have my fourteenth birthday in London, just as the queen has to go and die, and the whole court droop into mourning for years. Sometimes I feel that the whole world conspires against me, as if people want me to live and die an old lady spinster.

What is the point of being pretty if no nobleman is ever going to know me? How will anyone ever see how charming I can be if nobody ever sees me at all? If it were not for my love, my sweetest handsome love, Francis, Francis, Francis, I should utterly despair, and throw myself into the Thames before I am a day older.

But thank God, at least I do have Francis to hope for, and the world to play for. And God, if He truly does know everything, can only have made me so exquisite for a great future. He must have a plan for me? Fourteen and perfect? Surely He in His wisdom won't let me waste away in Lambeth?

Jane Boleyn, Blickling Hall, Norfolk, November 1539

It comes at last, as the days grow dark and I am starting to dread another winter in the country: the letter I have wanted. I feel as if I have waited for it for a lifetime. My life can begin again. I can return to the light of good candles, to the heat of sea-coal braziers, to a circle of friends and rivals, to music and good food and dancing. I am summoned to court, thank God, I am summoned back to court and I shall serve the new queen. The duke, my patron and my mentor, has found me a place in the queen's chamber once again. I shall serve the new Queen of England. I shall serve Queen Anne of England.

The name rings like a warning tocsin: Queen Anne, Queen Anne again. Surely, the councillors who advised the marriage must have had a moment when they heard the words Queen Anne and felt a shiver of horror? They must have remembered how unlucky the first Anne was for us all? The disgrace she brought to the king, and the ruin of her family, and my own loss? My unbearable loss? But no, I see a dead queen is quickly forgotten. By the time this new Queen Anne arrives, the other Queen Anne, my Queen Anne, my sister, my adored friend, my tormentor, will be nothing more than a rare memory – my memory. Sometimes I feel as if I am the only one in the whole country who remembers. Sometimes I feel as if I am the only one in the world who watches and wonders, the only one cursed with memory.

I still dream of her often. I dream that she is again young and laughing, careless of anything but her own enjoyment, wearing her hood pushed back from her face to show her dark hair, her sleeves fashionably long, her accent always so exaggeratedly French. The pearl 'B' at her throat proclaiming that the Queen of England is a Boleyn, as I am. I dream that we are in a sunlit garden, and George is happy, and I have my hand in his arm, and Anne is smiling at us both. I dream that we are all going to be richer than anyone could ever imagine, we will have houses and castles and lands. Abbeys will fall down to make stone for our houses, crucifixes will be melted for our jewellery. We will take fish from the abbey ponds, our hounds will range all over the church lands. Abbots and priors will give up their houses for us, the very shrines will lose their sanctity and honour us instead. The country will be made over to our glory, our enrichment and amusement. I always wake then, I wake and lie awake shaking. It is such a glorious dream; but I wake quite frozen with terror.

Enough now of dreaming! Once again I shall be at court. Once again I shall be the closest friend of the queen, a constant companion in her chamber. I shall see everything, know everything. I shall be at the very centre of life again, I shall be the new Queen Anne's lady in waiting, serving her as loyally and well as I have served the other three of King Henry's queens. If he can rise up and marry again without fear of ghosts, then so can I.

And I shall serve my kinsman, my uncle by marriage, the Duke of Norfolk, Thomas Howard, the greatest man in England after the king himself. A soldier, known for the speed of his marches and the abrupt cruelty of his attacks. A courtier, who never bends with any wind but always constantly serves his king, his own family, and his own interest. A nobleman with so much royal blood in his family that his claim to the throne is as good as any Tudor. He is my kinsman and my patron and my lord. He saved me from a traitor's death once, he told me what I should do and how to do it. He took me when I faltered and led me from the shadow of the Tower and into safety. Ever since then I am sworn to him for life. He knows I am his. Once again, he has work for me to do, and I shall honour my debt to him.

Anne, Cleves Town,
November 1539

I have it! I am to be it! I shall be Queen of England. I have slipped my jesses like a free falcon and I shall fly away. Amelia has her handkerchief to her eyes because she has a cold and is trying to look as if she has been crying at the news of my going. She is a liar. She will not be at all sad to see me leave. Her life as the only duchess left in Cleves will be better by far than being the younger sister to me. And when I am married – and what a marriage! – her chances of a good alliance are much improved. My mother does not look happy either, but her anxiety is real. She has been strained for months. I wish I could think it is for the loss of me but it is not. She is worried sick about the cost of this journey and my wedding clothes on my brother's treasury. She is Lord of the Exchequer as well as housewife to my brother. Even with England waiving the demand for a dowry, this marriage is costing the country more than my mother wants to pay.

'Even if the trumpeters come free, they will have to be fed,' she says irritably, as if trumpeters are an exotic and expensive pet that I, in my vanity, have insisted on, instead of a loan from my sister Sybilla who wrote to me frankly that it does her no good in Saxony if I set off to one of the greatest kings in Europe in little more than a wagon with a couple of guards.

My brother says very little. This is a great triumph for him and a

17

great step up in the world for his duchy. He is in a league with the other Protestant princes and dukes of Germany and they hope that this marriage will prompt England to join their alliance. If all the Protestant powers in Europe were united then they could attack France or the Hapsburg lands and spread the word of reform. They might get as far as Rome itself, they might curb the power of the Pope in his own city. Who knows what glory to God might come, if only I can be a good wife to a husband who has never been pleased before?

'You must do your duty to God as you serve your husband,' my brother says to me pompously.

I wait to see what exactly he means by this. 'He takes his religion from his wives,' he says. 'When he was married to a princess from Spain he was named Defender of the Faith by the Pope himself. When he married the Lady Anne Boleyn she led him away from superstition to the light of reform. With Queen Jane he became Catholic again and if she had not died he would have reconciled with the Pope, for sure. Now, although he is no friend of the Pope, his country is all but Catholic. He could become a Roman Catholic again in a moment. But if you guide him as you should do, he will declare himself as a Protestant king and leader, and he will join with us.'

'I will try my best,' I say uncertainly. 'But I am only twenty-four. He is a man of forty-eight and he has been king since he was a young man. He may not listen to me.'

'I know you will do your duty,' my brother tries to reassure himself; but as the time comes for me to leave, he grows more and more doubtful.

'You cannot fear for her safety?' I hear my mother mutter to him as he sits in the evening over his wine and stares at the fire as if he would foresee the future without me.

'If she behaves herself she should be safe. But God knows he is a king who has learned that he can do anything he wants in his own lands.'

'You mean to his wives?' she asks in a whisper.

He shrugs uneasily.

'She would never give him cause to doubt her.'

'She has to be warned. He will hold the power of life and death over her. He will be able to do what he likes to her. He will control her utterly.'

I am hidden in the shadows at the back of the room, and this revealing remark from my brother makes me smile. From this one phrase, I finally understand what has been troubling him for all these months. He is going to miss me. He is going to miss me like a master misses a lazy dog when he finally drowns it in a fit of temper. He has become so accustomed to bullying me, and finding fault with me, and troubling me in a dozen small daily ways, that now, when he thinks that another man will have the ordering of me, it plagues him. If he had ever loved me, I would call this jealousy; and it would be easy to understand. But it is not love that he feels for me. It is more like a constant resentment that has become such a habit to him that to have me removed, like an aching tooth, brings him no relief.

'At least she will be of service to us in England,' he says meanly. 'She is worse than useless here. She has to bring him to reformed religion. She has to make him declare as a Lutheran. As long as she doesn't spoil it all.'

'How should she spoil it?' my mother replies. 'She has only to have a child by him. There is no great skill in that. Her health is good and her courses regular, and at twenty-four she's a good age for childbearing.' She considers for a moment. 'He should desire her,' she says fairly. 'She is well-made, and she carries herself well, I have seen to that. He is a man who is given to lust and falling in love on sight. He will probably take great carnal pleasure in her at first, if only because she is new to him, and a virgin.'

My brother leaps up from his chair. 'Shame!' he says, his cheeks burning with more than the heat from the fire. Everyone stops talking at the sound of his raised voice, then quickly they turn away, trying not to stare. Quietly, I rise from my stool and get myself to the very back of the room. If his temper is rising, I had better slip away.

'Son, I meant nothing wrong,' Mother says, quick to placate him. 'I just meant that she is likely to do her duty and please him . . .'

'I can't bear the thought of her . . .' He breaks off. 'I cannot stomach it! She must not seek him out!' he hisses. 'You must tell her. She must do nothing unmaidenly. She must do nothing wanton. You must warn her that she must be my sister, your daughter, before she is ever a wife. She must bear herself with coldness, with dignity. She is not to be his whore, she is not to act the part of some shameless, greedy . . .'

'No, no,' my mother says softly. 'No, of course not. She isn't like that, William, my lord, dear son. You know she has been most strictly raised, in fear of God and to respect her betters.'

'Well, tell her again,' he cries. Nothing will soothe him, I had better get away. He would be beside himself if he knew that I have seen him like this. I put my hand behind me and feel the comforting warmth of the thick tapestry covering the rear wall. I inch along, my dark dress almost invisible in the shadows of the room.

'I saw her when that painter was here,' he says, his voice thick. 'Preening in her vanity, setting herself out. Laced . . . laced . . . tight. Her breasts . . . on show . . . trying to appear desirable. She is capable of sin, Mother. She is disposed to . . . She is disposed to . . . Her temperament is naturally filled with . . .' He cannot say it.

'No, no,' Mother says gently. 'She only wants to be a credit to us.'

'. . . Lust.'

The word has become detached, it drops into the silence of the room as if it might belong to anybody, as if it might belong to my brother and not to me.

I am at the doorway now, my hand gently lifting the latch, my other finger muffling its click. Three of the women of the court casually rise and stand before me to mask my retreat from the two

20

at the fireside. The door swings open on oiled hinges and makes no sound. The cold draught makes the candles at the fireside bob, but my brother and my mother are facing each other, rapt in the horror of that word, and do not turn around.

'Are you sure?' I hear her ask him.

I close the door before I hear him reply, and I go quickly and quietly to our chamber where the maids are sitting up by the fireside with my sister and playing cards. They scramble them off the table when I tear open the door and stride in, and then they laugh when they see it is me in their relief that they have not been caught out gambling: a forbidden pleasure for spinsters in my brother's lands.

'I'm going to bed, I have a headache, I'm not to be disturbed,' I announce abruptly.

Amelia nods. 'You can try,' she says knowingly. 'What have you done now?'

'Nothing,' I say. 'As always, nothing.'

I go through quickly to our privy chamber and fling my clothes into the chest at the foot of the bed and jump into bed in my shift, drawing the curtains around the bed, pulling the covers up. I shiver in the coldness of the linen, and wait for the order that I know will come.

In only a few moments, Amelia opens the door. 'You're to go to Mother's rooms,' she says triumphantly.

'Tell her I'm ill. You should have said I've gone to bed.'

'I told her. She said you have to get up and put on a cloak and go. What have you done now?'

I scowl at her bright face. 'Nothing.' I rise unwillingly from the bed. 'Nothing. As always, I have done nothing.' I pull my cloak from the hook behind the door and tie the ribbons from chin to knee.

'Did you answer him back?' Amelia demands gleefully. 'Why do you always argue with him?'

I go out without replying, through the silenced chamber and

down the steps to my mother's rooms in the same tower on the floor below us.

At first it looks as if she is alone, but then I see the half-closed door to her privy chamber and I don't need to hear him, and I don't need to see him. I just know that he is there, watching.

She has her back to me at first, and when she turns I see she has the birch stick in her hand and her face is stern.

'I have done nothing,' I say at once.

She sighs irritably. 'Child, is that any way to come into a room?'

I lower my head. 'My lady mother,' I say quietly.

'I am displeased with you,' she says.

I look up. 'I am sorry for that. How have I offended?'

'You have been called to a holy duty, you must lead your husband to the reformed church.'

I nod.

'You have been called to a position of great honour and great dignity, and you must forge your behaviour to deserve it.'

Inarguable. I lower my head again.

'You have an unruly spirit,' she goes on.

True indeed.

'You lack the proper traits of a woman: submission, obedience, love of duty.'

True again.

'And I fear that you have a wanton streak in you,' she says, very low.

'Mother, that I have not,' I say as quietly as her. 'That is not true.'

'You do. The King of England will not tolerate a wanton wife. The Queen of England must be a woman without a stain on her character. She must be above reproach.'

'My lady mother, I . . .'

'Anne, think of this!' she says, and for once I hear a real ring of earnestness in her voice. 'Think of this! He had the Lady Anne Boleyn executed for infidelity, accusing her of sin with half the court, her own brother among her lovers. He made her queen and then he unmade her again with no cause or evidence but his own will. He accused her of incest, witchcraft, crimes most foul. He is a man most anxious for his reputation, madly anxious. The next Queen of England must never be doubted. We cannot guarantee your safety if there is one word said against you!'

'My lady . . .'

'Kiss the rod,' she says before I can argue.

I touch my lips to the stick as she holds it out to me. Behind her privy chamber door I can hear him slightly, very slightly, sigh.

'Hold the seat of the chair,' she orders.

I bend over and grip both sides of the chair. Delicately, like a lady lifting a handkerchief, she takes the hem of my cloak and raises it over my hips and then my night shift. My buttocks are naked, if my brother chooses to look through the half-open door he can see me, displayed like a girl in a bawdy house. There is a whistle of the rod through the air and then the sudden whiplash of pain across my thighs. I cry out, and then bite my lip. I am desperate to know how many cuts I will have to take. I grit my teeth together and wait for the next. The hiss through the air and then the slice of pain, like a sword-cut in a dishonourable duel. Two. The sound of the next comes too fast for me to make ready, and I cry out again, my tears suddenly coming hot and fast like blood.

'Stand up, Anne,' she says coolly, and pulls down my shift and my cloak.

The tears are pouring down my face, I can hear myself sobbing like a child.

'Go to your room and read the Bible,' she says. 'Think especially on your royal calling. Caesar's wife, Anne. Caesar's wife.'

I have to curtsey to her. The awkward movement causes a wave of new pain and I whimper like a whipped puppy. I go to the door and open it. The wind blows the door from my hand and, in the gust, the inner door to her privy chamber flies open without warning.

In the shadow stands my brother, his face strained as if it were him beneath the whip of the birch, his lips pressed tightly together as if to stop himself from calling out. For one awful moment our eyes meet and he looks at me, his face filled with a desperate need. I drop my eyes, I turn from him as if I have not seen him, as if I am blind to him. Whatever he wants of me, I know that I don't want to hear it. I stumble from the room, my shift sticking to the blood on the backs of my thighs. I am desperate to get away from them both.

Katherine, Norfolk House, Lambeth, November 1539

'I shall call you wife.'

'I shall call you husband.'

It is so dark that I cannot see him smile; but I feel the curve of his lips as he kisses me again.

'I shall buy you a ring and you can wear it on a chain around your neck and keep it hidden.'

'I shall give you a velvet cap embroidered with pearls.'

He chuckles.

'For God's sake be quiet, and let us get some sleep!' someone says crossly from elsewhere in the dormitory. It is probably Joan Bulmer, missing these very same kisses that I now have on my lips, on my eyelids, on my ears, on my neck, on my breasts, on every part of my body. She will be missing the lover who used to be hers, and now is mine.

'Shall I go and kiss her goodnight?' he whispers.

'Ssshhh,' I reprove him, and I stop his reply with my own mouth.

We are in the sleepy aftermath of lovemaking, the sheets tangled around us, clothes and linen all bundled together, the scent of his hair, of his body, of his sweat all over me. Francis Dereham is mine as I swore he would be.

'You know that if we promise to marry before God and I give

you a ring, then it is as much a marriage as if we were wed in church?'
he asks earnestly.

I am falling asleep. His hand is caressing my belly, I feel myself
stir and sigh and I open my legs to invite his warm touch again.

'Yes,' I say, meaning yes to his touch.

He misunderstands me, he is always so earnest. 'So shall we do
it? Shall we marry in secret and always be together, and when I have
made my fortune, we can tell everyone, and live together as man
and wife?'

'Yes, yes.' I am starting to moan a little from pleasure, I am
thinking of nothing but the movement of his clever fingers. 'Oh,
yes.'

In the morning he has to snatch his clothes and run, before my
lady grandmother's maid comes with much hustle and ceremony to
unlock the door to our bedchamber. He dashes away just moments
before we hear her heavy footstep on the stairs; but Edward Waldgrave
leaves it too late and has to roll under Mary's bed and hope the
trailing sheets will hide him.

'You're merry this morning,' Mrs Franks says suspiciously as we
smother our giggles. 'Laugh before seven, tears before eleven.'

'That is a pagan superstition,' says Mary Lascelles, who is always
pious. 'And there is nothing for these girls to laugh about if they
considered their consciences.'

We look as sombre as we can, and follow her down the stairs to
the chapel for Mass. Francis is in the chapel, on his knees, as handsome as an angel. He looks across at me and my heart turns over.
It is so wonderful that he is in love with me.

When the service is done and everyone is in a hurry for their
breakfast I pause in the pew to adjust the ribbons on my shoe and
I see that he has dropped back to his knees as if deep in prayer. The
priest slowly blows out the candles, packs up his things, waddles
down the aisle and we are alone.

Francis comes across to me and holds out his hand. It is a most wonderfully solemn moment, it is as good as a play. I wish I could see us, especially my own serious face. 'Katherine, will you marry me?' he says.

I feel so grown up. It is I who am doing this, taking control of my own destiny. My grandmother has not made this marriage for me, nor my father. Nobody has ever cared for me, they have forgotten me, cooped up in this house. But I have chosen my own husband, I will make my own future. I am like my cousin Mary Boleyn, who married in secret a man that no-one liked and then picked up the whole Boleyn inheritance. 'Yes,' I say. 'I will.' I am like my cousin Queen Anne, who aimed at the highest marriage in the land when no-one thought it could be done. 'Yes, I will,' I say.

What he means by marrying, I don't know exactly. I think that he means I will have a ring to wear on a chain, which I can show to the other girls, and that we will be promised to one another. But to my surprise he leads me up the aisle towards the altar. For a moment I hesitate, I don't know what he wants to do, and I am no great enthusiast for praying. We will be late for breakfast if we don't hurry and I like the bread when it is still warm from the ovens. But then I see that we are acting out our wedding. I so wish that I had put on my best gown this morning, but it is too late now.

'I, Francis Dercham, do take thee, Katherine Howard, to be my lawful wedded wife,' he says firmly.

I smile up at him. If only I had put on my best hood, I would be perfectly happy.

'Now you say it,' he prompts me.

'I, Katherine Howard, do take thee, Francis Dereham, to be my lawful wedded husband,' I reply obediently.

He bends and kisses me. I can feel my knees go weak at his touch, all I want is for the kiss to last forever. Already, I am wondering if we were to slip into my lady grandmother's high-walled pew, we could go a little further than this. But he stops. 'You understand that we are married now?' he confirms.

'This is our wedding?'

'Yes.'

I giggle. 'But I am only fourteen.'

'That makes no difference, you have given your word in the sight of God.' Very seriously he puts his hand in his jacket pocket and pulls out a purse. 'There is one hundred pounds in here,' he says solemnly. 'I am going to give it into your safekeeping, and in the New Year I shall go to Ireland and make my fortune so that I can come home and claim you openly as my bride.'

The purse is heavy, he has saved a fortune for us. This is so thrilling. 'I am to keep the money safe?'

'Yes, as my good wife.'

This is so delightful that I give it a little shake and hear the coins chink. I can put it in my empty jewel box. 'I shall be such a good wife to you! You will be so surprised!'

'Yes. As I told you. This is a proper wedding in the sight of God. We are husband and wife now.'

'Oh, yes. And when you have made your fortune, we can really marry, can't we? With a new gown and everything?'

Francis frowns for a moment. 'You do understand?' he says. 'I know you are young, Katherine, but you must understand this. We are married now. It is legal and binding. We cannot marry again. This is it. We have just done it. A marriage between two people in the sight of God is a marriage as binding as one signed on a contract. You are my wife now. We are married in the eyes of God and the law of the land. If anyone asks you, you are my wife, my legally wedded wife. You do understand?'

'Of course I do,' I reply hastily. I don't want to look stupid. 'Of course I understand. All I am saying is that I would like a new gown when we tell everybody.'

He laughs as if I have said something funny and takes me in his arms again and kisses the base of my throat and nuzzles his face into my neck. 'I shall buy you a gown of blue silk, Mrs Dereham,' he promises me.

I close my eyes in pleasure. 'Green,' I say. 'Tudor green. The king likes green best.'

Jane Boleyn, Greenwich Palace, December 1539

Thank God I am here in Greenwich, the most beautiful of the king's palaces, back where I belong in the queen's rooms. Last time I was here I was nursing Jane Seymour as she burned up with fever, asking for Henry, who never came; but now the rooms have been repainted, and I have been restored and she has been forgotten. I alone have survived. I have survived the fall of Queen Katherine, the disgrace of Queen Anne and the death of Queen Jane. It is a miracle to me that I have survived but here I am, back at court, one of the favoured few, the very favoured few. I shall serve the new queen as I have served her predecessors, with love and loyalty and an eye to my own opportunities. I shall once again walk in and out of the best chambers of the best palaces of the land as my home. I am once again where I was born and bred to be.

Sometimes I can even forget everything that has happened. Sometimes, I forget I am a widow of thirty, with a son far away from me. I think I am a young woman again with a husband I worship, and everything to hope for. I am returned to the very centre of my world. Almost I could say: I am reborn.

The king has planned a Christmas wedding and the queen's ladies are being assembled for the festivities. Thanks to my lord duke, I am one of them, restored to the friends and rivals I have known since my childhood. Some of them welcome me back with a wry smile and a backhand compliment, some of them look askance at me. Not that they loved Anne so much – not they – but they were frightened by her fall and they remember that I alone escaped, it is like magic that I escaped, it makes them cross themselves and whisper old rumours against me.

Bessie Blount, the king's old mistress, now married far above her station to Lord Clinton, greets me kindly enough. I have not seen her since the death of her son Henry Fitzroy, who the king made a duke, Duke of Richmond, for nothing more than being a royal bastard, and when I say how sorry I am for her loss, shallow words of politeness, she suddenly grips my hand and looks at me, her face pale and demanding, as if to ask me wordlessly if I know how it was that he died? Will I tell her how he died?

I smile coolly and unwrap her fingers from my wrist. I cannot tell her because truly I don't know, and if I did know I would not tell her. 'I am very sorry for the loss of your son,' I say again.

She will probably never know why he died nor how. But neither will thousands. Thousands of mothers saw their sons march out to protect the shrines, the holy places, the roadside statues, the monasteries and the churches, and thousands of sons never came home again. The king will decide what is faith and what is heresy, it is not for the people to say. In this new and dangerous world it is not even for the church to say. The king will decide who will live and who will die, he has the power of God now. If Bessie really wants to know who killed her son she had better ask the king his father; but she knows Henry too well to do that.

The other women have seen Bessie greet me and they come forwards: Seymours, Percys, Culpeppers, Nevilles. All the great families of the land have forced their daughters into the narrow compass of the queen's rooms. Some of them know ill of me and some of them suspect worse. I don't care. I have faced worse than the malice of envious women, and I am related to most of them anyway, and rival to them all. If anyone wants to make trouble for me they had better remember that I am under the protection of my lord duke, and only Thomas Cromwell is more powerful than us.

The one I dread, the one I really don't want to meet, is Catherine Carey, the daughter of Mary Boleyn, my mean-spirited sister-in-law. Catherine is a child, a girl of fifteen, I should not fear her, but – to tell the truth – her mother is a formidable woman and never a great admirer of mine. My lord duke has won young Catherine a place at court and ordered her mother to send her to the fount of all power, the source of all wealth, and Mary, reluctant Mary, has obeyed. I can imagine how unwillingly she bought the child her gowns and dressed her hair and coached her in her curtsey and her dancing. Mary saw her family rise to the skies on the beauty and wit of her sister and her brother, and then saw their bodies packed in pieces in the little coffins. Anne was beheaded, her body wrapped in a box, her head in a basket. George, my George . . . I cannot bear to think of it.

Let it be enough to say that Mary blames me for all her grief and loss, blames me for the loss of her brother and sister, and never thinks of her own part in our tragedy. She blames me as if I could have saved them, as if I did not do everything in my power till that very day, the last day, on the scaffold, when in the end there was nothing anybody could do.

And she is wrong to blame me. Mary Norris lost her father Henry on the same day and for the same cause, and she greets me with respect and with a smile. She bears no grudge. She has been properly taught by her mother that the fire of the king's displeasure can burn up anyone, there is no point in blaming the survivors who got out in time.

Catherine Carey is a maid of fifteen, she will share rooms with other young girls, with my cousin and hers, Katherine Howard, Anne Bassett, Mary Norris, with other ambitious maids who know nothing and hope for everything. I will guide and advise them as a woman who has served queens before. Catherine Carey will not be whispering to her friends of the time that she spent with her Aunt Anne in the Tower, the last-moment agreements, the scaffold-step promises, the reprieve that they swore was coming and yet never came. She will not tell them that we all let Anne go to the block – her saintly mother as guilty as any other. She has been raised as a Carey but she is a Boleyn, a king's bastard and a Howard through and through; she will know to keep her mouth shut.

In the absence of the new queen we have to settle into the rooms without her. We have to wait. The weather has been bad for her journey and she is making slow progress from Cleves to Calais. They now think that she will not get here in time for a Christmas wedding. If I had been advising her I would have told her to face the danger, any danger, and come by ship. It is a long journey, I know, and the English Sea in winter is a perilous place, but a bride should not be late for her wedding day; and this king does not like to wait for anything. He is not a man to deny.

In truth, he is not the prince that he was. When I was first at court and he was the young husband of a beautiful wife, he was a golden king. They called him the handsomest prince in Christendom and that was not flattery. Mary Boleyn was in love with him, Anne was in love with him, I was in love with him. There was not one girl at court, nor one girl in the country, who could resist him. Then he turned against his wife, Queen Katherine, a good woman, and Anne taught him how to be cruel. Her court, her clever young merciless court, persecuted the queen into stubborn misery and taught the king to dance to our heretic tune. We tricked him into thinking that the queen had lied to him, then we fooled him into thinking that Wolsey had betrayed him. But then his suspicious mind, rootling like a pig, started to run beyond our control. He started to doubt us as well. Cromwell persuaded him that Anne had betrayed him, the Seymours urged him to believe that we were all in a plot. In the end the king lost something greater than a wife, even two wives; he lost his sense of trust. We taught him suspicion, and the golden boyish shine tarnished on the man. Now, surrounded by people who fear him, he has become a bully. He has become a danger, like a bear that has been baited into surly spite. He told the Princess Mary he would have her killed if she defied him, and then declared her a bastard and princess no more. The Princess Elizabeth, our Boleyn princess, my niece, he has declared illegitimate and her governess says that the child is not even properly clothed.

And lastly, this business with Henry Fitzroy, the king's own son: one day to be legitimised and proclaimed the Prince of Wales, the next day dead of a mystery illness and my own lord told to bury him at midnight? His portraits destroyed, and all mention of him forbidden? What sort of a man is it who can see his son die and be buried without saying a word? What sort of a father can tell his two little girls that they are no children of his? What sort of a man can send his friends and his wife to the gallows and dance when their deaths are reported to him? What kind of a man is this, to whom we have given absolute power over our lives and souls?

And perhaps even worse than all of this: the good priests hanged from their own church beams, the devout men walking to the stake to be burned, their eyes down, their thoughts on heaven, the up-risings in the North and the East, and the king swearing that the rebels could trust him, that he would be advised by them, and then the dreadful betrayal that put the trusting fools on gallows in their thousands around the country, that made my lord Norfolk the butcher of his countrymen. This king has killed thousands, this king goes on killing thousands of his own people. The world outside England says he has run mad and waits for our rebellion. But like frightened dogs in the bear pit we dare do no more than watch him and snarl.

He is merry now, anyway, despite the new queen's failure to arrive. I have yet to be presented to him but they tell me he will greet me and all her ladies kindly. He is at dinner when I steal into his rooms to see the new queen's portrait that he keeps in his presence chamber.

The room is empty, the portrait is on an easel lit by big square candles. She is a sweet-looking thing, it must be said. She has an honest face, a straight gaze from lovely eyes. I understand at once what he likes in her. She has no allure; there is no sensuality in her face. She does not look flirtatious or dangerous or sinful. She has no polish, she has no sophistication. She looks younger than her twenty-four years, I could even say she looks a little simple to my critical gaze. She will not be a queen as Anne was a queen; that is a certainty. This is not a woman who will turn court and country upside down to dance to a new tune. This is not a woman who will turn men half-mad with desire and demand that they write of love in poetry. And, of course, this is exactly what he wants now – never again to love a woman like Anne.

Anne has spoiled him for a challenge, perhaps forever. She set a fire under his court and in the end everything was burned up. He is like a man whose very eyebrows have been scorched, and I am the woman whose house is ashes. He does not want ever again to marry a desirable mistress. I never again want to smell smoke. He wants a wife at his side who is as steady as an ox at the plough, and then he can seek flirtation and danger and allure elsewhere.

'A pretty picture,' a man says behind me and I turn to see the dark hair and long, sallow face of my uncle, Thomas Howard, the Duke of Norfolk, the greatest man in the kingdom after the king himself.

I sweep him a deep curtsey. 'It is indeed, sir,' I say.

He nods, his dark eyes steady. 'Do you think it will prove to be a good likeness?'

'We'll know soon enough, my lord.'

'You can thank me for getting you a post in her household,' he says casually. 'It was my doing. I took it as a personal matter.'

'I do thank you very much. I am in your debt for my life itself. You know, you have only ever to command me.'

He nods. He has never shown me kindness, except the once,

one great favour: pulling me from the fire that burned down the court. He is a gruff man of few words. They say he only really loved one woman and that was Katherine of Aragon, and he watched her thrust down to poverty, neglect and death, in order to put his own niece in her place. So his affections are of little value, anyway.

'You will tell me how things go on in her rooms,' he says, nodding at the portrait. 'As you always have done.' He holds out his arm to me, he is giving me the honour of leading me into dinner. I curtsey again, he likes a show of deference, and I put my hand lightly on his arm. 'I shall want to know if she pleases the king, when she conceives, who she sees, how she behaves, and if she brings in any Lutheran preachers. That sort of thing. You know.'

I know. We walk to the door together.

'I expect her to try to lead him in the matter of religion,' he says. 'We can't have that. We can't have him turning any further to reform; the country won't tolerate it. You must look at her books and see if she is reading any forbidden writing. And watch her ladies to see if they are spying on us, if they report to Cleves. If any of them express any heresy I want to know at once. You know what you have to do.'

I do. There is not a member of this wide-ranging family who does not know their task. We all work to maintain the power and wealth of the Howards and we stand together.

I can hear the roar of the feasting court from the hall as we walk towards it, serving men with great jugs of wine and platters of meat marching in line to serve the hundreds of people who dine every day with the king. In the gallery above are the people who have come to watch, to see the great monster that is the inner court of the noblest people, a beast with a hundred mouths and a million schemes, and two hundred eyes watching the king as the only source of all wealth, all power, and all favour.

'You will find him changed,' the duke says very softly, his mouth to my ear. 'We all find him hard to please.'

I think of the spoiled boy who could be distracted in a moment with a joke or a bet or a challenge. 'He was always flighty.'

'He's worse than that now,' my lord says. 'His temper shifts without warning, he is violent; he will lash out against Cromwell and hit him in the face, he can turn in a moment. He can take a rage that turns him scarlet. Something that pleases him in the morning can anger him at dinner. You should be warned.'

I nod. 'They serve him on bended knee now.' I notice the new fashion.

He gives a short laugh. 'And they call him "Majesty",' he says. '"Your Grace" was good enough for the Plantaganets themselves; but not enough for this king. He has to be "Majesty" as if he were a god.'

'People do this?' I ask curiously. 'This extreme honour?'

'You will do it yourself,' he tells me. 'Henry will be as a god if he wishes, there is no-one who dares to deny him.'

'The lords?' I query, thinking of the pride of the great men of the kingdom who hailed this man's father as an equal, whose loyalty gave him his throne.

'You will see,' my lord says grimly. 'They have changed the laws of treason so that even to think of opposition is a capital offence. Nobody dares argue against him, there would be the knock on the door at midnight and a trip to the Tower for questioning and your wife a widow without even a trial.'

I look to the high table where the king is seated, a massive spreading bulk on his throne. He is cramming food into his mouth as we watch him, both hands up to his face, he is fatter than any man I have ever seen in my life before, his shoulders gross, his neck like an ox, his features dissolving into the moon-shaped vat of his face, fingers like swollen puddings.

'My God, he has blown up like a monster!' I exclaim. 'What has become of him? Is he sick? I would not have known him. God knows he is not the prince he was.'

'He is a danger,' my lord says, his voice no more than a breath. 'To himself in his indulgences, and to others in his temper. Be warned.'

I am shaken more than I show when I go to the table for the queen's ladies. They make a space for me and greet me by name, many of them calling me cousin. I feel the king's little piggy eyes on me and I sweep him a deep curtsey before I sit down on my stool. Nobody else pays any attention to the beast that the prince has become, it is like a fairytale and we are all blinded by an enchantment not to see the ruin of the man in this pig of a king.

I settle to my dinner and serve myself from the common platter, the best wine is poured into my cup. I look around the court. This is my home. I have known most of these people for all of my life, and thanks to the duke's care in marrying all the Howard children to his own advantage, I am related to most of them. Like most of them, I have served one queen after another. Like most of them, I have followed my royal mistress in the fashion of hoods: gable hood, French hood, English hood; and in the fashion of praying: papist, reformist, English Catholic. I have stumbled in Spanish and I have chattered in French, and I have sat in thoughtful silence and sewed shirts for the poor. There is not much about the Queens of England that I have not known, that I have not seen. And soon I shall see the next one and know all about her: her secrets, her hopes, and her faults. I shall watch her and I shall make my reports to my lord duke. And perhaps, even in a court grown fearful under a king who is swelling into a tyrant, even without my husband, and even without Anne, I shall learn to be happy again.

Katherine, Norfolk House, Lambeth, December 1539

And what shall I get for Christmas? I know I am to have an embroidered purse from my friend Agnes Restwold, a hand-copied page from a prayer book from Mary Lascelles (I'm so thrilled at the prospect of this I can hardly breathe) and two handkerchiefs from my grandmother. So far, so very dull indeed. But my dearest Francis is going to give me a shift of best embroidered linen, and I have woven him, with my own hands, and it has taken me days, an armband of my favourite colours. I am very pleased that he should love me so, and of course I love him too, but he has not bought me a ring as he promised, and he is sticking to his plan to go to Ireland to seek his fortune in the very next month, and then I shall be left all alone, and what is the point of that?

The court is at Greenwich for Christmas, I hoped it would be at Whitehall and then I might at least have gone to see the king eat his dinner. My uncle the duke is there, but he does not summon us; and although my grandmother went to dine she did not take me with her. Sometimes I think that nothing will ever happen for me. Nothing will ever happen at all and I will live and die an old spinster in my grandmother's service. I shall be fifteen next birthday and clearly no-one has given a single thought to my future. Who ever cares for me? My mother is dead and my father barely remembers my name. It is terribly sad. Mary Lumleigh is to be married next year, they are drawing up the contract now, and she makes much of herself and queens it over me, as though I cared for her and for her pimply betrothed. I should not want such a match if it were offered to me with a fortune attached, and so I told her, and so we have quarrelled and the lace collar she was going to give me for Christmas will be given to someone else, and I do not care about that either.

The queen should be in London by now but she has been so stupidly slow that she is delayed, so all my hopes of her great entry into London and a wonderful wedding have been put off too. It is as if the very fates themselves work to make me unhappy. I am doomed. All I want is a little dancing! Anyone would think that a girl of nearly fifteen, or at any rate fifteen next year, could go dancing once before she dies!

Of course we will have dancing here for Christmas, but that is not what I mean at all. What is the pleasure in dancing when everyone who sees you has seen you every day for a year before? What's the pleasure in a feast when every boy in the room is as familiar as the tapestries on the walls? Where's the joy in having a man's eyes on you when he is your own man, your own husband, and he would come to your bed whether you dance prettily or not? I try a special turn and curtsey that I have been practising and it does me no good at all. Nobody seems to notice except my grandmother, who sees everything, and she calls me out of the line and puts her finger under my chin and says: 'Child, there is no need to twinkle around like some slut of an Italian. We all watch you anyway.' By which I am supposed to understand that I should not dance like a lady, like an elegant young lady, with some style; but like a child.

I curtsey and say nothing. There is no point in arguing with my lady grandmother, she has such a temper she can send me from the room in a moment if I so much as open my mouth. I really do think I am very cruelly treated.

'And what's this I hear about you and young Master Dereham?' she suddenly asks. 'I thought I had warned you once already?'

'I don't know what you hear, Grandmother,' I say cleverly.

Too clever for her, because she raps my hand with her fan.

'Don't forget who you are, Katherine Howard,' she says sharply. 'When your uncle sends for you to wait on the queen, I take it you will not want to refuse because of some greensick flirtation?'

'Wait on the queen?' I go at once to the most important thing.

'Perhaps,' she says maddeningly. 'Perhaps she will have need of a maid in waiting if the girl has been gently raised and is not known to be an utter slut.'

I cannot speak, I am so desperate. 'Grandmother . . . I . . .'

'Never mind,' she says and waves me away back to the dancers. I clutch at her sleeve and beg to know more; but she laughs and sends me to dance. As she is watching me, I hop about like a little wooden doll, I am so correct in the steps and so polite in my deportment that you would think I had a crown on my head myself. I dance like a nun, I dance like a vestal virgin, and when I look up to see if she is impressed by my modesty she is laughing at me.

So that night, when Francis comes to the chamber door, I meet him on the threshold. 'You can't come in,' I say bluntly. 'My lady grandmother knows all about us. She warned me for my reputation.'

He looks shocked. 'But my love . . .'

'I can't risk it,' I insist. 'She knows far more than we thought. God knows what she has heard or who has told her.'

'We would not deny each other,' he says.

'No,' I say uncertainly.

'If she asks you, you must tell her that we are married in the eyes of God.'

'Yes, but . . .'

'And I shall come to you as your husband now.'

'You can't.' Nothing in this world is going to prevent me from being the new queen's maid in waiting. Not even my undying love for Francis.

41

He puts his hand around my waist and nibbles at the nape of my neck. 'I shall be going to Ireland within days,' he whispers softly. 'You will not send me away with my heart breaking.'

I hesitate. It would be very sad for his heart to break, but I have to be maid in waiting to the new queen, there is nothing more important than that.

'I don't want your heart to break,' I say. 'But I have to take a post in the queen's household, and who knows what might happen?'

He lets me go abruptly. 'Oh, so you think you're going to go to court?' he asks crossly. 'And flirt with some great lord? Or one of your noble cousins or someone? A Culpepper or a Mowbray or a Neville or someone?'

'I don't know,' I say. It is really marvellous how dignified I can be. You would think I was my grandmother. 'I cannot discuss my plans with you now.'

'Kitty!' he cries, he is torn between anger and lust. 'You are my wife, you are my promised wife! You are my own beloved!'

'I must ask you to withdraw,' I say very grandly, and I close the door in his face and run and take a flying leap into my bed.

'What now?' asks Agnes. At the far end of the dormitory they have drawn the curtains around the bed, some boy and some loose girl are lovemaking, and I can hear his eager panting and her sighing.

'Can't you be quiet?' I shout down the long room. 'It's really shocking. It is offensive to a young maid such as me. It's shocking. It really shouldn't be allowed.'

Anne, Calais,
December 1539

In all this long journey I have started to learn how I shall be when I am queen. The English ladies that my lord the king sent to be with me have spoken English to me every day, and my lord Southampton has been at my side at every town we have entered, and has prompted me and guided me in the most helpful way. They are a most formal and dignified people, everything has to be done by rote, by rule, and I am learning to hide my excitement at the greetings, the music, and the crowds who everywhere come out to see me. I don't want to seem like the country sister of a minor duke, I want to be like a queen, a true Queen of England.

At every town I have had a welcome of people thronging in the streets, calling out my name and bringing me posies and gifts. Most towns present me with a loyal address and give me a purse of gold or some valuable jewellery. But my arrival in my first English town, the port of Calais, is dwarfing everything that went before. It is a mighty English castle with a great walled town around it, built to withstand any attack from France, the enemy, just outside the powerfully guarded gates. We enter by the south gate that looks over the road towards the kingdom of France and we are greeted by an English nobleman, Lord Lisle, and dozens of gentlemen and noblemen, dressed very fine, with a small army of men dressed in red and blue livery.

I thank God for sending me Lord Lisle to be my friend and advisor in these difficult days for he is a kind man, with something of the look of my father. Without him, I would be speechless from terror as well as from my lack of English. He is dressed as fine as a king himself, and there are so very many English noblemen with him that they are like a sea of furs and velvet. But he takes my cold hand in his big warm grip and he smiles at me and says 'Courage'. I may not know the word till I ask my interpreter, but I know a friend when I see one, and I find a small peaky smile and then he tucks my hand into the crook of his arm and leads me down the broad street to the harbour. The bells are pealing a welcome to me, and all the merchants' wives and children are lining the streets to have a look at me and the apprentice boys and servants all shout, 'Anna of Cleves, hurrah!' as I go by.

In the harbour there are two huge ships, the king's own, one called the *Sweepstake*, which means something about gambling, and one named the *Lion*, both flying banners and sounding the trumpets as they see me approach. They have been sent from England to bring me to the king, and with them comes a huge fleet to escort me. The gunners fire off rounds, and the cannon roar, and the whole town is drenched in smoke and noise, but this is a great compliment and so I smile and try not to flinch. We go on to the Staple Hall where the mayor of the town and the merchants give me greetings in long speeches and two purses of gold and Lady Lisle, who is here to greet me with her husband, presents my ladies in waiting to me.

They all accompany me back to the king's house, the Chequer, and I stand as one after another comes forwards and says their name and presents their compliments and makes their bow or their curtsey. I am so tired and so overwhelmed by the whole day that I feel my knees start to weaken underneath me but still they come on, one after another. My lady Lisle stands beside me and says each name in my ear and tells me a little about them, but I cannot understand her words and, besides, there are too many strangers to take it all in. It is a dizzying crowd of people; but they are all smiling kindly at me, and they all bow so respectfully. I ought to be glad of such attention and not overwhelmed by it, I know.

As soon as the last lady, maid, servant and page has made their bow, and I can decently leave, I say that I should like to go to my privy chamber before we dine, and my interpreter tells them; but still I cannot be at peace. As soon as we walk into my private rooms there are more strange faces waiting to be presented as servants and members of my privy chamber. I am so exhausted by all these introductions that I say I should like to go to my bedchamber, but even here I cannot be alone. In comes Lady Lisle and other ladies and the maids in waiting to make sure that I have everything I need. A full dozen of them come in and pat the bed and straighten the curtains and stand about, looking at me. In absolute desperation I say that I want to pray and go into the little closet beside the bedchamber and close the door on their helpful faces.

I can hear them waiting outside, like an audience waiting for a fool to come out and juggle or play tricks: a little puzzled at the delay, but good-humoured enough. I lean back against the door and touch my forehead with the back of my hand. I am cold and yet I am sweating, as if I were ill with a fever. I must do this. I know I can do this, I know I can be Queen of England, and a good queen as well. I will learn their language; already I can understand most of what is said to me, though I stumble over speech. I will learn all these new names and their rank and the proper way to address them so that I won't always have to stand like a little doll with a puppet-master beside me, telling me what to do. As soon as I get to England I shall see about ordering some new clothes. My ladies and I, in our German dress, look like fat little ducks beside these English swans. They go about half-naked with hardly a hood on their heads at all, they flit about in their light gowns, while we are strapped into fustian as if we were lumpy parcels. I shall learn to be elegant, I shall learn to be pleasing, I shall learn to be a queen. I shall certainly learn to meet a hundred people without sweating for fear.

It strikes me now that they will be finding my behaviour very odd. First, I say I want to dress for dinner, and then I step into a room that is little more than a cupboard, and make them wait outside. I will seem ridiculously devout or, worse, they will know I am painfully shy. As soon as this occurs to me I freeze inside the little room. I feel such a country-born dolt. I hardly know how to find the courage to come out.

I listen at the door. It has gone very quiet outside, perhaps they have become tired of waiting for me. Perhaps they have all gone off to change their clothes again. Hesitantly, I open the door a crack and look out.

There is only one lady left in the room, seated at the window, calmly looking down into the yard below, watching. As she hears the betraying creak of the door she looks up and her face is kind and interested.

'Lady Anne?' she says, and she rises to her feet and curtseys to me.

'I . . .'

'I am Jane Boleyn,' she says, guessing rightly that I cannot remember a single name from the blur of this morning. 'I am one of your ladies in waiting.'

As she says her name I am utterly confused. She must be some relation to Anne Boleyn; but what is she doing in my chamber? Surely she cannot be here to wait on me? Surely she should be in exile, or in disgrace?

I look around for someone to translate for us, and she smiles and shakes her head. She points to herself and says 'Jane Boleyn,' and then she says, very slowly and steadily: 'I will be your friend.'

And I understand her. Her smile is warm and her face honest. I realise that she means that she will be a friend to me; and the thought of having a friend I can trust in this sea of new people and new faces brings a lump into my throat and I blink back the tears and I put out my hand to her to shake, as if I were a half-simple country-woman in the market place.

'Boleyn?' I stammer.

'Yes,' she says, taking my hand in her cool grip. 'And I know all about how fearful it is to be Queen of England. Who would know better than me how hard it can be? I will be your friend,' she says again. 'You can trust me.' And she shakes my hand with a warm grasp, and I believe her, and we both smile.

Jane Boleyn, Calais, December 1539

She will never please him, poor child, not in a lifetime, not in a thousand years. I am amazed that his ambassadors did not warn him, they have been thinking entirely of making a league against France and Spain, of a Protestant league against the Catholic kings, and thinking nothing of the tastes of King Henry.

There is nothing she can do to become the sort of woman that pleases him. His preference runs to quick-witted, dainty, smiling women with an air that promises everything. Even Jane Seymour, though she was quiet and obedient, radiated a docile warmth that hinted at sensual pleasure. But this one is like a child, awkward like a child, with a child's honest gaze and an open, friendly smile. She looks thrilled when someone bows low to her, and when she first saw the ships in the harbour she seemed about to applaud. When she is tired or overwhelmed she goes pale like a sulky child and looks ready to weep. Her nose goes red when she is anxious, like a peasant in the cold. If it were not so tragic this would be the highest of comedies, this gawky girl stepping into the diamond-heeled shoes of Anne Boleyn. What can they have been thinking of when they imagined she could ever rise to it?

But her very awkwardness gives me a key to her. I can be her friend, her great friend and ally. She will need a friend, poor lost girl, she will need a friend who knows the way around a court such as ours. I can introduce her to all the things she will need to know, teach her the skills she must learn. And who should know better than I, who have been at the heart of the greatest court that England ever had, and seen it burn itself up? Who better than me to keep a queen safe, who watched one destroy herself and destroy her family with her? I have promised to be this new queen's friend and I can honour that promise. She is young, only twenty-four years old, but she will grow. She is ignorant but she can be taught. She is inexperienced but life will correct that. I can do much for this quaint young woman, and it will be a real pleasure and an opportunity to be her guide and mentor.

Katherine, Norfolk House, Lambeth,
December 1539

My uncle is coming to see my grandmother and I must be ready in case he sends for me. We all know what is about to happen but I am as excited as if I were waiting for a great surprise. I have practised my walk towards him and my curtsey. I have practised my look of astonishment and my delighted smile at the wonderful news. I like to be prepared, I like to be rehearsed, and I have had Agnes and Joan play the part of my uncle until I am step-perfect in my approach, my curtsey and my genteel cry of joy.

The maids' room is sick of me, sick as if they had eaten a glut of green apples, but I tell them it is only to be expected, I am a Howard, of course I will be called to court, of course I will serve the queen and, sadly, of course they will be left behind; what a pity.

They say I will have to learn German, and there will be no dancing. I know this is a lie. She will live like a queen and if she is dull, I shall only shine more brightly in contrast. They say it is well-known that she will live in seclusion, and the Dutch eat no meat but only cheese and butter all day. I know this is a lie – why else would the queen's apartments at Hampton Court have been repainted but for her to have a court and guests? They say that all her ladies have already been appointed and half of them have already left to meet her in Calais. My uncle is coming to tell me that I have missed my chance.

This, finally, frightens me. I know that the king's nieces, Lady

Margaret Douglas and the Marchioness of Dorset, have agreed to be the chiefest of her ladies and I fear it is too late for me. 'No,' I say to Mary Lascelles, 'he cannot be coming to tell me I must stay here. He cannot be coming to tell me that I am too late, that there will be no place left for me.'

'And if he does then let it be a lesson to you,' she says firmly. 'Let it be a lesson to you to mend your ways. You don't deserve to go to the queen's court as light as you have been with Francis Dereham. No true lady should have you in her chambers when you have played the slut with such a man.'

This is so unkind that I give a little gasp and feel the tears coming.

'Now don't cry,' she says wearily. 'Don't cry, Katherine. You will only make your eyes red.'

Instantly, I hold my nose to stop the tears coming. 'But if he tells me I am to stay here and do nothing I shall die!' I say thickly. 'I will be fifteen next year, and then I will be eighteen, and then I will be nineteen and then I will be twenty and too old for marriage and I will die here, serving my grandmother, never having been anywhere, and never seen anything, and never danced at court.'

'Oh, nonsense!' she exclaims crossly. 'Can you never think of anything but your vanity, Katherine? Besides, some would think you have done quite enough already for a maid of fourteen.'

'Duthing,' I say, with my nose still pinched. I let it go and press my cool fingers against my cheeks. 'I have done nothing.'

'Of course, you will serve the queen,' she says scornfully. 'Your uncle is not likely to miss such a place for one of his family, however badly you have behaved.'

'The girls said . . .'

'The girls are jealous of you because you are going, you ninny. If you were staying they would be all over you with pretend sympathy.'

This is so true that even I can see it. 'Oh, yes.'

'So wash your face again and come to my lady's chamber. Your uncle will be here at any moment.'

I go as fast as I can, pausing only to tell Agnes and Joan and Margaret that I know full well I am going to court and that I never believed their spite for a moment, and then I hear them shouting: 'Katherine! Katherine! He is here!' and I dash down to my lady's own parlour and there he is, my uncle, standing before the fire and warming his backside.

It would take more than a fire to warm this man through. My grandmother says that he is the king's hammer; whenever there is hard and dirty work to do it is my uncle who leads the English army to batter the enemy into submission. When the North rose up to defend the old religion just two years ago when I was a little girl, it was my uncle who brought the rebels to their senses. He promised them a pardon and then cozened them to the gallows. He saved the king's throne and he saved the king the trouble of fighting his own battles and putting down a great rebellion. My grandmother says that he knows no other argument but the noose. She says he strung up thousands even though inwardly, he agreed with their cause. His own faith did not stop him. Nothing will stop him. I can see by his face that he is a hard man, a man not easily softened; but he has come to see me and I will show him what sort of niece he has.

I dip down into a deep curtsey, as we have practised over and over again in the maids' chamber, leaning a little forwards so that my lord can see the tempting curve of my breasts pressed at the top of my gown. Slowly I look up at his face before I rise, so that he sees me almost on my knees before him, giving him a moment to think about the pleasure of what I could be doing down there, my little nose almost against his breeches. 'My lord uncle,' I breathe as I rise, as if I were whispering it in his ear in bed. 'Give you a very good day, sir.'

'Good God,' he says bluntly, and my grandmother gives a little 'Huh' of amusement.

'She is a . . . a credit to you, ma'am,' he says as I rise without wobbling and stand before him. I clasp my hands behind my back to present my breasts to their full advantage, and I arch my back too so that he can admire the slimness of my waist. With my eyes modestly cast down I could be a schoolgirl except for the thrust of my body and the little half-hidden smile.

'She is a Howard girl through and through,' says my grandmother, who has no great opinion of Howard girls, known as we are for beauty and forwardness.

'I was expecting a child,' he says as if he is very pleased to find me grown.

'A very knowing child.' She gives me a hard look to remind me that nobody wants to know what I have learned while in her care. I widen my eyes innocently. I was seven years old when I first saw a maid bedding a pageboy, I was eleven when Henry Manox first got hold of me. How did she think I would turn out?

'She will do very nicely,' he says, after he has taken a moment to recover. 'Katherine, can you dance and sing and play the lute and so on?'

'Yes, my lord.'

'Read, write, in English and French, and Latin?'

I shoot an anguished look at my grandmother. I am tremendously stupid, and everyone knows it. I am so stupid that I don't even know if I should lie about it or not.

'Why would she need that?' she asks. 'The queen speaks nothing but Dutch, doesn't she?'

He nods. 'German. But the king likes an educated woman.'

The duchess smiles. 'He did once,' she says. 'The Seymour girl was no great philosopher. I think he has lost his taste for argument from his wives. Do you like an educated woman?'

He gives a little snort at this. The whole world knows that he and his wife have been parted for years, they hate each other so much.

'Anyway, what matters most is that she pleases the queen and pleases the court,' my uncle rules. 'Katherine, you are to go to court and be one of the new queen's maids in waiting.'

I beam at him.

'You are glad to go?'

'Yes, my lord uncle. I am very grateful,' I remember to add.

'You have been placed in such a position of importance to be a credit to your family,' he says solemnly. 'Your grandmother here tells me you are a good girl and that you know how to behave. Make sure that you do, and don't let us down.'

I nod. I dare not look at my grandmother, who knew all about Henry Manox, and who caught me once in the upper hall with Francis, with my hand down the front of his breeches and the mark of his bite on my neck, and called me a whore in the making and a stupid slut, and gave me a cuff that made my head ring, and warned me off him again at Christmas.

'There will be young men who may pay attention to you,' my uncle warns, as if I have never met a young man before. I dart a look at my grandmother but she is blandly smiling. 'Remember that nothing is more important than your reputation. Your honour must be without stain. If I hear any unbecoming gossip about you – and I mean anything, and you can be sure that I hear everything – then I will remove you immediately from court and send you not even here, but back to your step-grandmother's house in the country at Horsham. Where I will leave you forever. Do you understand?'

'Yes, my lord uncle.' It comes out in a terrified whisper. 'I promise.'

'I will see you at court almost daily,' he says. I am almost beginning to wish that I was not going. 'And from time to time I shall send for you to come to my rooms and tell me how you are getting on with the queen, and so on. You will be discreet and you will not gossip. You will keep your eyes open and your mouth shut. You will take advice from your kinswoman Jane Boleyn, who is also in the queen's rooms. You will endeavour to become close to the queen, you shall be her little friend. From the favour of princes comes wealth. Never forget it. This could be the making of you, Katherine.'

'Yes, my lord uncle.'

'And another thing,' he says warningly.

'Yes, uncle?'

'Modesty, Katherine. It is a woman's greatest asset.'

I sink into a curtsey, my head bowed, as modest as a nun. A laugh of derision from my grandmother tells me that she is not persuaded. But when I look up my uncle is smiling.

'Convincing. You can go,' he says.

I curtsey again and I flee from the room before he can say anything worse. I have been longing to go to court for the dancing and young men and he makes it sound like going into service.

'What did he say? What did he say?' They are all waiting in the great hall, desperate to know the news.

'I am to go to court!' I crow. 'And I am to have new gowns and new hoods and he says I will be the prettiest girl in the queen's chamber, and there will be dancing every night, and I daresay I will never see any of you ever again.'

Anne, Calais,
December 1539

The weather to cross the English Sea is, thank God, fair at last, after days of delay. I hoped that I would have a letter from home before we set sail, but though we have had to wait and wait for good weather for the crossing, no-one has written to me. I thought that Mother might have written to me; even if she is not missing me I thought she might have sent me some words of advice. I thought Amelia might already be hoping for a visit to England and might write me a letter of sisterly greeting. I could almost laugh at myself tonight, to think how low my spirits must be if I am wanting a letter from Amelia.

The only one I was certain of was my brother. I was sure I would have a letter from him. He never regained his temper with me, not in all the long preparation of leaving, and we parted on the terms that we have lived all our lives: on my side with a resentful fearfulness of his power, and on his side with an irritation that he cannot voice. I thought that he might write to me to appoint me with business to transact at the English court; surely I should be representing my country and our interests? But there are all the Cleves lords who are travelling with me, no doubt he has spoken or written to them. He must have decided that I am not fit to do business for him.

I thought at any rate that he was certain to write to me to lay down rules for my conduct. After all, he has spent his life dominating me, I did not think he would just let me go. But it seems I am free of him. Instead of being glad of that, I am uneasy. It is strange to leave my family, and none of them even send me Godspeed.

We are to set sail tomorrow in the early morning to catch the tide and I am waiting in my rooms in the king's house, the Chequer, for Lord Lisle to come for me when I hear something like an argument in the presence chamber outside. By luck my Cleves translator, Lotte, is with me and at a nod from me she crosses quietly to the door and listens to the rapid English speech. Her expression is intent, she frowns, and then, when she hears footsteps coming, she scurries back into the room and sits beside me.

Lord Lisle bows as he comes into the room but his colour is up. He smooths down his velvet jerkin, as if to compose himself. 'Forgive me, Lady Anne,' he says. 'The house is upside down with packing. I will come for you in an hour.'

She whispers his meaning to me and I bow and smile. He glances back at the door. 'Did she hear us?' he asks Lotte bluntly, and she turns to me to see me nod. He comes closer.

'Secretary Thomas Cromwell is of your religion,' he says quietly. Lotte whispers the German words into my ear so that I can be sure of understanding him. 'He has wrongly protected some hundreds of Lutherans in this city which is under my command.'

I understand the words, of course, but not their significance.

'They are heretics,' he says. 'They deny the authority of the king as a spiritual leader, and they deny the sacred miracle of the sacrifice of Jesus Christ, that his wine becomes blood. This is the belief of the Church of England. To deny it is a heresy punished with death.'

I put my hand gently on Lotte's arm. I know these are most perilous matters, but I don't know what I should say.

'Secretary Cromwell himself could be charged with heresy if the king knew that he had sheltered these men,' Lord Lisle says. 'I was telling his son, Gregory, that these men should be charged, whoever protects them. I was warning him that I cannot look to one side, I was warning him that good Englishmen think as I do, that God will not be mocked.'

'I know nothing of these English matters,' I say carefully. 'I wish only to be guided by my husband.' I think briefly of my brother who has charged me with bringing my husband away from these Papist superstitions into the clarity of reform. I think I shall have to disappoint him again.

Lord Lisle nods, he bows and steps back. 'Forgive me,' he says. 'I should not have troubled you with this. I just wanted to make clear that I resent Thomas Cromwell's protection of these people and that I am wholly loyal to the king and to his church.'

I nod, for what else can I say or do? And he goes out of the room. I turn to Lotte.

'That's not quite right,' she says very quietly. 'He did accuse the Master Cromwell of protecting Lutherans, but the son, Gregory Cromwell, accused him of being a secret Papist, and said that he would be watched. They were threatening each other.'

'What does he expect me to do?' I ask blankly. 'He can hardly think that I would judge on such a matter?'

She looks troubled. 'Perhaps to speak to the king? To influence him?'

'Lord Lisle as good as told me that in his eyes I am a heretic myself. I deny that the wine turns into blood. Anyone of any sense must know that such a thing cannot happen.'

'Do they really execute heretics in England?' the woman asks nervously.

I nod.

'How?'

'They burn them at the stake.'

At her aghast expression I am about to explain that the king knows of my faith and is supposed to be allying with my Protestant brother and his league of Protestant dukes; but there is a shout at the door and the ships are ready to leave.

'Come on,' I say with a sudden rush of bravado. 'Let's go anyway, whatever the dangers. Nothing can be worse than Cleves.'

Setting sail from an English port on an English ship feels like the start of a new life. Most of my companions from Cleves will leave me now, so there are more leave-takings, and then I board the ship and we cast off, the rowing barges take the ships into tow out of the harbour, and they raise the sails and they catch the wind and the sails start to creak and the ship lifts up as if it would take flight, and now, at this moment, I feel truly that I am a queen going to my country, like a queen in a story.

I go to the bow and stare over the side at the moving water, at the crest of white waves on the black sea, and wonder when I shall see my new home, my kingdom, my England. All around me are the other little lights on the ships that are sailing with us. It is a fleet of ships, fifty great vessels, the queen's fleet, and I am coming to realise the wealth and power of my new country.

We are to sail all the day, they say the sea is calm but the waves look very high and dangerous to me. The little ships climb up one wall of water and then belly down to the trough between the waves. Sometimes we lose sight of the other ships in the fleet altogether. The sails billow and creak as if they would tear, and the English sailors haul on ropes and dash around the deck like blasphemous madmen. I watch the dawn break, a grey sun over a grey sea, and I feel the immensity of the water all around me and even beneath me, then I go to rest in my cabin. Some of the ladies are sick, but I feel well. Lady Lisle sits with me for some of the day and some of the others, Jane Boleyn among them. I shall have to learn the names of all the others. The day goes slowly by, I go up on deck but all I can see are the ships around us, almost as far as I can see is the English fleet, keeping company with me. I should feel proud at this attention being paid to me, but more than anything else I feel uncomfortable at being the centre and the cause of so much trouble and activity. The sailors on the ship all pull off their caps and bow whenever I come out of the cabin, and two of the ladies always have to escort me, even if it is just to the prow of the ship. After a while, I feel so conspicuous, so restless, that I force myself to sit still in my cabin and watch the waves going up and down through the little window rather than inconvenience everyone by wandering about.

The first sight I have of England is a dark shadow on darkening seas. It is getting late by the time we come into a tiny port called Deal, but even though it is dark and raining, I am greeted by even more grand people. They take me to rest in the castle, and to eat, and there are hundreds, truly hundreds, of people who come to kiss my hand and welcome me to my country. In a haze I meet lords and their ladies, a bishop, the warden of the castle, some more ladies who will serve in my chamber, some maids who will be my companions. Clearly, I will never be alone again for another moment in all my life.

As soon as we have eaten we are all to move on, there is a strict plan as to where we shall stay and where we shall dine, but they ask me very courteously, am I ready to travel now? I learn quickly that this does not mean, in truth, would I like to leave? It means, that the plan says we should go now, and they are waiting for me to give my assent.

So even though it is evening and I am so tired I would give a fortune to rest here, I climb into the litter that my brother equipped for me at such begrudged expense, and the lords mount their horses and the ladies mount theirs and we rattle on the road in the darkness with soldiers before us and behind us as if we were an invading army, and I remind myself that I am queen now, and if this is how queens travel and how they are served then I must become accustomed to it, and not long for a quiet bed and a meal without an audience watching my every move.

We stay this night in the castle in Dover, arriving in darkness. The next day I am so weary I can hardly rise, but there are half a dozen maids holding my shift and my gown and my hairbrush and my hood, and maids in waiting standing behind them, and ladies in waiting behind them, and a message comes from the Duke of Suffolk as to whether I would like to journey on to Canterbury once I have said my prayers and broken my fast? I know from this that he is anxious that we should leave and that I should hurry to say my prayers and eat, and so I say that I shall be delighted, and that I myself am keen to press on.

This is clearly a lie since it has been raining all the night and now it is getting heavier and it is starting to hail. But everyone prefers to believe that I am anxious to see the king, and my ladies wrap me up as well as they can and then we trudge out of the courtyard with a gale blowing, and we set off up the road they call Watling Street to the town of Canterbury.

The archbishop himself, Thomas Cranmer, a gentle man with a kind smile, greets me on the road outside the city, and rides alongside my litter as we travel the last half a mile. I stare out through the driving rain; this was the great pilgrim road for the faithful going to the shrine of St Thomas à Becket at the cathedral. I can see the spire of the church long before I can see even the walls of the town, it is built so high and so beautiful, and the light catches it through dark clouds as if God was touching the holy place. The road is paved here and every other house alongside was built to accommodate pilgrims, who used to come from all over Europe to pray at this most beautiful shrine. This was once one of the great holy sites of the world – just a few short years ago.

It's all changed now. Changed as much as if they had thrown the church down. My mother has warned me not to remark on what we had heard of the king's great changes, nor on what I see – however shocking. The king's own commissioners went to the shrine of the great saint and took the treasure that had been offered at the shrine.

They went into the vaults and raided the very coffin that held the saint's body. It is said that they took his martyred body and threw it on the midden outside the city walls, they were so determined to destroy this sacred place.

My brother would say it is a good thing that the English have turned their backs on superstition and Popish practices, but my brother does not see that the houses for pilgrims have been taken over by bawdy houses and inns and there are beggars without anywhere to go all along the roads into Canterbury. My brother does not know that half the houses in Canterbury were hospitals for the poor and sick and that the church paid for poor pilgrims to stay and be nursed back to health and that the nuns and monks spent their lives serving the poor. Now our soldiers have to push their way through a murmuring crowd of people who are looking for the holy refuge that they were promised; but it has all gone. I take care to say nothing when our cavalcade turns through great gates and the archbishop dismounts from his horse to welcome me into a beautiful house that was clearly an abbey, perhaps only months ago. I look around as we go into a beautiful hall where travellers would have been freely entertained, and where the monks would have dined. I know that my brother wants me to lead this country still further away from superstition and papacy, but he has not seen what has been spoiled in this country in the name of reform.

The windows, which were once made of coloured glass to show beautiful stories, have been smashed so carelessly that the stone is broken and the tracery of stonework is all crushed. If a naughty boy did such a thing to windows he would be whipped. High in the vaulting roof were little angels and, I think, a frieze of saints, which has been knocked out by some fool with a hammer who cared for nothing. It is foolish, I know, to grieve for things of stone; but the men who did this godly work did not do it in a godly way. They could have taken the statues down and made good the walls after. But instead, they just knocked off the heads, and left the little angel bodies headless. How this serves the will of God, I cannot know.

I am a daughter of Cleves and we have turned against papacy and rightly; but I have not seen this sort of stupidity before. I can't think why men would believe that it is a better world where something beautiful is destroyed and something broken left in its place. Then they take me to my rooms, which clearly once belonged to the prior. They have been replastered and repainted and still smell of new limewash. And here I start to realise the real reason for religious reform in this country. This beautiful building, and the lands on which it stands, the great farms which pay it rent and the flocks of sheep which bear its wool, once all belonged to the church and to the Pope. The church was the greatest landowner in England. Now all that wealth belongs to the king. For the first time I realise that this is not just a matter of the worship of God. Perhaps it is nothing to do with God. There is the greed of man here too.

There is vanity as well, perhaps. For Thomas à Becket was a saint who defied a tyrant King of England. His body lay in the crypt of this most lavish cathedral, encased in gold and jewels, and the king himself – who ordered the throwing down of this shrine – used to come here to pray for help. But now the king needs no help, and rebels are hanged in this country, and the wealth and beauty must all belong to the king. My brother would say that this is a good thing and that a country cannot have two masters.

I am wearily changing my gown for dinner when I hear another roar of guns and although it is pitch black and nearly midnight Jane Boleyn comes smiling to tell me that there are hundreds of people in the great hall come to welcome me to Canterbury.

'Many gentlemen?' I ask her in my stilted English.

She smiles at once, she knows that I am dreading a long line of introductions.

'They just want to see you,' she says clearly, pointing to her eyes.

'You just have to wave.' She shows me a wave and I giggle at the masque that we play to each other while I learn her language.

I point to the window. 'Good land,' I say.

She nods. 'Abbey land, God's land.'

'Now the king's?'

She has a wry smile. 'The king is now head of the church, you understand? All the wealth –' she hesitates '– the spiritual wealth of the church is now his.'

'And the people are glad?' I ask. I am so frustrated by being unable to speak fluently. 'The bad priests are gone?'

She glances towards the door as if she would be sure that we cannot be overheard. 'The people are not glad,' she says. 'The people loved the shrines and the saints, they don't know why the candles are being taken away. They don't know why they cannot pray for help. But you should not speak of this to anyone but me. It is the king's will that the church should be destroyed.'

I nod. 'He is a Protestant?' I ask.

Her quick smile makes her eyes sparkle. 'Oh, no!' she says. 'He is whatever he wishes to be. He destroyed the church so that he could marry my sister-in-law; she believed in a reformed church and the king believed with her. Then he destroyed her. He has turned the church almost back to being Catholic, the Mass is almost completely restored – but he will never give back the wealth. Who knows what he will do next? What will he believe next?'

I understand only a little of this so I turn away from her and look out of the window at the driving rain and the pitch darkness. The thought of a king who can determine not only what life his people lead but even the nature of the God they worship makes me shiver. This is a king who has thrown down the shrine of one of the greatest saints in Christendom, this is a king who has turned the great monasteries of his country into private houses. My brother was quite wrong to command me to lead this king into right-thinking. This is a king who will have his own way, and I daresay nobody can stop or turn him.

'We should go to dinner,' Jane Boleyn says gently to me. 'Do not speak of these things to anyone.'

'Yes,' I say, and with her just one pace behind me I open my privy chamber door to the crowds of people waiting for me in my presence chamber and I face the sea of unknown smiling faces once more.

I am so delighted to be out of the rain and out of the darkness that I take a large glass of wine and eat heartily at dinner, even though I sit alone under a canopy and I am served by men who kneel to offer dishes to me. There are hundreds of people dining in the hall and hundreds more who peer in at the windows and doorways to see me as if I were some strange animal.

I will grow accustomed to this, I know that I have to; and I will. There is no point being a Queen of England and being embarrassed by servants. This stolen abbey is not even one of the great palaces of the land and yet I have never seen a place so wealthy with gildings and paintings and tapestries. I ask the archbishop if this is his own palace and he smiles and says his own house is nearby. This is a country of such great riches that it is almost unimaginable.

I do not get to my bed till the early hours of the morning and then we rise again, early, to travel on. But however early we start it still takes us forever to leave as every day there are more people coming with us. The archbishop and all his train, truly hundreds of them, are now travelling with me, and this day I am joined by more great lords who escort me into Rochester. The people line the streets to greet me and everywhere I go I smile and wave.

I wish I could remember everyone's name, but every time we stop anywhere some richly dressed man comes up and bows before me, and Lady Lisle, or Lady Southampton, or one of the other ladies whispers something in my ear, and I smile and extend my hand, and try to fix a fresh set of names into my mind. And they all look the same anyway: all dressed in rich velvet and wearing gold chains and with pearls or jewels in their hats. And there are dozens of them, hundreds of them, half of England has come to pay their compliments to me, and I cannot tell one man from another any more.

We dine in a great hall with much ceremony and Lady Browne, who is to be in charge of my maids in waiting, is presented to me. She introduces my maids by name and I smile at the unending line of Katherines and Marys and Elizabeths and Annes and Bessies and Madges, all of them pert and pretty under tiny hoods that show their hair in a way that my brother would blame as immodest, all of them dainty in little slippers, and all of them stare at me as if I were a wild white falcon landed in a chicken coop. Lady Browne especially stares me out of countenance, and I beckon Lotte and ask her to tell Lady Browne in English that I hope she will advise me about my dress and English fashions when we get to London. When she gives her my message, Lady Browne flushes and turns away and does not stare any more, and I fear that she was indeed thinking that my dress is very odd and that I am ugly.

Jane Boleyn, Rochester, December 1539

'Advise her about her dress!' Lady Browne hisses at me, as if it is my fault that the new Queen of England looks so outlandish. 'Jane Boleyn, tell me! Could she not have changed her dress in Calais?'

'Who could have advised her?' I ask reasonably. 'All her ladies dress the same, after all.'

'Lord Lisle could have advised her. He could have warned her that she couldn't come to England looking like a friar in fustian. How can I be expected to keep her maids in order when they are laughing their heads off at her? I nearly had to smack Katherine Howard. That child has been one day in royal service and already she is mimicking the queen's walk and, what is worse, she has her to the life.'

'Maids are always naughty. You will command them.'

'There is no time for dressmakers until she gets to London. She will have to go on as she has begun, even if she looks like a parcel. What is she doing now?'

'She is resting,' I say guardedly. 'I thought I would leave her in peace for a moment.'

'She is to be Queen of England,' her ladyship snaps. 'That is not a peaceful life for any woman.'

I say nothing.

'Should we say anything to the king? Shall I speak to my husband?' Lady Browne asks me, her voice very low. 'Should we not tell Secretary

Cromwell that we have . . . reservations? Will you say anything to the duke?'

I think quickly. I swear that I am not going to be the first to speak against this queen. 'Perhaps you should speak to Sir Anthony,' I say. 'Privately, as his wife.'

'Shall I tell him that we are agreed? Surely my lord Southampton realises that she is not fit to be queen. She is so graceless! And all but mute!'

'I have no opinion, myself,' I say rapidly.

She laughs at once. 'Oh, Jane Boleyn, you always have an opinion; not much ever escapes you.'

'Perhaps. But if the king has chosen her because she brings with her the Protestant alliance, if my lord Cromwell has chosen her because it makes us safe against Spain and France, then perhaps the fact that her hood is the size of a house will not matter to him. She can always change her hood. And I would not want to be the one to suggest to the king that the woman he has solemnly and unbreakably betrothed is not fit to be queen.'

That stops her in her tracks. 'You think I would be mistaken to criticise her?'

I think of the white-faced girl who peeped out of the closet in Calais, too shy and too frightened to sit in a room with her own court, and I find that I want to defend her against this unkindness. 'Well, I have no criticism to make of her,' I say. 'I am her lady in waiting. I may advise her as to her gowns or her hair if she asks me; but I would not have one word to say against her.'

'Or at any rate, not yet,' Lady Browne amends coldly. 'Until you see an advantage for yourself.'

I let it pass for just as I am about to answer the door opens and the guard announces: 'Mistress Catherine Carey, the queen's maid in waiting.'

It is her. My niece. I have to face the child at last. I find a smile and I hold out my hands to her. 'Little Catherine!' I exclaim. 'How you have grown!'

She takes my hands but she does not turn up her face to kiss my cheek. She looks at me quietly, as if she is taking the measure of me. The last time I saw her was when she stood behind her Aunt Anne the queen on the scaffold, and held her cloak as the queen put her head on the block. The last time she saw me was outside the courtroom when they called my name to go in to give evidence. I remember how she looked at me then: curiously. She looked at me so curiously, as if she had never seen such a woman before.

'Are you cold? How was your journey? Will you have some wine?' I am drawing her to the fire and she comes, but she is not eager. 'This is Lady Browne,' I say. Her curtsey is good, she is graceful. She has been well taught.

'And how is your mother? And your father?'

'They are well.' Her voice is clear with just a hint of the country in her speech. 'My mother sent you a letter.'

She brings it out of her pocket and hands it to me. I take it over to the light of the large square candle that we use in the royal household and break the seal.

Jane,

So starts Mary Boleyn, without a word of a title as if I did not hold the very name of her house in my name, as if I were not Lady Rochford while she lives at Rochford Hall. As if she did not have my inheritance and my house while I have hers, which is nothing.

Long ago I chose the love of my husband over the vanity and danger of the court, and we perhaps would all have been happier if you and my sister had done the same – God have mercy on her soul. I have no desire to return to court but I wish you and the new Queen Anne better fortune than before, and I hope that your ambitions bring you the happiness you seek, and not what some might think you deserve.

My uncle has commanded the attendance of my daughter Catherine at court and in obedience to him, she will arrive for the New Year. It is my instruction to her that she obeys only the king and her uncle, that she is guided only by my advice and her own good conscience. I have told her that, at the end, you were no friend to my sister nor my brother and advised her to treat you with the respect you deserve.

Mary Stafford

I am shaking after I have read this note and I re-read it again as if it might be different the second time. The respect I deserve? The respect I deserve? What did I do but lie and deceive to save the two of them till the very last moment, and then what did I do but protect the family from the disaster that they brought down on us? What could I do more? What should I have done differently? I obeyed the duke my uncle as I was bound to do, I did as he commanded me, and my deserts are these: that I am his faithful kinswoman and honoured as such.

Who is she to call me a woman who might have been a good wife? I loved my husband with every inch of my soul and being and I would have been everything to him if it were not for her and her sister and the net they made for him that he could not break, and that I could not break for him. Would he not be alive today if he had not gone down with his sister's disgrace? Would he not be my husband and the father of our son today, if he had not been named with Anne and beheaded with Anne? And what did Mary do to save him? What did she ever do but suit herself?

I could scream with sheer rage and despair that she should set these thoughts running again in my head. That she should doubt my love of George, that she should reproach me! I am lost for words at the malice of her letter, at the veiled accusation. What else could I have done? I want to shout into her face. You were there, you were hardly the saviour of George and Anne. What else could any of us have done?

But she was always like this, she and her sister; they always had a way to make me feel that they saw better, understood better, considered better. From the moment that I married George I was aware that his sisters were supposed to be finer young women than I: one the king's lover and then the other. One, in the end, the king's wife and Queen of England. They were born for greatness! The Boleyn Sisters! And I was only ever a sister-in-law. Well, so be it. I have not got where I am today, I have not borne witness and sworn oaths to be reprimanded by a woman who ran away at the first sign of danger and married a man to hide in the country and pray Protestant prayers that good times would come.

Catherine, her daughter, looks at me curiously. 'Did she show you this?' I ask, my voice shaking. Lady Browne looks at me, avidly inquisitive.

'No,' Catherine says.

I put it into the fire, as if it were evidence against me. The three of us watch it burn to grey ash. 'I will reply later,' I say. 'It was not at all important. For now, I will go and see that they have prepared your room.'

It is an excuse to get away from the two of them and the soft ash from the notepaper in the fire. I go quickly out and I call the maids and scold them for inattention, and then I go quietly to my own room and lean my hot forehead against the cool, thick glass. I shall ignore this slander, I shall ignore this insult, I shall ignore this enmity. Whatever its cause. I live in the heart of the court. I serve my king and my family. In time they shall all acknowledge me as the finest of the family, the Boleyn girl who served king and family to the end, never shrinking, never faltering, even if the king has grown fat and dangerous, and the family are all dead but me.

Katherine, Rochester,
31 December 1539

Now let me see, what do I have? What do I have now I am practically a grown-up lady at court?

I have three new gowns, which is good, but it is hardly a vast wardrobe for a girl who expects to be much observed and much commented on. I have three new hoods to match, which are very pretty but none of them are trimmed with anything more than gold lace and I see that many of the ladies of court have pearls and even precious stones on their hoods. I have some good gloves and a new cloak and a muff and a couple of lace collars, but I cannot say that I am overly indulged in my choice or quantity of clothes. And what is the point of being at court if I do not have a great deal of pretty things to wear?

For all my great hopes of court life, it is not proving to be very merry. We came down by boat from Gravesend in the worst weather I have ever seen, driving rain and terrible wind so my hood was all blown about and my hair a mess, and my new velvet cape got wet and I am sure it will be water-marked. The queen-to-be greeted us with a face as blank as a fish. They may say she is tired but she seems just amazed by everything, like some peasant come to town for the first time, she stares astounded at the commonest of sights. When people cheer for her she smiles and waves like a child at a travelling fair, but when she is called upon to greet a lord come to her court, she forever looks around for one of her Cleves companions and mutters to them in their stupid language, puts out her hand as if she was serving a joint of meat and says nothing in English at all.

When I was presented to her she barely looked at me, she looked at all of us new girls as if she did not know what we were doing in her chamber, nor what she should do with us. I thought she might at least ask for music and I have a song note-perfect and ready to sing but, absurdly, she said that she must pray and she went off and shut herself in her closet. My cousin Jane Boleyn says that she does that when she wants to be alone, and that it is a sign not of piety, but of her shyness, and that we must be kind to her and merry with her and she will soon learn our language and be less simple.

I can't see it myself. She has a shift under her gown that comes up nearly to her chin. She has a hood that must be a ton in weight crammed on her head, she is broad in the shoulders and she could be any size in the hips under that pudding-bowl of a gown. Lord Southampton seems very taken with her, but perhaps he is just relieved that the journey will soon be over and his job done. The English ambassadors who were at Cleves with her chat to her in her language and then she is all smiles and chatters back at them like a quacking duckling. Lady Lisle seems to like her. Jane Boleyn is often at her side. But I am afraid that this is not going to be a very merry court for me, and what is the point of a court at all if it is not merry with dancing and flirtation? Indeed, what is the point of anyone being a young queen at all if she is not going to be merry and vain and silly?

There is to be a bull-baiting after dinner and Lady Anne is shown to the window that overlooks the courtyard so that she can have the best view. As soon as she appears at the window a cheer goes up from the men in the yard below, even though they are bringing out the dogs and it is rare for common men to break off from gambling at such a moment. She smiles and waves to them. She is always easy with the ordinary people, and they like her for it. Everywhere we have been on the road she has a smile for the people who come out to see her, and she will blow a kiss to little children who throw posies of flowers in her litter. Everyone is surprised at this. Not since Katherine of Aragon have we had a queen who is so smiling and pleasant to the common people, and not since Aragon has England relished the novelty of a foreign princess. No doubt this one will learn to be easy with the court too, in time.

I stand beside her on one side and one of her German friends is on the other so that he can tell her what is being said. Lord Lisle is there, of course, and Archbishop Cranmer. He is devoting himself to being pleasing, of course. She may be Cromwell's candidate, and thus an asset for his rival; but his worst fear must have been that the king would bring in a Papist princess, and this reforming archbishop would see his church turned back to the old ways once more.

Some of the court are at the windows to see the baiting, some are gossiping quietly at the back of the room. I cannot hear exactly what is being said, but I think there are more than Lady Browne who think that the Lady Anne is not well-suited to the great position that she has been called on to fill. They judge her harshly for her shyness and her lack of speech. They blame her for her clothes and they laugh at her for not being able to dance or sing or play a lute. This is a cruel court, devoted to frivolity, and she is a girl easy to use as a butt for sarcasm. If this goes on, what will happen? She and the king are all but married. Nothing can stop the wedding. He can hardly send her home in disgrace, can he? For the crime of wearing a heavy hood? Not even the king can do that, surely? Not even this king can do it? It would bring Cromwell's treaty down about his ears, it would bring down Cromwell himself, it would leave England friendless facing France and Spain without any Protestant alliance at our back. The king will never risk it, I am sure. But I cannot imagine what will happen.

Down in the yard below they are getting ready to release the bull, his handler unclips the rope from the ring in his nose, skips out of the way, vaults over the boards and the men who have been sitting on the wooden benches rise to their feet and start to shout bets. The bull is a great animal with heavy shoulders and a thick, ugly head. He turns this way and that, spotting the dogs from one little eye and then the other. The dogs are none too eager to be the first to run in, they are afraid of him in his power and his strength.

I feel a little breathless. I have not seen a bull-baiting since I was last at court, I had forgotten what a savage excitement it is to see the yapping dogs and the great beast that they will pull down. It is rare to see a bull as big as this one, his muzzle scarred from earlier fights, his horns barely blunted. The dogs hang back and bark, sharp, persistent barks with the thrilling sound of fear behind them. He turns from one to another, threatening them with the sweep of his horns, and they fall back into a circle around him.

One rushes in, and at once the bull spins, you would not think such a great animal could move so quickly, his head ploughs low and there is a scream like a human cry from the dog as the horns buffet his body, his bones are broken for sure. He is down and cannot crawl away, he is yelping like a baby, the bull stands over him, his head down, and grinds the side of his great horn into the screaming dog.

I find I am crying out, though whether for the dog or for the bull I couldn't say. There is blood on the cobbles but the bull's attack has left him unguarded to the other dogs, and another darts in and takes a bite at his ear. He turns, but at once another fastens on his throat and hangs there for a moment, his white teeth bared and gleaming in the torchlight, while the bull bellows for the first time and the roar of it makes all the maids scream and me among them, and everyone is now crowding to the windows to see as the bull rakes his head round and the dogs fall back and one of them howls with rage.

I find I am trembling, crying out for the dogs to go on! Go on! I want to see more, I want to see all of it, and Lady Anne beside me is laughing, she is excited too, she points to the bull where his ear is bleeding, and I nod and say, 'He will be so angry! He will kill them for sure!' And then suddenly, a bulky man I don't know, a stranger smelling of sweat and wine and horses, pushes in front of us, into the window bay where we are standing, pushes rudely by me, and says to the Lady Anne, 'I bring you greetings from the King of England,' and he kisses her, full on the mouth.

At once I turn to shout for the guards. This is an old man of nearly fifty, a fat man, old enough to be her father. She thinks at once that he is some drunk fool who has managed to push his way into her chamber. She has greeted a hundred men, a thousand men, with a smile and an extended hand and now this man, wearing a marbled cape and a hood pulled over his head, comes up to her and pushes his face into hers and puts his slobbery mouth on hers.

Then I bite off my shout of alarm, I see his height, and I see the men who have come in with him in matching capes, and I know him at once for the king. At the same moment, like a miracle, at once he does not seem old and fat and distasteful. As soon as I know he is the king I see the prince that I have always seen, the one they called the handsomest prince in Christendom, the one that I was in love with myself. This is Henry, King of England, one of the most powerful men in the entire world, the dancer, the musician, the sportsman, the courtly knight, the lover. This is the idol of the English court, as big as the bull in the yard below us, as dangerous as a bull when wounded, as likely to turn on any challenger and kill.

I don't curtsey because he is in disguise. I learned from Katherine of Aragon herself that one should never see through his disguises, he loves to unmask and wait for everyone to exclaim that they had no idea who the handsome stranger was, that they admired him for himself, without knowing that he was our wonderful young king.

And so, because I cannot warn Lady Anne, the scene in our gallery becomes a baiting to equal what is going on, bloodily, in the court-yard below us. She pushes him away, two firm hands against his fat chest, and her face, sometimes so dull and stolid, is burning with colour. She is a modest woman, an untouched girl, and she is horri-fied that this man should come and insult her. She rubs the back of her hand over her face to erase the taste of his lips. Then, terribly, she turns her head and spits his saliva from her mouth. She says something in German that needs no translation, clearly it is a curse against this commoner who has presumed to touch her, to breathe his wine-scented breath into her face.

He stumbles back, he, the great king, almost falls back before her contempt. Never in his life has a woman pushed him away, never in his life has he ever seen any expression in any woman's face but desire and welcome. He is stunned. In her flushed face and bright, offended gaze he sees the first honest opinion of himself that he has ever known. In a terrible, blinding flash he sees himself as he really is: an old man, long past his prime, no longer handsome, no longer desirable, a man that a young woman would push roughly away from her because she could not stand his smell, because she could not bear his touch.

He reels back as if he has taken a mortal blow to the face, to his heart. I have never seen him like this before. I can almost see the thoughts running behind his stunned, flabby face. The sudden realisation that he is not handsome, the realisation that he is not desirable, the terrible realisation that he is old and ill and one day he will die. He is no longer the handsomest prince in Christendom, he is a foolish old man who thought that he could put on a cape and a hood and ride out to meet a girl of twenty-four, and she would admire the handsome stranger, and fall in love with the king.

He is shocked to his soul, and now he looks foolish and confused like a muddled grandfather. Lady Anne is magnificent, she is drawn up to her full height and she is angry, she is powerful, she is standing on her dignity and she shoots a look at him which dismisses him from her court as a man that no-one would want to know. 'Leave me,' she says in heavy-accented English, and she turns her shoulder on him as if she would push him away again.

She looks around the room for a guard to arrest this intruder, and she notices for the first time that no-one is springing to save her, we are all appalled, no-one knows what they can say or do to recover this moment: Lady Anne outraged, the king humbled in his own eyes, thrown down before us all. The truth of the king's age and decay is suddenly, painfully, unforgiveably apparent. Lord Southampton steps forwards but is lost for words; Lady Lisle looks at me and I see my shock mirrored in her face. It is a moment of such intense embarrassment that all of us – we skilled flatterers, courtiers, liars – are lost for words. The world we have been building for thirty years, around our prince who is ageless, eternally handsome, irresistibly desirable, has been shattered about our ears – and by a woman we none of us respect.

He turns wordlessly, he almost stumbles as he goes, his stinking leg giving way beneath him, and Katherine Howard, that clever, clever little girl, catches her breath in a gasp of absolute admiration and says to him: 'Ooh! Forgive me, sir! But I am new to court myself, a stranger like you. May I ask – who are you? What is your name?'

Katherine, Rochester,
31 December 1539

I am the only person to see him come in. I don't like bull-baiting, or bears, or cockfighting, or anything like that, I think it's just down-right nasty – and so I am standing a little back from the windows. And I am looking round, actually, I am looking at a young man that I had seen earlier, such a handsome young man with a cheeky smile, when I see the six of them come in, old men, they must all be thirty at the least, and the big old king at the front, and they are all wearing the same sort of cape, like a masquing costume, so I guess at once that it is him, and that he has come in disguise like a knight errant, silly old fool, and that he will greet her and she will pretend not to know him, and then there will be dancing. Really, I am delighted to see him because this makes it a certainty that there will be dancing and so I am wondering how I can encourage the handsome young man to be near me in the dance.

When he kisses her it all goes terribly wrong. I can see at once that she has no idea who he is, someone should have warned her. She thinks he is just some drunk old man who has staggered in to kiss her for a wager, and of course she is shocked, and of course quite repelled, because when he is in a cheap cloak and not surrounded by the greatest court in the world he does not look at all like a king. In truth, when he is in a cheap cloak and with his companions, also dressed poorly, he looks like some common

80

merchant, with a waddling walk and a red nose, who likes a glass of wine, and hopes to go to court and see his betters. He looks like the sort of man my uncle would not acknowledge if he called out in the street. A fat old man, a vulgar old man, like a drunk sheep farmer on market day. His face is terribly bloated, like a great round dish of dripping, his hair is thinning and grey, he is monstrously fat, and he has an old injury in his leg that makes him so lame that he rolls in his walk like a sailor. Without his crown he is not handsome, he looks like anybody's fat old grandfather.

He falls back, she stands on her dignity, rubbing her mouth to take the smell of his breath away, and then – it is so awful I could almost scream with shock – she turns her head and spits out the taste of him. 'Leave me,' she says and turns her back on him.

There is utter, dreadful silence, nobody says a word, and suddenly I know, as if my own cousin Anne Boleyn is at my side telling me, what I should do. I am not even thinking of the dancing and the young man, for once I am not even thinking of myself, and that almost never happens. I just think, in a flash, that if I pretend not to know him, then he can go on not knowing himself, and the whole sorry masque of this silly old man and his gross vanity will not tumble about our ears. I just feel sorry for him, to tell the truth. I just think that I can spare him this awful embarrassment of bouncing up to a woman and having her slap him down like a smelly old hound. If anyone else had said anything then I would have stayed silent. But nobody says anything and the silence goes on and on, unbearably, and he stumbles back, he almost falls back into me, and his face is all crumpled and confused and I am so sorry for him, poor humbled old fool, that I say, I coo: 'Ooh! Forgive me, sir! But I am new to court myself, a stranger like you. May I ask – who are you?'

Jane Boleyn, Rochester,
31 December 1539

Lady Browne is ordering the maids to their beds in a bellow as if she were a Yeoman of the Guard. They are over-excited and Katherine Howard among them is the centre of it all, as wild as any of them, a true Queen of the May. How she spoke to the king, how she peeped up at him from under her eyelashes, how she begged him, as a handsome stranger, new-come to court, to ask the Lady Anne for dancing, is being mimicked and re-enacted till they are drunk with their own laughter.

Lady Browne is not laughing, her face is like thunder, so I hustle the girls into bed and tell them that they are all very foolish and that they would do better to copy their lady, the Lady Anne, and show proper dignity, than mimic Katherine Howard's free and forward ways. They slip into their beds two by two like pretty angels and we blow out the candle and leave them in the darkness and lock the door. We have hardly turned away before we hear them whispering, but no power on earth can make girls behave well; and we do not even try.

'Are you troubled, Lady Browne?' I ask considerately.

She hesitates, she is longing to confide in someone, and I am here at her side, and known to be discreet.

'This is a bad business,' she says heavily. 'Oh, it all passed off pleasantly enough in the end, with the dancing and the singing and

Lady Anne recovered quickly enough as soon as you had explained to her; but this is a bad, bad business.'

'The king?' I suggest.

She nods and folds her lips over as if she would stop herself saying more.

'I am weary,' I say. 'Shall we take a glass of warm ale together before we go to our beds? Sir Anthony is staying here tonight, is he not?'

'God knows he won't join me in my rooms for hours,' she says unguardedly. 'I doubt if any of the king's circle will sleep tonight.'

'Oh?' I say. I lead the way into the presence chamber. The other ladies have gone to bed, the fire is burning low, but there is a jug of ale set at the fireside and half a dozen tankards. I pour us both a drink. 'Trouble?'

She sits in her chair and leans forwards to whisper. 'My lord husband tells me that the king swears that he will not marry her.'

'No!'

'He does. He does. He swears it. He says that he cannot like her.'

She takes a long draw on the ale and looks at me over the top of the mug.

'Lady Browne, you must have this wrong . . .'

'I have it from my husband this very night. The king seized him by the collar, almost by the throat, as soon as we retired, and said that the moment he saw Lady Anne, he had been struck with consternation, and that he saw nothing in her that he had been told.'

'He said that?'

'Those very words.'

'But he seemed so happy as we left?'

'He was as truly happy just as Katherine Howard was truly ignorant of his identity. He is as much a happy bridegroom as she is an innocent child. We are all actors here, but the king will not play the part of eager bridegroom.'

'He has to, they are betrothed and the contract signed.'

'He does not like her, he says. He cannot like her, he says, and he is blaming the men who made this marriage for him.'

I have to get this news to the duke, he has to be warned before the king gets back to London.

'Blaming the men who made the marriage?'

'And those who brought her to him. He is furious.'

'He will blame Thomas Cromwell,' I predict quietly.

'Indeed.'

'But what of the Lady Anne? Surely, he cannot refuse her?'

'There is some talk of an impediment,' she says. 'And that is why Sir Anthony and none of the others will have any sleep tonight. The Cleves lords should have brought a copy of an agreement to say that some old previous contract to marry has been withdrawn. Since they don't have it, perhaps there may be grounds to argue that the marriage cannot go ahead, it is not valid.'

'Not again,' I say, unguarded for a moment. 'Not the same objection that he put against Queen Katherine! We will all look like fools!'

She nods. 'Yes, the same. But better for her that an impediment is declared now and she is sent safely home, than she stays and marries an enemy. You know the king, he will never forgive her for spitting out his kiss.'

I say nothing. These are dangerous speculations.

'Her brother must be a fool,' I say. 'She has come a long way if he has not secured her safety.'

'I would not be in her shoes tonight,' Lady Browne says. 'You know I never thought she would please the king, and I told my husband so. But he knew best, the alliance with Cleves is vital, he tells me, we have to be protected from France and Spain, we have to be protected against the Papist powers. There are Papists who would march against us from every corner of Europe, there are Papists who would kill the king in his own bed, here in England. We have to strengthen the reformers. Her brother is a leader of the Protestant dukes and princes, that is where our future lies. I say:

"Yes, my lord; but the king will not like her. Mark my words: he will not like her." And then the king comes in, all ready for courtship, and she pushes him away from her as if he was a drunk tradesman.'

'He did not look kingly at that moment.' I will not say more than this cautious judgement.

'He was not at his best,' she says, as careful as I. Between us is the unsayable fact that our handsome prince has grown into a gross, ugly man, an old, ugly man; and for the first time we have all seen it.

'I must go to my bed,' she says, putting down her cup. She cannot bear even to think of the decay of the prince we have adored.

'I too.'

I let her go to her room and I wait till I hear her door close, then I quietly go to the great hall where, drinking heavily, and clearly nearly dead drunk, is a man in Howard livery. I crook my finger at him and he rises up quietly and leaves the others.

'Go to my lord duke,' I say to him quietly, my mouth to his ear. 'Go at once and get to him before he sees the king.'

He nods, he understands at once. 'Tell him, and tell him only, that the king does not like the Lady Anne, that he will try to declare that the marriage contract is invalid, and that he is blaming those who made this marriage and will blame anyone who insists on it.'

The man nods again. I think hard, in case there is anything I should add.

'That's all.' I need not remind one of the most skilled and unscrupulous men in England that our rival Thomas Cromwell was the architect and inspiration for this match. That this is our great chance to bring down Cromwell, as we brought down Wolsey before him. That if Cromwell is down then the king will need an advisor and who better than his commander in chief? Norfolk.

'Go at once, and get to the duke before he sees the king,' I say again. 'Our lord must not meet the king without warning.'

The man bows, he leaves the room at once, without saying goodbye to his drinking companions. By his swift stride he is clearly completely sober.

I go to my own room. My bedfellow for tonight, one of the other ladies in waiting, is already asleep, her arm outflung to my side of the bed. Gently, I lift it and slide in between the warm sheets. I don't sleep at once, I lie in the silence and listen to her breathing beside me. I am thinking about the poor young woman Lady Anne and the innocence of her face and the directness of her gaze. I am wondering if Lady Browne could possibly be right and this young woman could be in danger of her life simply by being the wife that the king does not want.

Surely not. Lady Browne is exaggerating for certain. This young woman is the daughter of a German duke, she has a powerful brother who will protect her. The king needs her alliance. But then I remember that this brother let her come to England without the one piece of paper which would secure her marriage, and I wonder that he should be so careless with her, to send her such a long way into such a bear pit with no protector.

Anne, on the road to Dartford, 1 January, 1540

Nothing could be worse, I feel such a fool. I am so glad to be travelling today, seated uncomfortably in the rolling litter, but at least alone. At least I don't have to face any sympathetic, secretly laughing faces, all buzzing with the disaster of my first meeting with the king.

But truly, how should I be blamed? He has a portrait of me, Hans Holbein himself humbled me to the ground with his unsmiling stare, so that the king had my portrait to scrutinise and criticise and study, he has a very good idea of who I am. But I have no picture of him except the picture in my mind that everyone has: of the young prince who came to his throne a golden youth of eighteen, the handsomest prince in the world. I knew well enough that he is all but fifty now. I knew that I was not marrying a handsome boy, not even a handsome prince. I knew I was marrying a king in his prime, even an ageing man. But I did not know what he was like. I had seen no new portrait of him to consider. And I was not expecting . . . that.

Not that he is so bad, perhaps. I can see the man he once was. He has broad shoulders, handsome in a man at any age. He still rides, they tell me, he still hunts except when some wound in his leg is troubling him, he is still active. He runs his country himself, he has not handed over power to more vigorous advisors, he has all his wits about him, as far as one can tell. But he has small, piggy eyes and a small, spoiled mouth, in a great ball of a moon face swelling with fat. His teeth must be very bad, for his breath is very foul. When he grabbed me and kissed me the stink of him was truly awful. When he fell back from me he looked like a spoiled child, ready to cry. But, I must be fair, that was a bad moment for both of us. I daresay, as I thrust him away from me, that I did not appear at my best either.

I wish to God I had not spat.

This is a bad beginning. A bad and undignified beginning. Really, he should not have come on me unprepared and without warning. All very well for them to tell me now that he loves disguising and masquing and pretending to be an ordinary man so that people can discover him with delight. They never told me this before. On the contrary, every day it has been dinned into my head that the English court is formal, that things must be done in a certain way, than I have to learn orders of precedence, that I must never be faulted by calling a junior member of a family to my side before a senior member, that these things matter to the English more than life itself. Every day before I left Cleves, my mother reminded me that the Queen of England must be above reproach, must be a woman of utter royal dignity and coldness, must never be familiar, must never be light, must never be overly-friendly. Every day she told me that the life of a Queen of England depends on her unblemished reputation. She threatened me with the same fate as Anne Boleyn if I was loose and warm and amorous like her.

So why should I ever dream that some fat old drunk would come up and kiss me? How would I ever dream that I am supposed to let an ugly old man kiss me without introduction or warning?

Still, I wish to God that I had not spat out the foul taste of him.

Anyway, perhaps it is not so bad. This morning he has sent me a present, a gift of rich sables, very expensive and very high quality. Little Katherine Howard, who is so sweet that she mistook the king for a stranger and greeted him kindly, has had a brooch of gold from him. Sir Anthony Browne brought the gifts this morning with a pretty speech, and told me that the king has gone ahead to prepare for our official meeting, which will happen at a place called Blackheath, outside the City of London. My ladies say that there will be no surprises between now and then, so I need not be on my guard. They say that this disguising is a favourite game of the king's and once we are married I must be prepared for him to come wearing a false beard or a big hat and ask me to dance, and we will all pretend not to know him. I smile and say how charming, though in truth I am thinking: how odd, and how childlike, and really, how very vain of him, how foolishly vain to hope that people will fall in love with him on sight as a common man, when he looks as he does now. Perhaps when he was young and handsome he could go about in disguise and people would welcome him for his good looks and charm; but surely, for many years now, many years, people must have only pretended to admire him? But I don't speak my thoughts. It is better that I say nothing now, having spoiled the game once already.

The girl who saved the day by greeting him so politely, little Katherine Howard, is one of my new maids in waiting. I call her to me in the bustle of departing this morning, and I thank her, as best I can manage in English, for her help.

She dips a little curtsey, and speaks to me in a rattle of English.

'She says that she is delighted to serve you,' my translator, Lotte, tells me. 'And that she has not been to court before, so she did not recognise the king either.'

'Why then did she speak to a stranger who had come without invitation?' I ask, puzzled. 'Surely, she should have ignored him? Such a rude man, pushing his way in?'

Lotte turns this into English, and I see the girl look at me as if there is more that divides us than language, as if we are on different worlds, as if I come from the snows and fly on white wings.

'*Was?*' I ask in German. I spread out my hands to her and raise my eyebrows. 'What?'

89

She steps a little closer, she whispers in Lotte's ear without ever taking her eyes from my face. She is such a pretty little thing, like a doll, and so earnest, that I cannot help smiling.

Lotte turns to me, she is near to laughing. 'She says that of course she knew it was the king. Who else would be able to get into the chamber past the guards? Who else is so tall and fat? But the game of the court is to pretend not to know him, and to address him only because he is such a handsome stranger. She says she may be only fourteen, and her grandmother says she is a dolt; but already she knows that every man in England loves to be admired, indeed, the older they are the vainer they get, and surely, men are not so different in Cleves?'

I laugh at her, and at myself. 'No,' I say. 'Tell her that men are not so different in Cleves but that this woman of Cleves is clearly a fool and I shall be guided by her in future even if she is only fourteen, whatever her grandmother calls her.'

Utter terror! Oh, God! Horror beyond my worst fears! I shall die of this, I shall. My uncle has come here, all the way from Greenwich, specially to see me, and summoned me to him. What on God's earth can he want with me? I am certain that my conversation with the king has come to his ears and he thinks the worst of it and will send me home to my grandmother for unmaidenly behaviour. I shall die. If he sends me to Lambeth I shall die of the humiliation. But if he sends me back to Horsham I shall be glad to die of boredom. I shall fling myself into the whatever it is called, the river there – the River Horsh, the River Sham – the duckpond if needs be, and drown, and they will be sorry when I am drowned and lost to all of them.

It must have been like this for my cousin Queen Anne when she knew she was to appear before him accused of adultery and knew he would not take her side. She must have been scared out of her wits, sick with terror, but I swear no worse than I am now. I could die of terror. I may just die of terror before I even see him.

I am to see him in my Lady Rochford's own room, the disgrace is obviously so bad that it has to be kept among us Howards, and when I go in, she is in the window-seat, so I suppose it is her who has told him all about it. When she smiles at me I scowl at her for a tale-bearing old tabby and I make a horrid face at her to let her know who I thank for my doom.

'Lord uncle, I beg of you not to send me to Horsham,' I say, the moment I am through the door.

He looks at me with a scowl. 'And good day to you, my niece,' he says icily.

I drop into a curtsey, I could almost fall to my knees. 'Please, my lord, don't send me back to Lambeth either,' I say. 'I beg of you. The Lady Anne is not displeased with me, she laughed when I told her . . .' I break off. I realise, too late, that to tell my uncle that I have told the king's betrothed wife that although he is fat and old he is also unspeakably vain, is perhaps not the cleverest thing to say. 'I didn't tell her anything,' I correct myself. 'But she is pleased with me and she says she will take my advice even though my grandmother thinks I am a dolt.'

His sardonic bark of laughter warns me that he agrees with my grandmother's verdict.

'Well, not my advice, exactly, sir; but she is pleased with me, and so is the king, for he sent me a gold brooch. Oh, please, uncle, if you let me stay I will never speak out again, I won't even breathe! Please, I beg of you. I am utterly innocent of everything!'

He laughs again.

'I am,' I say. 'Please, uncle, don't turn your face from me, please trust me. I shall be a good girl, I shall make you proud of me, I shall try to be a perfect . . .'

'Oh, hush, I am pleased with you,' he says.

'I will do anything . . .'

'I said, I am pleased with you.'

I look up. 'You are?'

'You seem to have behaved delightfully. The king danced with you?'

'Yes.'

'And talked with you?'

'Yes.'

'And seemed much taken with you?'

I have to think for a minute. I would not have called him exactly 'taken'. He was not like a young man whose eyes drift down from my face to peek at my breasts while he is talking to me, or who blushes when I smile at him. And besides, the king almost fell back into me when Lady Anne rebuffed him. He was still shocked. He would have spoken to anyone to hide his hurt and embarrassment.

'He did talk to me,' I repeat helplessly.

'I am very pleased that he honoured you with his attention,' my uncle says. He is speaking slowly as if he is a schoolmaster, and I should be understanding something.

'Oh.'

'Very pleased.'

I glance across at Lady Rochford to see if this is making any sense for her. She gives me a slight smile and a nod.

'He sent me a brooch,' I remind him.

He looks at me sharply. 'Valuable?'

I make a little face. 'Nothing to the sables that he sent Lady Anne.'

'I should hope not. But it was of gold?'

'Yes, and pretty.'

He turns to Lady Rochford. 'Is it?'

'Yes,' she says. They exchange a small smile, as if they understand each other well.

'Should His Majesty honour you by speaking with you again, you will endeavour to be very charming and pleasing.'

'Yes, my lord uncle.'

'From such little attentions do great favours flow. The king is not pleased with the Lady Anne.'

'He sent her sables,' I remind him. 'Very good ones.'

'I know. But that is not the point.'

It seems the point to me, but very cleverly I don't correct him but stand still and wait.

'He will see you daily,' my uncle says. 'And you may continue to please him. Then perhaps he will send you sables. Do you understand?'

This, about the sables, I do understand. 'Yes.'

'So if you want presents, and my approval, you will do your best to behave charmingly and pleasantly to the king. Lady Rochford here will advise you.'

She nods at me.

'Lady Rochford is a most skilled and wise courtier,' my uncle goes on. 'There can be few people who have seen more of the king throughout his life. Lady Rochford will tell you how you are to go on. It is our hope and our intention that the king will favour you, that he will, in short, fall in love with you.'

'Me?'

They both nod. Are they quite mad? He is an old old man, he must have given up all thoughts of love years ago. He has a daughter Princess Mary, far older than me, nearly old enough to be my mother. He is ugly, his teeth are rotten and his limp makes him waddle like a fat old goose. A man like this must have put all thoughts of love out of his head years ago. He might think of me as a granddaughter but not in any other way.

'But he is marrying Lady Anne,' I point out.

'Even so.'

'He is too old to fall in love.'

My uncle shoots such a scowl at me that I give a little squeak of terror.

'Fool,' he says shortly.

I hesitate for a moment. Can they really mean that they want this old king to be my lover? Should I say something about my virginity and my spotless reputation, which in Lambeth seemed to matter so very much?

'My reputation?' I whisper.

Again my uncle laughs. 'That doesn't matter,' he says.

I look towards Lady Rochford, who was supposed to be my chaperone in a lewd court and watch my behaviour and guard my precious honour.

'I can explain it all to you later,' she says.

I take it then that I should say nothing. 'Yes, my lord,' I say very sweetly.

'You are a pretty girl,' he says. 'I have given Lady Rochford money for you to have a new gown.'

'Oh, thank you!'

He smiles at my sudden enthusiasm. He turns to Lady Rochford. 'And I will leave a manservant with you. He can serve you and run errands. It seems that it may become worth my while to keep a man with you. Who would have thought it? Anyway, keep me informed as to how things go on here.'

She rises from her seat and curtseys. He goes out without another word. The two of us are left alone.

'What does he want?' I ask, utterly bewildered.

She looks at me as if she were measuring me for a gown, she looks me up and down. 'Never mind for now,' she says kindly. 'He is pleased with you, that's the main thing.'

Anne, Blackheath,
3 January 1540

This is the happiest day of my life, because today I have fallen in love. I have fallen in love, not like a silly girl falls in love, because a boy catches her eye or tells her some foolish story. I am in love and this love will last forever. I am in love with England this day, and the realisation has made this the happiest day of my life. This day I realise that I am to be queen of this country, this rich, beautiful country. I have been travelling through it like a fool, with my eyes shut – in all fairness, some of the time I have been travelling through it in darkness and in the worst weather that I could imagine – but today it is bright and sunny and the sky is so blue, blue as duck eggs, the air is fresh and bright, as exciting and cold as white wine. Today I feel like the gyrfalcon my father used to call me, I feel as if I am riding high on cool winds, looking down on this most beautiful country which will be mine. We ride from Dartford to Blackheath, the frost white and shining on the road all the way, and when we get to the park all the ladies of my court are presented to me, all dressed so beautifully and warm and friendly in their greetings. I am to have nearly seventy ladies altogether, the king's nieces and cousins among them, and they all greet me today as new friends. I am wearing my very best, and I know I look well, I think even my brother would be proud of me today.

96

They have made a city of tents of cloth of gold, flying brilliantly coloured flags, guarded by the king's own Yeomen of the Guard, men so tall and so handsome that they are a legend in England. While we wait for the king, we go inside and take a glass of wine and warm ourselves at the braziers, they are burning sea-coal for me, only the best, as I am to be a member of the royal family of England. The floors are lined with rich carpets and the tents hung with tapestries and silks for warmth. Then, when they say it is time, and everyone is smiling and chattering and almost as excited as I am, I mount my horse and ride out to meet him. I go out filled with hope. Perhaps, at this ceremonial meeting, I shall like him and he will like me.

The trees are tall and their bare black winter branches stretch out against the sky like dark threads on a tapestry of blue. The park extends for miles, so green and so fresh, sparking with melting frost, the sun is bright and pale yellow, almost burning white in the sky. Everywhere, held back by gaily coloured ropes, there are the people from London smiling and waving at me and calling blessings down on me, and for the first time in my life I am not Anne – the middle daughter of Cleves: less pretty than Sybilla, less charming than Amelia – but here I am Anne, the only Anne. They have taken me to their hearts. These odd, rich, charming, eccentric people are all welcoming me, as if they want a good queen and an honest queen, and they believe and I know that I can be such a queen for them.

I know very well that I am not an English girl like the late Queen Jane, God rest her soul. But having seen the court and the great families of England I think it might be a good thing that I am not an English girl. Even I can see that the Seymour family is high in favour now, and could easily become overmighty. They are everywhere, these Seymours, handsome and conceited, always emphasising their child is the king's only son and heir to the throne. If I were the king and it were my court, I should be wary of them. If they are allowed to govern the young prince, to dominate him because of their kinship to his mother, then the balance of this court will all be thrown to them. From what I can see, the king is not careful who he chooses for his favourites. I may be half his age but I know well enough that a ruler's favour must be measured. I have lived my life with the disfavour of the favourite son and I know how poisonous is whim in a ruler. This king is whimsical; but perhaps I can make his court more balanced, perhaps I can give his son a level-headed stepmother who can maintain the flatterers and the courtiers at a safe distance from the little boy.

I know his daughters have been estranged from him. Poor girls, I so hope to be of service to little Elizabeth, who never knew her mother and has spent her life under the shadow of disgrace. Perhaps I can bring her to court and keep her near me and reconcile her to her father. And the Princess Mary must be lonely, without her mother and knowing herself to be far from her father's favour. I can be kind to her, I can overcome her fear of the king and bring her to court as my kinswoman, she need not say 'stepmother', but perhaps I could be as a good sister to her. For the king's children at least I can be a great force for good. And if we are blessed, if I am blessed, and we have a child of our own then perhaps I shall give a little prince to England, a godly youth who can help to heal the divisions in this country.

There is a murmur of excitement from the crowd and I see all the heads turn away from me and back again. The king is coming towards us, and all my fears about him are gone in a moment. Now he is not pretending to be a common man, he is not hiding majesty in the disguise of a vulgar old fool, today he is dressed as a king and he rides as a king, in a coat embroidered with diamonds, with a collar of diamonds around his shoulders, on his head a hat of velvet sewn with pearls, and on the finest horse I think I have ever seen. He is magnificent, he looks like a god in the bright winter light, his horse curvetting on his own land, weighed down with jewels, surrounded by the royal guard with the trumpets singing out. He smiles when he draws near to me and we greet each other, and people cheer to see us together.

'I give you welcome to England,' he says slowly enough for me to understand, and I reply carefully in English: 'My lord, I am very glad to be here, and I shall try to be a good wife to you.'

I think I will be happy, I think it can be done. That first embarrassing mistake can be forgotten and put behind us. We will be married for years, we will be happy together for all our lives. In ten years from now, who will ever remember a little thing like that?

Then my chariot comes and I ride through the park to the palace of Greenwich, which is by the river, and all the barges on the river are dressed out in colours with flags flying and the London citizens are dressed in their very best. They have musicians out on the water and they are playing a new song called 'Merry Anna', written for me, and there are pageants on the boats to celebrate my coming, and everyone is smiling and waving at me; so I smile and wave back.

Our procession turns up the sweeping approach to Greenwich and I realise again what a country it is, this new home of mine. For this Greenwich is not a castle at all, not fortified in fear against an enemy who might come, it is a palace built for a country at peace, a great, rich, fair palace, as fine as anything in France. It faces the river and is the most beautiful building of stone and precious Venice glass that I have ever seen in my life. The king sees my delighted face and brings his horse alongside my chariot and leans down to tell me that this is just one of his many palaces, but his favourite, and that in time, as we travel around the country, I shall see the others, and that he hopes I shall be happy with them all.

They take me to the queen's rooms to rest, and for once I do not want to hide in the private rooms, but instead I am glad to be here, with my ladies around me in my privy chamber, and more of them waiting in the great presence chamber outside. I go into the private robing room and change into my taffeta gown, which they have trimmed with the sables that the king gave me for the New Year. I think I have never had such a fortune on my back in my life before. I lead my ladies down to dinner feeling as if I am queen already and at the entrance to the great dining hall the king takes me by the hand and leads me around the tables, where everyone bows and curtseys and we smile and nod, hand-clasped, like husband and wife already.

I am starting to recognise people, and to know their names without prompting, so now the court is not such a friendless blur. I see Lord Southampton, who looks tired and troubled, as well he might be for the work he has done for me in bringing me here. His smile is strained and, oddly, his greeting is cool. He glances away from the king as if there is some trouble brewing, and I remember my resolution to be a fair queen in this court that is commanded by whim. Perhaps I will learn what is troubling Lord Southampton, perhaps I can help him.

The king's foremost advisor, Thomas Cromwell, bows to me and I recognise him from my mother's description as the man, more than any other, who sought alliance with us and with the Protestant dukes of Germany. I would have expected him to greet me more warmly, since my marriage is the triumph of his planning, but he is quiet and self-effacing and the king leads me past him with only a short word.

Archbishop Cranmer is dining with us as well, and I recognise Lord Lisle and his wife. He too is looking weary and guarded, and I remember his fears in Calais of the divisions in the kingdom. I smile warmly at him. I know that there is work for me to do in this country. If I can save one heretic from the fires then I will have been a good queen and I am sure I can use my influence to bring this country to peace.

I am starting to feel that I have friends in England, and when I look down the hall and see my ladies, Jane Boleyn, kind Lady Browne, the king's niece Lady Margaret Douglas and little Katherine Howard among them, I start to feel that this indeed can be my new home, and that the king is indeed my husband, his friends and his children shall be my family, and that I shall be happy here.

Katherine, Greenwich Palace,
3 January 1540

Just as I have always dreamed, there is to be dancing after dinner in a beautiful chamber filled with the most handsome young men in the world. And better than my greatest dreams I have a new gown and pinned to the gown, as obviously, as noticeable as possible, is my new gold brooch given to me by the King of England himself. I finger it all the time, almost as if I were pointing at it and saying to people: 'What d'you think of that then? Not bad for practically my very first day at court.' The king is on his throne looking powerful and fatherly, and Lady Anne is as pretty as she can be (given that awful dress) beside him. She might as well have just thrown the sables in the Thames as have them sewn on that taffeta tent. I am so distressed about such wonderful furs all but thrown away that it almost dims my pleasure for a moment.

But then I glance around the room – not in an immodest way, just glancing around as if looking for nothing in particular – and I see first one young, handsome boy and then another, half a dozen indeed that I would be glad to know better. Some of them are sitting together at a table, it is the pages' table, and every single one of them is a son of a good family, wealthy in their own right, and high in the favour of a lord. Dereham, poor Dereham, would be a nobody to them, Henry Manox would be their servant. These will be my new suitors. I can barely drag my eyes away from any one of them.

I catch a glance or two in my direction and know that prickle of excitement and pleasure that tells me that I am being watched, that I am desired, that my name will be mentioned, that a note will be passed to me, that the whole joyous adventure of flirtation and seduction will start again. A boy will ask my name, will send a message. I will agree to a meeting, there will be an exchange of looks and silly words over dancing and sports and dinner. There will be a kiss, there will be another, then slowly, deliciously, there will be a seduction and I shall know another touch, another boy's delicious kisses, and I shall fall head over heels in love again.

The dinner is delicious but I pick at my food because at court there is always someone watching you, and I don't want to seem greedy. Our table faces the front of the hall so it is natural that I look up to see the king at his dinner. In his rich clothes and great collar of gold you might mistake him for one of the old pictures over an altar; I mean, a picture of God. He is so grand and so broad and so weighted with gold and jewels, he sparkles like an old treasure mountain. There is a cloth of gold spread over his great chair, with embroidered curtains hanging down on either side, and every dish is served to him by a servant on his knees. Even the server who offers him a golden bowl to dip his fingers and wipe his hands does so on bended knee. There is another server altogether to hand him the linen cloth. They bow their heads as well when they kneel to him, as if he were of such unearthly importance that they cannot meet his eyes.

So when he looks up and sees me watching him, I don't know whether I should look away, or curtsey, or what. I am so confused by this that I give him a little smile and half look away and half look back again, to see if he is still watching, and he is. Then I think that this is just what I would do if I was trying to attract a boy, and that makes me blush and look down at my plate, and I feel such a fool. Then, when I look up, under my eyelashes as it happens, to see if he is still looking at me, he is gazing away down the hall and clearly has hardly noticed me at all.

My uncle Howard's sharp black gaze is on me though, and I am afraid he will frown; perhaps I should have curtseyed to the king when I first caught his eye. But the duke just gives a little approving nod and speaks to a man seated on his right. A man of no interest to me, he must be a hundred and ninety-two if he is a day.

I really am amazed at how old this court is, and the king is quite ancient. I always had the impression of it being a court of young people, young and beautiful and joyful; not such very old men. I swear that there cannot be a friend of the king's who is a day under forty years. His great friend Charles Brandon, who is said to be a hero of glamour and charm, is absolutely ancient, in his dotage at fifty. My lady grandmother talks about the king as if he was the prince that she knew when she was a girl, and of course this is why I have it all wrong. She is such an old lady that she forgets that long years have gone by. She probably thinks that they are all still young together. When she talks about the queen she always means Queen Katherine of Aragon, not Queen Jane or even the Lady Anne Boleyn. She just skips every queen since Katherine. Indeed, my grandmother was so frightened by the fall of her niece Anne Boleyn that she never speaks of her at all except as a terrible warning to naughty girls like me.

It wasn't always like that. I can just about remember first coming to my step-grandmama's house at Horsham and every second sentence was 'my niece the queen' and every letter to London asked her for a favour or a fee, a place for a servant, or the pickings of a monastery, asked her to turn out a priest or pull down a nunnery. Then Anne had a girl and there was a good deal of 'our baby the Princess Elizabeth' and hopes that the next baby would be a boy. Everyone promised me I would have a place at court in my cousin's household, I would be kin to the Queen of England, who knew where I might look for a husband? Another Howard cousin, Mary, was married to the king's bastard son Henry Fitzroy, and a cousin was intended for Princess Mary. We were so inter-married with the

Tudors that we would be royal ourselves. But then slowly, like winter coming when you don't at first notice the chill, there was less spoken of her, and less certainty about her court. Then one day my step-grandmother called the whole household into the great hall and said abruptly that Anne Boleyn (she called her that, no title, definitely no kinship), Anne Boleyn had disgraced herself and her family and betrayed her king and that her name and her brother's name would never again be mentioned.

Of course we were all desperate to know what had happened but we had to wait for servants' gossip. Only when the news finally came from London could I learn what my cousin Queen Anne had done. My maid told me, I can hear her now telling me, that Lady Anne was accused of terrible crimes, adultery with many men, her brother among them, witchcraft, treason, bewitching the king, a string of horrors from which only one thing stood out to me, an aghast little girl: that her accuser was her uncle, my uncle Norfolk. That he presided over the court, that he pronounced her death sentence and that his son, my handsome cousin, went to the Tower like a man might go to a fair, dressed in his best, to see his cousin beheaded.

I thought my uncle must be a man so fearsome that he might have been in league with the devil; but I can laugh at those childish fears, now that I am his favourite, so high in his favour that he has ordered Jane Boleyn, Lady Rochford, to take most particular care of me, and given her money to buy me a gown. Obviously, he has taken a great fancy to me, he likes me best of all the Howard girls he has placed at court, and thinks that I will advance the interests of the family by making a noble match or becoming friends with the queen, or charming to the king. I had thought him a man of fiendish heart-lessness but now I find him a kindly uncle to me.

There is a masque after dinner and some very funny clowning from the king's fool, and then there is some singing that is almost unbearably dull. The king is a great musician, I learn, and so most evenings we will have to endure one of his songs. There is a great deal of tra-la-la-ing and everyone listens very intently and applauds very loudly at the end. Lady Anne I think has no more opinion of it than me, but she makes the mistake of gazing round rather vacantly, as if she were quietly wishing to be elsewhere. I see the king glance at her, and then away, as if he is irritated by her inattention. I take the precaution of clasping my hands beneath my chin and smiling with my eyes half-closed as if I can hardly bear the joy of it. Such luck! He happens to glance my way again and clearly thinks his music has transported me. He gives me a broad, approving smile and I smile back and drop my eyes to the board as if fearful of looking at him for too long.

'Very well done,' says Lady Rochford, and I give her a little beam of triumph. I love, I love, I love court life. I swear it will quite turn my head.

Jane Boleyn, Greenwich Palace, 3 January 1540

'My lord duke,' I say, bowing very low.

We are in the Howard apartments at Greenwich Palace, a series of beautiful rooms opening the one into another, almost as spacious and beautiful as the queen's own rooms. I stayed here once with George, when we were newly wed, and I remember the view over the river, and the light at dawn when I woke, so much in love, and I heard the sound of swans flying overhead going down to the river on their huge creaking wings.

'Ah, Lady Rochford,' says my lord duke, his lined face amiable. 'I have need of you.'

I wait.

'You are friendly with the Lady Anne, you are on good terms?'

'As far as I can be,' I say cautiously. 'She speaks little English as yet but I have made a great effort to talk to her and I think she likes me.'

'Would she confide in you?'

'She would speak to her Cleves companions first, I think. But she sometimes asks me things about England. She trusts me, I think.'

He turns to the window and taps his thumbnail against his yellow teeth. His sallow face is creased in thought.

'There is a difficulty,' he says slowly.

I wait.

'As you heard, they have indeed sent her without the proper documents,' he says. 'She was betrothed when she was a child to Francis of Lorraine, and the king needs to see that this engagement was cancelled and put aside before he goes any further.'

'She is not free to marry?' I demand, astounded. 'When the contracts have been signed and she has come all this way and been greeted by the king as his bride? When the City of London has welcomed her as their new queen?'

'It is possible,' he says evasively.

It is absolutely impossible, but it is not my place to say so. 'Who says that she may not be free to marry?'

'The king fears to proceed. His conscience is uneasy.'

I pause, I cannot think fast enough to make sense of this. This is a king who married his own brother's wife, and then put her aside because he said the lifelong marriage was invalid. This is a king who put Anne Boleyn's head on the block as a matter of his own judgement under the exclusive guidance of God. Clearly, this is not a king who would be deterred from marrying a woman just because some German ambassador did not have the right piece of paper to hand. Then I remember the moment when she pushed him aside, and his face as he stepped back from her at Rochester.

'It is true then. He doesn't like her. He can't forgive her for her treatment of him at Rochester. He will find a way to get out of the marriage. He is going to claim pre-contract again.' One glance at the duke's dark face tells me that I have guessed right and I could almost laugh aloud at this new twist in the play that is King Henry's comedy. 'He doesn't like her and he is going to send her home.'

'If she confessed that she was pre-contracted she could go home again, without dishonour, and the king would be free,' the duke says quietly.

'But she likes him,' I say. 'At any rate, she likes him enough. And she can't go home again. No woman of any sense would go home again. Go back to be spoiled goods in Cleves when you could be

Queen of England? She would never want that. Who would marry her if he refuses her? Who could marry her if he declares her pre-contracted? Her life would be over.'

'She could clear herself of the pre-contract,' he says reasonably.

'Is there one?'

He shrugs. 'Almost certainly not.'

I think for a moment. 'Then how can she be released from something that does not exist?'

He smiles. 'That is a matter for the Germans. She can be sent home against her will, if she does not co-operate.'

'Not even the king can abduct her and fling her out of the kingdom.'

'If she could be entrapped into saying that there was a pre-contract.' His voice is like a whisper of silk. 'If it came from her own mouth that she is not free to marry . . .'

I nod. I begin to see the favour he would have of me.

'The king would be most grateful to the man who could tell him that he had a confession from her. And the woman who brought such a confession about would be most high in his favour. And in mine.'

'I am yours to command,' I say to give myself time to think. 'But I cannot make her lie. If she knows she is free to marry, then she would be mad to say otherwise. And if I claim that she has said otherwise, she has only to deny it. Then it is her word against mine and we are back to the truth again.' I pause as a fear occurs to me. 'My lord, I take it that there is no possibility of an accusation?'

'What sort of accusation?'

'Of some crime?' I say nervously.

'Do you mean she might be charged with treason?'

I nod. I will not say the word myself. I wish that I could never hear the word again. It leads to the Tower Green and the executioner's block. It took the love of my life from me. It ended the life we lived forever.

'How could it be treason?' he asks me, as if we do not live in a dangerous world where everything can be treason.

'The law has changed so much, and being innocent is no defence any more.'

Abruptly he shakes his head. 'There's no possibility of him accusing her, anyway. The King of France is entertaining the Holy Roman Emperor in Paris at this very moment. They could be planning a joint attack on us even as we speak. We can do nothing that might upset Cleves. We have to have an alliance with the Protestant princes or we risk standing alone to face a Spain and France that have united against us. If the English Papists rise again as they did before we will be finished. She has to confess herself betrothed to another and go home by her own free will so that we lose the girl and keep the alliance. Or if someone were to trap her into making a confession, that would be good enough. But if she persists in saying that she is free to marry and if she insists upon marriage, then the king will have to do it. We cannot offend her brother.'

'Whether the king likes it or not?'

'Though he hates it, though he hates the man who contrived it, and even though he hates her.'

I pause for a moment. 'If he hates her and yet marries her he will find some way to be rid of her later.' I am thinking aloud.

The duke says nothing but his eyelids hood his dark eyes. 'Oh, who can foretell the future?'

'She will be in the greatest of danger every day of her life,' I predict. 'If the king wants rid of her he will soon think that it is God's will that he is rid of her.'

'That is generally the way that God's will seems to be manifest,' the duke says with a wolfish grin.

'Then he will find her guilty of some offence,' I say. I will not say the word treason.

'If you care for her at all, you would persuade her to go now,' the duke says quietly.

I walk slowly back to the queen's rooms. She will not be advised by me, in preference to her ambassadors; and I am not free to tell her what I truly think. But if I had been her true friend I would have told her that Henry is not a man to take as a husband if he hates you before the wedding day. His malice towards women who cross him is fatal. Who would know better than me?

Anne, Greenwich Palace,
3 January 1540

The lady in waiting Jane Boleyn seems troubled and I tell her that she can sit beside me and I ask her, in English, if she is well.

She beckons my translator to come and sit with us, and she says that she is troubled by a matter of some delicacy.

I think it must be something about precedence at the wedding, they are so anxious about the order of the service and what jewels everyone may wear. I nod as if it is a serious matter and ask her if I may serve her.

'On the contrary; I am anxious to be of service to you,' she says, speaking quietly to Lotte. She translates for me, I nod. 'I hear that your ambassadors have forgotten to bring the contract that releases you from a previous betrothal.'

'What?' I speak so sharply that she guesses the meaning of the German word, and nods, her face as grave as my own.

'So they have not told you?'

I shake my head. 'Nothing,' I say in English. 'They tell nothing.'

'Then I am glad to speak with you before you are ill-advised,' she says rapidly and I wait as the words are translated. She leans forwards and takes my hands. Her clasp is warm, her face intent. 'When they ask you about your previous betrothal you must tell them that it was annulled, and that you have seen the document,' she says earnestly. 'If they ask why your brother failed to send it, you can say that you don't know, that it is not your responsibility to bring the papers – as indeed it was not.'

I am breathless; something about her intensity makes me feel fearful. I cannot think why my brother should be so careless of my marriage, then I remember his constant resentment of me. He has betrayed his own plan from malice; at the last moment he could not bear to let me go smoothly from him.

'I see you are shocked,' she says. 'Dearest Lady Anne, be warned by me, and never let them think for a moment that there is no document, that you have a previous betrothal still in place. You must tell a powerful and convincing lie. You must tell them that you have seen the documents and that your previous betrothal was definitely annulled.'

'But it was,' I say slowly. I repeat in English so she cannot be mistaken. 'I have seen the document. It is not a lie. I am free to marry.'

'You are certain?' she asks intently. 'These things can be done without a girl knowing what plans are made. No-one would blame you if you were at all uncertain. You can tell me. Trust me. Tell me the truth.'

'It was cancelled,' I say again. 'I know that it was cancelled. The betrothal was my father's plan; but not my brother's. When my father was ill and then died, then my brother ruled, and the betrothal was finished.'

'Why do you not have the document, then?'

'My brother,' I start. 'My foolish brother . . . My brother is careless of my well-being,' Lotte rapidly translates. 'And my father died so recently, and my mother is so distressed, there has been too much for him to do. My brother has the document in our records room, I myself have seen it; but he must have forgotten to send it. There was so much to arrange.'

'If you are in any doubt at all you must tell me,' she cautions me. 'And I can advise you what best we should do. You see from my coming to you and advising you that I am utterly loyal to you. But if there is any chance that your brother does not have the document you must tell me, Lady Anne, tell me for your own safety, and I will plan with you what we can best do.'

I shake my head. 'I thank you for your care of me but there is no need. I have seen the documents myself, and so have my ambassadors,' I say. 'There is no impediment, I know I am free to marry the king.'

She nods as if she is still waiting for something else. 'I am so glad.'

'And I want to marry the king.'

'If you wished to avoid the marriage, now you have seen him, you could do so,' she says very quietly. 'This is your chance to escape. If you did not like him, you could get safely home, with no word against you. I could help you. I could tell them that you had told me that you are not certain, that you may be pre-contracted.'

I withdraw my hands from hers. 'I do not want to escape,' I say simply. 'This is a great honour for me and my country, and a great joy for me.'

Jane Boleyn looks sceptical.

'Truly,' I say. 'I long to be Queen of England, I am coming to love this country and I want to make my life here.'

'Indeed?'

'Yes, on my honour.' I hesitate and then I tell her the greatest reason. 'I was not very happy at my home,' I admit. 'I was not highly regarded or well treated. Here I can be somebody, I can do good. At home I will never be more than an unwanted sister.'

She nods. Many women know what it is to be in the way while the great affairs of men go on without them.

'I want to have a chance,' I say. 'I want to have a chance to be the woman I can be. Not my brother's creature, not my mother's daughter. I want to stay here and grow into myself.'

She is silent for a moment, I am surprised at the depth of my own feeling. 'I want to be a woman in my own right,' I say.

'A queen is not free,' she points out.

'She is better than a duke's disliked sister.'

'Very well,' she says quietly.

'I suppose the king must be angry with my ambassadors for forgetting the papers?' I ask.

'I am sure that he is,' she says, her eyes slide sideways. 'But they will give their word that you are free to marry and I am sure it will all go ahead.'

'There is no possibility of the marriage being delayed?' I am surprised at my own feeling. I have such a strong sense that I can do much for this country, that I can be a good queen here. I want to start at once.

'No,' she says. 'The ambassadors and the king's council will resolve it. I am sure.'

I pause. 'He does want to marry me?'

She smiles at me and touches my hand. 'Of course he does. This is just a small difficulty. The ambassadors will undertake to produce the document and the marriage will go ahead. Just as long as you are certain that the document is there?'

'It is there,' I say, and I am speaking nothing but the truth. 'I can swear to it.'

Katherine, Greenwich Palace,
6 January 1540

I am to help the queen to dress for her wedding and I have to get up extremely early to get everything ready, I would rather not get up early, but it is nice to be singled out from the other girls who sleep so late and so lazy. Really it's very bad of them to lie in bed so late when some of us are up and working for Lady Anne. Truly, everyone but me is completely idle.

I lay out her dress as she is washing in her closet. Catherine Carey helps me spread out the skirt and the underskirts on the closed chest as Mary Norris goes for her jewels. The skirt is enormous, like a great fat spinning top, I would rather die than marry in a dress like this; the greatest beauty in the world could not help but look like a pudding, waddling out to be eaten. It is hardly worth being queen if you have to go around like a tent, I think. The cloth is extremely fine – cloth of gold – and it is heavy with the most wonderful pearls, and she has a coronet to wear. Mary has put it out before the mirror and if no-one else was here I would try it on, but already, though it is so early, there are half a dozen of us, servants and maids and ladies in waiting, and so I have to give it a little polish and leave it alone. It is very finely wrought, she brought it from Cleves with her and she told me that the spiky bits are supposed to be rosemary, which her own sister wore as a fresh herb in her hair at her wedding. I say it looks like a crown of thorns and her lady secretary gives me a sharp look and doesn't translate my remark. Just as well, really.

She will wear her hair loose and when she comes out of the bathroom she sits before her silver looking-glass, and Catherine brushes her hair with long, smooth strokes, like you would a horse's tail. She is fair-haired, to be just to her she is quite golden-haired, and wrapped in a bath sheet and glowing from her wash, she looks well this morning. She is a little pale, but she smiles at all of us, and she seems happy enough. If I were her I would be dancing for joy to be Queen of England. But I suppose she is not the dancing sort.

Off she goes for the wedding and we all fall in behind her in strict order of importance, which means that I am so far back it is hardly worth my while being there, nobody will be able to see me, even though I am wearing my new gown that is trimmed with silver thread, the most costly thing I have ever owned. It is a very pale grey-blue, and suits my eyes. I never looked better; but it is not my wedding and nobody pays any attention to me at all.

Archbishop Cranmer is to marry them: drone, drone, drone, like an old bee. He asks them if there is any reason why they cannot be married, and if we, the congregation, know of any impediment and we all say very cheerfully, 'no we don't', and I suppose only I am fool enough to wonder what would happen if someone said, 'stop the wedding, for the king has had three wives already and none of them died of old age!' but of course, nobody does.

If she had any sense, she should be alarmed. It is hardly a very reassuring record. He is a great man of course, and his will is the will of God, of course; but he has had three wives and all of them dead. It's not much of a prospect for a bride, when I come to think about it. But I don't think she thinks like that. Probably nobody thinks like this unless they are as stupid as me.

They are married and go off to hear Mass in the king's private closet and the rest of us wait around with nothing to do, which is, I find, one of the main activities at court. There is a very handsome young man whose name happens to be John Beresby and he manages to work his way through the people so that he is standing behind me.

'I am dazzled,' he says.

'I don't know what by,' I say pertly. 'It is hardly daybreak, it is so early.'

'Not by the sun, but by the greater light of your beauty.'

'Oh, that,' I say and give him a little smile.

'You are new to court?'

'Yes, I am Katherine Howard.'

'I am John Beresby.'

'I know.'

'You know? You have asked someone my name?'

'Not at all,' I say. Though it is a lie. I noticed him that first day at Rochester, and I asked Lady Rochford who he was.

'You have asked after me,' he says delightedly.

'Don't flatter yourself,' I say crushingly.

'Tell me that I may at least dance with you later, at the wedding feast.'

'Perhaps,' I say.

'I shall take that as a promise,' he whispers, and then the door opens and the king comes out with Lady Anne and we all curtsey very low because she is queen now, and a married woman, and I can't help but think that though that is very nice for her, it would have been much better if she had worn a gown with a long train.

Anne, Greenwich Palace,
6 January 1540

So it is done. I am Queen of England. I am a wife. I sit on the right hand of my husband the king at the wedding feast and I smile down the hall so that everyone, my ladies, the lords at their tables, the common people in the gallery, everyone can see that I am happy to be their queen and that I will be a good queen and a merry wife.

Archbishop Cranmer performed the service according to the rites of the Holy Catholic Church in England, so I feel a little uneasy in my conscience. This is not bringing the country closer to the reformed religion as I promised my brother and my mother that I would do. My advisor, the Count Overstein, stands beside me and when there is a break in the dinner I remark quietly to him that I hope he and the lords of Cleves are not disappointed at my failure to lead the king to reform.

He says that I will be allowed to practise my faith as I wish, in private, but the king does not want to be troubled with matters of theology on his wedding day. He says that the king seems firm in keeping the church that he has made, which is Catholic but denies the leadership of the Pope. The king is as opposed to reformers as he is to fervent Papists.

'But surely we could have found a form of words that could have suited both of us?' I remark. 'My brother was anxious that I should support the reform of the church in England.'

He makes a grimace. 'The reform of the church is not as we understood it,' he says, and from the closed line of his mouth I take it that he wants to say no more.

'Certainly, it seems to have been a profitable process,' I remark tentatively, thinking of the great houses that we stayed in on the way from Deal which were clearly former monasteries, or abbeys, and the medicine gardens around them being dug over for flowers, and the farms which fed the poor but are now being converted into parkland for hunting.

'When we were at home we thought it was a godly process,' he says shortly. 'We did not realise it was drenched in blood.'

'I cannot believe that to tear down the shrines where simple people liked to say their prayers can lead them closer to God,' I say. 'And what is the profit in forbidding them from lighting candles to remember their loved ones?'

'Earthly profit as well as spiritual,' he says. 'The church's tithes are not lifted, they are just paid to the king. But it is not for us to remark on how the country of England chooses to say its prayers.'

'My brother . . .'

'Your brother would have done better to look to his own record keeping,' he says, in sudden irritation.

'What?'

'He should have sent the letter which released you from your promise to marry the Duke of Lorraine's son.'

'It didn't matter that much, did it?' I ask. 'The king has said nothing of it to me.'

'We had to swear that we knew of its existence, and then we had to swear that it would be sent within three months, and then we had to swear that we ourselves would be hostage for it. If your brother does not find it and send it, God knows what will happen to us.'

I am aghast. 'They cannot hold you to ransom for my brother's record keeping? They cannot really think that there was an impediment?'

He shakes his head. 'They know full well that you are free to marry and that the marriage is valid. But for some reason known only to themselves, they choose to throw a doubt over it all, and your brother's error in letting us come without it has allowed that doubt. And we have been most cruelly embarrassed.'

I turn my eyes down. My brother's resentment of me goes against his own interests, goes against the interests of his own country, even against the interests of his own religion. I can feel my temper rise at the thought of him jeopardising my very marriage from his jealousy and spite. He is such a fool, he is such a wicked fool. 'He is careless,' is all that I say; but I hear my voice shake.

'This is not a king to be careless with,' the count warns.

I nod, I am very conscious of the king sitting in silence on my left. He cannot understand German but I do not want him to look at me and see me anything other than happy.

'I am sure I shall be very content,' I say, smiling, and the count bows and goes back to his place.

The entertainment is finished and the archbishop rises from his place at the table. My councillors have prepared me for this moment and when the king rises to his feet, I know that I have to get up too. The two of us follow my lord Cranmer to the king's great chamber and stand in the doorway while the archbishop walks around the room, swinging the censer and sprinkling the bed with holy water. This really is most superstitious and outlandish. I don't know what my mother would say; but I know she would not like it.

Then the archbishop closes his eyes and starts to pray. Beside me, Count Overstein whispers a rapid translation. 'He prays for the two of you to sleep well and not be troubled with demonic dreams.' I make sure that my expression is one of interest and devotion. But I can hardly keep my face straight. Are these the people who have closed down shrines to stop people praying for miracles and yet here in a palace they have to pray for protection against dreams of demons? What sense can one make of them?

'He prays that you will not suffer from infertility, nor the king from impotence, he prays that the power of Satan will not unman the king nor unwoman you.'

'Amen,' I say promptly, as if anyone could believe this nonsense. Then I turn to my ladies and they escort me from the room to my own chamber where I will change into my nightgown.

When I come back the king is standing with his court beside the great bed, and the archbishop is still praying. The king is in his nightshirt with a great handsome cloak lined with fur thrown over his shoulders. He has laid aside his hose and I can see the bulky bandage on his leg where he has an open wound. The bandage is clean and fresh, thank God, but even so the smell of the wound seeps into the bedchamber to mingle, sickeningly, with the smell of incense. The prayers seem to have been going on while we both changed our clothes. Really, you would have thought that we were safe from demonic dreams and impotence by now. My ladies step forwards and slip my cloak from my shoulders. I am dressed only in my nightshift before the whole court and I am so mortified and embarrassed that I could almost wish myself back at Cleves.

Lady Rochford quickly lifts the covers from the bed to shield me from their inquisitive stares and I slip between them and sit up with my back against the pillows. On the other side of the bed a young man, Thomas Culpepper, kneels for Henry to lean on his shoulder and another man takes the king's elbow to push him upwards. King Henry grunts like a weary carthorse as he hauls himself into bed. The bed dips at his great weight and I have to make an ungainly little wriggle and grab the side to stop myself rolling over towards him.

The archbishop raises his hands above his head for a final blessing and I look straight ahead. Katherine Howard's bright face catches my eye, she has her hands pressed together, held against her lips as if devoutly praying, but she is clearly struggling not to giggle. I pretend I have not seen her, for fear that she should set me laughing too, and when the archbishop completes his prayers I say: 'Amen.'

They all go then, thank God. There is no suggestion that they should watch the marriage being consummated, but I know that they will need to see the sheets in the morning and know that it has been done. This is the nature of the royal marriage. That, and marrying a man old enough to be your father, who you hardly know.

Jane Boleyn, Greenwich Palace,
6 January 1540

I am one of the last to leave and I close the door quietly on yet another marriage of the king's which I have seen progress through courtship to the marriage bed. Some, like that young fool Katherine Howard, would think that this is where the story ends, that this is the conclusion of everything. I know better. This is where the story of a queen begins.

Before this night there are contracts and promises, and sometimes hopes and dreams; rarely there is love. After this night there is the reality of two people working out their lives together. For some, it is a negotiation that cannot be done; my own uncle is married to a wife he cannot tolerate, they live apart now. Henry Percy married an heiress but could never free himself from his love for Anne Boleyn. Thomas Wyatt hates his wife with a vengeance, since he fell in love with Anne when she was a girl and he has never recovered. My own husband . . . but I will not think about my own husband now. Let me remember that I loved him, that I would have died for love of him – whatever he thought of me when we were put to bed together for the first time. Whoever he thought of when he had to do the deed with me. God forgive him for holding me in his arms and thinking of her. God forgive me for knowing that, and letting it haunt me. In the end, God forgive me for having my head turned and my heart turned so I liked nothing more than to lie in his arms and think of him with another woman – jealousy and lust brought me so low that it was my pleasure, a wicked sinful pleasure, to feel his touch on me and think of him touching her.

It is not a matter of four bare legs in a bed and the business done. She will have to learn to obey him. Not in the grand things, any woman can put on a bit of a show. But in the thousand petty compromises that come to a wife every day. The thousand times a day when one has to bite the lip and bow the head and not argue in public, nor in private, nor even in the quiet recesses of one's own mind. If your husband is a king, this is even more important. If your husband is King Henry, it is a life or death decision.

Everyone tries to forget that Henry is a ruthless man. Henry himself tries to make us forget. When he is being charming, or setting himself out to please, we like to forget that we are playing with a savage bear. This is not a man whose temperament is tamed. This is not a man whose mood is constantly sweet. This is not a man who can manage his feelings, he cannot keep constant from one day to another. I have seen this man love three women with an absolute passion. I have seen him swear to each of them an eternal, unchangeable fidelity. I have seen him joust under the motto 'Sir Loyal Heart'. And I have seen him send two to their deaths, and learn of the death of the third with quiet composure.

That girl had better please him tonight, and she had better obey him tomorrow, and she had better give him a son within a year, or I, personally, would not give a snap of my fingers for her chances.

Anne, Greenwich Palace,
6 January 1540

One by one they leave the room, and we are left in candlelight and an awkward silence. I say nothing. It is not for me to speak. I remember my mother's warning that whatever happens in England I must never, never give the king reason to think that I am wanton. He has chosen me because he has faith in the character of the women of Cleves. He has bought himself a well-mannered, self-controlled, highly disciplined Erasmian virgin and this is what I must be. My mother does not say outright that to disappoint the king could cost me my life, because the fate of Anne Boleyn has never been mentioned in Cleves since the day when the contract was signed to marry me to a wife-killer. Since my betrothal it is as if Queen Anne was snatched up to heaven in complete silence. I am warned, constantly warned, that the King of England will not tolerate lightness of behaviour in his wife; but no-one ever tells me that he might do to me what he did to Anne Boleyn. No-one ever warns me that I too might be forced to put my head down on the block to be beheaded for imaginary faults.

The king, my husband, in bed beside me, sighs heavily, as if he is weary, and for a moment I think that perhaps he will just fall asleep and this exhausting, frightening day will be over and I can wake tomorrow a married woman and start my new life as Queen of England. For a moment, I dare to hope that my duties for today will be done.

I lie, as my brother would want me to lie, like a frozen moppet. My brother had a horror of my body: a horror and a fascination. He commanded me to wear high necks, thick clothes, heavy hoods, big boots, so that all he could see of me, all anyone could see of me, was my overshadowed face and my hands from my wrists to my fingers. If he could have put me into seclusion like the Ottoman emperor with his imprisoned wives I think he would have done so. Even my gaze was too forward for him, he preferred me not to look directly at him; if he could, he would have had me veiled.

And yet, he constantly spied on me. Whether I was in my mother's chamber sewing under her supervision, or in the yard looking at the horses, I would glance up and see him staring at me with that look of irritation and . . . I don't know what . . . desire? It was not lust. He never wanted me as a man wants a woman; of course I know that. But he wanted me as if he would dominate me completely. As if he would like to swallow me up so that I should trouble him no more.

When we were children he used to torment all three of us: Sybilla, Amelia and myself. Sybilla, three years older than him, could run fast enough to get away, Amelia would dissolve into the easy tears of the baby of the family; only I would oppose him. I did not hit him back when he pinched me or pulled my hair. I did not lash out when he cornered me in the stable yard or a dark corner. I just gritted my teeth and when he hurt me, I did not cry. Not even when he bruised my thin little-girl wrists, not even when he drew blood with a stone thrown at my head. I never cried, I never begged him to stop. I learned to use silence and endurance as my greatest weapons against him. His threat and his power was that he would hurt me. My power was that I dared to act as if he could not. I learned that I could endure anything a boy could do to me. Later, I learned that I could survive anything that a man might do to me. Later still I knew that he was a tyrant and he still did not frighten me. I have learned the power of surviving.

When I was older and watched his gentleness and his command of Amelia and his pleasant respect to my mother I realised that my stubbornness, my obstinacy, had created this constant trouble between us. He dominated my father, imprisoned him in his own bedroom, usurped him. He did all this with the blessing of my mother and with a proud sense of his own righteousness. He allied with Sybilla's husband, two ambitious princelings together, and so he still rules Sybilla, even after her marriage. He and my mother have forged themselves into a powerful partnership, a couple to rule Juliers-Cleves. They command Amelia; but I could not be dominated or patronised. I would not be babied or ruled. For him I became an itch that he had to scratch. If I had wept, or begged, if I had collapsed like a girl or clung like a woman he could have forgiven me, adopted me, taken me under his protection and cared for me. I would have been his little pet, as Amelia is: his sweetheart, the sister that he guards and keeps safe.

But by the time I understood all this it was too late. He was locked into his frustrated irritation with me and I had learned the joy of stubbornly surviving, despite all odds, and going my own way. He tried to make a slave of me, but all he did was teach me a longing to be free. I desired my freedom as other girls desire marriage. I dreamed of freedom as other girls dream of a lover.

This marriage is my escape from him. As Queen of England I command a fortune greater than his, I rule a country bigger than Cleves, infinitely more populous and powerful. I shall know the King of France as an equal, I am stepmother to a granddaughter of Spain, my name will be spoken in the courts of Europe and if I have a son he will be brother to the King of England and perhaps king himself. This marriage is my victory and my freedom. But as Henry shifts heavily in the bed and sighs again like a weary old man, not like a bridegroom, I know, as I have known all along, that I have exchanged one difficult man for another. I shall have to learn how to evade the anger of this new man, and how to survive him.

'Are you tired?' he asks.

I understand the word tired. I nod, and say: 'Little.'

'God help me in this ill-managed business,' he says.

'I don't understand? I am sorry?'

He shrugs, I realise he is not speaking to me, he is complaining of something for the pleasure of grumbling aloud, just as my father used to do before his ill-tempered mutterings became madness. The disrespect of this comparison makes me smile and then bite my lip to hide my amusement.

'Yes,' he says sourly. 'You might well laugh.'

'Will you like wine?' I ask carefully.

He shakes his head. He lifts the sheet and the sickly smell of him blows over me. Like a man seeing what he has bought in a market, he takes the hem of my nightgown, lifts it up, pulls it past my waist and my breasts and leaves it, so that it is in a roll around my neck. I am afraid I look stupid, like a burgher with a scarf tied tight under the chin. My cheeks are burning with shame that he should just stare at my exposed body. He does not care for my discomfort.

He puts his hand down, and abruptly squeezes my breasts, slides his rough hand down to my belly, pinches the fat. I lie absolutely still so that he shall not think I am wanton. It is not hard to freeze in horror. God knows why anyone would feel wanton under such handling. I have stroked my horse with more affection than this cold-hearted groping. He rears up in the bed with a grunt of effort and pushes my thighs apart with a heavy hand. I obey him without making a sound. It is essential that he knows that I am obedient but not eager. He heaves himself over me and slumps between my legs. He is taking his full weight with his elbows planted on either side of my head, and with his knees, but even so his great flaccid belly, pressing down on me, is stifling me. The fat of his chest is pressing on my face. I am a good-sized woman but I am dwarfed underneath him. I fear that if he lies any more heavily I will not be able to breathe, it is quite unbearable. His panting breath on my face is foul from his rotting teeth, I hold my head rigid to stop myself from turning my face away from him. I find I am breathless, trying not to inhale the stink of him.

He puts his hand down between us and grabs on to himself. I have seen them with the horses in the stables at Duren and I know well enough what is going on in this hard fumbling. I snatch a breath sideways, and I brace myself for the pain. He gives a little grunt of frustration and I can feel his hand pumping away, but still nothing happens. He punches repeatedly at my thigh with his moving hand but that is all. I lie very still, I don't know what he wants to do, nor what he expects of me. The stallion at Duren went rigid and reared up. This king seems to be weakening.

'My lord?' I whisper.

He throws himself off me and grunts a word that I don't know. His head is buried in the richly embroidered pillow, he is still face down. I don't know if he has finished or is merely beginning. He turns his head to me. His face is very red and sweating. 'Anne . . .' he starts.

At that fatal name he stops, freezes into silence. I realise that he has said her name, the first Anne that he loved, that he is thinking of her, the lover that drove him to madness and whom he killed in jealous resentment.

'I, Anne of Cleves, am,' I prompt him.

'I know that,' he says shortly. 'Fool.'

With a great heave that pulls all the bedcovers off me, he turns around and lies with his back to me. The air released from the bed is stale with an awful smell. This is the smell of the wound on his leg, this is the smell of putrid flesh, this is the smell of him. It will scent my sheets for ever, till death us do part, I had better get used to it.

I lie very still. To put a hand on his shoulder would, I think, be wanton behaviour, and so I had better not, though I am sorry if he is weary and haunted by the other Anne tonight. I will have to learn not to mind about the smell and about the feeling of being pressed down. I shall have to do my duty.

I lie in the darkness and look up at the rich canopy of the bed above me. In the dimming light which gets darker as each square block candle, one by one, gutters and goes out, I can see the glint of gold thread and the rich colours of the silks. He is an old man, poor old man, forty-eight years old, and it has been a long and exhausting day for us both. I hear him sigh again and then the sigh turns into a deep, bubbling snore. When I am certain that he is asleep I put my hand lightly on his shoulder where the thick damp linen of his nightshirt covers the fat sweaty bulk of him. I am sorry that he should fail this night, and if he had stayed awake, and if we had spoken the same language, and were able to tell each other the truth, then I would have told him that even though there is no desire between us that I hope to be a good wife to him and a good queen for England. That I feel pity for him in his old age and weariness, and that no doubt when he is rested and less tired we will be able to make a child, the son that we both want so much. Poor sick old man, I would have given much to be able to tell him not to worry, that it will come out all right, that I do not want a young handsome prince, that I will be kind to him.

Katherine, Greenwich Palace,
7 January 1540

The king was already gone before we arrived in the chamber on the day after the wedding, so I missed seeing the King of England in his nightshirt on his wedding morning, though I had set my heart on it. The maids of work went in with her ale, and wood for her fire, and water to wash in, and we waited until we were called to help her dress. She was sitting up in bed with her nightcap on and a neat plait down her back, not a hair out of place. She didn't look like a girl who has made merry all night, I must say. She looked exactly the same as when we put her to bed last night, quite calm and pretty in that cow-like way, and pleasant enough with everyone, not asking for any special favours and not complaining of anything. I was by the bed and since nobody was taking any notice of me I twitched up the sheet and had a quick look.

I didn't see a thing. Exactly so. Not one solitary thing. Speaking as a girl who has had to smuggle a sheet down to the pump and wash it quickly and sleep on it damp more than once, I know when a man and a maid have used a bed for more than sleeping. Not this bed. I would put my precious reputation on the fact that the king did not have her and she did not bleed. I would put the Howard fortune on a bet that they slept just as we left them, when we put them to bed, side by side like a pair of little dolls. The bottom sheet was not even rumpled, never mind soiled.

I would bet Westminster Abbey that nothing has happened between them.

I knew who would want to know at once, Lady Nosy-Parker of course. I made a curtsey and went from the room as if I were running an errand and found her, just coming from her own chamber. As soon as she saw my face she snatched my hands and drew me back into her room.

'I bet you a fortune that he has not had her,' I say triumphantly, without a word of explanation.

One thing that I like about Lady Rochford is that she always knows what I am talking about. I never have to explain anything to her.

'The sheets,' I say. 'Not a mark on them, they're not even creased.'

'Nobody has changed them?'

I shake my head. 'I was first in, after the maids.'

She reaches in the cupboard by the bed and brings out a sovereign and gives it to me. 'That's very good,' she says. 'You and I, between us, should always be the first to know everything.'

I smile, but I am thinking about some ribbons I shall buy with the sovereign to trim my new gown and perhaps some new gloves.

'Don't tell anyone else,' she cautions me.

'Oh?' I protest.

'No,' she says. 'Knowledge is always precious, Katherine. If you know something that no-one else knows then you have a secret. If you know something that everyone else knows then you are no better than them.'

'Can't I at least tell Anne Bassett?'

'I'll tell you when you can tell her,' she says. 'Perhaps tomorrow. Now go back to the queen. I am coming in a minute.'

I do as I am told, and as I go out I see she is writing a note. She will be writing to my uncle to tell him that I believe that the king has not bedded his wife. I hope she tells him that it was I who thought this first and not her. Then there may be another sovereign to go with the first. I begin to see what he means about great places bring great favours. I have only been in royal service for a matter of days and already I am two sovereigns wealthier. Give me a month and I shall make my fortune.

Jane Boleyn, Whitehall Palace,
January 1540

We have moved to Whitehall Palace, where the wedding is to be celebrated by a week-long jousting tournament, and then the last of the visitors will go back to Cleves and we will all settle into our new lives with a new Queen Anne. She has never before seen anything on the scale or of the style of this tournament, and she is rather endearing in her excitement.

'Lady Jane, where I sit?' she demands of me. 'And how? How?'

I smile at her bright face. 'You sit here,' I say, showing her the queen's box. 'And the knights will come into the arena, and the heralds will announce them. Sometimes they will tell a story, sometimes recite a poem about their costume. Then they fight either on horseback, riding down the lists here; or hand-to-hand fighting with swords, on the ground.' I think how to explain.

I never know how much she understands now, she is learning to speak so quickly. 'It is the greatest tournament the king has planned in many years,' I say. 'It will last for a week. There will be days of celebrations with beautiful costumes and everyone in London will come to see the masques and the battles. The court will be at the forefront, of course, but behind them will be the gentry and the great citizens of London and then behind them the common people will come in their thousands. It is a great celebration for the whole country.'

'I sit here?' she says, gesturing at the throne.

I watch her take her seat. Of course, to me this box is filled with ghosts. The seat is hers now; but it was Queen Jane's before her, and Queen Anne's before that, and when I was a young woman, not even married, just a girl filled with hopes and ambitions and passionately in love, I served Queen Katherine, who sat in that very chair under her own canopy which the king had ordered should be sewn with little gold Ks and Hs for Katherine and Henry, and he himself had ridden out under the name Sir Loyal Heart.

'This new is?' she asks, patting the curtains that are swagged around the royal box.

'No,' I say, forced by my memories to tell the truth. 'These are the curtains that are always used. Look, you can see.' I turn the fabric over and she can see where other initials have been. They have cut the embroidery from the front of the curtains but left the old sewing at the back. Clearly one can see K and H, entwined with lovers' knots. Oversewn, beside each H, is an H&A. It is like summoning a ghost to see her initials here again. These were the curtains which kept the sun from her head that May Day tournament when it was so hot, and we all knew that the king was angry, and we all knew that the king was in love with Jane Seymour, but none of us knew what would happen next.

I remember Anne leaning over the front of the box and dropping her handkerchief down to one of the jousters, shooting a sidelong smile at the king to see if he was jealous. I remember the cold look on his face and I remember she went pale and sat back again. He had the warrant for her arrest in his doublet then, at that very moment; but he said nothing. He was planning to send her to her death but he sat beside her for much of the day. She laughed and she chattered and she gave out her favours. She smiled at him and flirted and she had no idea he had made up his mind that she would die. How could he do such a thing to her? How could he? How could he sit beside her, with his new lover standing smiling, behind them

136

both, and know that within days Anne would be dead? Dead, and my husband dead with her, my husband dying for her, my husband dying for love of her. God forgive me for my jealousy. God forgive her for her sins.

Seated in her place, her initials showing like a dark stain on the hidden underside of her curtains, I shudder as if someone has laid a cold finger on my neck. If any place is haunted it will be here. These curtains have been stitched and overstitched with the initials of three doomed, pretty girls. Will the court seamstresses be ripping out another A in a few years? Will this box host another ghost? Will another queen come after this new Anne?

'What?' she asks me, the new girl who knows nothing.

I point to the neat stitches. 'K: Katherine of Aragon,' I say simply. 'A: Anne Boleyn. J: Jane Seymour.' I turn the curtain right side round so that she can see her own initials standing proud and new on the fair side of the fabric. 'And now, Anne of Cleves.'

She looks at me with her straight gaze and for the very first time I think that perhaps I have underestimated this girl. Perhaps she is not a fool. Perhaps behind that honest face there is quick intelligence. Because she cannot speak my language I have talked to her as if she is a child and I have thought of her with the wit of a child. But she is not frightened by these ghosts – she is not even haunted by them, as I am.

She shrugs. 'Queens before,' she says. 'Now: Anne of Cleves.'

Either this is a high courage; or it is the stoicism of the very stupid.

'Are you not afraid?' I ask very quietly.

She understands the words, I know she does. I can see it in her stillness and the sudden attentive tilt of her head. She looks at me directly. 'Afraid of nothing,' she says firmly. 'Never afraid.'

For a moment I want to warn her. She is not the only brave girl to sit in this box to be honoured as queen and then end her life stripped of her title, facing death alone. Katherine of Aragon had the courage of a crusader, Anne the nerves of a whore. The king brought them both down to nothing. 'You must take care,' I say.

'I afraid of nothing, am,' she says again. 'Never afraid.'

Anne, Whitehall Palace,
January 1540

I was dazzled by the beauty of the palace of Greenwich, but I am shaken to my shoes by Whitehall. More like a town than a palace, it is a thousand halls and houses, gardens and courts, in which only the nobly born and bred seem to find their way around. It has been the home of the Kings of England forever, and every great lord and his family have their own houses built inside the half-dozen acres of the sprawling palace. Everyone knows a secret passage, everyone knows a quick route, everyone knows a door that is conveniently left open to the streets, and a quick way down to a pier on the river where you can get a boat. Everyone but me and my Cleves ambassadors, who are lost inside this warren a dozen times a day and who feel more stupid and more like peasants abroad each time.

Beyond the gates of the palace is the city of London, one of the most crowded, noisy, populous cities in the world. From dawn I can hear the street sellers calling, even from my set of rooms hidden deep inside the palace. As the day goes on the noise and business increases until it seems that there is nowhere in the world that can be at peace. There is a constant stream of people through the palace gates with things to sell and bargains to make and, from what Lady Jane tells me, a continual stream of petitions for the king. This is the true home of his Privy Council; his parliament sits just down the road at the Palace of Westminster. The Tower of London, the great fortified lodestone of every king's power, is just down the river. If I am to make this great kingdom my home I shall have to learn my way around this palace, and then find my way around London. There is no point in hiding in my closet, overwhelmed by the noise and the bustle, I have to get out into the palace and let the people – who crowd in their thousands from dawn till nightfall – look at me.

My stepson, Prince Edward, is on a visit to court, he can watch the jousting tomorrow. He is allowed to court only seldom for fear of taking an infection and never in the summertime for fear of the plague. His father worships the boy, for his own little fair head, I am sure; but also because he is the only boy, the only Tudor heir. A single boy is such a precious thing. All the hopes of this new line rest on little Edward.

Lucky that he is such a strong healthy child. He has hair of the fairest gold, and a smile that makes you want to catch him up and hug him. But he is strongly independent and would be most offended if I were to press my kisses on him. So when we go to his nursery I take care only to sit near him and let him bring his toys to me, one by one, and each one he puts into my hand, with great pleasure and interest. 'Glish,' he says. 'Maow.' And I never catch his little fat hand and plant a kiss in the warm palm, though he looks up at me with eyes as dark and as round as toffee and with a smile as sweet.

I wish I could stay in his nursery all day. It does not matter to him that I cannot speak English or French or Latin. He hands a carved wooden top to me and says solemnly, 'moppet,' and I reply, 'moppet,' and then he fetches something else. We neither of us need a great deal of language nor a great deal of cleverness to pass an hour together.

When it is time for him to eat he allows me to lift him up into his little seat, and sit beside him as he is served with all the honour and respect that his own father commands. They serve this little boy on bended knee, and he sits up and takes his share from any one of a dozen rich dishes as if he were king already.

I say nothing as yet, because it is early days for me as his step-mother; but after I have been here a while longer, perhaps after my coronation next month, I shall ask my lord the king if the boy cannot have a little more freedom to run about and play, and a plainer diet. Perhaps we can visit him more often in his own household, even if he cannot come to court. Perhaps I might be allowed to see him often. I think of him, poor little boy, without a mother to care for him, and I think that I might have the raising of him, and see him grow into a young man, a good young man to be King Edward for England. And then I could laugh at myself for the selfishness of duty. Of course I want to be a good stepmother and queen to him, but more than anything else I long to mother him. I want to see his little face light up when I come into the room, not just for these few days, but every day. I want to hear him say 'Kwan', which is all he can manage of 'Queen Anne'. I want to teach him his prayers and his letters and his manners. I want him for my own. Not just because he is motherless; but because I am childless and I want someone to love.

This is not my only stepchild, of course. But the Lady Elizabeth is not allowed to come to court at all. She is to stay at Hatfield Palace, some distance from London, and the king does not recognise her except as his bastard, got on Lady Anne Boleyn; and there are those who say she is not even that, but another man's child. Lady Jane Rochford – who knows everything – showed me a portrait of Elizabeth and pointed to her hair, which is red as coals in a brazier, and smiled as if to say that there could be little doubt that this is the king's child. But King Henry has made it his right to decide which children he shall acknowledge, and Lady Elizabeth will be brought up away from court as a royal bastard and married to a minor nobleman when she is of age. Unless I can speak to him first. Perhaps, when we have been married a while, perhaps if I can give him a second son, perhaps then he will be kinder to the little girl who needs kindness.

In contrast, the Princess Mary is now allowed to court, though Lady Rochford tells me that she has been out of favour for years, ever since the defiance of her mother. The refusal of Queen Katherine to let Henry go meant that he denied the marriage and denied their child. I have to try not to think the worse of him for this. It was too long ago, and I am not fit to judge. But to visit on a child the coldness earned by the mother seems to me to be cruel. Just so did my brother blame me for the love that my father felt for me. Of course the Princess Mary is a child no longer. She is a young woman and ready for marriage. I think she is in poor health, she has not been well enough to come to court and meet me, though Lady Rochford says that she is well enough but that she is trying to avoid the court because the king has a new betrothal in mind for her.

I cannot blame her for that, she was to be betrothed to my brother William at one time, and then to a Prince of France, and then to a Hapsburg prince. It is natural that her marriage should be a matter of continual debate until she is settled. What is more odd is the fact that no-one can ever know what they are getting when they buy her. There is no telling her pedigree, since her father has disowned her once and now recognises her again, but could disown her again at any time, since nothing has any weight with him but his own opinion, which he says is the will of God.

When I become more of a power and an influence with my lord the king I shall talk to him about settling the Princess Mary's position once and for all. It is not fair to her that she should not know whether she is princess or a nothing, and she will never be able to marry any man of any substance while her position is so unreliable. I daresay the king has not thought of it from her point of view. And there has been no-one to be an advocate for her. It would surely be the right thing to do, as his wife, to help him see the needs of his daughters, as well as the demands of his own dignity.

Princess Mary is a most determined Papist; and I have been raised in a country that rejects the abuses of Papists and calls for a purer church. We might be enemies over doctrine and yet become friends. More than anything, I want to be a good queen for England, and a good friend to her, and surely, she should understand that. Of all the things that people say of Katherine of Aragon, everyone knows that she was a good queen and a good mother. All I want to do is follow her example; her daughter might even welcome that.

Katherine, Whitehall Palace,
January 1540

I am summoned to practise a masque, a tableau to open the tournament. The king is going to come in disguised as a knight from the sea, and we are to be waves or fish or something like that in his train and dance for the queen and the court. His composer has the score of the music and there are to be six of us. I think we represent the muses, but I am not sure. Now I come to think of it, I don't even know what a muse is. But I hope that it is the sort of thing that has a costume made from very fine silks.

Anne Bassett is another dancer, and Alison, and Jane, Mary, Catherine Carey and me. Of the six of us probably Anne is the prettiest girl, she has the fairest blonde hair and big blue eyes and she has this trick, which I must learn, of looking down and looking up again as if she had heard something most interesting and indecent. If you tell her the price of a yard of buckram she will look down and back up, as if you have whispered that you love her. Only if someone else is watching, of course. If we are just on our own she doesn't bother with it. It does make her most engaging when she is trying hard. After her, I am certain that I am the prettiest girl. She is the daughter of Lord and Lady Lisle and a great favourite of the king's, who is very much taken with this up and down look and has promised to give her a horse, which I think a pretty good fee for doing nothing more than fluttering eyelashes. Truly, there is a fortune to be made at court if you know how.

I enter the room at a run because I am late and there is the king himself, with two or three of his greatest friends, Charles Brandon, Sir Thomas Wyatt and young Thomas Culpepper, standing with the musicians with the score in his hand.

I curtsey very low at once, and I see that Anne Bassett is there, in the forefront, looking very demure and with her are the four others, preening themselves like a nest of cygnets and hoping to catch the royal eye.

But it is me that the king smiles to see. He really does. He turns and says, 'Ah! My little friend from Rochester.'

Down I go into my curtsey again and up I come tilted forwards so that the men can get a good sight of my low neckline and my breasts and, 'Your Grace!' I breathe, as if I can hardly speak for lust.

I can see they all enjoy this and Thomas Culpepper, who has the most dazzling blue eyes, gives me a naughty wink as one Howard kinsman to another.

'Did you really not know me at Rochester, sweetheart?' the king asks. And he comes across the room and puts his finger under my chin and turns my face up to him as if I were a child, which I don't like much; but I make myself stand still and say: 'Truly, sire, I did not. I would know you again, though.'

'How would you know me again?' he says indulgently, like a kind father at Christmas.

Well, this has me stuck because I don't know. I don't have anything to say, I was simply being pleasant. I have to say something; but nothing at all comes to mind. So I look up at him as if my head were full of confessions but I dare say nothing, and to my enormous pleasure I can feel a little heat in my cheeks and I know that I am blushing.

I am blushing for nothing but vanity, of course, and the pleasure of being singled out by the king himself in front of that slut Anne

Bassett, but also for the discomfort of having nothing to say and not a thought in my head; but he sees the blush and mistakes it for modesty, and he at once tucks my hand in the crook of his arm and leads me away from the others. I keep my eyes down, I don't even wink back at Master Culpepper.

'Hush, child,' he says very kindly. 'Poor sweet child, I didn't mean to embarrass you.'

'Too kind,' is all I manage to murmur. I can see Anne Bassett looking after us as if she would kill me. 'I'm so shy.'

'Sweetest child,' he says more warmly.

'It was when you asked me . . .'

'When I asked you what?'

I take a little breath. If he were not king, I would know better how to play this. But he is the king, and this makes me uncertain. Besides he is a man old enough to be my grandfather, it seems quite indecent to flirt with him. Then I take a little glance upwards at him and I know I am right. He has got that look on his face. The look that so many men have when they look at me. As if they want to just swallow me up, just capture me, and have me in one gulp.

'When you asked me whether I would know you again,' I say in a thin, little-girl voice. 'Because I would.'

'How would you?' He bends down to hear me, and I suddenly realise in a rush of excitement that it does not matter that he is king. He is sweet on me like my lady grandmother's steward. It is exactly the same soft, doting look in his face. I swear I recognise it. I should do; I have seen it often enough. It is that stupid, wet look that old men have when they see me, rather nasty really. It is how old men look at women young enough to be their daughters and imagine themselves to be as young as their sons. It is how old men look when they lust for a woman who is young enough to be their daughter, and they know they should not.

'Because you are so handsome,' I say, looking directly at him, taking the risk and seeing what will happen. 'You are the handsomest man at court, Your Grace.'

He stands quite still, almost like a man who suddenly hears beautiful music. Like a man enchanted. 'You think I am the handsomest man at court?' he asks incredulously. 'Sweet child, I am old enough to be your father.'

Closer to my grandfather if truth be told, but I gaze up at him. 'Are you?' I pipe, as if I don't know that he is near to fifty and I am not yet fifteen. 'But I don't like boys. They always seem so silly.'

'They trouble you?' he demands instantly.

'Oh, no,' I say. 'I have nothing at all to do with them. But I would rather walk and talk with a man who knows something of the world. Who can advise me. Someone I can trust.'

'You shall walk and talk with me this very afternoon,' he promises. 'And you shall tell me all your little troubles. And if anyone has troubled you, anyone, no matter how great: he shall answer to me for it.'

I sink into a curtsey. I am so close to him that I almost brush his breeches with my bent head. If that doesn't cause a little stirring, then I shall be very surprised. I look up at him and I smile up at him and I give a tiny little shake of my head as if in wonderment. I think to myself that this really is awfully good. 'Such an honour,' I whisper.

Anne, Whitehall Palace, 11 January 1540

This is a most wonderful day, I feel that I am queen indeed. I am seated in the royal box, my own box, the queen's box, in the newly built gatehouse at Whitehall, and in the jousting ground below me is half the nobility of England, with some great gentlemen from France and Spain come also to show their courage and to seek my favour.

Yes, my favour, for though I am inside still Anne of Cleves, not much regarded and neither the prettiest nor the sweetest of the Cleves girls, on the outside I am now Queen of England and it is amazing how much taller and more beautiful I turn out to be once I have a crown on my head.

The new gown does much to help with my confidence. It is made in the English style and, although I feel dangerously naked with a low-cut gown and no neckpiece of muslin to come up to my chin, at last I am looking more like the other ladies and less like a newcomer to court. I am even wearing a hood in the French style though I have it pulled forwards to hide my hair. It feels very light and I have to remember not to toss my head about and laugh at the sense of freedom. I do not want to seem too changed, too loose in my behaviour. My mother would be terribly shocked by my appearance, I don't want to let her down, nor my country.

Already, I have young men asking for my favour to ride in the lists, bowing low and smiling up at me with a special warmth in their eyes. With meticulous care, I keep my dignity and I award my favour only to those who already carry the king's regard, or those who carry his wagers. Lady Rochford is a safe advisor in these matters, she will keep me away from the danger of causing offence, and the far greater danger of causing scandal. I never forget that a Queen of England must be above any whisper of flirtation. I never forget that it was at a joust, such as this one, when one young man and then another carried the queen's handkerchief and that day was ended with their arrest for adultery, and her merry day was ended on the block.

This court has no memory of that; though the men who gave evidence and handed down the sentence of her death are here today in the bright sunshine, smiling and shouting orders into the jousting ring, and those who survived, like Thomas Wyatt, smile at me as if they have not seen three other women in the place where I sit now.

The arena is lined with painted boards and marked out with poles painted in the Tudor green-and-white stripes, standards fluttering at every flagpole. There are thousands of people here, all dressed in their best and looking for entertainment. The place is noisy with people shouting their wares, the flower girls singing out their prices, and the chink of coins as bets change hands. The citizens cheer me whenever I glance in their direction, and their wives and their daughters wave their handkerchiefs and call, 'Good Queen Anne!' to me when I raise my hand to acknowledge their attention. The men throw their hats in the air and bellow my name, and there is a constant stream of noblemen and gentry to the royal box to bow over my hand and introduce their ladies, come to London especially for the tournament.

The arena is sweet with the smell of a thousand nosegays and freshly dampened clean sand, and when the horses enter at a gallop, skid to a standstill and rear, they kick up a golden spray. The knights are glorious in their armour, each piece burnished to shine like silver and most of them gorgeously engraved and inlaid with rich metals. Their standard bearers carry flags of brilliant silks embroidered with special mottoes. There are many who come as mystery knights, with their visors down and strange and romantic names bellowed out as their challenge, some of them are accompanied by a bard who tells their tragic story in poetry, or sings their song before the joust. I was afraid that it would be a day of fighting and that I wouldn't understand what was going on, but it is as good as the most beautiful pageant to see the fine horses come into the lists, the handsome men in their pride, and the crowds of thousands cheering them on.

They promenade before they start and there is a tableau to welcome them to the arena. The king himself is the centre of the scene, dressed as a knight from Jerusalem and the ladies of my court are in his train, dressed in costume and sitting on a great wagon that comes in towed by horses who are draped in yards of blue silk. They represent the sea, I can tell, but what the ladies are supposed to be is beyond me. Given the brilliant smile of little Katherine Howard as she stands at the front, her hand raised to shield her bright eyes, I think she is supposed to be lookout mermaid, or something of that nature, perhaps a siren. Certainly she is swathed in white muslin drapery which might represent sea foam and she has accidentally let it fall so that one lovely shoulder is showing, as if she is emerging naked from the sea.

When I have a little more command of the language I shall talk to her about taking care with her reputation and modesty. She does not have a mother, who died when she was a little child, and her father is a careless spendthrift who lives abroad in Calais. She was brought up by a step-grandmother, Jane tells me, so perhaps she has not had anyone to warn her that the king is most alert to any sort of improper behaviour. Her dress today is perhaps allowed, since it is part of a tableau; but the way it is sliding down to show her slim white back is, I know, very wrong.

The ladies dance in the arena and then curtsey and escort the king to my box and he comes to sit beside me. I smile and give him my hand, it is as if we are part of the pageant, and the crowd roars their pleasure to see him kiss my hand. It is my part to smile very sweetly and curtsey to him and welcome him to his great reinforced seat which towers over mine. Lady Jane sees that he is served with a cup of wine and some sweetmeats, and she nods to me that I am to take my seat beside him.

The ladies retreat as half a dozen knights, all in dark armour and flying a sea-blue flag, ride in, so I imagine that they are the tide or Neptune or something. I feel very ignorant not understanding all the meaning of this, but it hardly matters for once they ride around the ring and the heralds bawl out their titles and the crowds roar their approval the jousting will start.

The crowds are packed into the tiered seating and the poorer people are crammed into the spaces between. Every time a knight comes to present his arms to me there is a great bellow of approval from the crowd and they shout 'Anna! Anna Cleves!' over and over again. I stand and smile and wave my thanks, I cannot imagine what I have done to earn such public acclaim, but it is so wonderful to know that the people of England have taken to me, just as naturally and easily as I have taken to them. The king stands up beside me and takes my hand before them all.

'Well done,' he says shortly to me, and then he goes from the box. I look to Lady Jane Boleyn, in case I should go with him. She shakes her head. 'He will have gone to talk with the knights,' she says. 'And the girls of course. You stay here.'

I take my seat and see that the king has appeared in his own royal box opposite to mine. He waves at me, and I wave at him. He sits, and I sit a few moments after him.

'You are already beloved,' Lord Lisle says quietly to me in English, and I grasp what he means.

'Why?'

He smiles. 'Because you are young.' He pauses for my nod of comprehension. 'They want you to have a son. Because you are pretty, and because you smile and wave at them. They want a pretty, happy queen who will give them a son.'

I shrug a little at the simple ways of these most complicated people. If all they want is for me to be happy, that is easy. I have never been so happy in my life. I have never been so far from my mother's disapproval and my brother's rages. I am a woman in my own right, with my own place, with my own friends. I am queen of a great country that I think will grow yet more prosperous and more ambitious. The king is a whimsical master of a nervous court, even I can see that; but here too I might be able to make a difference. I might give this court the steadiness that it needs, I might even be able to advise the king to have more patience. I can see my life here, I can imagine myself as queen. I know I can do this. I smile at Lord Lisle who has been distant from me over these last few days and who has not been his usual kindly self.

'Thank you,' I say. 'I hope.'

He nods.

'You are well?' I ask awkwardly. 'Happy?'

He looks surprised at my question. 'Er, yes. Yes, Your Grace.'

I think for the word I need. 'No trouble?'

For a moment I see it, the fear that crosses his face, the momentary thought of confiding in me. Then it is gone. 'No trouble, Your Grace.'

I see his eyes drift across the jousting arena to the opposite side where the king is sitting. Lord Thomas Cromwell is at his side, whispering in his ear. I know that in a court there are always factions, a king's favour comes and goes. Perhaps Lord Lisle has offended the king in some way.

'I know you good friend to me,' I say.

He nods. 'God keep Your Grace, whatever comes next,' he says and steps away from my chair to stand at the back of the box.

I watch the king stand and go to the front of his box. A pageboy keeps him steady on his lame leg. He takes his great gauntlet and holds it above his head. The people in the crowd fall silent, their eyes on this, their greatest king, the man who has made himself king, emperor and Pope. Then, cleverly, when all the attention is on him, he bows to me and gestures with his gauntlet. The crowd roars its approval. It is for me to start the joust.

I rise from my great chair with the gold canopy over my head. Either side of the box the curtains billow in the Tudor colours of green and white, my initials are everywhere, my crest is everywhere. The other initials of all the other queens are only on the underside of the curtains and they don't show. To judge from today, there has only ever been one queen: myself. The court, the people, the king, all conspire to forget the others and I am not going to remind them. This joust is for me as if I were the very first of Henry's queens.

I raise my hand and the whole arena goes silent. I drop my glove and at either end of the jousting line the horses dive forwards as the spurs strike their sides. The two riders thunder towards each other, the one on the left, Lord Richman, lowers his lance a little later, and his aim is good. With a tremendous thud like an axe going into a tree, the lance catches his opponent in the very centre of his breastplate and the man bellows out and is thrown violently backwards off his horse. Lord Richman rides to the end of the line and his squire catches the horse as his lordship pushes back his dark visor and looks at his opponent, thrown down into the sand.

Among my ladies, Lady Lisle gives a little scream and rises to her feet.

Unsteadily, the young man rises, his legs tottering.

'He is hurt?' I ask in a quiet undertone to Lady Rochford.

She is avidly watching. 'He may be,' she says, a delighted exultant tone in her voice. 'It is a violent sport. He knows the risks.'

'Is there a . . .' I do not know the English word for doctor.

'He is walking.' She points. 'He is unhurt.'

They have his helmet off, he is white as a sheet, poor young man. His brown curly hair is dark with sweat and sticking to his pale face.

'Thomas Culpepper,' Lady Rochford tells me. 'A distant kinsman of mine. Such a handsome boy.' She gives me a sly smile. 'Lady Lisle had given him her favour, he has a desperate reputation with the ladies.'

I smile down at him as he takes a few shaky strides to come before the queen's box and bows low to me. His squire has a hand on his elbow to help him up from his bow.

'Poor boy,' I say. 'Poor boy.'

'I am honoured to fall in your service,' he says. His words are obscured by the bruise on his mouth. He is a devastatingly handsome young man, even I, raised by the strictest of mothers, have a sudden desire to take him away from the arena and bathe him.

'With your permission, I shall ride for you again,' he says. 'Perhaps tomorrow, if I can mount.'

'Yes, but take care,' I say.

He gives me the most rueful sweet smile, bows and steps to one side.

He limps from the arena and the victor of this first joust takes a slow canter around the outside circle, his lance held upright, acknowledging the shouts from the crowd who have won their bets on him. I look back at my ladies and Lady Lisle is gazing after the young man as if she adores him and Katherine Howard, with a cape thrown around her costume, is watching him from the back of the box.

'Enough,' I say. I have to learn to command my ladies. They have to behave as my mother would approve. The Queen of England and her ladies must be above question. Certainly the three of us should not be gawping after a handsome young man. 'Katherine, get dressed at once. Lady Lisle, where your husband his lordship?'

They both nod, and Katherine whisks away. I sit back on my throne while another champion and his challenger ride into the ring.

This time the poem is very long and in Latin, and my hand creeps to my pocket where a letter rustles. It is from Elizabeth, the six-year-old princess. I have read it and re-read it so often that I know I have her meaning, indeed, I almost have every word by heart. She promises me her respect as a queen and her entire obedience to me as her mother. I could almost weep for her, dear little girl, creating these great solemn phrases and then copying them over and over until the handwriting is as regular as any royal clerk. Clearly, she hopes to come to court and indeed, I do think that she might be allowed to enter my household. I have maids in waiting who are not very much older than her and it would be such a pleasure to have her with me. Besides, she lives all but alone, in her own household with her governess and nurse. Surely the king would prefer her to be near us, to be supervised by me?

There is a fanfare of trumpets and I look up to see the riders drawn to one side and saluting as the king limps across the arena to the front of my box. The pages spring to open the doors so that he can mount the steps. He has to be heaved up by a young man on either side. I know enough about him by now to know that this, before a watching crowd, will make him bad-tempered. He feels humiliated and self-conscious and his first desire will be to humiliate someone else. I stand and curtsey to greet him, I never know whether I should put out my hand or reach forwards in case he wants to kiss me. Today, before the crowd that likes me, he draws me to him and kisses me on the mouth and everyone cheers. He is clever at this; he always does something to please the crowd.

He sits on his chair and I stand beside him.

'Culpepper took a hard knock,' he says.

I don't quite understand this so I say nothing to it. There is an awkward silence and clearly it is my turn to speak. I have to think hard to find something to say and the correct English words. Finally I have it: 'You like to joust?' I ask.

The scowl he turns on me is quite terrifying, his eyebrows are drawn down so hard that they almost cover his furious little eyes. I have clearly said utterly the wrong thing and offended him very deeply. I gasp, I don't know what I have said that is so very bad.

'Excuse me, forgive . . .' I stammer.

'I like to joust?' he repeats bitterly. 'Indeed yes, I would like to joust, but for being crippled with pain with a wound that never heals, that is poisoning me every day, that will be the death of me. Probably in a matter of months. That makes it agony to walk and agony to stand and agony to ride, but no fool thinks of it.'

Lady Lisle steps forwards. 'Sire, Your Grace, what the queen means to say is, do you like to watch the joust?' she says quickly. 'She did not mean to offend you, Your Grace. She is learning our language with remarkable speed, but she cannot help small errors.'

'She cannot help being as dull as a block,' he shouts at her. Spittle from his pursed mouth sprays her face but she does not flinch. Steadily she sinks into a curtsey and stays down low.

He looks her over but does not tell her to rise. He leaves her in her discomfort and turns to me. 'I like to watch it because it is all that is left for me,' he says bitterly. 'You know nothing; but I was the greatest champion. I took on all-comers. Not once, but every time. I jousted in disguise so that no-one did me any favours, and even when they rode as hard as they could I still defeated them. I was the greatest champion in England. Nobody could defeat me, I would ride all day, I would break dozens of lances. Do you understand that, you dullard?'

Still shaken, I nod, though in truth, he speaks so fast and so angrily that I can understand hardly any of this. I try to smile but my lips are trembling.

'No-one could beat me,' he insists. 'Ever. Not one knight. I was the greatest jouster in England, perhaps in the world. I was unbeatable and I could ride all day and dance all night, and be up the next day at dawn to go hunting. You know nothing. Nothing. Do I like to joust? – good God, I was the heart of chivalry! I was the darling of the crowd, I was the toast of every tournament! There was none like me! I was the greatest knight since those of the round table! I was a legend.'

'No-one who saw you could ever forget it,' Lady Lisle says sweetly, raising her head. 'You are the greatest knight that ever entered a ring. Even now I have never seen your equal. There is no equal. None of them in these days can equal you.'

'Hmm,' he says irritably, and falls silent.

There is a long, awkward pause and there is nobody in the jousting arena to divert us, and everyone is waiting for me to say something pleasant to my husband, who sits in silence, scowling at the herbs on the floor.

'Oh, get up,' he says crossly to Lady Lisle. 'Your old knees will lock up if you stay down for much longer.'

'I have letter,' I say quietly, trying to change the subject to something less controversial to him.

He turns and looks at me, he tries to smile, but I can see he is irritated by me, by my accent, by my halting speech.

'You have letter,' he repeats, in harsh mimicry.

'From Princess Elizabeth,' I say.

'Lady,' he replies. 'Lady Elizabeth.'

I hesitate. 'Lady Elizabeth,' I say obediently. I take out my precious letter and show it to him. 'May she come here? May she live with me?'

He twitches the letter from my hand, and I have to stop myself from snatching it back. I want to keep it. It is my first letter from my little stepdaughter. He screws up his eyes to stare at it then he snaps at his pageboy who hands him his spectacles. He puts them on to read but he shades his face from the crowd so that the common people shall not know that the King of England is losing the sight of his squinty eyes. He scans the letter quickly, then he hands it with the spectacles to his page.

'Is my letter,' I say quietly.

157

'I shall reply for you.'

'Can she come to me?'

'No.'

'Your Grace, please?'

'No.'

I hesitate, but my stubborn nature, learned under the hard fist of my brother, a bad-tempered, spoiled child just like this king, urges me on.

'So, why not?' I demand. 'She writes me, she asks me, I wish to see her. So why not?'

He rises to his feet and leans on the back of the chair to look down on me. 'She had a mother so unlike you, in every way, that she ought not to ask for your company,' he says flatly. 'If she had known her mother she would never ask to see you. And so I shall tell her.' Then he rises to his feet and stamps down the stairs, out of my box, and across the arena to his own.

Jane Boleyn, Whitehall Palace, February 1540

I have been expecting this summons to confer with my lord the duke at some stage during the tournament but he did not send for me. Perhaps he too remembers the tournament at May Day and the fall of her handkerchief and the laughter of her friends. Perhaps even he cannot hear the trumpet sound without thinking of her white-faced and desperate on that hot May Day morning. He waits until the tournament is over and life in the palace of Whitehall has returned to normal and then he tells me to come to his rooms.

This is a palace for plotting, all the corridors twist round and about each other, every courtyard has a little garden at the centre where one may meet by accident, every apartment has at least two entrances. Not even I know all the secret ways from the bedrooms to hidden water gates. Not even Anne did, not even my husband, George, who stole away so often.

The duke commands me to come to him privately after dinner and so I slip away from the dining hall and go the long way round in case anyone is watching me before entering his rooms without knocking, in silence.

He is seated at his fireside. I see by the servant clearing the plates that he has dined alone and eaten better than we did in the hall, I imagine. The kitchens are so far from the dining hall in this old fashioned palace that the food is always cold. Everyone who has private rooms has their food cooked for them in their own chambers. The duke has the best rooms here, as he does almost everywhere. Only Cromwell is better housed than the head of our house. The Howards have always been the first of families, even when their girl is not on the throne. There is always dirty work to be done and that is our speciality. The duke waves the server away and offers me a glass of wine.

'You can sit,' he says.

I know by this honour that the work he has for me will be confidential and perhaps dangerous. I sit and sip my wine.

'And how are matters in the queen's rooms?' he asks agreeably.

'Well enough,' I reply. 'She is learning more of our language every day, and she understands almost everything now, I think. Some of the others underestimate her understanding. They should be warned.'

'I hear the warning,' he nods. 'And her temper?'

'Pleasant,' I say. 'She shows no signs of missing her home, indeed she seems to have a great affection and interest in England. She is a good mistress to the younger maids, she watches them and considers them, and she has high standards; she keeps good command in her rooms. She is observant but not overly religious.'

'She prays like a Protestant?'

'No, she follows the king's order of service,' I say. 'She is meticulous in it.'

He nods. 'No desire to return to Cleves?'

'None that she has ever mentioned.'

'Odd.'

He waits. This is his way. He stays silent until one feels obliged to comment.

'I think there is bad feeling between her and her brother,' I volunteer at last. 'And I think Queen Anne was beloved of her father who was sick from drink at the end of his life. It sounds as if the brother took his place and his authority.'

He nods. 'So no chance of her being willing to step down from the throne and go home?'

I shake my head. 'Never. She loves being queen and she has a fancy to be a mother to the royal children. She would have Prince Edward at her side if she could, and she was bitterly disappointed that she could not see the Prin – the Lady Elizabeth. She hopes to have children of her own and she wants to gather her stepchildren around her. She is planning her life here, her future. She will not go willingly, if that is in your mind.'

He spreads his hands. 'Nothing is in my mind,' he lies.

I wait for him to tell me what he wants next.

'And the girl,' he says. 'Our young Katherine. The king has taken a liking to her, hasn't he?'

'Very much so,' I agree. 'And she is as clever with him as a woman twice her age. She is very skilled. She appears completely sweet and very innocent, and yet she displays herself like a Smithfield whore.'

'Charming indeed. Does she have ambitions?'

'No, only greed.'

'She has no thought that the king has married his wives' maids in waiting before now?'

'She is a fool,' I say shortly. 'She is a skilled flirt because that is her great delight, but she can plan no more than a lapdog.'

'Why not?' He is momentarily diverted.

'She has no thought of the future, she cannot imagine beyond the next masque. She will do tricks for sweets, but she does not dream that she might learn to hunt and pull down the greatest prize.'

'Interesting.' He bares his yellow teeth in a smile. 'You are always interesting, Jane Boleyn. And so: to the king and queen. I escort him to her room every other night. Do you know if he has yet managed to do the act?'

'We are all certain that he has not,' I say. I lower my voice though I know I am safe in these rooms. 'I think he is unmanned.'

'Why d'you think that?'

I shrug. 'It was the case in the last months with Anne. We all know that.'

He gives a short laugh. 'We know it now.'

It was George, my George, who told the world that the king was impotent when he was on trial for his life. Typical of George, with nothing left to lose, to say the unsayable, the one thing he should have kept secret. He was daring to the very steps of the scaffold.

'Does he show her that he is discontented? Does she know that she does not please him?'

'He is courteous enough, but cold. It's as if he doesn't even think of her with pleasure. As if he cannot get pleasure from anything.'

'D'you think he could do it with anyone else?'

'He is old,' I start; but the quick glare from the old duke reminds me that he is no stripling himself. 'That should not prevent him, of course. But he is sick with the pain of his leg and I think that this is worse recently. Certainly, it smells worse and he limps very heavily.'

'So I see.'

'And he is costive.'

He makes a face. 'As we all know.' The latest movement of the king's bowels is of constant concern to the court, for their own interest as much as his; when he is bound his temper is much worse.

'And she does nothing to arouse him.'

'She discourages him?'

'Not exactly, but my guess is that she does nothing to help him.'

'Is she mad? If she wants to stay married it all depends on her getting a son from him.'

I hesitate. 'I believe that she has been cautioned against appearing light or wanton.' I can hear a little gurgle of laughter in the back of my voice. 'Her mother and her brother are very strict, I think. She has been severely brought up. Her great concern seems to be not to give the king cause to complain that she is amorous or hot-blooded.'

He lets out a crack of laughter. 'What are they thinking of? Would you send a king like this a block of ice, and expect him to thank you?' Then he sobers again. 'So do you believe that she is a virgin still? He has managed nothing?'

'Yes, sir, I think she is.'

'She will be anxious about these matters, I suppose?'

I take a sip of wine. 'She has taken no-one into her confidence, as far as I know. Of course she may speak to her own countrywomen in their language but they are not intimate, there is no whispering in corners. Perhaps she is ashamed. Perhaps she is discreet. I think she is keeping the king's failure as a secret between the two of them.'

'Commendable,' he says dryly. 'Unusual in a woman. D'you think she would talk to you?'

'She might. What do you want her to say?'

He pauses. 'The alliance with Cleves may no longer be so important,' he says. 'The friendship between France and Spain is weakening. Who knows? it may be falling apart even as we speak. So if they are not allies, then we no longer need the friendship of the Lutherans of Germany against the united Papists of France and Spain.' He pauses. 'I am going to France myself, on the king's command, to the court of King Francis to find how friendly he is with Spain. If King Francis tells me that he has no love of Spain, that he is weary of them and their perfidy, then he might choose to join with England against them. In such a case we wouldn't need the friendship of Cleves, we wouldn't need a Cleves queen on the throne.' He pauses for emphasis. 'In such a case we would be better with an empty throne. We would do better if our king was free to marry a French princess.'

My head is spinning, as it often does when I talk with the duke. 'My lord, are you saying that the king could make an alliance with France now, and so he does not need the Queen Anne's brother as his friend any more?'

'Exactly so. Not only does he not need him, the friendship of Cleves could become an embarrassment. If France and Spain are not arming against us, we don't need Cleves, we don't want to be tied up with Protestants. We might ally with either France or Spain. We might want to join the great players again. We might even reconcile with the Pope. If God were with us then we might get the king forgiven, restore the old religion and bring the church in England back under the rule of the Pope. Anything, as always with King Henry, is possible. In all of the Privy Council there was only one man who thought that Duke William would prove to be a great asset, and that man may be about to fall.'

I gasp. 'Thomas Cromwell is about to fall?'

He pauses. 'The most important diplomatic mission, that of discovering the feeling in France, has been given to me, not Thomas Cromwell. The king's thoughts that the reform of the church has gone too far are shared with me, not with Thomas Cromwell. Thomas Cromwell made the Cleves alliance. Thomas Cromwell made the Cleves marriage. It turns out that we don't need the alliance and that the marriage is not consummated. It turns out the king does not like the Cleves mare. *Ergo* (that means therefore, my dear Lady Rochford), *ergo* we might dispense with the mare, the marriage, with the alliance, and with the broker: Thomas Cromwell.'

'And you become the king's chief advisor?'

'Perhaps.'

'You would advise him into alliance with France?'

'God willing.'

'And speaking of God, he reconciles with the church?'

'The Holy Roman Church,' he corrects me. 'Please God we can see it restored to us. I have long wanted it restored, and half the country feels as I do.'

'And so the Lutheran queen is no more?'

'Exactly, she is no more. She stands in my way.'

'And you have another candidate?'

He smiles at me. 'Perhaps. Perhaps the king has already chosen himself another candidate. Perhaps his fancy has alighted and his conscience will follow.'

'Little Kitty Howard.'

He smiles.

I speak out bluntly: 'But what of the young Queen Anne?'

There is a long silence. 'How would I know?' he says. 'Perhaps she will accept a divorce, perhaps she will have to die. All I know is: she is in my way and she will have to go.'

I hesitate. 'She is without friends in this country and most of her countrymen have gone home. She has no support or counsel from her mother or her brother. Is she in danger of her life?'

He shrugs. 'Only if she is guilty of treason.'

'How could she be? She cannot speak English, she knows no-one but those people we have presented to her. How could she plot against the king?'

'I don't know yet.' He smiles at me. 'Perhaps I will one day ask you to tell me how she has played the traitor. Perhaps you will stand before a court and offer evidence of her guilt.'

'Don't,' I say through cold lips.

'You have done it before,' he taunts me.

'Don't.'

Katherine, Whitehall Palace,
February 1540

I am brushing the queen's long fair hair as she sits before her silvered mirror. She is looking at her reflection but her eyes are quite blank, she is not seeing herself at all. Fancy that! Having such a wonderful looking-glass that it will give a perfect reflection, and not looking at yourself! I seem to have spent my life trying to get a view of myself in silver trays and bits of glass, even leaning over the well at Horsham, and here she is before a perfectly made looking-glass and she is not entranced. Really, she is most peculiar. Behind her, I admire the movement of the sleeve of my gown as my hands move up and down, I bend down a little to see my own face and tip my head to one side to see the light catch my cheek then I tip it the other way. I try a small smile, then I raise my eyebrows as if I am surprised.

I glance down and find she is watching me, so I giggle and she smiles.

'You are a pretty girl, Katherine Howard,' she says.

I flutter my eyelashes at our reflected images. 'Thank you.'

'I am not,' she says.

One of the awkward things about her not knowing how to speak properly is that she says these dreadfully flat statements and you can't quite tell how you should reply. Of course she is not as pretty as me, but on the other hand she has lovely hair, thick and shiny, and she has a pleasant face and good, clear skin and really quite beautiful eyes. And she should remember that almost no-one at court is as pretty as me, so she need not reproach herself for that.

She has no charm at all but that is partly because she is so stiff. She can't dance, she can't sing, she can't chatter. We are teaching her to play cards and everything else, like dancing and music and singing, of which she has absolutely not a clue; but in the meantime she is fearfully dull. And this is not a court where dull goodness counts for much. Not at all, really.

'Nice hair,' I say helpfully.

She points to her hood on the table before her, that is so very large and heavy. 'Not good,' she says.

'No,' I agree with her. 'Very bad. You like try mine?' One of the really funny things about trying to talk to her is that you start speaking like she does. I do it for the maids when we are supposed to be sleeping at night. 'You sleep now,' I say into the darkness and we all scream with laughter.

She is pleased at this offer. 'Your hood? Yes.'

I take the pins out and I lift it off my head. I take a little glance at myself in the mirror as my hood comes off and my hair tumbles down. It reminds me of dear Francis Dereham, who used to love to take off my hood and rub his face in my loose hair. Seeing myself do this in a good mirror with a true likeness for the first time in my life I understand how desirable I was to him. Really, I can't blame the king for looking at me as he does, I can't blame John Beresby or the new page who is with Lord Seymour. Thomas Culpepper could not take his eyes off me at dinner last night. Truly, I am in extraordinarily good looks since I have come to court, and every day I seem to be prettier.

Gently I hold out the hood for her and when she takes it I stand behind her to gather back her hair as she sets the hood on her head.

It makes a tremendous improvement; even she can see it. Without the heavy square frame of her German hood sitting like a roof slap on her forehead, her face becomes at once rounder and prettier.

But then she pulls my pretty hood forwards so it is practically on her eyebrows, just like she wore her new French hood at the joust. She looks quite ridiculous. I give a little tut of irritation, and push it so that it is far back on her head, and then I pull some waves of hair forwards to show the fair shiny thickness of it.

Regretfully, she shakes her head and pulls the hood forwards again, tucking her lovely hair out of sight. 'It is better so,' she says.

'Not as pretty, not as pretty! You have to wear it set back. Set back!' I exclaim.

She smiles at my raised voice. 'Too French,' is all she says.

She silences me. I suppose she is right. The last thing any Queen of England can dare to look is too French. The French are the absolute last word in immodesty and immorality and a previous English queen educated in France, quintessentially French, was my cousin Anne Boleyn who brought the French hood to England and took it off only to put her head on the block. Queen Jane wore the English hood in a triumph of modesty. It is like the German hood, quite ghastly, only a little lighter and slightly curved, and that's what most ladies wear now. Not me: I wear a French hood and I wear it as far back as I dare and it suits me, and it would suit the queen too.

'You wore it at the joust and nobody dropped dead,' I urge her. 'You are queen. Do what you like.'

She nods. 'Maybe,' she says. 'The king likes this?'

Well, yes, he likes this hood but only because I am under it. He is such a doting old man that I think he would like me if I wore a jester's cap on my head and danced about in motley, shaking a pig's bladder with bells.

'He likes it well enough,' I say carelessly.

'He likes Queen Jane?' she asks.

'Yes. He did. And she wore an awful hood, like yours.'

'He comes to her bed?'

Saints, I don't know where this is going but I wish that Lady Rochford were here. 'I don't know, I wasn't at court then,' I say.

'Honestly, I lived with my grandmother. I was just a girl. You could ask Lady Rochford, or any of the old ladies. Ask Lady Rochford.'

'He kiss me goodnight,' she says suddenly.

'That's nice,' I say faintly.

'He kiss me good morning.'

'Oh.'

'That all.'

I look around the empty dressing chamber. Normally there should be half a dozen maids in here, I don't know where they can all be. They just wander off sometimes, there is nothing so idle as girls, really. I can see why I irritate everybody so much. But now I really need some help with this embarrassing confession and there is no-one here at all.

'Oh,' I say feebly.

'Just that: kiss, goodnight, and then kiss, good morning.'

I nod. Where are the idle sluts?

'No more,' she says, as if I am so stupid that I don't understand the really disastrous thing she is telling me.

I nod again. I wish to God someone would come in. Anyone. I should even be glad to see Anne Bassett right now.

'He cannot do more,' she says bluntly.

I see a dark colour rising up her face, the poor thing is blushing with embarrassment. At once I stop feeling awkward and I feel such pity for her; really, this is as bad for her to tell me as it is for me to hear. Actually, it must be worse for her to say than for me to hear, since she is having to tell me that her husband feels no desire for her, and she doesn't know what to do about it. And she is a very shy, very modest woman; and God knows, I am not.

Her eyes are filling with tears as her cheeks are growing red. The poor thing, I think. The poor, poor thing. Fancy having an ugly old man for a husband and him not being able to do it. How disgusting would that be? Thank God I am free to choose my own lovers and Francis was as young and sleek-skinned as a snake, and kept me awake all night with his unstoppable lust. But she is stuck with a sick old man and she will have to find a way to help him.

'Do you kiss him?' I ask.

'No,' she says shortly.

'Or . . .' I mime a stroking motion with my right hand lightly clenched at hip level; she knows well enough what I mean.

'No!' she exclaims, quite shocked. 'Good God, no.'

'Well, you have to do that,' I tell her frankly. 'And let him see you, leave the candles burning. Get out of bed and undress.' I make a little gesture to indicate how she should let her shift slide off her shoulders, slither down over her breasts. I turn away from her and look over my shoulder with a little smile, slowly I bend over, still smiling over my shoulder. No man can resist that, I know.

'Stop,' she says. 'Not good.'

'Very good,' I say firmly. 'Must be done. Must have baby.'

She turns her face one way and the other, like a poor trapped animal. 'Must have baby,' she repeats.

I mime for her the opening of a shift, I stroke my hand down from my breasts to my fanny. I close my eyes and sigh as if in the grip of tremendous pleasure. 'Like this. Do this. Let him watch.'

She looks at me with her serious face very grave. 'I cannot,' she says quietly. 'Katherine, I cannot do anything like that.'

'Why not? If it would help? If it would help the king?'

'Too French,' she says sadly. 'Too French.'

Anne, Hampton Court, March 1540

This great court is on the move, from the palace at Whitehall to another of the king's houses, called Hampton Court. No-one has described it to me but I am expecting to see a good-sized farmhouse in the country. In truth, I am hoping for a smaller house where we can live more simply. The palace of Whitehall is like a little town inside the city of London and twice a day, at least, if I were not guided by my ladies I should get lost. The noise is constant, of people coming and going, striking deals, having arguments, musicians practising, tradesmen offering their goods, even pedlars come to sell things to the housemaids. It is like a village filled with people who have no real work to do but gossip and spread rumours and cause trouble.

All the great tapestries, carpets, musical instruments, treasures, plate, glasses and beds are packed on a train of wagons, on the day of our departure, as if a city were on the move. All the horses are saddled, and the falcons settled in their special wagons, standing on their posts with wickerwork screens around them, their hooded heads turning eagerly, this way and that, the pretty feathers at the top of the hood bobbing like a knight's jousting crest. I watch them and think that I am as blind and as powerless as them. We have both been born to be free, to go where we want, and here we both are, captives of the king's pleasure, waiting for his command.

The dogs are whipped in by their huntsmen, they spill around the courtyards, yelping and tumbling over in their excitement. All the great families pack their own goods, order their own servants, prepare their own horses and luggage train and we fall into procession, early in the morning like a small army, to ride out through the gates of Whitehall and along the river, to Hampton Court.

For once, God be praised, the king is merry, in high spirits. He says he will ride with me and my ladies and he can tell me about the countryside as we go by. I do not have to go in a litter as I did when I first came to England; I am now allowed to ride and I have a new gown for riding in with a long skirt that drapes down either side of the saddle. I am not a skilled rider, for I was never properly taught. My brother only let Amelia and me ride the safest fat horses in his small stable, but the king has been kind to me and given me a horse of my own, a gentle mare with steady paces. When I touch her with my heel she will go forwards into a canter but when fear makes me jerk on the reins she goes back into a courteous walk. I love her for this obedience, as she helps me hide my fear in this fearless court.

It is a court that loves riding and hunting and galloping out. I should look like a fool if it were not for little Katherine Howard who can ride only a little better than me, and so with her to keep me company the king goes along slowly between the two of us, and tells us both to tighten our reins and sit up straighter, and praises our courage and progress.

He is so kind and pleasant that I stop fearing that he will think me a coward and I start to ride with more confidence, and to look about me, and to enjoy myself.

We leave the city by winding roads, so narrow that we can only go two abreast, and all the people of the city are leaning out of the overhanging windows to see us go by, the children shouting and running alongside our train. On the broad highways we take up both sides of the road and the market vendors in the central section shout blessings and pull off their caps as we ride by. The place is rich with life, a cacophony of noise from people shouting their wares and the thunderous rumble of cart wheels on cobblestones. The city stinks with its own special smell of manure from the thousands of animals kept in the alleys, the offal of butchers' shops and fishmongers, the reek of the leather tanning, and the constant drift of smoke. Every now and then there is a great house, set amongst the squalor, indifferent to the beggars at its doors. High walls shield it from the street and I can just see the tops of great trees in the enclosed gardens. The noblemen of London build their great houses next to hovels and rent their doorways to pedlars. It is so loud and so confusing that it makes me dizzy and I am glad to rattle through the great gates and find myself outside the city wall.

The king shows me the old moats that have been dug in the past to defend London from invaders.

'No men come now?' I ask him.

'There is no trusting any man,' he says grimly. 'The men would come from the North and the East if they had not felt the hammer of my anger already; and the Scots would come if they thought they could. But my nephew King James fears me, as well he should, and the Yorkshire rabble have been taught a lesson they will not forget. Half of them are in mourning for the other half who are dead.'

I say no more for fear of spoiling his happy mood, and Katherine's horse stumbles and she gives a little gasp and clutches the horse's mane, and the king laughs at her and calls her a coward. Their talk leaves me free to look about me.

Beyond the city walls are bigger houses set back from the road with little gardens before them or close-planted little fields. Everyone has a pig in their field, and some people have cows or goats as well as hens in their gardens. It is a rich country, I can see it in the faces of the people who have the shining round cheeks and the smiles of the well fed. Another mile from the city and we come into countryside of open fields and little hedgerows and neat farms and sometimes little villages and hamlets. At every crossroads there is a shrine that has been destroyed, sometimes a statue of the mother of Christ stands with her head casually knocked off and still a little fresh posy of flowers at her feet; not all the English are convinced by the changes in the law. In every other village a small monastery or abbey is being remodelled or broken down. It is extraordinary to see the change that this king has made to the face of his country in a matter of years. It is as if oak trees had been suddenly banned and every great sheltering and beautiful tree had been savagely felled overnight. The king has plucked the heart out of his country and it is too soon to see how it will live and breathe without the holy houses and the holy life that have guided it forever.

The king breaks off from his conversation with Katherine Howard and says to me: 'I have a great country.'

I am not such a fool to comment that he has destroyed or stolen one of its greatest treasures.

'Good farms,' I say, 'and . . .' I stop for I do not know the English word for the beasts. I point to them.

'Sheep,' he says. 'This is the wealth of this country. We supply the wool to the world. There is not a coat made in Christendom that is not woven with English wool.'

This is not quite true, for in Cleves we shear our own sheep and weave our own wool, but I know that the English wool trade is very great, and besides, I don't want to correct him.

'Grandmama has our flock on the South Downs,' Katherine pipes up. 'And the meat is so good, sire. I will ask her to send you some.'

'Will you, pretty girl?' he asks her. 'And shall you cook it for me?'

She laughs. 'I could try, sir.'

'Now confess, you cannot dress a joint or make a sauce. I doubt you have ever been so much as inside a kitchen.'

'If Your Grace wants me to cook for you, then I will learn,' she says. 'But I admit you might eat better with your own cooks.'

'I am quite sure of it,' he says. 'And a pretty girl like you does not need to cook. I am sure you have other ways to enchant your husband.'

Their speech is too quick for me to quite follow but I am glad that my husband is merry and that Katherine has the way of managing him. She chatters to him like a little girl and he finds her amusing, as an old man might pet a favoured granddaughter.

I let them talk together, and go on looking around me. Our road now runs beside the wide, fast-flowing river which is busy with boatmen, barges of the noble families, wherry boats, barges of trade travelling laden into London, and fishermen with rods out for the good river fish. The watermeadows, still wet with the winter floods, are lush and shiny with pools of standing water. A great heron lifts up slowly from a mere as we go past and flaps his great wings and flies west before us, tucking his long legs up.

'Is Hampton Court a little house?' I ask.

The king spurs his horse forwards to talk to me. 'A great house,' he says. 'The most beautiful house in the world.'

I doubt very much that the French king who built Fontainebleau or the Moors who built the Alhambra would agree, but since I have not seen either palace I won't correct him. 'Did you build it, Your Grace?' I ask.

As soon as I speak I discover that it is once again the wrong thing to say. I thought it would encourage him to tell me about the planning and building of it; but his expression, which was so smiling and handsome, suddenly darkens. Little Katherine quickly answers.

'It was built for the king,' she says. 'By an advisor who proved to be a false counsellor. The only good thing he did was make a palace fit for His Majesty. Or at least, that's what my grandmother told me.'

His face lightens, he laughs aloud. 'You speak truly, Mistress Howard, indeed, though you must have been a child when Wolsey betrayed me. He was a false counsellor and the house that he built and gave to me is a fine one.' He turns to me. 'It is mine now,' he says less warmly. 'That is all you need to know. And it is the finest house in the world.'

I nod and ride forwards. How many men have offended this king, in the long years of his rule? He drops back for a moment and speaks to his Master of Horse who is riding beside the young man Thomas Culpepper, talking and laughing together.

The riders ahead of us turn from the road and I see the great gateway before us. I am stunned at the sight of it. It really is a tremendous palace, of beautiful scarlet brick, the most expensive of all building materials, with arches and quoins of shining white stone. I had no idea that it was so great and fine. We ride through the huge stone gate and down the sweeping road towards it, under the entry gate and our horses' hooves sound like thunder on the cobbles of the great inner yard. Inside is a great court, and the servants coming out of the house fling open the huge double doors so that I can see the hall beyond. They line up, like a guard of honour, in the liveries of the royal Tudor house, according to their rank, row on row of men and women dedicated to our service. This is a house for hundreds of people, a massive place built for the pleasure of the court. Again, I am overwhelmed, the wealth of this country too much for me.

'What happened to the man who built the house?' I ask Katherine as we dismount in the great courtyard, amid the noise of the court, the seagulls calling on the river beyond the house, the rooks cawing on the turrets. 'What happened to the counsellor who offended the king?'

'That was Cardinal Wolsey,' she says quietly. 'He was found guilty of acting against the king and he died.'

'He died too?' I ask. I find I dare not ask what blow felled the builder of this kingly house.

'Yes, died and disgraced,' she says shortly. 'The king turned on him. Sometimes he does, you know.'

Jane Boleyn, Hampton Court, March 1540

I am back in my old rooms at Hampton Court and sometimes, when I go from the garden to the queen's rooms, it is as if time has stood still and I am still a bride with everything to hope for, my sister-in-law is on the throne of England, expecting her first child, my husband has just been given the title of Lord Rochford, and my nephew will be the next King of England.

Sometimes, when I pause by one of the wide-paned windows and look down to the garden running down to the river I think I might almost see Anne and George walking down the gravelled paths, her hand tucked in his, their heads close together. I think I might watch them again, as I used constantly to watch them then, and see his little gestures of affection, his hand in the small of her aching back, her head brushing his shoulder. When she was with child she used to cling to him for comfort and he was always tender with her, the sister who might be carrying the next King of England in her belly. But when I was big with my child, it was during our last months together and he never took my hand or felt any sympathy for my fatigue. He never put his hand on my swelling belly to feel the baby move, he never put my hand in his arm and encouraged me to lean on him. There was so much that we never did together that I miss now. If we had been happily married I could not be more filled with regret at the loss of him.

We had so much left unfinished and unsaid between the two of us; and it will never be said or finished now. When he was dead I sent his son away. He is being raised by friends of the Howards and he will enter the church, I have no ambition for him. I lost the great Boleyn inheritance that I was amassing for him, and there is no credit to be had from his family name; only shame. When I lost the two of them, Anne and George, I lost everything.

My lord the Duke of Norfolk is returned from his mission to France and closets himself with the king for hours. He is in the highest of favour, anyone can see that he has brought the king good news from Paris. If I could not see the rise of our family in the swagger of our men, in our ally Archbishop Gardiner's added air of authority, in the appearance of rosaries and crucifixes at belts and throats, I would see it in the decline of the party of reform: Thomas Cromwell's ill-concealed bad temper, the quiet thoughtfulness of Archbishop Cranmer, the way they seek to see the king and cannot get an interview with him. If I read the signs correctly then our party, the Howards and the Papists, are in the ascendant once more. We have our faith, we have our traditions, and we have the girl that is taking the king's eye. Thomas Cromwell has sucked the church dry, he has no more wealth to offer the king, and his girl, the queen, may learn English but cannot learn how to flirt. If I were an undecided courtier I would find a way to befriend the Duke of Norfolk and join his side.

He summons me to his rooms. I go to him down the familiar corridors, the smell of lavender and rosemary around my feet from the strewing herbs, the light from the river falling through the great windows ahead of me, and it is as if their ghosts are running just ahead of me, down the panelled gallery, as if her skirt has just flicked out of sight around the corner, as if I can hear my husband's easy laughter still on the sunlit air. If I went a little faster I would catch them – and so even now, it is just as it always was. I always felt that if only I could go a little faster I would catch them, and learn the secrets they shared.

I hurry despite myself but when I round the corner the panelled corridor is empty but for the Howard guards at the door and they have seen no ghosts. I have lost the two of them, as I always did. They are too fast for me in death as they were in life. They didn't wait for me, they never wanted me with them. The guards knock and swing open the door for me, and I go in.

'How is the queen?' the duke asks abruptly from his seat behind a table, and I have to remember that it is a new queen and not our beloved, infuriating Anne.

'She is in good spirits and good looks,' I say. But she will never be the beauty that our girl was.

'Has he had her?'

This is crude, but I assume he is tired from his journey and has no time for the courtesies.

'He has not. As far as I can tell, he is still incapable.'

There is a long pause while he rises from his chair and goes to the window to look out. I think of when we stood here before, when he asked me about Anne and George, when he looked out of the window to see them walking on the gravelled paths down to the river. I wonder if he can see them still, even now, as I can. He asked me then if I envied her, if I would be prepared to act against her. He said I might save my husband by putting her at risk. He asked me if I loved George more than her. He asked me if I would mind very much if she were dead.

His next question breaks into the memories that I wish I could forget. 'Do you think he might have been . . .' He pauses. 'Ill-wished?'

Ill-wished? I can hardly believe what I am hearing. Is the duke seriously suggesting that the king is impotent with his wife as a result of a curse, or a spell, or an ill-wishing? Of course law of the land says that impotence in a healthy man can only be caused by the action of a witch; but in real life everyone knows that illness or old age can render a man feeble and the king is grossly fat, almost paralysed with pain and sick as a dog in both body and soul. Ill-wishing? The last time the king claimed to be a victim of ill-wishing, the woman he accused was my sister-in-law Anne, who went to the block, guilty of witchcraft, the evidence being the king's impotence with her and her lust with other men.

'You cannot think that the queen . . .' I break off. 'No-one could think that *this* queen . . . that yet another queen . . .' The suggestion is so preposterous and so fraught with danger I cannot even put it into words. 'The country would not stand . . . nobody would believe it . . . not again . . .' I break off. 'He can't go on doing this . . .'

'I am thinking nothing. But if he is unmanned then someone must be ill-wishing him. Who could it be, if not her?'

I am silent. If the duke is collecting evidence of the queen ill-wishing her husband, then she is a dead woman.

'He has no desire for the queen at the moment,' I begin. 'But surely it is nothing worse than that? Desire may come. After all, he is not a young man, he is not a well man.'

He nods. I am trying to judge what he wants to hear. 'And he has desire for others,' I go on.

'Ah, this proves the accusation,' he says slickly. 'It could be that he has been ill-wished only when he lies with the queen, so that he cannot be a man with her, so he cannot give England a son and heir.'

'If you say so,' I agree. Pointless to say that it is far more likely that since he is old and often ill, he has not the lust that he used to have; and only a little slut like Katherine Howard with her tricks and her charm can arouse him.

'So who would ill-wish him?' he persists.

I shrug. Whoever I name should say their farewells, for if charged with witchcraft against the king, then they are dead. There can be no proof of innocence and no plea of not guilty; under the new laws any treasonous intent, any thought is a crime as grave as the deed itself. King Henry has passed a law against his people thinking, and his people dare not think that he is wrong. 'I don't know who would do such wickedness,' I say firmly. 'I cannot imagine.'

'Does the queen entertain Lutherans?'

'No, never.' This is true, she is most careful to conform to English ways and takes Mass according to the rules of Archbishop Cranmer, as if she were another Jane Seymour, born to serve.

'Does she see Papists?'

I am astounded by this question. This is a girl from Cleves, the heartland of reform. She was raised to think of Papists as Satan on earth. 'Of course not! She was born and bred a Protestant, she was brought here by the Protestant set, how would she entertain Papists?'

'Is Lady Lisle intimate with her?'

My swift glance to his face tells him of my shock.

'We have to be ready, we have to be prepared. Our enemies are everywhere,' he cautions me.

'The king himself appointed Lady Lisle to her household and Anne Bassett, her daughter, is one of his own favourites,' I say. 'I have no evidence against Lady Lisle.' Because there is none, and there could never be any.

'Or Lady Southampton?'

'Lady Southampton?' I repeat incredulously.

'Yes.'

'I know of nothing against Lady Southampton either,' I say.

He nods. We both know that evidence, especially of witchcraft and ill-wishing, is not hard to create. It is a whisper, and then an accusation, and then a shower of lies, and then a show trial and then a sentence. It was done before to rid the king of a wife he did not want, a woman who could be sent to the block without her family lifting a finger to save her.

He nods, and I wait for long moments in silent dread, thinking that he may order me to frame evidence that will be the death of an innocent woman, thinking what I can say if he makes such a terrible demand of me. Hoping that I can find the courage to refuse him, knowing that I will not. But he says nothing, so I curtsey to him and move towards the door; perhaps he has finished with me.

'He will find evidence of a plot,' he predicts as my hand is on the brass latch.

'He will find evidence against her, you know.'

At once I freeze. 'God help her.'

'He will find evidence that either the Papists or the Lutherans have set a witch in his household to unman him.'

I try to keep my face expressionless; but this is such a disaster for the queen, perhaps such danger for me, that I can feel my panic rising at my uncle's calm words.

'Better for us if he names Lutherans as the traitors,' he reminds me. 'And not our party.'

'Yes,' I agree.

'Or if he does not seek her death he will get a divorce on the grounds that she was pre-contracted, if that fails he will get a divorce on the grounds that he did not desire her and so he did not consent to the wedding.'

'He said "I do" before witnesses,' I whisper. 'We were all there.'

'Inwardly, he did not consent,' he tells me.

'Oh.' I pause. 'He says this now?'

'Yes. But if she denies that she was pre-contracted then he can still claim that he cannot consummate the marriage because witch-craft by his enemies is working against him.'

'These Papists?' I ask.

'Papists like her friend Lord Lisle.'

I gasp. 'He would be accused?'

'It is possible.'

'Or Lutherans?' I whisper.

'Lutherans like Thomas Cromwell.'

My face shows him my shock. 'He is a Lutheran now?'

He smiles. 'The king will believe what he wishes,' he says silkily. 'God will guide him in his wisdom.'

'But who does he think has unmanned him? Who is the witch?'

It is the most important question to ask, especially for a woman. It is always the most important thing for a woman to know. Who will be named as the witch?

'Do you have a cat?' he asks, smiling.

I can feel myself grow icy with terror, as if my breath is snow. 'I?' I repeat. 'I?'

The duke laughs. 'Oh, don't look like that, Lady Rochford. No-one will accuse you while you are under my protection. Besides, you don't have a cat, do you? No familiar tucked away? No wax dolls? No midnight Sabbaths?'

'Don't joke,' I say unsteadily. 'It is not a laughing matter.'

At once he sobers. 'You are right, it is not. So who is the witch who is unmanning the king?'

'I don't know. None of her ladies. None of us.'

'Perhaps it might be the queen herself?' he suggests quietly.

'Her brother would defend her,' I gabble. 'Even if you do not need his alliance, even if you have come home from France with a promise of their friendship, you surely cannot risk her brother's enmity? He could raise the Protestant league against us.'

He shrugs. 'I think you will find he may not defend her. And I have indeed secured the friendship of France, whatever happens next.'

'I congratulate you. But the queen is the sister of the Duke of Cleves. She cannot be named as a witch and strangled by a village blacksmith and buried at a crossroads with a stake through her heart.'

He spreads his hands as if he had nothing to do with these decisions. 'I don't know. I merely serve His Majesty. We will have to see. But you should watch her closely.'

'I am to watch her for witchcraft?' I can hardly keep the incredulity from my voice.

'For evidence,' he says. 'If the king wants evidence, of anything, then we Howards will give it to him.' He pauses. 'Won't we?'

I am silent.

'As we always have done.' He waits for my assent. 'Won't we?'

'Yes, my lord.'

Katherine, Hampton Court, March 1540

Thomas Culpepper, my kinsman, in the king's service and high in his favour for no better reason than his pretty face and his deep blue eyes, is a rogue and a promise breaker, and I shall see him no more.

I first saw him years ago, when he came to visit my step-grandmother at Horsham and she would make a fuss over him and swear he would go far. I daresay he didn't even see me then, though now he swears that I was the prettiest maid at Horsham and always his favourite. It's true that I saw him. I was in love with Henry Manox then, the nobody; but I could not help but notice Thomas Culpepper. I think even if I were betrothed to the greatest man in the land I would notice Thomas Culpepper. Anybody would. Half the ladies of the court are driven mad for love of him.

He has dark curly hair and eyes that are very blue, and when he laughs his voice cracks on his laughter in a way which is so funny that it makes me want to laugh, just for hearing it. He is the most handsome man at court, without doubt. The king adores him because he is witty and merry and a wonderful dancer and a great huntsman and as brave as a knight in a jousting tournament. The king has him at his side, night and day, and calls him his pretty boy and his little knight. He sleeps in the king's bedchamber to serve him in the night and he has hands so gentle that the king would rather he dress the wound on his leg than any apothecary or nurse.

All the girls have seen how much I like him and they swear that we should marry, being cousins, but he has no money to his name and I have no dowry and so how would that ever serve us? But if I were to choose one man in the world to marry, it would be him. A naughtier smile I have never seen in my life and when he looks at me, it feels as if he is undressing me and then stroking me all over.

Thank God that now I am one of the queen's ladies and she such a strict and modest queen there will be none of that, though if he had come to the dormitory at Lambeth I swear he could have come to my bed and found a warm welcome there. I should have thrown my handsome Francis back to Joan Bulmer if I had been given a chance at a boy like Tom Culpepper.

He is back at court after resting at his home from his wounding in the joust. He took a bad blow but he says he is young, and young bones mend quickly. It is true, he is young and as filled with life as a hare, leaping for no reason in a spring field. You only have to look at him to see the joy going through his veins. He is like quicksilver, he is like a spring wind blowing. I am glad he has come back to court, even in Lent he makes the place more merry. But just this very morning he has made me wait an hour for him in the queen's garden when I should have been in her rooms and when he came late he said he could not stay but had to run to wait upon the king.

This is not how I am to be treated and I shall teach him so. I shall not wait for him again, I shall not even agree to meet him next time he asks me. He will have to ask me more than once, I swear it. I shall give up flirtation for Lent and it will serve him right. Indeed, perhaps I shall grow thoughtful and serious and never flirt with anyone again.

Lady Rochford asks me why I am in such a temper when we go in to dine and I swear to her that I am as happy as the day is long.

'Mind your smiles then,' she says as if she doesn't believe me for a moment. 'For my lord duke is back from France and he will be looking for you.'

I lift my chin at once and I smile at her quite dazzlingly, as if she has just said something very witty. I even give a little laugh, my court laugh, 'ha ha ha', very light and elegant, as I have heard the other ladies do. She gives a little nod.

'That's better,' she says.

'What was the duke doing in France, anyway?' I ask.

'You are taking an interest in affairs of the world?' she asks quizzically.

'I am not a complete fool,' I say.

'Your uncle is a great man in the favour of the king. He went to France to secure the friendship of the French king so that our country is not faced with the danger of the Holy Fa–, I mean the Pope, the emperor and the King of France all in alliance against us.'

I smile that Jane Boleyn herself should nearly say 'Holy Father', which we can't say any more. 'Oh, I know about that,' I say cleverly. 'Because they want to put Cardinal Pole on our own throne, out of wickedness.'

She shakes her head. 'Don't speak of it,' she warns me.

'They do,' I insist. 'And that is why his poor old mother and all the Poles are in the Tower. For the Cardinal would call on the Papists of England to come against the king, just as they did before.'

'They won't come against the king any more,' she says dryly.

'Because they know they are wrong now?'

'Because most of them are dead,' she says shortly. 'And that was your uncle's doing too.'

Anne, Hampton Court, March 1540

I was told the court would observe the period of Lent with great solemnity. I was assured that we would eat no red meat at all. I was expecting to dine on fish for the whole of the forty days but I discover, the very first night at dinner, that English consciences are easy. The king is tender to his own needs. Despite the fast of Lent there is an enormous range of dishes marching into the hall held high above the heads of the servers, and they come first to the royal table and the king and I take a little from each, as is the custom, and send them out to our friends and favourites around the hall. I make sure I send them to my ladies' table and to the great ladies of court. I make no mistake about this and I never send my favourite dish to any man. This is no empty politeness, the king watches me. Every word I speak at dinner, everything I do, his bright little eyes almost hidden by his fat cheeks follow everything, as if he would like to catch me out.

To my surprise there is chicken, in pies and fricassees, roasted with mouth-watering herbs, carved from the bone; but in this season of Lent it is not called meat. For the purposes of the Lenten fast, the king has ruled that chicken counts as fish. There are all the game birds (also not meat, according to God and the king) beautifully presented, enfolded one within another for the flavour and tenderness. There are rich dishes of eggs (which are not meat), and there is indeed fish: trout from the ponds and wonderful fish dishes from the Thames and deep sea fish, brought by the fishermen who go far out to sea to feed this greedy court. There are freshwater crayfish and stargazy pies with little tasty whitebait heads all peeping out through a thick pastry crust. And there are great dishes of spring vegetables which are rarely served at court, and I am glad to have them on my plate in this season. I shall eat lightly now, and anything that I especially enjoy will be brought to me again for a private dinner in my chamber later. I have never been fed so richly or so well in my life, my Cleves maid has had to let out the stomacher of my gown and there was much arch comment about me growing and blooming, as if to suggest that it is a baby making me fatter. I cannot contradict them without exposing myself, and the king my husband, to even worse comment, so I had to smile and listen to them tease me as if I were a wife wedded and bedded and hoping to be with child; and not a virgin untouched by her husband.

Little Katherine Howard came in and said that they were all ridiculous and that the good butter of England had made me gain a little weight and they were blind if they did not see how well it suits me. I was so grateful to her for that. She is a foolish, frivolous little thing but she has the cleverness of a stupid girl, since, like any stupid girl, she only thinks about one thing, and so she has become very expert in that. And the one thing that she thinks about? All the time, every moment of every day, Kitty Howard thinks about Kitty Howard.

We surrender other pleasures for the time of Lent. There are no court entertainments of the merry kind, though there are readings of holy texts after dinner, and the singing of psalms. There are no masquings nor mumming and no jousts of course. I am greatly relieved by this because, best of all, it means that there is no possibility of the king coming in disguised. The memory of our first disastrous meeting still lingers with me, and I fear it stays with him too. It was not that I did not recognise him that was so offensive; it was the blatant fact that at first sight I was utterly repelled by him. Never since that day, by word, deed, or even look, have I let him know that I find him so unpleasant: fat, very old, and the stink of him turns my stomach. But however much I hold my breath and smile, it is too late to make amends. My face, when he tried to kiss me, told him everything in that moment. The way I pushed him off me, the way I spat the taste of him from my mouth! I still bow my head and flush hot at the terrible embarrassment. All this has left an impression with him that no later good manners can erase. He saw the truth of my view of him in that one swift glimpse, and – what is worse – he saw himself through my eyes: fat, old, disgusting. Sometimes I fear his vanity will never recover from this blow. And since his vanity is damaged I think his potency has gone with it. I am certain that his manhood was destroyed by my spit on the floor, and there is nothing I can do to recall it.

And that is another thing we give up for Lent. Thank God. I shall look forward to this time every year. For various blessed feast days and forty wonderful days every year of my married life, there will be forty nights when the king will not come to my chamber, when I will not smile at his entrance, and try to arrange myself in such a way that it is easy for him to lever his great bulk above me, and try to show my willingness but not wantonness in a bed that stinks of the festering wound of his leg, in half-darkness, with a man who cannot do the task.

The burden of this insulting misery night after night is utterly defeating me, it is humbling me to dust. I wake every morning in despair; I feel humiliated, though the failure is all his. I lie awake in the night and hear him fart and groan with the pain of his swollen belly and I wish myself away, almost anywhere rather than in his bed. I shall be so glad to be spared, for these forty days, the terrible ordeal of his attempt and his failing and my lying awake and knowing that tomorrow night he will try again, but still he will not be able to do it, and that each time he fails he blames me a little more and likes me even less.

At least we can have this time when we are allowed a little peace. I need not worry how I should help him. He need not work above me like a great heaving boar. He will not come to my room, I can sleep in sheets that smell of lavender instead of pus.

But I know that this time will end. Easter will come with the celebrations; my coronation which was planned for February and put off for our grand entrance into London, will now take place in May. I must take this time as a welcome rest from the presence of my husband, but I must use this time to make sure that when he comes back to my chamber we can deal better together. I must find a way to help him to come to my bed, and for me to help him to do the act.

Thomas Cromwell must be the man to help me. Kitty Howard's advice is what I should have expected of her: the seductive skills of a naughty girl. How she must have behaved before she was taken into my rooms I dare not imagine. When I am a little more settled myself I shall have to talk to her. A girl – a child – such as her should not know how to drop a shift and smile over a naked shoulder. She must have been very badly guarded and very ill-advised. The ladies of my court must be as above criticism as myself. I shall have to tell her that whatever flirtatious tricks she knows she must put them aside. And she cannot teach them to me. I cannot have a shadow of suspicion over my behaviour. A queen has died in this country for less.

I wait for the dinner to end and for the king to leave his place and walk between the tables, greeting men and women as he goes. He is affable tonight, his leg must be less painful. It is often hard to tell what ails him, for he is bad-tempered for so many different reasons, and if I inquire after the wrong cause, that can give offence too.

As I see him walk away I look down the hall and I catch Thomas Cromwell's eye. I crook my finger and he comes to me, and I rise and take his arm and let him lead me away from the dining table and to a window overlooking the river, as if we are admiring the view and the icy night with a dozen sparkling stars.

'I need help, Master Secretary,' I say.

'Anything,' he says. He is smiling but his face is strained.

'I cannot please the king,' I say in the words I have rehearsed. 'Help me.'

At once, he looks quite sick with discomfort. He glances around him as if he would shout for help for himself. I am ashamed to be speaking so to a man, but I have to get good advice from somewhere. I cannot trust my women, and to speak to my advisors from Cleves, even Lotte, would be to alert my mother and brother whose servants they are. But this is not a true marriage, this is not a marriage in deeds as well as words. And if it is not a marriage then I have failed in my duty to the king, to the people of England, and to myself. I have to make this marriage a real one. I have to do it. And if this man can tell me what is wrong then he must do so.

'These are . . . private matters,' he says, his hand half-covering his mouth as if to stop any words coming out. He is pulling at his lip.

'No. This is the king,' I say. 'This is England. Duty, not private.'

'You should be advised by your women, by your Mistress of Maids.'

'You made the wedding,' I say, groping for words. 'Help me make it true.'

'I am not responsible . . .'

'Be my friend.'

He glances around as if he would like to run away, but I will not release him.

'These are early days.'

I shake my head. 'Fifty-two days.' Who has counted the days more carefully than me?

'Has he explained his dislike of you?' he demands suddenly. The English is too fast for me, and I don't understand the words.

'Explained?'

Cromwell makes a little noise of irritation at my stupidity and glances around as if he would summon one of my countrymen to translate. Then he checks himself as he remembers that this must be a complete secret.

'What is wrong with you?' he says very simply and very quietly, his mouth to my ear.

I realise that my face is stunned, and quickly I turn to the window before the court can see my shock and distress.

'It is me?' I demand. 'He says it is me?'

His little dark eyes are anguished. He cannot answer me for shame; and that is how I know. It is not that the king is old or tired or sick. It is that he does not like me, that he does not desire me, perhaps even that I disgust him. And I guess from Thomas Cromwell's scrunched-up, worried little face that the king has already discussed his repulsion with this nasty little man.

'He tell you he hate me?' bursts out of me.

His agonised grimace tells me that 'yes', the king has told this man that he cannot force himself to be my lover. Perhaps the king has told others, perhaps all his friends. Perhaps all this time the court has been laughing behind their white hands at the ugly girl from Cleves who came to marry the king and now repels him.

The humiliation of this makes me give a little shudder and turn away from Cromwell, and I do not see his bow and his swift retreat as he rushes to get away from me as you would avoid a person with poisonous bad luck.

I spend the rest of the evening in a daze of misery, I cannot put words to my shame. If I had not served such a hard apprenticeship at my brother's court of Cleves I should have fled to my bedroom and cried myself to sleep. But I long ago learned to be stubborn, and long ago learned to be strong, and I have faced the dangerous dislike of a powerful ruler before, and survived.

I keep myself alert, like a wakened frightened falcon. I do not droop and I do not let my pleasant smile slip from my face. When it is time for the ladies to retire I curtsey to the king my husband without betraying for a moment my anguish that he finds me so disgusting that he cannot do to me what men can do to beasts of the field.

'Goodnight, Your Grace,' I say.

'Goodnight, sweetheart,' he says with such easy tenderness that for a moment I want to cling to him as my only friend at this court and tell him of my fear and unhappiness. But he is already looking beyond me, away from me. His glance is idly resting on my ladies and Katherine Howard steps forwards and curtseys to him and then I lead them all away.

I say nothing during the slow taking off of my gold collar, my bracelets, my rings, net, my hood, my sleeves, my stomacher, the two skirts, the padding, the petticoats and the shift. I say nothing when they throw my nightdress over my head and I sit before the mirror and they brush my hair and plait it and pin my nightcap on my head. I say nothing when Lady Rochford lingers and asks kindly if I need anything, if she can be of service to me, if my mind is easy tonight.

My priest comes in, and the ladies and I kneel together for the night-time prayers, and my thoughts beat in rhythm to the familiar words while I cannot help but think that I disgust my husband and have done from the very first day.

And then I remember it again. That first moment at Rochester when he came in all puffed up in his vanity and looking so very ordinary, exceptional only in that he stepped up to me, just like a drunken tradesman might do. But this was not a drunken old man of the country town, this was the King of England playing knight errant and I humiliated him before the whole court and I think he will never forgive me.

His dislike of me springs from that moment, I swear it. The only way that he can bear the memory of it is to say, like a hurt child: 'Well, I don't like her either'. He recalls me pushing him away and refusing to kiss him and now he pushes me away and refuses to kiss me. He has found a way to redress the balance by naming me as the undesirable one. The King of England, especially this king, cannot be seen to be the undesirable one, especially to himself.

The priest finishes the prayers and I rise to my feet as the maids troop from the room, their heads bowed, as sweet as little angels in their nightcaps. I let them go. I ask for no-one to wake with me though I know I will not sleep this night. I have become an object of disgust, just as I was in Cleves. I have become an object of disgust to my own husband and I cannot see how we shall reconcile and make a child while he cannot bear to touch me. I have become an object of disgust to the King of England and he is a man of utter power and no patience.

I am not weeping for the insult to my beauty because now I have a far greater worry. If I am an object of disgust to the King of England and he is a man of utter power and no patience, what might he do to me? This is a man who killed one beloved wife with studied cruelty, the second that he adored he executed with a French sword; and the third, who had given him a son, he left to die of poor nursing. What might he do to me?

Jane Boleyn, Hampton Court, March 1540

That she is not happy is a certainty, but she is a discreet young woman, wiser by far than her years, and she cannot be led into confidences. I have been as kind and as sympathetic as I can to her, but I don't want her to feel that I am probing for my own sake; and I don't want to make her feel any worse than she must do already. For certain she must feel very friendless and strange in a country where she is only starting to grasp the language and where her husband shows such obvious relief when he can avoid her, and such blatant attention to another girl.

Then in the morning, after Mass, she comes to me as the girls are preening themselves before going to breakfast. 'Lady Rochford, when will the princesses come to court?'

I hesitate. 'Princess Mary,' I remind her. 'But only Lady Elizabeth.'

She gives a little 'ach' noise. 'Yes. So. Princess Mary and Lady Elizabeth.'

'They usually come to court for Easter,' I say helpfully. 'And then they can see their brother, and they can greet you. We were surprised that they did not greet you on your entry to London.' I stop myself. I am going too fast for her. I can see her frown as she struggles to follow my speech. 'I am sorry,' I say more slowly. 'The princesses should come to court to meet you. They should greet their stepmother. They should have welcomed you to London. Usually they come to court for Easter.'

She nods. 'So. I may invite them?'

I hesitate. Of course, she can; but the king will not like her taking the power upon herself in this way. However, my lord duke will not object to any trouble between the two of them, and it is not my job to warn her.

'You can invite them,' I say.

She nods to me. 'Please write.'

I go to the table and pull the little writing box towards me. The quills are ready-sharpened, the ink in the little pot, the sand in the sifter for scattering on the wet ink, and there is a stick of sealing wax. I love the luxury of court, I love to pick up the quill and take a sheet of paper and wait for the queen's orders.

'Write to the Princess Mary that I should be glad to see her at court for Easter and that she will be welcome as a guest in my rooms,' she says. 'Is that the right way to say it?'

'Yes,' I say, writing rapidly.

'And write to the governess of the Lady Elizabeth that I shall be glad to see her at court too.'

My heart beats a little faster, like it does at a bear-baiting. She will walk straight into trouble if she sends these letters. These are an absolute challenge to the absolute power that is Henry. Nobody issues invitations in his household but he, himself.

'Can you send these for me?' she asks.

I am almost breathless. 'I can,' I say. 'If you wish.'

She puts out her hand. 'I shall have them,' she says. 'I shall show them to the king.'

'Oh.'

She turns to hide a little smile. 'Lady Rochford, I would never do anything against the king's wishes.'

'You have the right to have what ladies you please at your court,' I remind her. 'It is your right as queen. Queen Katherine always insisted that she appoint her own household. Anne Boleyn too.'

'These are his daughters,' she says. 'So I shall ask him before I invite them.'

I bow, she leaves me with nothing to say. 'Will there be anything else?' I ask her.

'You may go,' she says pleasantly, and I walk from the room. I am rather conscious that she tricked me into giving her bad advice, and she knew of it all along. I must remember that she is far more astute than any of us ever credit.

A page in Norfolk livery is idling outside the queen's rooms. He passes me a folded note and I step into one of the window embrasures. Outside the garden is bobbing with yellow Lenten lilies, daffodils, and in a chestnut tree which is studded with fattening sticky buds there is a blackbird singing. The spring is coming at last, the queen's first spring in England. The summer days of picnics and jousts and hunting and pleasure trips, boating on the river and the summer progress around the great palaces will start again. Perhaps the king will learn to tolerate her, perhaps she will find a way to please him. I shall see it all. I shall be in her rooms, where I should be. I lean against the polished panelling to read my note. It is unsigned, like every note from the duke.

The king will keep company with the queen only until the moment that France quarrels with Spain. It is agreed. Her time with us can be measured in days. Watch her. Gather evidence against her. Destroy this.

I look around for the boy. He is leaning against the wall and idly tossing a coin, catching one side up and then the other. I beckon him to me. 'Tell your master that she wants the princesses at court,' I say quietly in his ear. 'That is all.'

Katherine, Hampton Court,
March 1540

The king is most angry at dinner tonight, I can tell from the way that he leads in the queen and he does not glance over to me as he usually does. I am sorry about this because I have a new gown (another one!) in creamy yellow, and it is gathered under the bust so that my breasts are on display in the most ravishing and shameless way. But it is a waste of time and trouble trying to please a man. When you are at your very best his mind is elsewhere, or when he agrees to meet you he has to go off somewhere else, with less than half a decent excuse. Tonight, the king is so cross with the queen that he hardly looks at me and I have wasted my new gown for nothing. On the other hand, there is a most delicious young man sitting at the Seymour table who is clearly appreciating the gown and the contents; but I have no time for young men any more, sworn as I am to a life of self-denial starting this Lent. I see Tom Culpepper trying to catch my eye but I don't even look at him. I will not easily forgive him for promising to meet me and then failing me. I shall probably live and die a spinster and it will be his fault.

Why the king is angry, and what she has done, I don't know until after dinner when I go up to the table to take her a handkerchief that she had embroidered to give to the king. It is a new fashion and very elegant. She certainly can sew. If a man prized a wife for her sewing she would be his very favourite. But she never even gives it to him, for as I come up he suddenly turns to her and says: 'We shall have a merry court for Easter.'

She would have been better advised to say, 'yes', and leave it at that. But she says, 'I am glad. I wish for the Lady Elizabeth and the Princess Mary to come to court.'

He looks furious, and I see her hands grip together on the table before her. 'Not the Lady Elizabeth,' he says gruffly. 'You should not wish for her company nor she for yours.'

This is too fast for her and I see her puzzled little frown, but she understands well enough that he is saying, 'no'.

'Princess Mary,' she says quietly. 'She is my stepdaughter.'

I can hardly breathe, I am so amazed at her daring to reply. Fancy having him snarl at you like that and then standing your ground!

'I cannot think why you should want to summon a determined Papist to court,' he says icily. 'She is no friend of your faith.'

The queen understands the tone well enough even if she does not quite comprehend the words.

'I her stepmother am,' she says simply. 'I guide her.'

He gives a sharp bark of laughter and I am afraid of him, even if she is not. 'She is all but your own age,' he says unkindly. 'I don't think she will want any mothering from the likes of you. She was mothered by one of the greatest princesses of Christendom, and when I parted them they defied me rather than huddle together for love. D'you think she will need a girl her own age to take care of her? When she and her mother let death part them rather than deny their faith? D'you think she'll want a mother now who can't even speak English? She can talk to you in Latin or Greek or Spanish or French or English, but not German. And what do you have? Oh, yes, only High German.'

I know I should say something to distract his temper, but he is so spiteful and so sharp that he frightens me. I can't say anything, I stand there like a fool and wonder how she can find the strength not to faint in her chair.

She is flushed scarlet with embarrassment, from the neck of her gown to her heavy hood, I can see the blush under her muslin shift and under the collar of gold and her neckpiece. It is painful to see her embarrassment before his anger and I wait for her to burst into tears and run from the room. But she does not.

'I learn English,' she says with quiet dignity. 'All the time. And I her stepmother am.'

The king gets up from the table so fast that his heavy gold chair scrapes on the floor and almost tips over. He has to steady himself on the table. His face is red and there is a pulse beating at his temple. I am half-dead of terror just looking at him, but she is still seated, her hands gripped together on the table before her. She is like a little block of wood, rigid with fear but not moving, not crumbling. He glares down at her as if to frighten her into silence; but she speaks.

'I shall do my duty. To our children, and to you. Forgive me if I offend.'

'Invite her,' he snarls and he stamps from the high table to the door behind the throne which leads to his private rooms. He hardly ever uses this door, so there is no-one there to open it for him and he has to throw it open himself, and then he is gone, and we are all left dumbstruck.

She looks at me and I see that her stillness is not calm, she is frozen with terror. Now he has gone and the court scrambling to their feet to bow to the slammed door, and we are all alone.

'It is the queen's right to invite ladies to her household,' she says unsteadily.

'You won,' I say disbelievingly.

'I shall do my duty,' she says again.

'You won,' I repeat incredulously. 'He said: "invite her".'

'It is the right thing,' she says. 'I do my duty, for England. I shall do my duty to him.'

Anne, Hampton Court,
March 1540

I am waiting in my rooms at Hampton Court for my new ambassador who arrived late last night and is to come to see me this morning. I had thought that the king would see him before I did, but there are no plans for a royal greeting yet.

'Is that right?' I ask Lady Rochford.

She looks a little uncertain. 'Ambassadors usually have a special reception to introduce them to the court and all the king's council,' she says. She spreads her hands as if to say she does not know why the ambassador from Cleves is to be treated differently. 'It is Lent,' she suggests. 'He should not have come during Lent but at Easter.'

I turn to the window so she cannot see the irritation in my face. He should have travelled with me, and come to England when I did. Then I would have had a representative with the king from the moment that I set foot in England, and one who would have stayed with me. Counts Overstein and Olisleger were my escorts but they knew they would leave me and go home, and they were not experienced in foreign courts. I should have had an ambassador at my side from the first day. If he had been with me at Rochester when I insulted the king at our first meeting . . . But this is pointless to regret. Perhaps now that he is here, he will find a way to help me.

There is a knock at the door and the two guards swing it open. 'Herr Doktor Carl Harst,' the guard announces, labouring over the title, and the Cleves ambassador comes into the room, looks around for me, and bows low. All the ladies in waiting curtsey while looking him over and noting, in a breeze of critical whispers, the worn shine on the collar of his velvet jacket and the scuffed heels on his boots. Even the feather in his bonnet looks as if it has had a hard journey overland from Cleves. I can feel myself flush with shame that this man should be representing my country to the wealthiest and most frivolous court in Christendom. He will make himself laughable, and me with him.

'Herr Doktor,' I say and stretch out my hand for him to kiss.

I can see he is taken aback by my fashionable dress, my English hood set neatly on my hair, the rich rings on my fingers and the gold chains at my waist. He kisses my hand and says in German: 'I am honoured to present myself to you, Your Grace. I am your ambassador.'

Dear God, he looks more like a poor clerk. I nod.

'You have broken your fast?' I ask.

He makes a little embarrassed face. 'I . . . er . . . I could not quite . . .'

'You have not eaten?'

'I could not find the hall, Your Grace. I am sorry. The palace is very large and my rooms are some way from the main building, and there was no-one . . .'

They have put him somewhere halfway to the stables. 'You did not ask someone? There are thousands of servants?'

'I don't speak English.'

I am truly shocked. 'You don't speak English? How will you conduct the business of our country? Nobody here speaks German.'

'Your brother the duke thought that the councillors and the king would speak German?'

'He knows full well that they do not.'

'And he thought I would learn English. I already speak Latin,' he adds defensively.

I could cry, I am so disappointed. 'You must certainly have some breakfast,' I say, trying to recover myself. I turn to Kitty Howard who, as usual, is lingering at my side eavesdropping. She is welcome to our conversation so far. If she can speak German well enough to spy then she can translate for this useless ambassador. 'Mistress Howard, would you send one of the maids for some bread and cheese for the ambassador? He has not broken his fast. And some small ale.'

As she goes I turn back to him. 'Do you have any letters for me from my home?'

'Yes,' he says. 'I have instructions from your brother, and your mother sends her maternal love and hopes you are a credit to your home and have not forgotten her loving discipline.'

I nod. I would prefer it if she had sent me a competent ambassador who could also have been a credit to my home, rather than this chilly blessing, but I take the package of letters that he holds out to me, and he settles to his breakfast at one end of the table and I read my letters at the other end.

I read the letter from Amelia first. She starts with a list of the compliments that have been paid to her and how happy she is with her own court at Cleves. She likes to be in sole possession of our rooms. She tells me of her new gowns, and of dresses that were mine but have been adapted for her use. This is to form her trousseau, for she is to be married. I give a little gasp at this and Lady Rochford says kindly: 'Not bad news I hope, Your Grace?'

'My sister is to be married.'

'Oh, how lovely. A good match?'

It is nothing compared to my good fortune, of course. I should be laughing at the small scale of Amelia's triumph. But I have to blink back tears before I can answer. 'She is to marry my brother-in-law. My older sister Sybilla is already married to the Duke of Saxony, and she is to go to their court and marry his younger brother.' And so become a happy little neighbouring family, I think bitterly.

So they are all together: mother, brother, two sisters and their two husbands, and only I am sent far away to wait for letters which bring me no joy but just continue the sense of exclusion and unkindness that my brother has dealt me all my life.

'Not a match like yours then.'

'There is no other match like mine,' I say. 'But she will like to live with my sister, and my brother likes to keep the others close.'

'No sables for her,' Kitty Howard points out, and makes me smile at her unending shameless greed.

'No, that is the main thing of course.' I smile at her. 'Nothing matters more than sables.'

I put Amelia's letter aside, I cannot bring myself to read her confident predictions of family Christmases and joining together for hunting in summer, and celebrating birthdays and bringing up their children, the Saxony cousins all together in the same happy nursery.

I open the letter from my mother instead. If I had hoped for some comfort here I would be disappointed. She has spoken with Count Olisleger and she is filled with anxiety. He tells her that I have been dancing with men not my husband, that I wore a gown without a muslin filet up to my ears. She hears that I have put aside Cleves dress and am wearing an English hood. She reminds me that the king married me because he wanted a Protestant bride of impeccable behaviour and that he is a man of jealous and difficult temperament. She asks me if I want to dance my way to Hell, and reminds me that there is no sin worse than wantonness in a young woman.

I put down the letter and go to the window to look out over the beautiful garden of Hampton Court, the ornate walkways near to the palace and the paths, running down to the river with the pier and the royal barges rocking at their moorings. There are courtiers walking with the king in the garden, dressed as richly as if they were going to a joust. The king, a head taller than any man in his train and broad as a bull, is wearing a cloak of cloth of gold, and a bonnet of velvet which sparkles, even at this distance, with diamonds. He is leaning on the shoulder of Thomas Culpepper, who is dressed in the most glorious dark green cloak pinned with a diamond brooch. Cleves with its uniform of fustian and broadcloth, seems a long way away. I will never be able to explain to my mother that I do not peacock in English fashions for the sake of vanity, but only so that I do not seem more despicable and more repellent than I already am. If the king puts me aside, God knows that it will not be for dressing too fine. It will be because I disgust him, and I seem to do that whether I wear my hood like my grandmother, or like pretty little Kitty Howard. Nothing I can do can please the king; but my mother could spare herself the trouble of cautioning me that my life depends upon pleasing him. I already know that. And it cannot be done. At any rate, I cannot do it.

The ambassador has finished eating. I return to the table and motion to him that he may stay seated while I read my last letter, from my brother.

Sister, he starts. *I have been much troubled by the report of Counts Overstein and Olisleger as to your reception and behaviour at the court of your new husband, King Henry of England. Your mother will deal with matters of clothing and decorum, I can only beg that you listen to her and do not allow yourself to be led into behaviour that can only embarrass us, and shame yourself. Your tendency to vanity and ill-conditioned behaviour is known to us all; but we hoped that it would remain a family secret. We beg you to reform, especially now that the eyes of the world are upon you.*

I skip the next two pages, which are nothing but a list of the times that I have disappointed him in the past and warnings that a false step at the English court could have the gravest consequences. Who would know this better than I?

Then I read on.

This letter is to introduce the ambassador who will represent our country to King Henry and his council. You will extend to him every assistance. I expect you to work closely with him to further our hopes for this alliance that has so far disappointed us. Indeed, the King of England seems to think that he has made a very vassal of Cleves and now he is hoping for our alliance against the emperor, with whom we have no quarrel and are not likely to make one to oblige your husband or you. You should make this clear to him.

I understand that a senior Englishman, the Duke of Norfolk, has enjoyed a visit to the French court and there is no doubt in my mind but that England is drawing closer to France. This is the very thing that you were sent to England to prevent. Already, you are failing your country of Cleves, failing your mother, and me. The ambassador should advise you as to how you can do your duty and not forget it in the pleasures of the flesh.

I have provided him with transport to England and a servant to attend him, but you will have to pay him directly. I assume, from what I hear of your jewels and your new clothes and other ungodly extravagances including, I am told, expensive sables, that you can well afford to do this. Certainly, you would do better to spend your new-found wealth on the future of your country than on items of personal vanity and adornment which can only attract contempt. Just because you have been raised to a high position does not mean that you can neglect your conscience as you have done in the past. I urge you most earnestly to mend your ways, Sister. As the head of your house I advise you to abjure vanity and wantonness.

Trusting that this letter finds you in good health as it leaves me, certainly I hope that it finds you in good spiritual health, Sister. Luxury is no substitute for a good conscience, as you will find if you are spared to grow old.

As prays your loving brother

William.

I put down the letter and I look at the ambassador. 'Tell me, at least, that you have done this work before, that you have been an ambassador in another court.'

It is my fear that he is some Lutheran preacher that my brother has decided to employ.

'I served your father at the court of Toledo and Madrid,' Dr Harst replies with some dignity. 'But never before at my own expense.'

'My brother's finances are a little difficult,' I say. 'At least you can live for free at court here.'

He nods. 'He indicated to me that you would pay my salary.'

I shake my head. 'Not I. The king gives me my court and my ladies and my clothes, but no money as yet. That can be one of the questions that you raise with him.'

'But as the crowned Queen of England . . .'

'I am married to the king, but not crowned queen,' I say. 'Instead of my coronation in February I had a formal welcome into London, and now I expect to be crowned after Easter. I have not yet been paid my allowance as queen. I have no money.'

He looks a little anxious. 'I take it there is no difficulty? The coronation will go ahead?'

'Well, you will have brought the papers that the king requires?'

'What papers?'

I can feel my temper rising. 'The papers that prove that my earlier betrothal was annulled. The king demanded them, Counts Overstein and Olisleger swore that they would send them. They swore on their honour. You must have them.'

His face is quite aghast. 'I have nothing! Nobody said anything about these papers to me.'

I am stammering in my own language, I am so distraught. 'But there could be nothing more important! My wedding was delayed because there was fear of a pre-contract. The emissaries from Cleves swore that they would send the evidence as soon as they got home. They had to offer themselves as hostages. They must have told you. You must have them! They offered themselves as security!'

'They said nothing to me,' he repeats. 'And the duke your brother insisted that I delayed my journey to meet with them. Can they have forgotten such a thing?'

At the mention of my brother the fight goes out of me. 'No,' I say wearily. 'My brother agreed to this marriage but does not assist me. He does not seem to care for my embarrassment. Sometimes I fear that he has sent me to this country just to humiliate me.'

He is shocked. 'But why? How can such a thing be?'

I pull myself back from indiscretion. 'Oh, who knows? Things occur between children in the nursery and are never forgotten or forgiven. You must write to him at once and tell him that I have to have the evidence that shows my earlier betrothal was annulled. You have to persuade him to send it. Tell him that without it, I can do nothing, I can have no influence on the king. Tell him that without it we appear guilty of double dealing. The king could suspect us, and he would be right to suspect us. Ask my brother if he wants my very marriage to be questioned? If he wants me sent home in disgrace? If he wants this marriage annulled? If he wants me crowned queen? Because every day that we delay we give the king grounds for suspicion.'

'The king would never . . .' he begins. 'Everybody must know . . .'

'The king will please himself,' I say fiercely. 'That is the first thing that you learn in this court. The king is king, and head of the church, he is a tyrant who answers to nobody. He rules men's bodies and their souls. He speaks for God in this country. He himself believes that he knows God's will, that God speaks directly through him, that he is God on earth. He will do exactly what he wishes and he will decide if it is right or wrong, and then he will say that God wills it. Tell my brother that he puts me in very real danger and discomfort if he fails me in this one small thing. He has to send the documents or I fear for myself.'

Katherine, Hampton Court, March 1540

Easter morning and a happy Easter for me. I so hate Lent – for whatever have I to do penance for, or regret? Next to nothing. But I hated Lent even worse this year when it meant no dancing at court and no music except the dreariest of hymns and psalms; and worst of all no masquing and no plays. But for Easter we shall at last be merry. The Princess Mary is to come to court and we are all desperate to know how she likes her new stepmother. We are already laughing in anticipation of that greeting as the queen tries to be a mother to a child only one year her junior, tries to speak to her in German, tries to guide her to the reformed religion. It will be as good as a play. Princess Mary is said to be very grave and sad and pious; while the queen is light-hearted and merry in her rooms and born and bred a Lutheran or an Erasmian or one of those sorts of things, reformed, anyway. So we are all on the tips of our toes to get a good view from the window as the Princess Mary rides up to the front of the palace, and then we all scuttle like a flock of frantic hens to get into the queen's rooms before the Princess Mary is shown up the stairs. We fling ourselves into the seats around the room and try to look as if we are quietly sewing and listening to a sermon, and the queen says, 'Naughty girls,' with a smile and then there is the knock on the door, and in comes the princess, and – such a surprise – she has the Lady Elizabeth with her, by the hand.

Up we all pop and drop into very careful curtseys, we have to curtsey to the Princess Mary low enough to indicate our respect to a Princess of the Blood Royal, and rise up before the Lady Elizabeth can take the credit since she is only a bastard of the king, and perhaps not his at all. But I give her a smile and poke out my tongue at her as she goes past me for she is only a little girl, poor little poppet, only six years old, and besides, she is my cousin, but with the most distressing hair you can imagine, red as a carrot. I should die if I had hair like that, but it is her father's hair and that must be worth having for a child whose parentage is in doubt.

The queen rises to greet her two stepdaughters and she gives them each a kiss on both cheeks and then she draws them into her privy chamber and closes the door on all of us, as if she would be alone with them. So we have to wait about outside with no music and no wine and no merriment at all, and worst of all, no idea what is going on behind the closed door. I take a little stroll towards the privy chamber; but Lady Rochford frowns me away and I raise my eyebrows and say, 'What?' as if I have no idea that she is preventing me from eavesdropping.

Within minutes anyway we can all hear the laughter and the chatter of little Elizabeth, and within half an hour they throw open the door and out they come and Elizabeth has hold of the queen's hand and Princess Mary, who was so dour and sad when she came in, is smiling and looking quite flushed and pretty. The queen presents us by name one after another and Princess Mary smiles graciously at each of us, knowing half of us to be her sworn enemy, and then at last they call for refreshments and the queen sends a message to the king to tell him that his daughters are come to court and are in her rooms.

Now things improve even more, for the next thing is that the king himself is announced and all the men come in with him, and I sink into a curtsey but he goes past me with hardly a second glance to greet his daughters.

He is very fond of them, he has some sugared plums in his pocket for the little Lady Elizabeth and he speaks kindly and gently to Princess Mary. He sits by the queen and she puts her hand over his and says something quietly in his ear and clearly they are a merry little family which would be very sweet if he were a wise old grandfather with his three pretty granddaughters around him, as one might almost think.

I feel a little sour and irritated by all this, since no-one is paying the least attention to me, and then Thomas Culpepper – whom I have not forgiven for one moment – comes up to me and kisses my hand and says, 'Cousin.'

'Oh, Master Culpepper,' I exclaim as if I am surprised to see him. 'Are you here?'

'Where else could I be? Is there a prettier girl in the room?'

'I don't know, I'm sure,' I say. 'The Princess Mary is a beautiful young lady.'

He makes a face. 'I am talking about a girl that can turn a man's heart upside down.'

'I don't know of a girl like that for you, since I don't know of any girl that could make you keep an appointment on time,' I say sharply.

'You cannot still be cross with me,' he says, as if this is a great wonder. 'Not a girl like you, who could have any man she wanted with a snap of her fingers. You cannot be cross with someone as unimportant as me when I am commanded away from you, though my heart was breaking at the thought of leaving you.'

I give a little crow of laughter, and put my hand over my mouth as the queen glances over to me. 'Your heart was never breaking,' I say. 'You have none.'

'It was,' he insists. 'Broken in two. But what could I do? The king commanded my attendance but my heart lies with you. I had to break my heart and do my duty, and now you still will not forgive me.'

'I don't forgive you because I don't believe a word of it,' I say cheerfully. I look towards the queen and I see that the king is now watching us. Carefully, I turn my head a little away from Thomas Culpepper and withdraw slightly. It will not do to seem too engaged with him. I glance under my eyelashes and indeed the king is looking at me. He beckons me to him with a crook of his finger, and I ignore Thomas Culpepper and step up to the royal chair.

'Your Grace?'

'I am saying that we should have some dancing. Will you partner the Princess Mary? The queen tells me you are the best of her dancers.'

So now, who capers like an Italian? I flush hot with pleasure and I wish with all my heart that my grandmother could see me now, being ordered to dance by the king himself on the recommendation of the queen.

'Of course, Your Grace.' I curtsey beautifully; I cast down my eyes modestly as well, since everyone is watching me, and I put out my hand to the Princess Mary. Well, toll-loll, she doesn't exactly leap up to take it, and she walks to the centre of the room to form the first line of the dance with me as if she were not much honoured by her partner. I toss my head a little at her grave face and summon the other girls, who form a line behind us. The musicians strike a chord and we start to dance.

And who would have thought it? She's rather a good dancer. She moves gracefully and she holds her head high. Her feet twinkle through the steps, she has been wonderfully taught. I give a little sway of my hips just to make sure that the King, and every man in the room, keeps his eyes on me, but to be honest, I am sure that half of them are watching the princess, whose colour rises as she dances and who is smiling by the time we have gone through the chain part of the dance and the walking your partner down the archway. I try to look modestly pleased with the success of my partner but I am afraid I look as if I am sucking lemons. I can't be a foil to someone else's performance, I just can't. It's not my nature, I just don't aspire to second place.

So we finish with a curtsey and the king rises to his feet and calls *'Brava! Brava!'* which is Latin or German or something for hurrah, and I smile and try to look quietly pleased while he comes towards us and takes the princess by the hand and kisses her on both cheeks and tells her he is delighted with her.

I stand back, as modest as a little flower, but as green with envy as a spike of grass at all the praise being showered on the dull creature; but then he turns to me, and bends down to whisper in my ear. 'And you, sweetheart, dance like a little angel. Any partner of yours would look the better for being at your side. Will you ever dance for me, d'you think? Just on your own, for my pleasure?'

And I, looking up at him, fluttering my eyelashes down as if I am overwhelmed by him, say: 'Oh, Your Grace! I should quite forget my steps if I were to dance for you. I would have to be guided, every step of the way. You would have to lead me wherever you wanted.'

So he says: 'Pretty little thing, I know where I would lead you, if I could.'

Oh, do you? I think. Well, you naughty old man. Can't muster a salute for your own wife and yet whispering to me.

The king steps back and leads the Princess Mary back to the queen and the musicians strike a chord and the young men of the court step forwards for their partners. I feel a hand take mine and I turn around with my eyes cast down as if I am shy at being asked. 'No need to trouble yourself with that,' says my uncle Norfolk coldly. 'I want a word with you.'

Rather shocked that it is not handsome young Thomas Culpepper, I let him escort me to the side of the chamber and there is Lady Rochford, as if waiting, of course she is waiting, and I am between the two of them and my heart sinks down into my little dancing shoes, I am sure, I am certain-sure that he is going to send me home for flirting with the king.

'What d'you think?' he asks Lady Rochford over my head.

'Uncle, I am innocent,' I say, but no-one pays any attention to me.

'Possible,' she says.

'I'd say certain,' he returns.

They both look at me as if I were a cygnet for the carving.

'Katherine, you have taken the king's eye,' my uncle says.

'I have done nothing,' I squeak. 'Uncle, I swear I am innocent.' I give a little gasp when I hear myself. I am thinking of Anne Boleyn, who said those very words to him and found no mercy. 'Please . . .' I whisper. 'Please, I beg you . . . Truly I have done nothing . . .'

'Keep your voice down,' says Lady Rochford, glancing around, but nobody is paying us any attention, nobody is going to call me away.

'You have taken his fancy, now you have to take his heart,' he goes on, as if I had said nothing. 'You have done beautifully so far; but he is a man of a certain age and he doesn't want a little slut on his knee, he likes to fall in love, he likes the pursuit better than the capture. He wants to think he is courting a girl of unblemished reputation.'

'I am! Truly, I am! Unblemished!'

'You have to lead him on and bring him on and yet forever draw back.'

I wait, I have no idea what he wants of me.

'In short he is not just to lust for you, he has to fall in love with you.'

'But why?' I ask. 'So that he gets me a good husband?'

My uncle leans forwards, his mouth to my ear. 'Listen, fool. So that he makes you his wife, his own wife, the next Queen of England.'

My exclamation of surprise is silenced by Lady Rochford, who pinches the back of my hand sharply. 'Ow!'

'Listen to your uncle,' she says. 'And keep your voice down.'

'But he is married to the queen,' I mutter.

'He can still fall in love with you,' my uncle says. 'Stranger things have happened. And he has to know that you are a virgin untouched, a little rose, that you are a good enough girl to be Queen of England.'

I glance back towards the woman who already is the Queen of England. She is smiling down at the Lady Elizabeth, who is doing a little hopping dance in time to the music. The king is tapping his good foot in time to the beat, even Princess Mary looks happy.

'Perhaps not this year, perhaps not next,' my uncle says. 'But you must keep the king interested and you must lead him into honourable love. Anne Boleyn led him on and held him off, and kept him coming on for six years, and she started when he was in love with his wife. This is not the work of a day, this is a masterpiece, it will be your life's work. You are not to give him the least idea that he could make you his mistress. He has to honour you, Katherine, as if you were a young lady fit only for marriage. Can you do that?'

'I don't know,' I say. 'He is king. Doesn't he know everybody's thoughts anyway? Doesn't God tell him?'

'God help us, the girl is an idiot,' my uncle mutters. 'Katherine, he is a man like any other, only now, in his old age, more suspicious and more vindictive than most. He has enjoyed an easier life than most, he has been idle for all his days. He has had kindness everywhere he has ever gone, no-one has said "no" to him since he got rid of Katherine of Aragon. He is used to having his own way in everything. This is the man you have to delight, a man brought up to indulgence. You have to make him think you are special, he is surrounded by women who pretend to adore him. You have to do something special. You have to make him aroused and yet keep his hands off you. This is what I am asking you to do. You can have new gowns and Lady Rochford's help but this is what I want. Can you do it?'

'I can try,' I say doubtfully. 'But what happens then? When he is in love and aroused but trusting? What happens then? I can hardly tell him that I am hoping to be queen while I serve the queen.'

'You leave that to me,' he says. 'You do your part and I will do mine. But you have to do your part. Just as you are: but a little more, a little more warmly. I want you to bring him on.'

I hesitate. I am longing to say yes, I am longing for the gifts that will come my way and the fuss that everyone will make of me if I am seen to take the king's eye. But Anne Boleyn, my cousin, this man's niece, must have felt that too. He may have given her the very same advice, and look where it got her. I don't know how much of a part he played in helping her to the throne, nor whether he helped her on to the scaffold. I don't know if he will take better care of me than he did of her. 'What if I can't do it?' I ask. 'What if something goes wrong?'

He smiles down at me. 'Are you telling me that you doubt for a moment that you can make any man fall in love with you?'

I try to keep my face grave; but my own vanity is too much for me and I smile back at him. 'Not really,' I say.

Jane Boleyn, Hampton Court, March 1540

We are riding to London, to the palace of Westminster for the opening of parliament. But this riding back to London is not the same as when we were riding out. Something has happened. I feel as if I am an old hound, the pack leader, who can lift her grizzled head and smell the change in the wind. When we rode out, the king was between the queen and young Kitty Howard and anyone looking at them would have seen him distribute his smiles between his wife and her friend. Now, to me, perhaps only to me, the scene is quite different. Once again the king rides between the queen and her little favourite but this time his head is turned, all the time, to his left. It's as if his round face has swivelled on the fleshy neck and got stuck. Katherine holds his attention like a dancing mayfly holds the attention of the fat, gaping carp. The king is goggling at Katherine Howard as if he cannot take his eyes from her; and the queen, on his right, and even the Princess Mary on her other side, cannot divert him, cannot distract him, can do nothing but provide a shield for his infatuation.

I have seen this before – my God – so many times. I have been at Henry's court since I was a maid and Henry was a boy, and I know him: a boy in love, a man in love, and now an old fool in love. I saw him run after Bessie Blount, after Mary Boleyn, after her sister Anne, after Madge Shelton, after Jane Seymour, after

Anne Bassett, and now this: this pretty child. I know how Henry looks when he is besotted: a bull, ready to be led by the nose. He is at this point now. If we Howards want him, we have him. He is caught.

The queen reins back to speak with me, and leaves Katherine Howard, Catherine Carey, Princess Mary and the king riding together before us. They barely turn their heads to see that she has gone. She is becoming a cipher, a person of no significance.

'The king likes Kitty Howard,' she observes to me.

'And Lady Anne Bassett,' I say equably. 'Young people make him merry. You have enjoyed the company of the Princess Mary, I think.'

'No,' she says shortly, there is no diverting her. 'He likes Katherine.'

'No more than any other,' I persist. 'Mary Norris is a favourite.'

'Lady Rochford, be my friend: what am I to do?' she asks me simply.

'Do? Your Grace?'

'If he has a girl . . .' She breaks off to find the right word. 'A whore.'

'A lover,' I correct her rapidly. 'Whore is a very bad word, Your Grace.'

She raises her eyebrows. 'Ach, so? Lover.'

'If he takes a lover, you must pay no attention.'

She nods. 'This is what Queen Jane do?'

'Yes indeed, Your Grace. She did not notice.'

She is silent for a second. 'They do not think her a fool for this?'

'They thought her queenly,' I say. 'A queen does not complain of her husband the king.'

'That is what Queen Anne do?'

I hesitate. 'No. Queen Anne was very angry, she made much noise.' God spare us ever again from the storm that broke over our heads on the day that Anne found Jane Seymour squirming and giggling on the king's lap. 'The king was then angry with her. And . . .'

'And?'

'It is dangerous to anger the king. Even if you are queen.'

She is silent at this, it has not taken her long to learn that the court is a death-trap for the unwary.

'Who was the king's lover then? When Queen Anne made much noise?'

This is rather awkward to tell the king's new wife. 'He was courting Lady Jane Seymour, who became queen.'

She nods. I have learned that when she looks most stolid and stupid it is then that she is thinking the most furiously.

'And Queen Katherine of Aragon? She makes a noise?'

I am on firmer ground here. 'She never once complained to the king. She always greeted him with a smile, whatever she had heard, whatever she feared. She was always a most courteous wife and queen.'

'But he took a lover? Just the same? With such a queen at his side? Her, a princess that he had married for love?'

'Yes.'

'And was that lover Lady Anne Boleyn?'

I nod.

'A lady in waiting? Her own lady in waiting?'

I nod again at the remorseless march of her logic.

'So both his two queens were ladies in waiting? He see them in the queen's rooms? He meet them there.'

'That is so,' I say.

'He meets them while the queen watches. He dances with them in her rooms. He agrees that they should meet later?'

I cannot deny it. 'Er, yes.'

She looks ahead to where Katherine Howard is riding close to the king and watches as he leans over and puts his hand on hers, as if to correct how she is holding the reins. Katherine looks up at him as if his touch is an honour she can hardly bear. She leans slightly towards him, yearning, we both hear her breathless little giggle.

'Like that,' she says flatly.

I can think of nothing to say.

'I see,' says the queen. 'I understand now. And a wise woman say nothing?'

'She says nothing.' I hesitate. 'You cannot prevent it, Your Grace. Whatever comes of it.'

She bows her head and to my surprise I see a tear fall on to the pommel of her saddle and she covers it quickly with her gloved finger. 'Yes, I can do nothing,' she whispers.

We have been settled in our apartments at Westminster for only a few days when I am summoned to the rooms of my kinsman the Duke of Norfolk. I go at midday, before we dine, and I find him pacing about his rooms, not his usual contained self at all. It is so unusual to see him disturbed that I am at once alert to danger. I do not enter the room but stay by the wall, as I would if I had opened the wrong door in the Tower and found myself among the king's lions. I stay by the door and my hand rests on the door knob.

'Sir?'

'Have you heard? Did you know? Cromwell is to be an earl? A damned earl?'

'He is?'

'Did I not just say so? Earl of Essex. Earl of bloody Essex! What do you think of that, madam?'

'I think nothing, sir.'

'Have they consummated the marriage?'

'No!'

'Do you swear? Are you certain? They must have done. He's got it up at last and he's paying his bawd. He must be pleased with Cromwell for something!'

'I am utterly certain. I know they have not. And she is unhappy, she knows he is attracted to Katherine, and she is anxious about that. She spoke to me of it.'

'But he is rewarding the minister who gave him the queen. He must be pleased with the marriage, something must have pleased him. He must have learned something, he must be turning from us for some reason. He is rewarding Cromwell, and Cromwell brought him the queen.'

'I swear to you, my lord, I have held nothing back from you. The king has been coming to her bed almost every night since the end of Lent but it is no better than it was before. The sheets are clean, her hair is still in plaits, her nightcap straight every morning. She cries sometimes, during the day, when she thinks no-one is watching. This is not a well-loved woman, this is a hurt girl. I swear she is a virgin still.'

The duke rounds on me in his rage. 'Then why would he make Cromwell Earl of Essex?'

'It must be for some other reason.'

'What other reason? This is Cromwell's great triumph, this alliance with the Protestant dukes and the king, this alliance against France and Spain, sealed with this marriage with the Flanders girl. I have an alliance with the King of France at my fingertips. I have filled the king's head with suspicions against Cromwell. Lord Lisle has told him that Cromwell favours reformers, has hidden heretics away in Calais. Cromwell's favourite preacher is to be accused of heresy. Everything is piling up against him but then he gets an earldom. Why is that? The earldom is his reward. Why would the king reward him if he is not pleased with him?'

I shrug my shoulders. 'My lord uncle. How should I know?'

'Because you are here to know!' he shouts at me. 'You are put at court and kept at court and dressed and fed at court so that you shall know everything, and so that you shall tell me! If you know nothing, what is the point of you being here? What was the point of sparing you from the scaffold?'

I feel my face grow stiff with fear at his anger. 'I know what goes on in the queen's rooms,' I say softly. 'I cannot know what happens in the Privy Council.'

'You dare to say that I should know? That I am remiss?'

Mutely, I shake my head.

'How should anybody know what the king thinks when he keeps his own counsel and rewards the man whose face he has been slapping in public for the past three months? How should anyone know what is happening when Cromwell is blamed for the worst marriage the king has ever made and is now to lord it around us as earl, as damned Earl of damned-to-hell Essex?'

I find that I am pressed back against the wall and the silky feel of the tapestry is behind my outspread hands. I can feel the fabric grow damp with my cold sweat.

'How is anybody to know what the hell is in the king's mind when he is by turns as cunning as a crow and as mad as a hare?'

I shake my head in silence. That he should name the king in the same breath as madness is as good as treason. I will not repeat it even here, safe in Howard rooms.

'At any rate, you are sure that he still likes Katherine?' the duke says more quietly.

'Hotly. There is no doubt in my mind.'

'Well, tell her to keep him at arm's length. We gain nothing if she becomes his whore, but he stays married to the queen.'

'There can be no doubt . . .'

'I doubt everything,' he says flatly. 'And if he beds her and then beds the queen and gets a son on her and thanks Cromwell for the addition to his nursery then we are ruined, along with the little slut.'

'He will not bed the queen,' I say, returning to my only certainty.

'You don't know anything,' he says rudely. 'All you know is what can be gleaned from keyholes and privy chamber whispers, out of the chamber sweepings and the midden. You know everything that can be found in the dirt of life, you know nothing of policy. I tell you, he is rewarding Cromwell with rank beyond his dreams for bringing him the Cleves queen; and your plans and my plans are all thrown down. And you are a fool.'

There is nothing I can say to this so I wait for him to tell me to leave, but he turns to the window and pauses, looking out and gnawing his thumbnail. After a little while a page comes to tell him that he is required at the House of Lords and he goes out without another word to me. I curtsey, but I don't think he even sees me.

When he is gone, I should go too but, I do not leave. I walk around his room. When the room is quiet and no-one comes to the door, I draw back the chair. Then I sit behind his table in his big carved chair with the crest of the Howards, hard and uncomfortable behind my head. I wonder what it would have been like if George had lived and his uncle had died and George had been the great man of this family and I might have sat here, beside him, in my own right. We might have had matching chairs at this great table, and hatched our own plans, our own schemes. We might have made a great house of our own and raised our own children in it. We would have been brother and sister-in-law to the queen, our children would have been cousins to the next king. George would have been a duke for sure, I would have been a duchess. We would have been wealthy, the greatest family in the kingdom. We might have grown old together, he would have prized me for my advice and my fierce loyalty, I would have loved him for his passion and his good looks, and his wit. He would have turned to me, in the end he would surely have turned to me. He would have tired of Anne and her temper. He would have learned that a steady love, a faithful love, a wife's love is the best.

But George died, and so did Anne, both of them dead before they could learn to value me. And all that is left of the three of us is me, the only survivor, wishing for the Boleyn inheritance, perching in the Howard chair, dreaming that they are still alive and that there is greatness before us, instead of loneliness and old age, petty plots and disgrace and death.

Katherine, Westminster Palace, April 1540

I am on my way to the queen's rooms just before dinner when I feel a gentle hand on my sleeve. I think at once that it is John Beresby or Tom Culpepper and I turn with a laugh, to tell him to let me go, when I see that it is the king, and I swoop into a curtsey.

He says, 'You know me then,' and I see that he is wearing a big hat and a big cape and thinks himself quite unrecognisable. I don't say: you are the fattest man at court, of course I know you. You must be the only man who is six feet tall and more than four feet round. You are the only man who stinks like mouldy meat. I say: 'Your Grace, oh, Your Grace, I think I would know you at any time, anywhere.'

He steps forwards, out of the shadows, and there is no-one else with him, which is extraordinary. Usually he has half a dozen men with him wherever he is. Whatever he is doing. 'How do you know me?' he asks.

I have a little trick now which is, whenever he speaks to me like this, I imagine it is Thomas Culpepper, the utterly delicious Thomas Culpepper, and I think how I would answer him to enchant him, and I smile as I would for Thomas, and I say the words I would use to him, to the king. So I say easily: 'Your Grace, I dare not tell you,' thinking, 'Thomas, I dare not tell you.'

And he says: 'Tell me.'

And I say: 'I cannot.'

And he says: 'Tell me, pretty Katherine.'

This could go on all day, so I change the tune and say: 'I feel so ashamed.'

And he says: 'There's no need to feel ashamed, sweetheart. Tell me how you know me.'

And I say, thinking of Thomas: 'It is a scent, Your Grace. It is a scent like a perfume, a goodly smell that I love, like a flower like jasmine or roses. And then there is a deeper smell, like the sweat of a good horse when it is hot from hunting, then there is a smell like leather, and then a sort of tang like the sea.'

'I smell like this?' he asks and there is wonder in his voice, and I realise, with a little shock, that of course this will hit home since in truth he smells of pus from his leg, poor man, and often of farting since he is so costive, and this stink goes with him everywhere so that he has to carry a pomader all the time to block it out from his own nose, but he must know that to everyone he smells of decay.

'You do to me,' I say faithfully, thinking hard of Thomas Culpepper and the clean smell of his brown curly hair. 'There is a scent of jasmine and sweat and leather and salt.' I look down and lick my lips, just lightly, nothing bawdy. 'I always know you by this.'

He takes me by the hand and he draws me to him. 'Sweet maid,' he breathes. 'Oh God, sweet maid.'

I give a little gasp as if I am afraid, but I look up at him as if I would be kissed. This is rather nasty, really. He is awfully like my step-grandmother's steward at Horsham – very old. Old enough to be my grandfather almost, and his mouth is trembling and his eyes are wet. I admire him because he is the king, of course. He is the greatest man in the world and I love him as my king. And my uncle has made clear that there are new dresses involved if I can lead him on. But it is not very nice when he holds me round the waist and puts his mouth wetly on my neck, and I can feel his spittle cold on my skin.

'Sweet maid,' he says again, and he nuzzles me with a moist kiss, which is like being sucked by a fish.

'Your Grace!' I say breathlessly. 'You must let me go.'

'I will never let you go!'

'Your Grace, I am a maid!'

This works wonderfully well, he lets me go a little way and I can step back and though he takes both my hands, at least I don't have him breathing down the front of my gown.

'You are a sweet maid, Katherine.'

'I am an honest maid, sire,' I say breathlessly.

He has tight hold of my hands and he draws me to him. 'If I were a free man would you be my wife?' he asks simply.

I am so surprised by the speed of this, that I cannot say a word. I just look at him as if I were a complete milkmaid, and stupid as a dairy cow. 'Your wife? Your wife, sire?'

'My marriage is not a true one,' he says quickly, all the time he is pulling me closer, his hand sliding round my waist again. I think that the words are just to dazzle me while he backs me into the corner and gets a hand up my skirt, so I keep moving and he keeps talking. 'My marriage is invalid. For several reasons. My wife was pre-contracted and not free to marry. My conscience warned me of this and for my soul's sake I cannot lie with her in a holy union. I know in my deepest heart that she is another man's wife.'

'Is she?' Surely, he can't imagine I am fool enough to believe this for a moment.

'I know it, my conscience warns me. God speaks to me. I know it.'

'Does He? Do you?'

'Yes,' he says firmly. 'And so I did not fully consent at my wedding. God knew of my doubts then; and I have not lain with her. So the marriage is no marriage and I will soon be free.'

So he does think me fool enough, because he has fooled himself. Good God, what men can do to their brains when their cocks are hard. It is truly amazing.

'But what will happen to her?' I ask.

'What?' His hand, which is creeping up my stomacher to my breast, is halted at the thought.

'What will happen to the queen?' I ask. 'If she is no queen any more?'

'How should I know?' he says, as if it is nothing to do with him. 'She should not have come to England if she was not free to marry. She is a promise-breaker. She can go home again.'

I don't think that she will want to go home again, not to that brother of hers, and she has taken a liking to the royal children, and to England. But his hand is pulling urgently on my waist and he is turning me to face him.

'Katherine,' he says longingly. 'Tell me that I can think of you? Or is there another young man? You're a young woman, surrounded by temptation in a lascivious court, a dirty-minded, lustful court with many bad, filthy-headed boys, I suppose one of them will have taken your fancy? Promised you some fairing for a kiss?'

'No,' I say. 'I told you. I don't like boys. They are all too silly.'

'You don't like boys?'

'Not at all.'

'So what do you like?' he asks. His voice is lilting with admiration of himself. He knows the reply in this song.

'I daren't say.' His hand is creeping up from my waist again, in a moment he will be fondling my breast. Oh, Thomas Culpepper, I wish to God this was you.

'Tell me,' he says. 'Oh, tell me, pretty Katherine, and I will give you a present for being an honest girl.'

I snatch a quick breath of clean air. 'I like you,' I say simply, and one hand clamps – smack – on my breast and the other pulls me towards him and his mouth comes down on mine, all wet and sucking, and it is really very horrible; but on the other hand I have to wonder what present I get for being an honest girl.

He gives me the estates of two convicted murderers: that is, a couple of houses and some goods, and some money. I can't believe it. That I should have houses, two houses, and land, and money of my own!

I have never had such wealth in my life, and never any gift so easily earned. I have to acknowledge: it was easily earned. It is not nice to lead on a man who is old enough to be my father, almost old enough to be my grandfather. It is not very nice to have his fat hand rubbing at my breasts and his stinking mouth all over my face. But I must remember that he is the king, and he is a kind old man and a sweet, doting old man, and I can close my eyes most of the time and pretend that it is someone else. Also, it is not very nice to have dead men's goods, but when I say this to Lady Rochford she points out that we all have dead men's goods one way or another, everything is either stolen or inherited, and a woman who hopes to rise in the world can't afford to be particular.

Anne, Westminster Palace, April 1540

I thought that I would be crowned as part of the May Day celebrations but we are already less than a month away and no-one has ordered any gowns or planned the order of the coronation, so I begin to think it won't be this May Day, it can't be. In the absence of any better advisor I wait until the Princess Mary and I are walking back from the Lady Chapel to the palace, and I ask her what she thinks. I have grown to like her more and more and trust her opinion. Also, because she has been the child and then the exile of this court, she knows better than most what it is to live here and yet know yourself to be an outsider.

At the very word 'coronation' she gives me a quick look of such concern that I cannot take another step. I freeze to the spot and cry: 'Oh, what have you heard?'

'Dear Anne, don't cry,' she says quickly. 'I beg your pardon. Queen Anne.'

'I'm not crying.' I show her my shocked face. 'I am not.'

At once we both look round to see if anyone is watching us. This is how it is at court, always the glance over your shoulder for the spy; truth told only in whispers. She steps closer to me and I take her hand and put it through my arm and we walk together.

'It can't be this May Day because we would have had everything planned and ready by now if he was going to crown you,' she says.

'I thought that in Lent, myself. But it's not so bad. It means nothing. Queen Jane wasn't crowned either. He would have crowned her if she had lived, once she had given him an heir. He will be waiting for you to tell him that you are with child. He will be waiting for you to have a child and then there will be the christening and then your coronation after that.'

I flush deeply at this and say nothing. She takes a glance at my face and waits until we have gone up the stairs, through my presence chamber, through my privy chamber and to my little withdrawing chamber where nobody comes without invitation. I close the door on the curious faces of my ladies and we are alone.

'There is a difficulty?' she says with careful tact.

'Not of my making.'

She nods but neither of us wants to say more. We are both virgins in our mid-twenties, old for spinsters, afraid of the mystery of male desire, afraid of the power of the king, both living on the edge of his acceptance.

'You know, I hate May Day,' she says suddenly.

'I thought it was one of the greatest days of celebration of the year?'

'Oh, yes, but it is a savage celebration, pagan: not a Christian one.'

This is part of her Papist superstition and I am going to laugh for a moment but the gravity of her face stops me.

'It's just to welcome the coming of spring,' I say. 'There is no harm in it.'

'It is the time for putting off the old and taking on the new,' she says. 'That's the tradition and the king lives it to the full, like a savage. He rode in a May Day tournament with a love message to Anne Boleyn on his standard, and then he put my mother aside for the Lady Anne on a May Day. Less than five years later, it was her turn: the Lady Anne was the new Queen of the Joust, with her champions fighting for her honour before her royal box. But the knights were arrested that afternoon and the king rode away from her without even saying goodbye, and that was the end of the Lady Anne, and the last time she saw him.'

'He didn't say goodbye?' For some reason, this seems to me the worst thing of all. No-one had told me this before.

She shakes her head. 'He never says goodbye. When his favour has gone then he goes swiftly too. He never said goodbye to my mother either, he rode away from her and she had to send her servants after him to wish him Godspeed. He never told her that he would not return. He just rode out one day, and never came back. He never said goodbye to the Lady Anne. He rode away from the May Day tournament and sent his men to arrest her. Actually, he never even said goodbye to Queen Jane, who died in giving him his son. He knew she was fighting for her life but he did not go to her. He let her die alone. He is hard-hearted but he is not hard-faced; he cannot stand women crying, he cannot stand goodbyes. He finds it easier to turn his heart, and turn his face, and then he just leaves.'

I give a little shudder, and I go to the windows and check that they are tight shut, I have to stop myself from closing the shutters against the hard light. There is a cold wind coming off the river, I can almost feel it chilling me as I stand here. I want to go out to the presence chamber and surround myself with my silly girls, with a pageboy playing the lute, and the women laughing. I want the comfort of the queen's rooms around me, even though I know that three other women have needed their comfort before, and they are all dead.

'If he turn against me, as he turn against the Lady Anne, I would have no warning,' I say quietly. 'Nobody at this court is my friend, no-one even tell me that danger is coming.'

Princess Mary does not attempt to reassure me.

'It could be, like for the Lady Anne, a sunny day, a tournament, and then the men at arms come and there is no escape?'

Her face is pale. She nods. 'He sent the Duke of Norfolk against me to order my obedience. The good duke, who had known me from childhood and served my mother loyally, with love, said to my face that if he were my father he would swing me by the heels and split my head open against the wall,' she says. 'A man I had known from childhood, a man who knew me to be a Princess of the Blood, who had loved my mother as her most loyal servant. He came with my father's goodwill, under his orders, and he was ready to take me to the Tower. The king sent his executioner against me and let him do what he would.'

I take a handful of priceless tapestry, as if the touch of it can comfort me. 'But I am innocent of offence,' I say. 'I have done nothing,'

'Neither had I,' she replies. 'Neither had my mother. Neither had Queen Jane. Perhaps even the Lady Anne was innocent too. We all saw the king's love turn to spite.'

'And I have never had it,' I say quietly to myself in my own language. 'If he could abandon his wife of sixteen years, a woman he had loved, how readily, how easily can he dispose of me, a woman he has never even liked?'

She looks at me. 'What will become of you?'

I know my face is bleak. 'I don't know,' I say honestly. 'I don't know. If the king allies with France and takes Kitty Howard as his lover then I suppose he will send me home.'

'If not worse,' she says very softly.

I give a rueful smile. 'I don't know what could be worse than my home.'

'The Tower,' she says simply. 'The Tower would be worse. And then the scaffold.'

The silence that follows those words seems to last a long time. Without speaking I rise up from my chair and go to the door that leads out to my public rooms and the princess steps back to let me precede her. We go through the withdrawing room in silence, both of us haunted by our own thoughts, and enter through the small door of my rooms to a great bustle and fuss. Servants are running from gallery to chamber carrying goods. A dining table is being set up in my presence chamber and it is laid with the gold and silver plate of the royal treasury.

'What is happening now?' I ask, bewildered.

'His Majesty the King has announced that he will dine in your rooms,' Lady Rochford bustles forwards and curtseys to tell me.

'Good.' I try to sound as if I am very pleased but I am still filled with dread at the thought of the king's spite and the Tower and the scaffold. 'I am honoured to invite His Grace by my rooms.'

'*To* my rooms,' Princess Mary corrects me quietly.

'To my rooms,' I repeat.

'Shall you change your gown for dinner?'

'Yes.' I see that my ladies in waiting have already put on their best, Kitty Howard's cap is so far back on her head she might as well dispense with it altogether, and she is loaded with chains of gold strung with little seed pearls. She has diamonds dancing in her ears, she has pearls wound round and round her neck. She must have come into some money from somewhere. I have never seen her wear more than a little chain of thin gold before. She sees me looking at her and she sweeps me a curtsey and then spins on the spot so I can admire the effect of a new gown of rose silk with an underskirt of deep pink.

'Pretty,' I say. 'New?'

'Yes,' she says, and then her eyes slide away like a child caught out in thieving and I know at once that all this finery has come from the king.

'Shall I come and help you dress?' she asks, almost apologetically.

I nod and she and two of the other maids in waiting follow me into my inner privy chamber. My gown for dinner is already laid out and Katherine runs to the chest and takes out my linen.

'So fine,' she says approvingly, smoothing the white-on-white embroidery on my shifts.

I slip on the shift and sit before the mirror so that Katherine can

235

brush my hair. Her touch is gentle as she twists my hair up into a gold-encrusted net, and we only disagree when she puts my hood far back on my head. I put it right and she laughs at me. I see our faces side by side in the mirror, and her eyes meet mine, as innocent as a child, without any shadow of deceit. I turn and speak to the other girls. 'Leave us,' I say.

From the glances they exchange as they go, I see that her new riches are common knowledge and everyone knows where those pearls come from, and they are expecting a jealous storm to break on Kitty Howard's little head.

'The king likes you,' I say to her bluntly.

The smile has faded from her eyes. She shifts from one little pink-slippered foot to another. 'Your Grace . . .' she whispers.

'He does not like me,' I say. I know I am too blunt but I have not the words to dress this up like a lying Englishwoman.

Her colour rises up from her low-cut neckline to burn in her cheeks. 'Your Grace . . .'

'Do you desire him?' I ask. I don't have the words to disguise the question in a lengthy conversation.

'No!' she says instantly, but then she bows her head. 'He is the king . . . and my uncle says, indeed, my uncle orders me . . .'

'You are not free?' I suggest.

Her grey eyes meet mine. 'I am a girl,' she says. 'I am only a young girl, I am not free.'

'Can you refuse to do what they want?'

'No.'

There is a silence between us, as we both come to realise the simple truth that is being spoken. We are two women who have recognised that we cannot control the world. We are players in this game but we do not choose our own moves. The men will play us for their own desires. All we can do is try to survive whatever happens next.

'What will happen to me, if the king wants you for his wife?' I know, as the words come awkwardly into my mouth, that this is the central, unsayable question.

She shrugs. 'I don't know. I don't think anyone knows that.'

'Would he have me killed?' I whisper.

To my horror she does not start back in terror and exclaim a denial. She looks at me very steadily. 'I don't know what he will do,' she says again. 'Your Grace, I don't know what he wants nor what he can do. I don't know the law. I don't know what he is able to do.'

'He will command you to his side,' I say through cold lips. 'I see that. Wife or whore. But will he send me to the Tower? Will he have me killed?'

'I don't know,' she says. She looks like a frightened child. 'I can't tell. Nobody tells me anything except that I have to please him. And I have to do that.'

Jane Boleyn, Westminster Palace, May 1540

The queen is in the royal box high above the jousting lists and though she is pale with anxiety she carries herself like a queen indeed. She has a smile for the hundreds of Londoners who have flocked to the palace to see the royal family and the nobles, the mock battles, the pageants, and the jousts. There are to be six challengers and six defenders and they circle the arena with their entourage and their shields and their banners and the trumpets scream out the fanfare and the crowd shouts their bets and it is like a dream with the noise and the heat and the glare of the sun beating off the golden sand in the arena.

If I stand at the rear of the royal box and half-close my eyes I can see ghosts today. I can see Queen Katherine leaning forwards and waving her hand to her young husband, I can even see his shield with this motto: Sir Loyal Heart.

Sir Loyal Heart! I would laugh if the king's changeable heart had not been the death of so many. Loyal only to its own desires is the king's heart, and this day, this May Day, it has changed again, like the spring wind, and is blowing another way.

I step to one side and a ray of sunshine peeping through a gap in the awning dazzles me and for a moment I see Anne at the front of the box, my Anne, Anne Boleyn with her head flung back in laughter and the white line of her throat exposed. It was a hot May

Day that year, Anne's last year, and she blamed the sun when she was sweating with fear. She knew that she was in trouble but she had no idea of her danger. How should she have known? We none of us knew. We none of us dreamed that he would put that long, lovely neck down on a block of wood and hire a French swordsman to hack it off. How should anyone dream that a man would do that to the wife he had adored? He broke the faith of his kingdom to have her. Why would he then break her?

If we had known . . . but it is pointless to say: if we had known.

Perhaps we would have run away. Me, and George my husband, and Anne his sister, and Elizabeth her daughter. Perhaps we might have run away and been free of this terror and this ambition and this lust for this life that is the English court. But we did not run. We sat like hares, cowering in the long grass at the sound of the hounds, hoping that the hunt would pass by; but that very day the soldiers came for my husband and for my beloved sister-in-law Anne. And I? I sat mum, and let them go, and never said one word to save them.

But this new young queen is no fool. We were afraid, all three of us; but we did not know how very afraid we should have been. But Anne of Cleves knows. She has spoken with her ambassador and she knows there is to be no coronation. She has spoken with the Princess Mary and knows that the king can destroy a blameless wife by sending her far away from court, to a castle where the cold and damp will kill her if the poison does not. She has even spoken to little Katherine Howard and now she knows that the king is in love. She knows that ahead of her there must be shame and divorce at the least, execution at the worst.

Yet here she sits, in the royal box, with her head held high, dropping her handkerchief to signify the start of a charge, smiling with her usual politeness on the victor, leaning forwards to put the circlet of bay leaves on his helmet, to give him a purse of gold as his prize. Pale under her modest, ugly hood, doing her duty as Queen of the

Joust as she has done her duty every day since she set foot in this country. She must be sick to her belly with terror but her hands on the front of the box are gently clasped and do not even tremble. When the king salutes her she rises up from her chair and curtseys respectfully to him, when the crowd calls her name she turns and smiles and raises her hand when a lesser woman would scream for rescue. She is utterly composed.

'She knows?' asks a quiet voice in my ear, and I turn to the Duke of Norfolk. 'Can she possibly know?'

'She knows everything but what is going to become of her,' I say.

He looks at her. 'She cannot know. She cannot have understood. She must be too stupid to understand what is going to happen to her.'

'She isn't stupid,' I say. 'She is incredibly courageous. She knows everything. She has more courage than we know.'

'She'll need it,' he says unsympathetically. 'I am taking Katherine away from court.'

'Taking her away from the king?'

'Yes.'

'Is that not a risk? Will you deprive the king of the girl of his choice?'

The duke shakes his head. He cannot hide his triumph. 'The king himself has told me to take her from court. He will marry Katherine as soon as he is rid of Anne. It is he who wants Katherine taken away. He wants her away from court so that she is not exposed to gossip while this false queen is ended.' He bites down on a smile, he is almost laughing. 'He wants no shadow of gossip attached to Katherine's unsullied name.'

'The false queen?' I pick out the strange new title.

'She was not free to marry. The marriage was never valid, it has not been consummated. God guided his conscience and he did not fulfil his vows. God prevented him from consummating the marriage. The marriage is false. The queen is false. It is probably treason to make a false declaration to the king.'

I blink. It is the king's right, as God's representative on earth, to rule on such matters but sometimes us mortals are a little slow to follow the whimsical changes of God. 'It is over for her?' I make a little gesture to the girl at the front of the box who stands now to acknowledge the salute of the champion, and raises her hand and smiles at the crowd who shouts her name.

'She is finished,' the duke says.

'Finished?'

'Finished.'

I nod. I suppose this means that they will kill her.

Anne, Westminster Palace, June 1540

My brother has finally sent the documents that show that indeed I was never married before I came to England, that my marriage to the king was my first wedding, and it is valid, as I know, as everybody knows. The documents arrived by messenger today, but my ambassador cannot present them. The king's Privy Council is in almost constant meeting, and we cannot find out what they are discussing. Having insisted on having this document, they now cannot be troubled even to see it; and what this new indifference means I cannot guess.

God knows what they are planning to do with me, my horror is that they will accuse me of something shameful and I will die in this distant land, and my mother will believe that her daughter died a whore.

I know that terrible trouble is brewing because of the danger that has come to my friends. Lord Lisle, who welcomed me so kindly to Calais, has been arrested and no-one can tell me the charges he faces. His wife has disappeared from my rooms, without saying goodbye. She did not come to ask me to intercede for him. This must mean either that he is to die without trial – dear God, perhaps he is dead already – or that she knows I have no influence with the king. Either way this is a disaster for him and for me. Nobody can tell me where Lady Lisle is hiding, and, in truth, I am afraid to ask. If her husband is charged with treason then any suggestion that he was a friend of mine will count against me.

Their daughter, Anne Bassett, is still in my service but she claims that she is ill and has taken to her bed. I wanted to see her but Lady Rochford says that it is safer for the girl if she is allowed to be alone. So her bedroom door is shut and the shutters in her room are closed. Whether she is a danger to me or I am to her, I dare not ask.

I have sent for Thomas Cromwell who, at least, is blessed with the king's favour since he was made Earl of Essex only a few weeks ago. Thomas Cromwell at least must stand my friend while my women whisper behind their hands and everyone at court is poised for disaster. But my lord Cromwell has, so far, sent me no reply. Someone surely must tell me what is happening.

I wish we were back at Hampton Court. It is hot today, and I feel cooped up, like a gyrfalcon in a crowded mews, a white falcon, hardly of this world: a bird as white as the winter snows and born to be free in the cold, wild places. I could wish myself back at Calais or even Dover when the road ahead of me lay to London and to my future as Queen of England, and I was full of hope. I could wish myself almost anywhere but here, looking through the little leaded window panes to a bright blue sky, wondering why my friend Lord Lisle is in the Tower of London, and why my supporter Thomas Cromwell does not reply to my urgent request that he come to me at once. Surely he can come and tell me why the council has been meeting in all but secret for days? Surely he will come and tell me why Lady Lisle has disappeared and why her husband is under arrest? Surely he will come soon?

The door opens and I start up, expecting him; but it is not Cromwell, nor his man, but little Katherine Howard, her face wan and her eyes tragic. She has her travelling cape over her arm and as soon as I see it I feel a wave of nausea from sheer terror. Little Kitty has been arrested, she too has been charged with some crime. Quickly I go to her and take her hands.

'Kitty? What is it? What is the charge?'

'I'm safe,' she gasps. 'It's all right. I am safe. I am just to go home to my grandmother, for a while.'

'But why? What do they say you have done?'

Her little face is twisted with distress. 'I am not to be your maid in waiting any more.'

'You are not?'

'No. I have come to say goodbye.'

'What have you done?' I cry out. Surely this girl, not much more than a child, cannot have committed any crime? The worst thing that Katherine Howard is capable of is vanity and flirtation, and this is not a court that punishes such sins. 'I will not let them take you away. I defend you. I know you are good girl. What do they say against you?'

'I have done nothing,' she says. 'But they tell me it is better for me to be away from court while all this is happening.'

'All what? Oh, Kitty, tell me quickly, what you know?'

She beckons me and I bend down so that she can whisper in my ear. 'Anne, Your Grace I mean, dearest queen. Thomas Cromwell has been arrested for treason.'

'Treason? Cromwell?'

'Ssh. Yes.'

'What has he done?'

'He conspired with Lord Lisle and the Papists to put the king under an enchantment.'

My mind is spinning, and I don't fully understand what she is saying. 'A what? What is that?'

'Thomas Cromwell made a spell,' she says.

When she sees I still do not understand the word she gently takes my face and draws it down so that she can whisper in my ear again. 'Thomas Cromwell employed a witch,' she says softly, without any inflection. 'Thomas Cromwell hired a witch to destroy His Majesty the king.'

She leans back to see if I understand her now and the horror in my face tells her that I do.

'They know this for true?'

She nods.

'Who is the witch?' I breathe. 'What has she done?'

'She has put the king under a spell so he is unmanned,' she says. 'She has cursed the king so that he shall not have a son by you.'

'Who is the witch?' I demand. 'Who is Thomas Cromwell's witch? Who has unmanned the king? Who do they say she is?' Katherine's little face is pinched with fear. 'Anne, Your Grace, my dearest queen, what if they say it is you?'

I live almost withdrawn from the world, emerging from my rooms only to dine before the court when I try to appear serene, or, better still, innocent. They are questioning Thomas Cromwell and the arrests go on, other men are accused of treason against the king, accused of employing a witch to blight his manhood. There is a network of plotters unfolding. Lord Lisle is said to have been the focus in Calais, he aided the Papists and the Pole family who have long wanted to recapture the throne from the Tudors. His second in command at the fortress has fled to Rome to serve under Cardinal Pole, which proves the guilt. They say that Lord Lisle and his party have worked with a witch to make sure that the king should not have a fruitful marriage with me, shall not make another heir to his reformed religion. But at the same time, it is said that Thomas Cromwell was aiding the Lutherans, the reformers, the evangelicals. It is said he brought me in to marry the king and ordered a witch to unman the king so that he could put his own line on the throne. But who is the witch? the court asks itself. Who is the witch who was friends with Lord Lisle, and was brought to England by Thomas Cromwell? Who is the witch? What woman is indicated by both of these nightmares of evil? Ask it again, what woman was brought to England by Thomas Cromwell; but is friends with Lord Lisle?

Clearly, there is only one woman.

Only one woman, brought to England by Thomas Cromwell, befriended by Lord Lisle, unmanning the king so that he was impotent on the night of his wedding and every night thereafter.

No-one has named the witch yet, they are gathering evidence.

Princess Mary's departure has been brought forwards and I have only a moment with her as we wait for them to bring the horses round from the stables.

'You know I am innocent of any wrongdoing,' I say to her under cover of the noise of the servants running around and her guards calling for their horses. 'Whatever you hear in the future about me, please believe me: I am innocent.'

'Of course,' she says levelly. She does not look at me. She is Henry's daughter, she has served a long apprenticeship in learning not to betray herself. 'I shall pray for you every day. I shall pray that they all see your innocence as I do.'

'I am certain that Lord Lisle is innocent too,' I say.

'Without doubt,' she replies in the same abrupt way.

'Can I save him? Can you?'

'No.'

'Princess Mary, on your faith, can nothing be done?'

She risks a sideways glance at me. 'Dearest Anne, nothing. There is nothing to do but to keep our own counsel and pray for better times.'

'Will you tell me something?'

She looks around and sees that her horses have not yet come. She takes my arm and we walk a little way towards the stable yard as if we are looking to see how long they will be. 'What is it?'

'Who is this Pole family? And why does the king fear the Papists when he defeated them so long ago?'

'The Poles are the Plantagenet family, of the House of York, some would say the true heirs to the throne of England,' she says. 'Lady Margaret Pole was my mother's truest friend, she was as a mother to me, she is utterly loyal to the throne. The king has her in the Tower now, with all of her family that he could capture. They are accused of treason, but everyone knows they have committed no offence but being of Plantagenet blood. The king is so fearful for his throne that I think he will not allow this family to live. Lady Margaret's two grandsons, two little boys, are in the Tower also, God help them. She, my dearest Lady Margaret, she will not be allowed to live. Others of the family are in exile, they can never come home.'

'They are Papists?' I ask.

'Yes,' she says quietly. 'They are. One of them, Reginald, is a cardinal. Some would say they are the true kings of the true faith of England. But that would be treason and you would be put to death for saying it.'

'And why does the king fear the Papists so much? I thought England was converted to the reformed faith? I thought the Papists were defeated?'

Princess Mary shakes her head. 'No. I should think fewer than half the people welcome the changes and many wish for the old ways back again. When the king denied the authority of the Pope and destroyed the monasteries there was a great rising of men in the north of the country, determined to defend the church and the holy houses. They called it the Pilgrimage of Grace and they marched under the banner of the five wounds of Jesus Christ. The king sent the hardest man in the kingdom against them at the head of the army, and he feared them so badly that he called for a parley, spoke with sweet words, and promised them a pardon and a parliament.'

'Who was that?' Already I know.

'Thomas Howard, Duke of Norfolk.'

'And the pardon?'

'As soon as the army had disbanded, he beheaded the leaders and hanged the followers.' She speaks with as little inflection as if she is complaining that the luggage wagon is badly packed. 'He promised a parliament and a pardon on the king's sacred word. He gave his own word too, on his honour. It meant nothing.'

'They are defeated?'

'Well, he hanged seventy monks from the roof timbers of their own abbey,' she says bitterly. 'So they won't defy him again. But no, I believe the true faith will never be defeated.'

She turns us so that we are strolling back to the door again. She smiles and nods at someone who calls 'safe journey' to her, but I cannot smile too.

'The king fears his own people,' she says. 'He fears rivals. He even fears me. He is my father and yet sometimes I think he has gone half-mad with mistrust. Any fear he has, however foolish, is real to him. If he so much as dreams that Lord Lisle has betrayed him, then Lord Lisle is a dead man. If someone suggests that his troubles with you are part of a plot, then you are in the gravest of danger. If you can get away, you should do. He cannot tell fear from truth. He cannot tell nightmares from reality.'

'I am Queen of England,' I say. 'They cannot accuse me of witchcraft.'

She turns to face me for the first time. 'That won't save you,' she says. 'It didn't save Anne Boleyn. They accused her of witchcraft and they found the evidence and they found her guilty. She was as much queen as you.' She suddenly laughs as if I have said something funny, and I see that some of my ladies have come out of the hall and are watching us. I laugh too but I am sure anyone could hear the fear in my voice. She takes my arm. 'If anyone asks me what we were talking about when we walked out and back to the steps again, I shall say that I was complaining that I would be late, and I was afraid of being tired.'

'Yes,' I agree but I am so frightened that I am shaking as if I were chilled with cold. 'I shall say you were looking to see when they would be ready.'

Princess Mary presses my arm. 'My father has changed the laws of this land,' she says. 'It is now a crime of treason, punishable by death, even to think ill of the king. You don't have to say anything, you don't have to do anything. Your own secret thoughts are treason now.'

'I am queen,' I maintain stubbornly.

'Listen,' she says bluntly. 'He has changed the process of justice too. You don't have to be condemned by a court. You can be condemned to death on a Bill of Attainder. That is nothing more than the king's order, supported by his parliament. And they never refuse to support him. Queen or beggar, if the king wants you dead he just has to order it now. He does not even have to sign the warrant for an execution, he only has to use a seal.'

I find I am clenching my jaw to stop my teeth from chattering. 'What do you think I should do?'

'Get away,' she says. 'Get away before he comes for you.'

After she has gone I feel as if my last friend has left court. I go back to my rooms and my ladies set up a table of cards. I let them start to play and then I summon my ambassador and take him into the window bay where we cannot be overheard, to ask him if anyone has questioned him about me. He says they have not, he is ignored by everyone, isolated as if he were carrying the plague. I ask him if he could hire or buy two fast horses and keep them outside the castle walls in case of my sudden need. He says he has no money to hire or buy horses, and in any case the king has guards on my doors night and day. The men who I thought were there to keep me safe, to open the doors to my presence chamber, to announce my guests, are now my gaolers.

I am very afraid. I try to pray but even the words of the prayers are a trap. I cannot appear as if I am becoming a Papist, a Papist like Lord Lisle is now said to be; and yet I must not appear to have held to my brother's religion; the Lutherans are suspected of being part of Cromwell's plot to ruin the king.

When I see the king I try to behave pleasantly and calmly before him. I dare not challenge him, nor even protest my innocence. Most frightening of all is his manner to me, which is now warm and friendly, as if we were acquaintances about to part after a short journey together. He behaves as if our time together has been an enjoyable interlude that is now naturally drawing to a close.

He will not say goodbye to me, I know that. Princess Mary has warned me of that. There is no point waiting for the moment when he tells me that I am to face an accusation. I know that one of these evenings when I rise from the dinner table and curtsey to him and he kisses my hand so courteously will be the last time I ever see him. I may walk from the hall with my ladies following me to find my rooms filled with soldiers and my clothes already packed, my jewels returned to the treasury. It is a short journey from the palace of Westminster to the Tower, they will take me by river in the darkness and I will go in by the watergate, and I will leave by the block on Tower Green.

The ambassador has written to my brother to say that I am desperately frightened; but I do not hope for a reply. William will not mind me being sick with fear, and by the time they learn of the charges against me it will be too late to save me. And perhaps William would not even choose to save me. He has allowed this peril to come about, he must have hated me more than I ever knew.

If anyone is to save me, it will have to be me, myself. But how can a woman save herself against the charge of witchcraft? If Henry tells the world that he is impotent because I have unmanned him, how can I prove differently? If he tells the world that he can lie with Katherine Howard but not with me, then his case is proved and my denial is just another instance of satanic cunning. A woman cannot prove her innocence when a man bears witness against her. If Henry wants me strangled as a witch then nothing can save me. He claimed that Lady Anne Boleyn was a witch and she died for it. He never said goodbye to her, and he had loved her with a passion. They just came for her one day and took her away.

I am waiting now, for them to come for me.

Jane Boleyn, Westminster Palace, June 1540

A note, dropped into my lap by one of the servers at dinner as he leans over to clear the meat platter, bids me go to my lord at once, and as soon as dinner is over, I do as I am told. These days, the queen goes into her bedroom straight after dinner, she will not miss me from the nervous huddle of those of us that are left in her depleted rooms. Katherine Howard is missing from court, gone back to her grandmother's house at Lambeth. Lady Lisle is under house arrest for her husband's grave crimes, they say she is quite frantic with distress and fear. She knows he will die. Lady Rutland is quiet and goes to her own rooms at night, she must be fearful too; but I don't know what accusation she might face. Anne Bassett has gone to stay with her cousin under the pretence of illness, Catherine Carey has been sent for by her mother, Mary. She asks permission for Catherine to come home as she is unwell. I could laugh at the transparent excuse. Mary Boleyn was always skilled at keeping herself and hers far from trouble. A pity she never exerted herself for her brother. Mary Norris has to help her mother in the country with some special tasks. Henry Norris's widow saw the scaffold last time the king plotted against his wife. She won't want to see her daughter climb the steps that her husband trod.

We are all of us guarded in our speech and retiring in our behaviour. The bad times have come to King Henry's court once more, and everyone is afraid, everyone is under suspicion. It is like living in a nightmare, every man, every woman knows that every word they say, every gesture they make, might be used in evidence against them. An enemy might work up an indiscretion into a crime, a friend might trade a confidence for a guarantee of safety. We are a court of cowards and tale bearers. Nobody walks any more, we all tiptoe, nobody even breathes, we are all holding our breath. The king has turned suspicious of his friends and nobody can be sure that they are safe.

I creep to my lord duke's rooms, walking in the shadows, and I open the door and slip in, in silence. My lord duke is standing by the window, the shutters open to the warm night air, the candles on his desk bobbing their flames in the draught. He looks up and smiles when I enter the room, I could almost think that he is fond of me.

'Ah, Jane, my niece. The queen is to go to Richmond with a much-reduced court, I want you to go with her.'

'Richmond?' I hear the quaver of fear in my own voice and I take a breath. This means house arrest while they inquire into the allegations against her. But why are they sending me in with her? Am I to be charged too?

'Yes. You will stay with her and keep a careful note of who comes and goes, and anything she says. In particular, you are to be alert for Ambassador Harst. We think he can do nothing, but you would oblige me by seeing that she has no plans to escape, sends no messages, that sort of thing.'

'Please . . .' I stop myself, my voice has come out weak. I know this is not the way to deal with him.

'What?' He is still smiling but his dark eyes are intent.

'I cannot prevent her escaping. I am one woman, alone.'

He shakes his head. 'The ports are closed from tonight. Her ambassador has discovered that there is not a horse to buy or hire in the whole of England. Her own stables are barred. Her rooms closed. She won't be able to escape or send for help. Everyone in her service is her gaoler. You just have to watch her.'

'Please let me go and serve Katherine,' I take a breath to say. 'She will need advice if she is to be a good queen.'

The duke pauses for thought. 'She will,' he says. 'She is an idiot, that girl. But she can come to no harm with her grandmother.'

He taps his thumbnail against his tooth, considering.

'She will need to learn to be a queen,' I say.

He hesitates. We two have known Queens of England who were queens indeed. Little Katherine is not fit to touch their shoes, let alone walk in them, years of training would not make her regal. 'No she won't,' he says. 'The king doesn't want a great queen beside him any more. He wants a girl to pet, a little filly, a young brood-mare for his seed. Katherine need be nothing more than obedient.'

'Then let me say the truth: I don't want to go to Richmond with Queen Anne. I don't want to bear witness against this queen.'

His sharp, dark eyes look up quickly at me. 'Witness of what?' he demands.

I am too weary to fence. 'Witness of whatever you want me to see,' I say. 'Whatever the king want me to say, I don't want to say it. I don't want to bear witness against her.'

'Why not?' he asks, as if he did not know.

'I am sick of trials,' I say from the heart. 'I am afraid of the king's desires now. I don't know what he wants. I don't know how far he will go. I don't want to give evidence at a queen's trial – not ever again.'

'I am sorry,' he says without regret. 'But we need someone to swear that she had a conversation with the queen in which the queen made it clear that she was a virgin untouched, absolutely untouched, and moreover quite ignorant of any doings between a man and a maid.'

'She has been in bed with him night after night,' I say impatiently. 'We all put her to bed the first night. You were there, the Archbishop of Canterbury was there. She was raised to conceive a son and bear

254

an heir, she was married for that single purpose. She could hardly be ignorant of the doings of a man and a maid. No woman in the world has endured more unsuccessful attempts.'

'That is why we need a lady of unimpeachable reputation to swear it,' he says smoothly. 'Such an unlikely lie needs a plausible witness: you.'

'Any of the others can do that for you,' I protest. 'Since the conversation never happened, since it is an impossible conversation, surely it does not matter who says that it took place?'

'I should like our name entered as witness,' the duke says. 'The king would be pleased to see our service. It would do us good.'

'Is it to prove her a witch?' I ask bluntly. I am too weary of my work and sick of myself to pick my way around my ducal uncle tonight. 'Is it, in fact, to prove her a witch and have her sent to her death?'

He draws himself up to his full height and looks down his nose at me. 'It is not for us to predict what the king's commissioners might find,' he says. 'They will sift the evidence, and give the verdict. All you will provide is a sworn statement, sworn on your faith before God.'

'I don't want her death on my conscience.' I can hear the desperation in my voice. 'Please. Let someone else swear to it. I don't want to go with her to Richmond and then swear a lie against her. I don't want to stand by while they take her to the Tower. I don't want her to die on the basis of my false evidence. I have been her friend, I don't want to be her assassin.'

He waits in silence till my torrent of refusals is finished, then he looks at me and smiles again, but now there is no warmth in his face at all. 'Certainly,' he says. 'You will swear only to the statement that we will have prepared for you, and your betters will decide what is to be done for the queen. You will keep me informed of whom she sees and what she does in the usual way, my man will go with you to Richmond. You will watch her with care. She is not to escape.

And when it is over, you will be Katherine's lady in waiting, you will have your place at court, you will be lady in waiting to the new Queen of England. That will be your reward. You will be the first lady at the new queen's court. I promise it. You will be head of her privy chamber.'

He thinks he has bought me with this promise but I am sick of this life. 'I can't go on doing this,' I say simply. I am thinking of Anne Boleyn, and of my husband, and of the two of them going into the Tower with all the evidence against them, and none of it true. I am thinking of them going to their death knowing that their family had borne witness against them, and their uncle passed the death sentence. I am thinking of them, trusting in me, waiting for me to come to give evidence for their defence, confident in my love for them, certain that I would save them. 'I cannot go on doing this.'

'I should hope not,' he says primly. 'Please God that you will never do it again. In my niece Katherine, the king has at last found a true and honourable wife. She is a rose without a thorn.'

'A what?'

'A rose without a thorn,' the duke repeats. He keeps his face perfectly straight. 'That is what we are to call her. That is what he wants us to call her.'

Katherine, Norfolk House, Lambeth, June 1540

Now, let me see, what do I have? I have the murderers' houses that the king first gave me, and their lands. I have the jewels I earned by a quick squeeze in a quiet gallery. I have half a dozen gowns, paid for by my uncle, most of them new, and hoods to match. I have a bedchamber of my own at my grandmother's house and my own presence chamber too, and a few maids in waiting but no ladies as yet. I buy dresses almost every day, the merchants come across the river with bolts of silk as if I were a dressmaker on my own account. They fit me with gowns and they mutter with their mouths filled with pins that I am the most beautiful, the most exquisite girl ever to be stitched into a too-tight stomacher. They bend to the floor to hem up my gown and say that they have never seen such a pretty girl, a very queen among girls.

I love it. If I were more thoughtful, or a graver soul, then I know I would be troubled by the thought of my poor mistress the queen and what will become of her, and the disagreeable thought that soon I shall marry a man who has buried three wives and maybe will bury his fourth, and is old enough to be my grandfather, as well as very smelly . . . but I cannot be troubled with such worries. The other wives did as they had to do, their lives ended as God and the king willed; it is really nothing to me. Even my cousin Anne Boleyn shall be nothing to me. I shall not think of her, nor of our uncle pushing her on to the throne and then pushing her on to the scaffold. She had her gowns and her court and her jewels. She had her time of being the finest young woman at court, she had her time of being the favourite of her family and the pride of us all; and now I shall have mine.

I will have my time. I will be merry. I am as hungry as she was, for the colour and the wealth, for the diamonds and the flirting, the horses and the dancing. I want my life, I want the very, very best of everything; and by luck, and by the whim of the king (whom God preserve), I am to have the very, very best. I had hoped to be spotted by one of the great men of the court and chosen for his kinswoman and given in marriage to a young nobleman who might rise through the court. That was the very pinnacle of my hopes. But instead, everything is to be different. Much better. The king himself has seen me, the King of England desires me, the man who is God on earth, who is the father of his people, who is the law and the word, desires me. I have been chosen by God's own representative on earth. No-one can stand in his way and no-one would dare deny him. This is no ordinary man who has seen me and desired me, this is not even a mortal. This is a half-god who has seen me. He desires me and my uncle tells me it is my duty and my honour to accept his proposal. I will be Queen of England – think of that! I will be Queen of England. Then we shall see what I, little Kitty Howard, can count as my own!

Actually, in truth I am torn between terror and excitement at the thought of being his consort and his queen, the greatest woman in England. I have a vain thrill that he wants me, and I make sure that I think about that, and ignore my sense of disappointment that although he is almost God, he is only a man like any other, and a very old man at that, and an old man who is half-impotent at that, an old man who cannot even do the job in the jakes, and I must play him as I would any old man who in his lust and vanity happened to desire me. If he gives me what I want, he shall have my favour,

I cannot say fairer than that. I could almost laugh at myself, granting the greatest man in the world my little favour. But if he wants it, and if he will pay so highly for it, then I am in the market like any huckster: selling myself.

Grandmother, the duchess, tells me that I am her clever, clever girl and that I will bring wealth and greatness to our family. To be queen is a triumph beyond our most ambitious dreams, but there is a hope even beyond that. If I conceive a son and give birth to a boy, then our family will rise as high as the Seymours. And if the Seymour boy Prince Edward were to die (though God forbid, of course), but *if* he were to die then my son would be the next King of England and us Howards would be kinsmen to the king. Then we would be the royal family, or as good as, and then we would be the greatest family in England, and everyone would have to thank me for their good fortune. My uncle Norfolk would bow his knee to me and bless me for my patronage. When I think of this, I giggle and cannot daydream any more, for sheer delight.

I am sorry to my heart for my mistress Queen Anne. I would have liked to stay as her maid and to see her become happy. But what cannot be, cannot be, and I would be foolish indeed to mourn over my own good fortune. She is like those poor men executed so that I can have their lands, or the poor nuns thrown from their homes so that we can all be richer. Such people have to suffer for our benefit. I have learned that this is the way of the world. And it's not my fault that the world is a hard place for others. I hope she finds happiness as I will do. Perhaps she will go home to her brother in wherever-it-is. Poor dear. Perhaps she will marry the man that she was betrothed to marry. My uncle tells me that she was very wrong to come to England when she knew she was bound to marry another man. This was a very shocking thing to do and I am surprised at her. She always seemed such a well-behaved young woman, I cannot believe that she would do such a naughty thing. Of course when my uncle speaks of a prior betrothal I cannot help but think of my poor, dear Francis Dereham. I have never mentioned the promises we exchanged, and really, I think it best that I just forget all about it, and pretend that it never happened. It is not always easy to be a young woman in this world that is full of temptation for sure, and I do not criticise Queen Anne for being betrothed to another and then marrying the king. I wouldn't do it myself, of course, but since Francis Dereham and I were not properly married, nor even properly betrothed, I do not consider it. I didn't have a proper gown, so clearly it wasn't a proper wedding or binding vows. All we did was the daydreaming of little children and a few innocent kisses. No more than that, really. But she could do worse, if she is sent home, than to marry her first love. I myself shall always think of Francis with affection. One's first love is always very sweet, probably sweeter than a very old husband. When I am queen I shall do something very kind for Francis.

Anne, Westminster Palace,
10 June 1540

Dear God, save me, dear God, save me, every one of my friends or allies is in the Tower and I do not doubt but they will soon come for me. Thomas Cromwell, the man given the credit for bringing me to England, is arrested, charged with treason. Treason! He has been the king's servant, he has been his dog. He is no more capable of treason than one of the king's greyhounds. Clearly, the man is no traitor. Clearly, he has been arrested to punish him for making my marriage. If this charge brings him to the block and the executioner's axe, then there can be little doubt that I will follow.

The man who first welcomed me into Calais, my dearest Lord Lisle, is charged with treason and also with being a secret Papist, party to a Papist plot. They are saying that he welcomed me as queen because he knew that I would prevent the king from conceiving a son. He is arrested and charged with treason for a plot that names me as one of the elements. It is no defence that he is innocent. It is no defence that the plot is absurd. In the cellars of the Tower are terrible rooms where wicked men go about cruel work. A man will say anything after he has been tortured by one of them. The human body cannot resist the pain that they can inflict. The king allows the prisoners to be torn, legs from body, arms from shoulders. Such barbarity is new to this country; but it is allowed now, as the king turns into a monster. Lord Lisle is gently born, quietly spoken. He cannot tolerate pain, surely he will tell them what they wish, what-ever it is. Then he will go to the block a confessed traitor, and who knows what they will have made him confess about me?

The net is closing around me. It is so close now that I can almost see the cords. If Lord Lisle says that he knew I would make the king impotent, then I am a dead woman. If Thomas Cromwell says he knew that I was betrothed and that I married the king when I was not free to do so, then I am a dead woman. They have my friend Lord Lisle, they have my ally Thomas Cromwell. They will torture them until they have the evidence they need, and then come for me. In all of England, there is only one man who might help me. I don't have much hope but I have no other friend. I send for my ambas-sador, Carl Harst.

It is a hot day and the windows are all standing wide open to the air from the garden. From outside I can hear the sound of the court boating on the river. They are playing lutes and singing and I can hear the laughter. Even at this distance I can hear the sharp note of forced merriment. The room is cool and in shadow but we are both sweating.

'I have hired horses,' he says in our language, in a hiss of a whisper. 'I had to go all over the city to find them and in the end I bought them from some Hanseatic merchants. I have borrowed money for the journey. I think we should go at once. As soon as I can find a guard to bribe.'

'At once,' I nod. 'We must go at once. What do they say of Cromwell?'

'It is barbaric. They are savages. He walked into the Privy Council with no idea that there was anything wrong. His old friends and fellow noblemen stripped him of his badges of office, of his Order of the Garter. They pecked at him like crows tear at a dead rabbit. He was marched away like a felon. He will not even stand trial, they need call no witnesses, they need prove no charges. He will be beheaded by a Bill of Attainder, it needs only the word of the king.'

'Might the king not say the word? Will he not grant him mercy? He made him earl only weeks ago to show his favour.'

'A feint, it was nothing but a feint. The king showed his favour only so that his spite falls more heavily now. Cromwell will beg for mercy, sure of forgiveness, he will find none. He is certain to die a traitor's death.'

'Did the king say farewell to him?' I ask, as if it is an idle question.

'No,' the ambassador says. 'There was nothing to warn the man. They parted as on any ordinary day, with no special words. Cromwell came into the meeting of the council as if nothing was out of the ordinary. He thought that he had come to command the meeting as Secretary of State, in his pomp and his power, and then, in moments, he found himself under arrest and his old enemies laughing at him.'

'The king did not say goodbye,' I say in a sort of quiet horror. 'It is as they say. The king never says goodbye.'

Jane Boleyn, Westminster Palace, 24 June, 1540

We are seated in the queen's room in silence, sewing shirts for the poor. Katherine Howard is missing from her place, she has been staying with her grandmother at Norfolk House, Lambeth all this week. The king visits her almost every evening, he takes his dinner with them as if he were a private man, not king at all. He is rowed across the river in the royal barge, he goes openly, he takes no trouble to conceal his identity.

The whole of the city is buzzing with the belief that only six months into the marriage the king has taken a mistress in the Howard girl. The spectacularly ignorant claim that since the king has a lover, therefore the queen must be pregnant, and everything is well in this most blessed world: a Tudor son and heir in the queen's belly and the king taking his own amusement elsewhere as he always does. Those of us who know better do not even take the pleasure of correcting those who know nothing. We know that Katherine Howard is guarded like a vestal virgin now, against the king's feeble seductive powers. We know that the queen is still untouched. What we don't know, what we cannot know, is what is going to happen.

In the absence of the king, the court has become unruly and when Queen Anne and we ladies go to our dinner, the throne is empty at the head of the room and there is no rule. The hall is avid, like a buzzing hive, seething with gossip and rumour. Everyone wants to be on the winning side, but no-one knows which that will turn out to be. There are gaps at the great tables where some of the families have left court altogether, either from fear, or from distaste at the new terror. Anyone who is known for Papist sympathies is in danger, and has gone to his country estates. Anyone who is in favour of reform fears that the king has turned against it with a Howard girl favourite again and Stephen Gardiner composing the prayers, which are just as they were when they came from Rome, and the reforming Archbishop Cranmer is quite out of fashion. Left behind at court are the opportunist and the reckless. It is as if the whole world is becoming unravelled with the unravelling of order. The queen pushes her food around her plate with her golden fork, her head bowed low so as to avoid the bright, curious stares of the people who have come to see a queen abandoned on her throne, deserted in her palace, who come in their hundreds to see her, avid to see a queen on her last night at court, perhaps her last night on earth.

We return to our rooms as soon as the board is cleared, there are no entertainments for the king after dinner because he is never here. It is almost as if there is no king, and in his absence no queen, and no court. Everything is changed, or waiting fearfully for more change. Nobody knows what will happen, and everyone is alert to any sign of danger.

And there is talk, all the time, of more arrests. Today, I heard that Lord Hungerford has been taken to the Tower, and when they told me of his crimes it was as if I had walked from the midday sun into an ice house. He is accused of unnatural behaviour, as my husband was: sodomy with another man. He is accused of forcing his daughter, as my husband George was accused of incest with his sister Anne. He is accused of treason and foretelling the king's death, just like George and Anne, charged together. Perhaps his wife will be invited to witness against him, just as they asked me to do. I shiver at the thought of this, it takes me all my willpower to sit quietly in the queen's room and make my stitches neat on the hems. I can hear a drumming in my ears, I can feel the blood heating my cheeks as if I am ill with a fever. It is happening again, King Henry is turning on his friends again.

This is a blood-letting again, a scatter of charges against those the king wants out of his sight. Last time Henry sought vengeance, the long days of his hatred took my husband, four others, and the Queen of England. Who can doubt but that Henry is about to do it again? But who can know who he will take?

The only sound in the queen's rooms is the little patter of a dozen needles piercing rough cloth, and the whisper of the thread being pulled through. All the laughter and music and gaming that used to fill the arched room has been silenced. None of us dares to speak. The queen was always guarded, careful in her speech. Now, in these fearful days, she is more than discreet, she is struck dumb, in a state of silent terror.

I have seen a queen in fear of her life before; I know what it is like to be at the queen's court when we are all waiting for something to happen. I know how the queen's ladies glance furtively, when they know in their hearts that the queen will be taken away, and who knows where else the blame will fall?

There are several empty seats in the queen's rooms. Katherine Howard has gone, and the rooms are a quieter, duller place without her. Lady Lisle is partly in hiding, partly seeking out the few friends who dare to acknowledge her, sick with crying. Lady Southampton has made an excuse to go away. I think that she fears her husband will be caught in the trap that is being set to catch the queen. Southampton was another friend of the queen's when she first came to England. Anne Bassett has managed to be ill since the arrest of her father, and has gone to her kinswoman. Catherine Carey has been taken from court, without a word of notice, by her mother who knows all about the fall of queens. Mary Norris has been summoned away by her mother who will also find these events too familiar. All of those who promised the queen their unending, undying friendship are now terrified that she will claim it and they will go down with her fall. All her ladies are afraid that they may be caught in the trap that is being primed to catch the queen.

All of us, that is, except those who already know that they are not the victims but the trap itself. The king's agents at the court of the queen are Lady Rutland, Catherine Edgecombe, and me. When she is arrested we three will give evidence against her. Thus will we be safe. At least we three will be safe.

I have not yet been told what evidence I shall give, just that I will be required to swear to a written statement. I am beyond caring. I asked the duke my uncle if I might be spared and he says that on the contrary I should be glad that the king should put his faith in me again. I think I can say or do no more. I shall give myself up to these times, I shall bob along like a bit of driftwood on the tide of the king's whim. I shall try to keep my own head above the water and pity those that drown beside me. And, if I am honest, I may keep my own head up by pushing another down, and snatching at their air. In a shipwreck, it is every drowning man for himself.

There is a thunderous knock at the door and a girl screams. We all jump to our feet, certain the soldiers are at the door, we are waiting for the word of our arrest. I look quickly at the queen and she is white, whiter than salt, I have never seen a woman blanch so pale except in death. Her lips are actually blue with fear.

The door opens. It is my uncle, the Duke of Norfolk, looking long-faced and cadaverous with his black hat on his head like a hanging judge.

'Your Grace,' he says and comes in and bows low to her.

She sways like a silver birch tree. I go to her side and take her arm to keep her steady. I feel her shudder at my touch, and I realise that she thinks I am arresting her, holding her while my uncle pronounces sentence.

'It's all right,' I whisper; but of course I do not know that it is all right. For all I know there are half a dozen of the royal guard standing out of sight in the corridor.

She holds her head high, and she raises herself up to her full height. 'Goot evening,' she says in her funny way. 'My lord duke.'

'I am come from the Privy Council,' he says, as smooth as funeral silk. 'I regret to say that the plague has broken out in the city.'

She frowns slightly, trying to follow the words, these are not what she was expecting. The ladies stir, we all know there is no plague.

'The king is anxious for your safety,' he says slowly. 'He commands you to move to Richmond Palace.'

I feel her sway. 'He comes also?'

'No.'

So everyone will know that she has been sent away. If there was plague in the city, then King Henry would be the last man in the world to be boating up and down on the Thames tra-la-la-la-ing with his lute and a new love song all the way to the Lambeth horse ferry. If there were sickness in the evening mists curling off the river then Henry would be away to the New Forest, or to Essex. He has an utter terror of illness. The prince would be despatched to Wales, the king would be long gone.

So anyone who knows the king knows that this report of plague is a lie, and that the truth must be that this is the start of the queen's ordeal. First, house arrest, while the inquiry goes on, then a charge, then a court hearing, then judgement, the sentence, and death. Thus it was for Queen Katherine, for Queen Anne Boleyn, so it will be for Queen Anne of Cleves.

'I will see him before I leave?' she asks, poor little thing, her voice is trembling.

'His Grace bade me come to tell you to leave tomorrow morning. He will visit you, without doubt, at Richmond Palace.'

She staggers and her legs buckle beneath her; if I were not holding her up she would fall. The duke nods at me, as if commending a job well done, then he steps back and bows, and takes himself from the room as if he were not Death himself, come for the bride.

I lower the queen into her chair and send one of the girls for a glass of water, and another running to the cellarer for a glass of brandy. When they come back I make her drink from one glass and then the other, and she lifts up her head and looks at me.

'I must see my ambassador,' she says huskily.

I nod, she can see him if she likes; but there will be nothing he can do to save her. I send one of the pages to find Dr Harst. He will be dining in the hall, he finds his way in every mealtime to one of the tables at the back. The Duke of Cleves has not paid him enough to set up his own house like a proper ambassador; the poor man has to scrounge like a mouse at the royal board.

He comes in at a run, and recoils when he sees her, seated in her chair, doubled over, as if she has been knifed in the heart.

'Leave us,' she says.

I drift to the end of the room but I don't go right outside. I stand as if I am guarding the door from the others coming in. I dare not leave her alone, even if I won't understand what is being said. I cannot risk her giving him her jewels and the two of them slipping away through the private door to the garden and the path to the river, even though I know there are sentries on the piers.

They mutter in their own language, and I see him shake his head. She is crying, trying to tell him something, and he pats her hand, and pats her elbow, and does everything but pat her head like a whipper-in might soothe a fretting bitch. I lean back against the door. This is not the man who can overthrow our plans. This man is not going to rescue her; we need not fear him. This man will still be desperately worrying about what he can do to save her as she climbs the scaffold. If she is counting on him for help, then she is as good as dead already.

Anne, Richmond Palace, July 1540

I think the waiting is the worst; and now waiting is all I do. Waiting to hear what charge they will frame against me, waiting for my arrest, and racking my brains for what defence I can make. Dr Harst and I are agreed that I must leave the country, even if it means losing my claim to the throne, breaking the contract of marriage and wrecking the alliance with Cleves. Even if it means that England will join with France in a war against Spain. To my horror, my failure to succeed in this country may mean that England is free to go to war in Europe. The one thing I hoped to bring to this country was peace and safety but my failure with the king may send them to war. And I cannot prevent it.

Dr Harst believes that my friend Lord Lisle and my sponsor Thomas Cromwell are certain to die, and that I will be next. There is nothing now I can do to save England from this outbreak of tyranny. All I can do for myself is try to save my own skin. There is no predicting the charge and no guarding against it. There will be no formal accusation in a courtroom, there will be no judges and no jury. There will be no chance to defend myself from whatever charge they have invented. Lord Lisle and Lord Cromwell will die under a Bill of Attainder, all it requires is the signature of the king. The king, who believes he is guided by God, has become a god with the full power of life and death. There can be no doubt that he is planning my death too.

I hesitate, like a fool I wait for a few days, hoping that it is not as bad as it seems. I think that the king might be well-advised by men who can see reason. I pray that God might speak to him in words of common sense and not reassure him that his own desires should be paramount. I hope that I might hear from my mother, to tell me what I should do. I even hope against hope for a message from my brother saying that he will not let them try me, he will prevent my execution, that he is sending an escort to bring me home. Then, on the very day that Dr Harst said he would come with six horses and I should be ready to leave, he comes to me, without horses, his face very grave, and says that the ports are closed. The king is letting no-one in or out of the country. No ships are allowed to sail at all. Even if we could get to the coast – and to run away would be a confession of guilt – we would not be able to sail. I am imprisoned in my new country. There is no way of getting home.

Like a fool I had thought that my difficulty would be getting past the guards at my door, getting horses, getting away from the palace without someone raising a hue and cry and coming after us. But no, the king is all-seeing, like the god he thinks he is. Getting away from the palace would have been hard enough, but now we cannot take a ship for home. I am marooned on this island. The king holds me captive.

Dr Harst thinks this means that they will come for me at once. The king has closed the whole country so that he can have me tried, found guilty, and beheaded, before my own family can even hear of my arrest. No-one in Europe can protest or cry shame! No-one in Europe will even know until it is over and I am dead. I believe this to be true. It must be within a few days, perhaps even tomorrow.

I cannot sleep. I spend the night at the window watching for the first light of dawn. I think this will be my last night on earth and I regret more than anything else that I have wasted my life. I spent all my time obeying my father and then my brother, I squandered these last months in trying to please the king, I did not treasure the little spark that is me, uniquely me. Instead I put my will and my thoughts beneath the will of the men who command me. If I had been the gyrfalcon that my father called me I would have flown high, and nested in lonely, cold places, and ridden the free wind. Instead I have been like a bird in a mews, always tied and sometimes hooded. Never free and sometimes blind.

As God is my witness, if I live through this night, through this week, I shall try to be true to myself in the future. If God spares me I shall try to honour him by being me, myself; not by being a sister or a daughter or a wife. This is an easy promise to make for I don't think I will be held to it. I don't think God will save me, I don't think Henry will spare me. I don't think I will have any life beyond next week.

As it grows light and then golden with the morning sun of summertime, I stay at my seat at the window, and they bring me a cup of small ale and a slice of bread and butter as I watch the river for the flutter of the standard and the steady dip and sweep of oars, for the coming of the royal barge to take me to the Tower. Any beat of a drum, drifting over the water to keep the rowers in time, and I can hear my heart echoing its thudding in my ears, thinking that it is them, come for me today. Funny then that when they finally come, not until mid-afternoon, it is not a troop but only a single man, Richard Beard, who arrives without warning in a little wherry, when I am walking in the garden, my hands cold in my pockets and my feet clumsy with fear. He finds me in the privy garden when I am walking among the roses, bending my head down to the blooms but unable to smell the perfume of the full-blown flowers. From a distance I must look to him like a happy woman, a young queen in a garden of roses. Only as he comes close does he see the whiteness of my blank face.

'Your Grace,' he says and bows low, as if to a queen.

I nod.

'I have brought a letter from the king.' He offers me the letter. I take it but I do not break the seal. 'What does it say?' I ask.

He does not pretend that it is a private matter. 'It is to tell you that after months of doubt the king has decided to examine his marriage to you. He fears that it is not valid because you were already contracted to marry. There is to be an inquiry.'

'He says we are not married?' I ask.

'He fears that you were not married,' he corrects me gently.

I shake my head. 'I don't understand,' I say stupidly. 'I don't understand.'

They all come then: half the Privy Council arrive with their entourage and servants, they all come to tell me that I must agree to an inquiry. I don't agree. I won't agree. They are all to stay the night here with me at Richmond Palace. I won't dine with them, I shall not agree. I shall never agree.

In the morning they tell me that three of my ladies are to be summoned to appear before the inquiry. They refuse to tell me what they will be asked, they will not even tell me who will be made to go and testify against me. I ask them for copies of the documents that are to be the evidence laid before the inquiry and they refuse to let me see anything. Dr Harst complains of this treatment, and writes to my brother; but we know that the letters will never get through until it is too late, the ports are sealed and there is no news leaving England at all. We are alone, I am alone. Dr Harst tells me that before her trial, there was an inquiry into Anne Boleyn's conduct. An inquiry: just as they will make into my conduct. The ladies of her chamber were questioned as to what she had said and done, just as mine will be. The evidence from that inquiry was used at her trial. The sentence was passed against her, and the king married Jane Seymour, her maid in waiting, within the month. They will not even hold a trial for me, it will be done on the king's signature: nothing more. Am I really going to die so that the king can marry little Kitty Howard? Can it really be possible, that I am to die so that this old man can marry a girl that he could bed for little more than the price of a gown?

Jane Boleyn, Westminster Palace, 7 July 1540

We come into the city of London by royal barge from Richmond, it is all done very fine for us, the king is sparing no trouble to make sure we are comfortable. There are three of us, Lady Rutland, Catherine Edgecombe and myself: three little Judases come to do our duty. With us, as escort, is Lord Southampton, who must feel he has some ground to regain with the king since he welcomed Anne of Cleves into England and said that she was pretty and merry and queenly. With him are Lord Audley and the Duke of Suffolk, eager to play their parts and curry favour. They will give their evidence against her to the inquiry after we have given ours.

Catherine Edgecombe is nervous, she says she does not know what she is to say, she is afraid of one of the churchmen cross-questioning her, and trapping her into saying the wrong thing, heavens, even the truth might slip out if she were to be harried – how dreadful would that be! But I am as much at ease as a bitter old fishwife gutting mackerel. 'You won't even see them,' I predict. 'You won't be cross-questioned. Who would challenge your lies? It's not as if there will be anyone wanting the truth, it's not as if there will be anyone speaking in her defence. I imagine you won't even have to speak. It will all be drawn up for us, we'll just have to sign it.'

'But what if it says . . . what if they name her as a . . .' She breaks off and looks downriver. She is too afraid even to say the word 'witch'.

'Why would you even read it?' I ask. 'What does it matter what it says above your signature? You agreed to sign it, didn't you? You didn't agree to read it.'

'But I would not have her harmed by my evidence,' she says, the ninny.

I raise my eyebrows but I say nothing. I don't need to. We all know that we have set out in the king's barge, on a lovely summer day, to be rowed up the river to destroy a young woman who has done nothing wrong.

'Did you just sign something? When you? Before?' she asks tentatively.

'No,' I say. There is a salt taste of bile in my mouth so strong that I want to spit over the side into the green, swift water. 'No. It was not done as well as this for Anne and my husband. See how we are improving in these ceremonies? Then, I had to go into court before them all and swear on the Bible and give my evidence. I had to face the court and say what I had to say against my own husband and his sister. I had to face him and say it.'

She gives a little shudder. 'That must have been dreadful.'

'It was,' I say shortly.

'You must have feared the worst.'

'I knew that my life would be saved,' I say crudely. 'And I imagine that is why you are here today, as I am, as is Lady Rutland. If Anne of Cleves is found guilty and dies, then at least we will not die with her.'

'But what will they say she has done?' Catherine asks.

'Oh, it will be us who say.' I give a harsh laugh. 'It will be us who accuse her. It will be us who make the accusation and swear to the evidence. It will be us who will say what she has done. They will just say that she will have to die for it. And we will find out her crime soon enough.'

Thank God, thank God, I have to sign nothing that blames her for the king's impotence. I don't have to give evidence that she cast a spell on him or bewitched him, or lay with half a dozen men, or gave birth in secret to a monster. This time, I have to say nothing like that. We all sign the same statement, which says only that she told us that she lay down with him every night as a maid and rose every morning as a maid, and that from what she said to us it was clear that she is such a fool that she never knew that there was anything wrong. We are supposed to have advised her that to be a wife required more than a kiss goodnight, and a blessing in the morning, we are supposed to have said that she wouldn't get a son this way; and she is supposed to have said that she was content to know no more. All this chatter is supposed to have taken place in her room between the four of us, conducted in fluent English without a moment's hesitation and no interpreter.

I seek out the duke before the barge takes us back to Richmond. 'They do realise that she doesn't talk like this?' I say. 'The conversation that we have all sworn took place could never have happened? Anyone who has been in the queen's rooms would know this at once for a lie. In real life we muddle along with the few words that she knows, and we repeat things half a dozen times before we all understand each other. And anyone who knows her would know that she would never ever speak of this with all of us together. She is far too modest.'

'It doesn't matter,' he says grandly. 'They needed a statement to say that she is a virgin, as she ever was. Nothing more.'

For the first time in weeks, I think that they might spare her. 'Is he just putting her aside?' I ask. I hardly dare to hope. 'Is he not accusing her of unmanning him?'

'He will be rid of her,' he says. 'Your statement today will serve to show her as a most deceptive and cunning witch.'

I gasp. 'How have I incriminated her as a witch?'

'You have written that she knows he is unmanned, and even in her chamber with her own women she has pretended that she knows nothing about what passes between a man and wife. As you say yourself, who could believe her claim? Who ever speaks like that? What woman put into a king's bed would know so little? What woman in the world is that ignorant? Clearly she must be lying, so clearly she is hiding a conspiracy. Clearly she is a witch.'

'But . . . but . . . I thought this statement was supposed to show her as innocent?' I stammer. 'A virgin with no knowledge?'

'Exactly,' he says. The duke allows himself a dark gleam of a smile. 'That is the beauty of it. You, all three of you highly regarded ladies of her chamber, have sworn to a statement that shows her either as innocent as the Virgin Mary, or as deeply cunning as the witch Hecate. It can be used either way, exactly as the king requires. You have done a good day's work, Jane Boleyn. I am pleased with you.'

I go to the barge saying nothing more; there is nothing I can say. He guided me once before and perhaps I should have listened to my husband, George, and not to his uncle. If George were here with me now perhaps he would advise me to go quietly to the queen and tell her to run away. Perhaps he would say that love and loyalty are more important than making one's way at court. Perhaps he would say that it is more important to keep faith with those that one loves than please the king. But George is not with me now. He will never now tell me that he believes in love. I have to live without him; for the rest of my life I will have to live without him.

We go back to Richmond. The tide is with us and I wish the barge would go more slowly and not rush us home to the palace where she will be watching for the barge and looking so very pale.

'What have we done?' asks Catherine Edgecombe dolefully. She is looking towards the beautiful towers of Richmond Palace, knowing that we will have to face Queen Anne, that her honest gaze will go from one of us to the other, and that she will know that we have been gone all day on our jaunt to London to give evidence against her.

'We have done what we had to do. We may have saved her life,' I say stubbornly.

'Like you saved your sister-in-law? Like you saved your husband?' she asks me, sharp with malice.

I turn my head away from her. 'I never speak of it,' I say. 'I never even think of it.'

Anne, Richmond Palace,
8 July 1540

It is the second day of the inquiry to conclude whether my marriage to the king is legal or not. If I were not so low in my spirits I would laugh at them sitting down in solemn convocation to sift the evidence they have themselves fabricated. We must all know what the result will be. The king has not called the churchmen, who take his pay and serve in his own church, who are all that is left now the faithful are hanging on scaffolds all around the walls of York, for them to tell him that he is inspired by nothing but lust for a pretty face, and that he should go down on his knees for forgiveness of his sins and acknowledge his marriage to me. They will oblige their master and deliver a verdict that I was pre-contracted, that I was never free to marry, that our marriage is therefore annulled. I have to remember that this is an escape for me, it could have been so much worse. If he had decided to put me aside for misconduct, they would still have heard evidence, they would still have found against me.

I see an unmarked barge coming up to the great pier and I see the king's messenger, Richard Beard, leap ashore before the ropes are even tied. Lightly he comes up the pier, looks towards the palace and sees me. He raises his hand and comes briskly over the lawns towards me. He is a busy man, he has to hurry. Slowly, I go to meet him. I know that this is the end for my hopes of being a good queen for this country, a good stepmother to my children, a good wife to a bad husband.

Silently, I hold out my hand for the letter he carries for me. Silently he gives it to me. This is the end of my girlhood. This is the end of my ambitions. This is the end of my dream. This is the end of my reign. Perhaps it is the end of my life.

Jane Boleyn, Richmond Palace,
8 July 1540

Who would have thought she would take it so hard? She has been crying like a broken-hearted girl, her useless ambassador patting her hands, and muttering to her in German like some old dark-feathered hen, that ninny Richard Beard standing on his dignity but looking like a schoolboy, agonisingly embarrassed. They start on the terrace where Richard Beard gives her the letter, then they bring her into her room when her legs give way beneath her, and they send for me as she cries herself into a screaming fit.

I bathe her face with rosewater, and then give her a glass of brandy to sip. That steadies her for a moment and she looks up at me, her eyes as red-rimmed as those of a little white rabbit.

'He denies the marriage,' she says brokenly. 'Oh, Jane, he denies me. He had me painted by Master Holbein himself, he chose me, he asked for me to come, he sent his councillors for me, he brought me to his court. He excused the dowry, he married me, he bedded me, now he denies me.'

'What does he want you to do?' I ask urgently. I want to know if Richard Beard has a guard of soldiers coming behind him, if they are going to take her away tonight.

'He wants me to agree to the verdict,' she says. 'He promises me a . . .' She breaks into tears on the word 'settlement'. These are hard words for a young wife to hear. 'He promises fair terms if I cause no trouble.'

I look at the ambassador, who is puffed up like a cockerel at the insult, and then I look at Richard Beard.

'What would you advise the queen?' Beard asks me. He is no fool, he knows who pays my hire. I will sing to Henry's tune, in four-part harmony if need be, he can be sure of that.

'Your Grace,' I say gently. 'There is nothing that can be done except to accept the will of the king and the ruling of his council.'

She looks at me trustingly. 'How can I?' she asks. 'He wants me to say that I was married before I married him, so we were not married. These are lies.'

'Your Grace.' I bend very low to her and I whisper, so that only she can hear. 'The evidence about Queen Anne Boleyn went from an inquiry, just like this one, to the court room and then to the scaffold. The evidence about Queen Katherine of Aragon went from an inquiry just like this one, took six years to hear, and in the end she was alone and penniless and died in exile from her friends and from her daughter. The king is a hard enemy. If he offers you any terms, any terms at all, you should take them.'

'But . . .'

'If you do not release him he will be rid of you anyway.'

'How can he?' she demands.

I look at her. 'You know.'

She dares me to say it. 'What will he do?'

'He will kill you,' I say simply.

Richard Beard moves away so that he can deny he ever heard this. The ambassador glares at me, uncomprehending.

'You know this,' I say.

In silence, she nods.

'Who is your friend in England?' I ask her. 'Who will defend you?'

I see the fight go out of her. 'I have none.'

'Can you get a message to your brother? Will he save you?' I know he will not.

'I am innocent,' she whispers.

'Even so.'

Katherine, Norfolk House, Lambeth, 9 July 1540

I cannot, I cannot believe it: but it is so. My grandmother has just told me, and she has just had it from my uncle Norfolk, and he was there, and so he knows. They have done it. They have examined all the evidence and announced that the king's marriage to Queen Anne of Cleves was never valid and they are both free to marry someone else, as if they had never been married to each other at all.

I am amazed. All that wedding, and the gown, and the beautiful jewels and gifts, and us all carrying the train and the wedding breakfast and the archbishop . . . none of it counted. How can that be? The sables! They didn't count either. This is what it is to be king. He wakes up in the morning and decides he is to marry and he does. Then he wakes up the morning after and decides he doesn't like her, and *voilà!* (this is French, it means something like: gracious, look at that!), *voilà!* He is not married. The marriage was never valid and they are now to be seen as brother and sister. Brother and sister!

Only a king could do such a thing. If it were done by an ordinary person you would think him a madman. But since he is king nobody can say that this is madness, and not even the queen (or whatever she happens to be now) can say this is madness. We all say: 'Oh, yes, Your Majesty', and he comes to dinner with my grandmother and me tonight and he will propose to marry me and I will say: 'Oh, yes, Your Majesty, thank you very much', and never, never

285

say that this is mad, and the work of a madman, and the world itself is mad that it does not turn on him.

For I am not mad. I may be very stupid, and I may be very ignorant (though I am learning French, *voilà!*) but at least I don't think that if you stand in front of the archbishop and say 'I do', then that doesn't count six months later. But I do see that I live in a world that is ruled by a madman and governed by his whims. Also, he is the king and head of the church, and God speaks to him directly, so if he says that something is the case then who is going to say no to him?

Not I, at any rate. I may have my thoughts (however stupid I am assured they are), I may have my stupid thoughts in – what did she say? – 'a head that can only hold one nonsensical idea at a time'; but I know that the king is mad, and the world is mad. The queen is now to be his sister, and I am to be his wife and the new queen. I am to be queen of England. I, Kitty Howard, am to marry the King of England and to be his queen. *Voilà* indeed.

I cannot believe it is true. And, I wish someone had thought of this: what real gain is there in it for me? For I have thought about this now. What should prevent him waking up one morning and saying that I too was pre-contracted and that our royal marriage is not valid? Or that I am unfaithful, and he had better behead me? What should prevent him taking a fancy to a stupid, pretty maid in waiting of mine, and putting me to one side for her?

Exactly! I don't think this has occurred to anyone but me. Exactly. Nothing can prevent him. And those people like my grandmother, who are so free with their insults and their slaps, who say that it is a tremendous honour and a fine step up for a ninny like me, might well consider that a fool can be jumped up, but a fool can also be thrown down; and who is going to catch me then?

Anne, Richmond Palace,
12 July 1540

I have written to say that I agree with the findings of the inquiry, and they have all witnessed it, one after another, the great men who came here to argue with me, the ladies that I had called my friends when I was Queen of England and they were desperate to serve in my court. I have admitted that I was pre-contracted, and not free to marry, I have even apologised for this.

This is a dark night for me in England. The darkest night I have ever faced. I am not to be queen. I can stay in England at the king's unreliable favour, while he marries the little girl who was my maid in waiting, or I can go home penniless, to live with my brother whose spite and negligence has brought me to this. I am very much alone tonight.

This is the most beautiful palace in the kingdom, overlooking the river in its own great park. It was built by the king's father as a great show palace in a peaceful, beautiful country. This wonderful place is to be part of the payment the king offers to be rid of me. And I am to have the Boleyn inheritance, their family house: the pretty castle of Hever. No-one but me seems to find this amusing: that Henry should bribe me with the other Queen Anne's childhood home, which he owns only because he beheaded her. Also, I can have a generous allowance. I shall be the first lady of the kingdom, second only to the new queen, and regarded as the king's sister. We shall all be friends. How happy we shall be.

I don't know how I shall live here. To tell the truth, I cannot imagine how my life will be after tonight, this dark night. I cannot go home to my brother, I should be shamed as a whipped dog if I were to go home to him and say that the King of England has put me aside, calling in archbishops to get his freedom from me, preferring a pretty girl, my own maid in waiting, to me. I cannot go home and say this. I cannot go home and face this shame. What they would say to me, how I would live as spoiled goods at my brother's court, I cannot imagine. It is not possible.

So I shall have to stay here. There is no refuge for me anywhere else. I cannot go to France or to Spain or even to a house of my own somewhere in Germany. I have no money to buy such a place and if I leave England I will have no rich allowance, they will pay me no rents. My lands will be given to someone else. The king insists that I live on his generosity in his kingdom. I cannot hope for another husband to offer me a home either. No man will marry me, knowing that I have laid under the king's heavy labourings for night after night and that he could not bring himself to do it. No man will find me desirable knowing that the king's manhood shrivelled at the sight of me. The king has volunteered to his friends that he was repelled by my fat belly and by my slack breasts and by the smell of me. I am shamed to the ground by this. Besides, since every churchman in England has agreed that I was bound to marry the son of the Duke of Lorraine, that will be an obstacle to any marriage I might want in the future. I will have to face a single life, without lover, or husband, or companion. I will have to face a lonely life, without family. I will never have a child of my own, I will never have a son to come after me, I will never have my own daughter to love. I will have to be a nun without a convent, a widow with no memories, a wife of six months and a virgin. I will have to face life in exile. I will never see Cleves again. I will never see my mother again.

This is a hard sentence for me. I am a young woman of only

twenty-five. I have done nothing wrong. And yet I shall be alone forever: undesirable, lonely and in exile. Truly, when a King is a god to himself and follows his own desires, the suffering falls on others.

It is done. It took all of six days. Six days. The king has rid himself of his queen, his lawfully wedded queen, so that he can now marry me. My grandmother says I should prepare myself for the greatest position in the land and consider what ladies I shall choose to serve me, and who I shall favour with the places and fees at my disposal. Clearly, my Howard relations must come first. My uncle says that I must remember to take his advice in all things and not be a stupid jade like my cousin Anne. And I must remember what happened to her! As if I am likely to forget.

I have looked sideways under my eyelashes at the king, and smiled at him, curtseyed bending forwards so that he can see my breasts, and worn my hood back so he can see my face. Now everything has gone faster than I could have imagined, everything is happening too fast. Everything is happening whether I want it or not.

I am to be married to King Henry of England. Queen Anne has been put aside. Nothing can save her, nothing can stop the king, nothing can save me – oh, I shouldn't have said that. I should have said: nothing can prevent my happiness. That is what I meant to say. Nothing can prevent my happiness. He calls me his rose. He calls me his rose without a thorn. Whenever he says it, I think it is just the sort of pet-name that a man might give to his daughter. Not a lover's name. Not a lover's name at all.

Anne, Richmond Palace, 13 July 1540

And so it is over. Unbelievably, it is over. I have put my name to the agreement that says I was pre-contracted and not free to marry. I have agreed that my marriage should be annulled and suddenly it is no more. Just like that. This is what it is to be married to the voice of God when He speaks against you. God warns Henry that I am pre-contracted. Henry warns his council. Then the marriage is no more, though he swore to be my husband and came to my bed and tried – how hard did he try! – to consummate the marriage. But it turns out it was God preventing his success (not witchcraft but the hand of God), and so Henry says it will not be.

I write to my brother at the king's command and tell him that I am no longer married and that I have consented to my change of state. Then, the king is not satisfied by my letter and I am ordered to write it again. If he wants, I will write it a dozen times. If my brother had protected me as he should have done, as my father would have wanted him to do, this could never have happened. But he is a spiteful man and a poor kinsman, he is a bad brother to me; and I have been unprotected since the death of my father. My brother's ambition made him use me, his spite let me fall. He would not have let his horse go to such a buyer as Henry of England, and be broken so.

The king has commanded me to return his wedding ring to him.

I obey him in this as I do in all things. I write a letter to go with it. I tell him that here is the ring he gave to me and that I hope he will have it broken into pieces for it is a thing which has no force or value. He will not hear my anger and my disappointment in these words for he does not know me nor think of me. But I am both angry and disappointed and he can have his wedding ring, and his wedding vows, and he can have his belief that God speaks to him, for they are all part of the same thing: a chimera, a thing which has no force or value.

And so it is over.

And so it begins for little Kitty Howard.

I wish her joy of him. I wish him joy of her. A more ill-matched, ill-conceived, ill-starred marriage could hardly be imagined. I cannot envy her. From the bottom of my heart, even tonight, when I have so much to complain of, when I have so much to blame her for: even now I do not envy her. I can only fear for her, poor child, poor, silly child.

I may have been alone, without friends, before the indifference of the king, but God knows the same will be true of her. I was poor and humble when he chose me and the same is true of her. I was part of a faction of his court (though I did not know it) and the same is even more true of her. When another pretty girl comes to court and takes his eye, how shall she make him cleave to her? (And be very sure they will send their pretty girls by the dozen.) When the king's health fails him and he cannot get a child on her, will he tell her that it is the failing of an old man, and ask her forgiveness? No, he will not. And when he blames her, who will defend her? When Lady Rochford asks her, who can she call on as a friend?, what will she answer? Who will be Katherine Howard's friend and protector when the king turns against her?

Queen Katherine, Oatlands Palace,
28 July 1540

Well, I must say that it is all well and good to be married but I have not had half the wedding that she had. There was no great reception for me at Greenwich, and no riding out on a beautiful horse and being greeted by him with all the nobles of England behind him. There was no sailing in barges down the river while the City of London went mad with joy either, so those who think that to marry the king is a very merry thing should note my wedding, which was – to be blunt – a hole-in-the-corner business. There! I've said it, and anyone who thinks different can't have been here. And actually, that would be most people in the world – for next to no-one was here.

I said to Lady Rochford, the day before: 'Please find out from the groom of the chamber or the Lord Chamberlain or somebody what it is we are to do. Where I am to stand, and what I am to say and what to do.' I wanted to practise. I like to practise if I am going to appear before people and everyone will watch me. I should have been warned by her response.

'Nothing much to practise,' she said dourly. 'Your bridegroom is well-rehearsed at least. You will just have to repeat the vows. And there will be hardly any audience for you at all.'

And how right she was! There was the Bishop of London officiating (thank you so much, not even a real archbishop for me), there was the king, not even wearing a special waistcoat, in an old coat – isn't that next to insulting? – there was me in the finest gown that I could order; but what could I do in little more than a fortnight? And not even a crown on my head!

He gave me some very good jewels, I sent for the goldsmith to value them at once and they are indeed very fine, though some of them I know for a fact were brought by Katherine of Aragon from Spain, and who wants jewels that belonged to a friend of your grandmother? I have no doubt that there will be sables as good as Queen Anne's to follow, and already I have commanded the dressmakers to make me new gowns and there will be gifts from everyone in the world, as soon as everyone knows, as soon as everyone is told.

But there is no denying that it was not as great a wedding as I had expected, and it was not a patch on hers. I thought we would have planned it for months, and there would be processions and my important entry to London, and I should have spent my first night in the Tower and then processed to Westminster Abbey through streets which were swathed in cloth of gold, with people singing songs about me. 'Fair Katherine', I thought they would sing. 'Rose of England.'

But no, instead there is a mere bishop, there is the king, there am I in a bewitching gown of grey-green silk which shifts colours as I move, and a new hood, and his pearls at least, and there is my uncle and grandmother as witnesses, and a couple of men from his court, and then we go to dine; and then . . . And then! . . . It is unbelievable! Nobody talks of anything but the beheading of Thomas Cromwell.

At a wedding breakfast! Is that what a bride wants to hear on her wedding day? There are no healths drunk and no speeches made to me, and scarcely any celebration. Nobody pays me any compliments at all, there is no dancing and no flirtation and no flattery. They can talk of nothing else but Thomas Cromwell because he has been beheaded today. On my wedding day! Is this how the king celebrates his wedding? With the death of his chief advisor and best friend? It's not a very nice gift for a girl on her wedding day, is it? It's not as if I am whoever she is in the Bible who wanted someone's head for a wedding gift. All I really wanted for a wedding gift were sables, not the news that the king's advisor has been beheaded, calling for mercy.

But it is all the old people talk about, no-one consults my feelings at all, they are utterly delighted with it, of course, and so they talk over the top of me, as if I were a child instead of the new Queen of England, and they talk about the alliance with France and say that King Francis will help us with the Pope. And nobody asks me for my opinion at all.

The king grips my hand beneath the shield of the table and leans towards me and whispers, 'I cannot wait for tonight, my rose, my finest jewel,' which is hardly very inspiring when I think that Thomas Culpepper had to help him to his seat, and will no doubt have to heave him into my bed.

In short, I am the happiest woman in the world, praise God. But just a little discontented tonight.

And I am out of my usual ways. At this time of night when I was in the queen's chamber we would all be getting ready to dine in the hall and we would be looking one another over and teasing each other if anyone had done their hair very well, or was dressed very fine. Someone would always accuse me of trying to attract one boy or another and I would always blush and say, 'No! Not at all!' as if I were shocked at the thought of it. And the queen would come out of her bedroom and laugh at us all and then she would lead us into the hall and it would all be very merry. Half the time there would be a young man with an eye to me, in the last few weeks there has been Thomas Culpepper always smiling at me, and all the girls around me would nudge me and tell me to look for my honour. Of course he does not even look at me now, obviously there is no amusement for a queen, you would think I was as old as my husband.

It was more than merry; it was busy and gay and young. There was always a crowd of us, all together, all happy and sharing a jest. And if the jest wore a little sour from time to time, with jealousy or malice, then there was always another person to complain to, and a little group to form, and a little quarrel to run. I like being in a gang of girls, I like the maidens' chamber, I like being one of the queen's ladies and all of us being together.

It is all very well being Queen of England but I have no friends. It just seems to be me, and these old people: Grandmother, my uncle, the king and his old men of the Privy Council. The young men in the king's service don't even smile at me now, you would think they didn't even like me. Thomas Culpepper bows his head when I come near him and doesn't meet my eyes. And the old people talk among themselves about the things that interest old people: the weather, the bad end of Thomas Cromwell, his estates and money, the state of the church and the danger of Papists and heretics, the danger of the men of the North who still long for their monasteries. And I sit here like a well-behaved daughter, like a well-behaved granddaughter actually, and it is all I can do not to yawn.

I turn my head one way to appear as if I am listening to my uncle, and then I turn the other to the king. I don't hear any of them, to tell truth. It is all buzz, buzz above me, and there are no musicians and no dancing and nothing to amuse me but the conversation of my husband, and what bride ever wanted that?

Then Henry says, very soft and sweet, that it is time for us to retire, and thank God Lady Rochford comes in and takes me away from the rest of them, and she has a new and beautiful nightshift for me with a matching cape to go over the top, and I change my gown in the queen's own dressing room because I am queen now.

'God save you, Your Grace,' she says. 'But you have risen very high indeed.'

'I have, Lady Rochford,' I say, most solemnly. 'And I shall keep you by me if you advise me and help me in the future as you have done in the past.'

'Your uncle has commanded me to do just that,' she says. 'I am to be head of your privy chamber.'

'I shall appoint my own ladies,' I say, very haughty.

'No, you won't,' she says pleasantly. 'Your uncle has already made the chief appointments.'

I check that the door is closed behind her. 'How is the queen?' I ask her. 'You have just come from Richmond, haven't you?'

'Don't call her queen.' She stops me at once. 'You're the queen now.'

I tut at my own stupidity. 'I forgot. How is she, anyway?'

'She was very sad when I left,' she says. 'Not for the loss of him, I don't think. But for the loss of all of us. She liked the life as Queen of England, she liked the rooms and being with us, and everything about it.'

'I liked it too,' I say wistfully. 'I miss it too. Lady Rochford, does she blame me very much, d'you think? Did she say anything against me?'

Lady Rochford ties my nightgown at the neck. There are little seed pearls embroidered on the ties, it is a most heartwarming gown, it will comfort me on my wedding night to know that I am wearing a gown that costs a small fortune in pearls. 'She doesn't blame you,' she says kindly. 'Silly girl. Everyone knows that this was not of your doing – except that you are young and pretty and no-one can blame you for that. Not even her. She knows that you did not plan her fall and her unhappiness, any more than you are responsible for the death of Thomas Cromwell. Everyone knows that you don't matter at all in this.'

'I am queen,' I say, rather nettled. 'I should think I matter more than anyone.'

'You are the fifth queen,' she points out, quite unmoved by my irritation. 'And to be honest, there has been none worth the name of queen since the first one.'

'Well, I am the queen now,' I say stoutly. 'And that is all that matters.'

'Queen of the day,' she says, going behind me to spread out the little train of my nightshift. It too is heavy with seed pearls, it is the most gorgeous of gowns. 'A mayfly queen, God save your little majesty.'

Jane Boleyn, Oatlands Palace,
30 July 1540

The king, having won his rose without a thorn, is determined to keep her close. Half the court don't even know that the wedding has taken place, left behind at Westminster, out of touch with everything that is happening here. This is the king's private circle, his new wife, her family, and only his most trusted friends and advisors; I am among them.

Once again I have proved my loyalty, once again I am the confidante who will tell everything. Once again I can be put into the queen's chamber, into her most secret heart, I can be put there and trusted to betray. I have been trusted friend to Queen Katherine, Queen Anne, Queen Jane and then Queen Anne; and I have seen all of them fall from favour or die during my service. If I were a superstitious woman I would think of myself as a plague wind that blows death warmly, with affection, like the breath of a whisper.

So I am not superstitious, and I don't trouble myself to think of the part I have played in these deaths and shames and disgraces. I have done my duty by the king and by my family. I have done my duty even when it cost me everything: my own true love and my honour. Why, my own husband . . . but there is no point in thinking of George tonight. He would be pleased anyway: another Howard girl on the throne of England, a Boleyn in the most favoured place. He was the most ambitious of us all. He would be the first to say that it was worth any lie to get a place at court, to join the king's most favoured circle. He would be the first to understand that there are times when the truth is a luxury that a courtier cannot afford.

I think he would be surprised how far the king has gone, how easily he steps from power, to great power, into absolute power. George was not a fool; I think if he were here now he would be warning that the king without any bridle on his will is not a great king (as we assure him) but a monster. I think when George died he knew that the king had stretched to the limits of tyranny and would go further.

As seems to be the pattern for the king's weddings, this one is followed by a round of executions. The king settles his scores with old enemies, and those who favoured the previous wife. The death of the Earl of Hungerford and his foolish soothsayer seems to put away the whisper of witchcraft. He was accused of all sorts of necromancy and wild sexual misdoings. A couple of Papists are to die for their part in the Lisle plot, the Princess Mary's tutor among them. That will sadden her, and serve as a warning for her too. The friendship of Anne of Cleves has given her no protection; she is friendless again, she is in danger again. All Papists and Papist sympathisers are in danger. She had better be warned. The Howards are back in power and they support the king, who is making a clean sweep of his old enemies to mark his happiness with the new Howard girl. He also kills a handful of Lutherans: a warning to Anne of Cleves and those who thought that she would lead him to reform. When she kneels to pray at her bedside at Richmond Palace tonight she will know that she has been spared by a hair's breadth. He will want her to live the rest of her life in fear.

Katherine, I notice, kneels to pray but does not close her eyes, I would swear she does not say so much as a Hail Mary. She clasps her long white fingers together and she kneels and draws breath but there is no thought of God in her mind. No thought of anything at all, would be my bet. There is never much in that pretty head. If she is praying for anything it is for sables like Queen Anne had for her betrothal.

Of course she is too young to be a good queen. She is too young to be anything but a silly girl. She knows nothing of charity to the poor, nothing of the duties of her great position, nothing about running a great household, let alone running a country. When I think that Queen Katherine was named regent and commanded England I could laugh out loud. This child could not command a pet dove. But she is pleasant and agreeable to the king. The duke her uncle has coached her pretty well in obedience and politeness, and it is my task to watch for the rest. She dances very prettily for the king, and she sits quietly beside him while he talks to men old enough to be her grandfather. She smiles when he addresses a remark to her, and she lets him pinch her cheek or hug her waist without grimace. At dinner the other night he could not keep his hands off her breasts and she blushed but did not pull away when he pawed at her before all the company. She has been raised in a hard school, the duchess is known for a heavy hand with her girls. The duke will have threatened her with the axe if she does not obey the king in thought and word and deed. And, to do her justice, she is a sweet thing anyway, she is glad of the king's presents, and glad to be queen. It is easy for her to be pretty and pleasing to him. He does not ask for much now. He does not want a wife of high intelligence and moral purpose like Queen Katherine. Nor one with a wit of fire like Anne. He just wants to enjoy her slim young body and get a baby on her.

It is as well the court is not here, in these early days of their marriage. Her family and those who profit from the marriage can look away from him pulling her about, her little hand lost in his grip, her determined smile when he stumbles on his bad leg, her rosy blush of embarrassment when his hand wanders to her crotch under the dinner table. Anyone who was not profiting from this mismatch wedding would find it disturbing to see such a pretty child dished up for such an old man. Anyone speaking honestly would call it a sort of rape.

Fortunate then, that there is no-one here who would ever speak honestly.

Anne, Richmond Palace,
6 August 1540

He is to visit me for dinner. Why, I cannot think. The royal groom of the household came yesterday and told my steward that the king would have the pleasure of dining with me today. I asked those ladies who are still with me if anyone had any news from the court, and one of them said that she had heard that the king was at Oatlands Palace, all but alone, hunting to take his mind off the terrible betrayal of Thomas Cromwell.

One of them asked me if I thought the king was coming to beg my pardon and to ask me to come back to him.

'Is it possible?' I ask her.

'If he was mistaken? If the inquiry was mistaken?' she asks. 'Why else would he come and see you, so soon after the end of the marriage? If he still wants to end the marriage, why would he dine with you?'

I go outside to the beautiful gardens and walk a little way, my head buzzing with thoughts. It does not seem possible that he should want to take me back, but there is no doubt that if he has changed his mind he can take me back, just as easily as he could put me aside.

I wonder if it would be possible for me to refuse to go back to him. I would want to return to the court and to be restored to my position, of course. But there is a freedom to being a single woman that I might learn to enjoy. I have never in my life before been Anne of Cleves, Anne by myself, not a sister, not a daughter, not a wife, but Anne: pleasing myself. I swore if I was spared death then I would live my life, my own life, not a life commanded by others. I order dresses in colours that I think suit me, I don't have to observe my brother's code of modesty, nor the court fashions. I order dinner at the time and with the food that I like; I don't have to sit down in front of two hundred people who watch every single thing I do. When I want to ride out I can go as far and as fast as I like, I don't have to consider my brother's fears or my husband's competitive spirit. If I call for musicians in the evening I can dance with my ladies or hear them sing, we don't always have to follow the king's tastes. We don't have to marvel at his compositions. I can pray to a god of my own faith in the words that I choose. I can become myself, I can be: me.

I had thought that my heart would leap at the chance to be queen again. My chance to do my duty by this country, by its people, by the children who I have come to love, and perhaps even to win my mother's approval and to fulfil my brother's ambitions. But I find, to my own amusement, as I examine my thoughts – and at last I have the privacy and peace to examine my thoughts – that it may be a better thing to be a single woman with a good income in one of the finest palaces in England than to be one of Henry's frightened queens.

The royal guards come first, and then his companions, handsome and overdressed as always. Then he comes in with a touch of awkwardness, limping slightly on his sore leg. I sink down in a low curtsey and I can smell the familiar stink of his wound as I come up. Never again will I have to wake with that smell on my sheets, I think, as I step forwards and he kisses me on the forehead.

He looks me up and down, frankly, as a man appraising a horse. I remember that he told the court that I smell and that my breasts are slack and I can feel my colour rising. 'You look well,' he says begrudgingly. I can hear the pique behind his praise. He was hoping I would pine with unrequited love, I am sure.

'I am well,' I say calmly. 'Glad to see you.'

He smiles at that. 'You must have known I would never treat you unfairly,' he says, happy at the thought of his own generosity. 'If you are a good sister to me then you will see I shall be kind to you.'

I nod and bow.

'Something's different about you.' He takes a chair and gestures that I may sit on the lower chair beside him. I sit and smooth the embroidered skirt of the blue gown over my knees. 'Tell me. I can judge a woman just by the look of her; I know that there is something different about you. What is it?'

'A new hood?' I suggest.

He nods. 'It becomes you. It becomes you very well.'

I say nothing. It is French-cut. If the Howard girl has returned to court he will be accustomed to the very height and folly of fashion. In any case, now I no longer wear the crown, I can wear what I please. It's funny, if I was of a mind to laugh, that he should prefer me dressed to my own taste, than when I tried to please his. But what he likes in a woman he would not like in a wife. Katherine Howard may discover this.

'I have some news.' He looks around at my small court of companions, his gentlemen standing about. 'Leave us.'

They go out as slowly as they dare. They are all longing to know what will happen next. I am certain that it will not be an invitation to me to return to him. I am certain that it will not be; and yet I am breathless to know.

'Some news that may distress you,' he says to prepare me. At once I think that my mother has died, far away, and without a chance for me to explain how I failed her.

'No need to cry,' he says quickly.

I put my hand to my mouth and nip my knuckles. 'I am not crying,' I say steadily.

'That's good,' he says. 'And besides, you must have known it would happen.'

'I didn't expect it,' I say foolishly. 'I didn't expect it so soon.' Surely they should have sent for me if they knew she was gravely ill?

'Well, it is my duty.'

'Your duty?' I want so much to know if my mother spoke of me in her last days that I hardly hear him.

'I am married,' he says. 'Married. I thought I should tell you first, before you hear it from some gossip.'

'I thought it was about my mother?'

'Your mother? No. Why would it be about your mother? Why would I trouble myself about your mother? It is about me.'

'You said bad news.'

'What could be worse for you than to know that I have married another woman?'

Oh, a thousand things, a thousand things, I think, but I don't say the thought aloud. The relief that my mother is alive rushes through me and I have to grip the arms of my chair to steady myself and to look as grave and as bereft as I know he will want me to look. 'Married,' I say flatly.

'Yes,' he says. 'I am sorry for your loss.'

So it is indeed done. He will not return to me. I will never again be Queen of England. I cannot care for little Elizabeth, I cannot love Prince Edward, I cannot please my mother. It is indeed over. I have failed in what I was sent to do and I am sorry for it. But, dear God, I am safe from him, I shall never be in his bed again. It is indeed utterly finished and over. I have to keep my eyes down and my face still so that he does not see my beam of joy at this freedom.

'To a lady of a most noble house,' he continues. 'Of the Norfolk house.'

'Katherine Howard?' I ask, before his boasting makes him look more ridiculous than I already think him.

'Yes,' he says.

'I wish you much happiness,' I say steadily. 'She is . . .' At that precise and dreadful moment I cannot find the English word. I want to say 'charming' but I cannot think of the word. 'Young,' I finish lamely.

He shoots me a quick, hard look. 'That is no objection to me.'

'None at all,' I say quickly. 'I meant to say, charming.'

He thaws. 'She is charming,' he agrees, smiling at me. 'I know you liked her when she was in your rooms.'

'I did,' I say. 'She was always pleasant company. She is a lovely girl.' I nearly say 'child' but catch myself in time.

He nods. 'She is my rose,' he says. To my horror his eyes fill with the sentimental tears of an old bully. 'She is my rose without a thorn,' he says thickly. 'I feel that I have found her at last, the woman I have waited for all my life.'

I sit in silence. This is an idea so bizarre that I cannot find any words, English or German, to reply. He has been waiting all his life? Well, he has not been waiting very patiently. During the time of his long vigil he has seen off three, no, four wives, me among them. And Katherine Howard is very far from a rose without a thorn. She is, if anything, a little daisy: delightful, sweet-faced, but ordinary. She must be the most common commoner ever to sit on a better woman's throne.

'I hope you will be very happy,' I say again.

He leans towards me. 'And I think we will have a child,' he whispers. 'Hush. It's early days yet. But she is so very young, and she comes from fertile stock. She says she thinks it is so.'

I nod. His smug confiding to me, who was bought and put in his bed to endure him labouring hopelessly above me, pushing himself against me, patting my stomach and pulling at my breasts, repels me so much I can hardly congratulate him on achieving with a girl what he failed to do with me.

'So let us dine,' he says, releasing me from my embarrassment, and we rise and he takes my hand as if we were still married, and leads me into the great hall of Richmond Palace, which was his father's favourite new-built palace and is now mine. He seats himself alone, on a throne raised higher than any other, and I am seated not at his side – as I was when I was queen – but down the hall at a little distance, as if to remind the world that everything has changed and that I will never sit at his side as queen again.

I don't need reminding. I know this.

Katherine, Hampton Court,
August 1540

Now let me see, what do I have?

I have eight new gowns ready made and another forty (forty! I can't believe it myself!) in the making and I am very displeased the dressmakers are so late with them, for it is my intention to wear a different gown to dinner every day of my life from now until the day I die, and to change my gown three times a day. That would be three new gowns a day which would be hundreds a year and since I may live till fifty years old that will be . . . well, I can't work it out but it is very many indeed. Thousands.

I have a collar of diamonds with matching cuffs of diamonds and gold and a matching set of earrings.

I have sables, like she had for her present, and they are better than hers, thicker and of a glossier pelt. I asked Lady Rochford and she definitely confirmed that they are better than hers. So that is one worry gone from my mind.

I have my own barge (think of it!), my own barge with my own motto engraved on it. Yes, I have a motto too, and it is 'No other will but his', which my uncle devised and my grandmother said was laying it on by the bucket; but the king likes it and says it was just what he was thinking. I didn't quite understand it at first but it means that I have no other will than his – that is, the king's will. Once I understood that, I saw at once why any man would like it, if he were fool enough to believe that anyone would devote their entire body and soul to another.

I have my own rooms here at Hampton Court and these are the queen's rooms! Unbelievable! The very rooms where I used to be a maid in waiting are now my rooms and now there are people waiting on me. The very bed where I used to put the queen to sleep and wake her in the morning is now my big bed. And when the court is jousting, the very same curtains that were her curtains around the royal box are now mine and now they are embroidered with H and K, just as they were once embroidered for her with H and A. Anyway, I have ordered new. It feels like dead men's shoes to me and I don't see why I should put up with it. Henry says I am an extravagant little kitten and that these curtains have been used in the queen's box since his first wife, and I say that is exactly why I might want a change. So, *voilà!* I will have new curtains too.

I have a court of ladies of my choosing; well, some of them I choose. At any rate, I have a court of ladies of my family. My greatest lady is the king's ward, Lady Margaret Douglas, practically a princess, to wait on me! Not that she does much waiting, I must say. Anybody would think I wasn't queen the way she looks down her nose. Then I have a handful of duchesses, my stepmother and my two sisters are my ladies in waiting, as well as dozens of other Howard women that my uncle has placed about me. I never knew I had so many cousins. The rest are my old room-mates and girlfriends from Norfolk House days who have popped up to sup from my bowl now that my portion is very rich, and who have to mind me now, though they did not mind me then. But I tell them that they can be my friends but they have to remember I am queen and I have to be on my dignity.

I have two lapdogs which I have called, for a private joke, Henry and Francis – by which I mean my two lapdog lovers from the old days, Henry Manox and Francis Dereham. When I named them, Agnes and Joan screamed with laughter, they were with me at Norfolk

House and they knew exactly who I was thinking of. Even now, every time I call the two dogs to my side, the three of us laugh out loud to think of those two lads chasing me and now I am queen of England. What those men must think, when they remember they had their hands up my skirt and down my stomacher! It is too scandalous to dare to remember. I should think they laugh and laugh; I do at the very memory.

I have a stable full of my own horses and my own favourite mare who is called Bessy. She is very sweet and steady and the most adorable boy in the stable keeps her exercised for me so that she doesn't get fat or naughty. He is called Johnny and he flushes like a little poppy when he sees me, and when I let him help me down from riding I rest my hands on his shoulders and watch his face burn.

If I were a vain silly girl (as my uncle persists in thinking) which, thank God, I am not, I should have my head turned by the flattery of the court from everyone to Johnny in the yard to Archbishop Gardiner. Everyone tells me that I am the best wife that the king ever had, and the wonder of it all is that this is almost certainly true. Everyone tells me I am the most beautiful queen in the world – and this is probably true too – though no great claim when I cast my eye around Christendom. Everyone tells me that the king has never loved anyone as much as he loves me; and this is true, for he tells me so himself. Everyone tells me that all the court is in love with me, and this is certainly true, for I walk everywhere in a small hail of love-notes and requests, and promises. The young noblemen that I used to eye when I was just a maid in waiting, and hope for assignations and flirtation, are now my own court; they have to adore me from a distance, which is really the most delicious thing. Thomas Culpepper is sent to me by the king himself in the morning and the evening to exchange greetings, and I know, I just know that he has fallen completely in love with me. I tease him and laugh at him and see his eyes follow me and it is all utterly delightful. Everywhere I go, I am attended by the finest young men in the land, they joust for my amusement, they dance with me, they dress up and entertain me, they hunt with me, they sail with me, they walk with me, they play games and sports for my praise, they do everything but sit up on their hind legs and beg for my favour. And the king, bless him, says to me, 'Run along, pretty girl, go and dance!' and then sits back and watches me as one handsome – oh, so handsome – young man after another dances with me and the king smiles and smiles like a kindly old uncle, and when I come back and sit at his side he whispers: 'Pretty girl, the fairest girl of the court, they all want you; but you are mine.'

It is like my dreams. I have never been happier in my life. I did not know I could be so happy. It is like the childhood I never had, to be surrounded by handsome playmates, my old friends from the days at Lambeth, with all the money in the world to spend, a circle of young men all desperate for my attention, and watched overall by a tender, loving man like a kindly father who never lets anyone say an unkind word to me and plans amusements and gifts for me every day of my life. I must be the happiest girl in England. I tell the king this and he smiles and chucks me under the chin and tells me that I deserve it, for without doubt, I am the best girl in England.

And it is true, I earn this pleasure, I am not idle; I have my duties to do, and I do them as well as I can. All the work of the queen's rooms I leave to others of course, my lord Chamberlain deals with all the requests for help and justice and petitions – I should not be bothered with such things, and anyway, I never know what I am supposed to do with all the paupers and homeless nuns and distressed priests. Lady Rochford takes care of the running of my rooms, and making sure that everything is done as well as Queen Anne had it done; but the servicing of the king falls to me alone. He is old and his appetite in the bedroom is strong but the execution is not easy for him at his great age and because he is so very fat. I have to use all my little tricks to help him along, poor old soul. I let him watch me slip off my nightgown, I make sure the candles stay lit. I sigh in his ear as if I am swooning with desire, a thing that all men love to believe. I whisper to him that all the young men of the court are nothing compared to him, that I despise their silly, youthful faces and light desires, that I want a man, a real man. When he has taken too much to drink or is too weary to get himself above me I even do a trick that my dearest Francis taught me, and sit astride him. He loves that, he has only had whores do that for him before, it is a forbidden pleasure, that God doesn't allow for some reason. So it thrills him that a pretty wife with her hair let down over her shoulders should rear above him and torment him like a Smithfield harlot. I don't complain of having to do this, actually it is far nicer for me than being crushed beneath him with the smell of his breath and the stench of his rotting leg making me sick as I moan with pretend pleasure.

This is not easy. Being the wife of a king is not all dancing and parties in the rose garden. I work as hard as any dairymaid, but I work at night in secret and nobody must ever know what it costs me. Nobody must ever know that I am so disgusted that I could vomit, nobody must ever know that it almost breaks my heart that the things I learned to do for love are now done to excite a man who would be better off saying his prayers and going to sleep. Nobody knows how hard I earn my sables and my pearls. And I can never tell them. It can never be said. It is a deep, deep secret.

When he has finished at last, and is snoring, that is oddly the only time of the day that I feel dissatisfied with my great good fortune. Often then I get up, I feel restless and stirred up. Am I going to spend every night of my womanhood seducing a man old enough to be my father? Almost my grandfather? I am just fifteen years old; am I never going to taste a sweet kiss again from a clean mouth, or feel the smoothness of young skin, or have a hard, muscled chest bearing down on me? Shall I spend the rest of my life jigging up and down on something helpless and limp and then crying out with pretended delight when it slowly, flaccidly stirs beneath me? When he farts in his sleep, a great royal trumpet which adds to the miasma under the bedclothes, I get up in a bad temper and go out to my private chamber.

And always, like my good angel, Lady Rochford is there, waiting for me. She understands how it is, she knows what I have to do and how, some nights, it leaves me feeling irritable and sore. She has a cup of hot mead and some little cakes ready for me, she seats me in a chair by the fire and puts the warm cup in my hand, and brushes my hair slowly and sweetly until the anger passes and I am calm again.

'When you get a son you will be free of him,' she whispers so quietly that I can hardly hear her. 'When you are sure you have conceived a child he will leave you alone. No more false alarms. When you tell him you are with child you must be certain, and then you will have nearly a year at peace. And after you have had a second son your place will be assured and you can take your own pleasures and he will not know and not mind.'

'I shall never have pleasure again,' I say miserably. 'My life is over before it has even begun. I am only fifteen and I am tired of everything.'

Her hands caress my shoulders. 'Oh, you will,' she says certainly. 'Life is long, and if a woman survives she can take her pleasures one way or another.'

Jane Boleyn, Windsor Palace,
October 1540

Supervising this privy chamber is no sinecure, I must say. Under my command I have girls who in any decent town would be whipped at the cart tail for whores. Katherine's chosen friends from Lambeth are without doubt the rowdiest sluts that ever came from a noble household where the lady of the house could not be troubled to mind them. Katherine has insisted that her friends from the old days should be invited to her privy chamber and I can hardly refuse, especially since the senior ladies of her privy chamber are no company for her, but are mostly old enough to be her mother and have been foisted on her by her uncle. She needs some friends of her own age but these chosen companions are not biddable girls from good families, they are women, lax women, the very companions who let her run wild and set her the worst example, and they will go on with their loose ways too if they can, even in the royal rooms. It is utterly unlike Queen Anne's rule, and soon everyone will notice. I cannot imagine what my lord duke is thinking, and the king will give his child-bride anything she asks. But a queen's chamber should be the finest, most elegant place in the land, not a tiltyard for rough girls with the language of the stables.

Her liking for Katherine Tylney and Margaret Morton I can understand, though they are equally loud-mouthed and bawdy; and Agnes Restwold was a confidante from the old days. But I don't believe she wanted Joan Bulmer to come into her service. She never mentioned her name once; but the woman wrote a secret letter and seems to have left her husband and wheedled her way in, and Katherine is either too kind-hearted, or too fearful of what secrets the woman might spill, to refuse her.

And what does that mean? That she allows a woman to come into her chamber, the privy chamber, the best place in the land, because she can tell secrets of Katherine's childhood? What can have taken place in the girl's childhood that she cannot risk it being spoken? And can we trust Joan Bulmer to keep it quiet? At court? At a court such as this? When all the gossip is always centred on the queen herself? How am I to rule over this chamber when one of the girls at least has a secret so powerful hanging over the queen's head that she can claim admittance?

These are her friends and companions and there is really no way to improve them; but I had hoped that the senior ladies who have been appointed to wait on her might set a more dignified tone, and make a little headway against the childish chaos that Katherine enjoys. The most noble lady of the chamber is Lady Margaret Douglas, only twenty-one years old, the king's own niece; but she is barely ever here. She simply vanishes from the queen's rooms for hours at a time, and her great friend Mary, Duchess of Richmond, that was married to Henry Fitzroy, goes with her. God knows where. They are said to be great poets and great readers, which is no doubt to their credit. But who are they reading and rhyming with all the day? And why can I never find them? The rest of the queen's ladies are all Howard women: the queen's older sister, her aunt, her step-grandmother's daughter-in-law, a network of Howard kin including Catherine Carey, who has reappeared promptly enough to benefit from the rise of a Howard girl. These are women who care only for their own ambitions, and do nothing to help me manage the queen's rooms so that they at least appear as they should be.

But things are not as they should be. I am certain that Lady Margaret is meeting someone; she is a fool and a passionate fool. She has crossed her royal uncle once already, and been punished for a flirtation which could have been far worse. She was married to Thomas Howard, one of our kin. He died in the Tower for his attempt to marry a Tudor, and she was sent to live at the nunnery of Syon until she begged the king's pardon and said she would only marry at his bidding. But now she is wandering out of the queen's rooms in the middle of the morning and doesn't come back until she arrives with a rush to go into dinner with us, straightening her hood and giggling. I tell Katherine that she should watch her ladies and make sure that their conduct befits a royal court, but she is hunting or dancing or flirting herself with the young men of the court and her behaviour is as wild as anyone's, worse than most.

Perhaps I am over-anxious. Perhaps the king would indeed forgive her anything; this summer he has been like a young man besottedly in love. He has taken her all round his favourite houses on the summer progress and he has managed to hunt with her every day, up at dawn, dining in tented pavilions in the woods at midday, boating on the river in the afternoon, watching her shooting at the butts, or at a tennis tournament, or betting on the young men tilting at the quintain all the afternoon and then a late dinner and a long night of entertainment. Then he takes her to bed and the poor old man is up at dawn again the next day. He has smiled on her as she has twirled and laughed and been embraced by the most handsome young men at his court. He has staggered after her, always beaming, always delighted with her, limping for pain and stuffing himself at dinner. But tonight he is not coming to dinner and they say he has a slight fever. I should think he is near to collapse from exhaustion. He has lived these last months like a young bridegroom when he is the age of a grandfather. Katherine gives him not a second thought and goes into dinner alone, arm-in-arm with Agnes, Lady Margaret arriving in the nick of time to slip in behind her; but I see my lord duke is absent. He is waiting on the king. He, at least, will be anxious for his health. There is no benefit to us if the king is sick and Katherine is not with child.

Katherine, Hampton Court, October 1540

The king won't see me, and it's as if I have offended him, which is tremendously unfair because I have been an absolutely charming wife for months and months without stopping, two months at least, and never a cross word from me though God knows I have reason. I know well enough that he has to come to my room at night and I endure it without saying a word, I even smile as if I desire him; but does he really have to stay? All night? And does he really have to smell so very badly? It is not just the stink of his leg but he trumps like a herald at a joust and though it makes me want to giggle, it's disgusting really. In the morning I throw my windows open to be rid of the stink of him, but it lingers in the bed linen and in the hangings. I can hardly bear it. Some days I think, I really think, I cannot bear another day of it.

But I have never complained of him and he can have no complaint of me. So why will he not see me? They say that he has a fever and he doesn't want me to see him when he is unmanned. But I can't help but be afraid that he is tired of me. And if he is tired of me, no doubt he will say that I was married to someone else and my wedding will be put aside. I feel very discouraged by this and though Agnes and Margaret say that he could never tire of me, that he adores me and anyone can see that, they weren't here when he put Queen Anne aside and that was done so easily and so smoothly that we hardly knew it was happening. Certainly, she didn't know it was happening. They don't realise how easy it is for the king to be rid of one his queens.

I send a message to his rooms every morning and they always send back and say that he is on the mend; and then I have a great fear that he is dying, which would not be surprising for he is so terribly old. And if he dies what will happen to me? And do I keep the jewels and the gowns? And am I still queen even if he is dead? So I wait until the end of dinner and I beckon the king's greatest favourite, Thomas Culpepper, to step up to the top table, and he comes to my side at once, so deferential and graceful, and I say very seriously, 'You may sit down, Master Culpepper,' and he takes a stool beside me and I say, 'Please tell me truly, how is the king?'

He looks at me with his honest blue eyes, he is desperately handsome it has to be said, and he says: 'The king has a fever, Your Grace, but it is from weariness, it is not the wound on his leg. You need not fear for him. He would be grieved if he caused you a moment's worry. He is overheated and exhausted, nothing more.'

This is so kind that I feel myself become quite sentimental. 'I have worried,' I say a little tearfully. 'I have been very anxious for him.'

'You need not be,' he says gently. 'I would tell you if there was anything wrong. He will be up and about within days. I promise it.'

'My position . . .'

'Your position is impossible,' he exclaims suddenly. 'You should be courting your first sweetheart, not trying to rule a court and shape your life to please a man as old as your grandfather.'

This is so unexpected from Thomas Culpepper, the perfect courtier, that I give a little gasp of surprise and I make the mistake of telling the truth, as he has done.

'Actually, I can only blame myself. I wanted to be queen.'

'Before you knew what it meant.'

'Yes.'

There is a silence. I am suddenly aware that we are before the whole of the court and that everyone is looking at us. 'I may not talk to you like this,' I say awkwardly. 'Everyone watches me.'

'I would serve you in any way I can,' he says quietly. 'And the greatest service I can do for you now is to go right away from you. I don't want to make grist for the gossips.'

'I shall walk in the gardens at ten tomorrow,' I say. 'You could come to me then. In my privy gardens.'

'Ten,' he agrees and bows very low and goes back to his table, and I turn and talk to Lady Margaret as if nothing in particular had happened.

She gives me a little smile. 'He is a handsome young man,' she says. 'But nothing compared to your brother Charles.'

I look down the hall to where Charles is dining with his friends. I have never thought of him as handsome, but then I hardly ever saw him until I came to court. He was sent away for his upbringing when he was a boy, and then I was sent to my step-grandmother. 'What an odd thing to say,' I remark. 'You surely cannot like Charles.'

'Good gracious, no!' she says and she flushes up quite scarlet. 'Everyone knows I'm not allowed even to think about a man. Ask anyone! The king would not allow it.'

'You do like him!' I say delightedly. 'Lady Margaret, you sly thing! You are in love with my brother.'

She hides her face in her hands and she peeps at me through the fingers. 'Don't say a word,' she begs me.

'Oh, all right. But has he promised marriage?'

She nods shyly. 'We are so much in love. I hope you will speak for us to the king? He is so strict! But we are so very much in love.'

I smile down the hall at my brother. 'Well, I think that's lovely,' I say kindly. I so like being gracious to the king's niece. 'And what a wonderful wedding we can plan.'

Anne, Richmond Palace, October 1540

I have had a letter from my brother, an utterly mad letter, it distresses me as much as it angers me. He complains of the king in the wildest of terms, and commands me either to return home, insist on my marriage, or never more be a sister to him. He offers me no advice as to how I am to insist on my marriage, clearly he does not even know that the king has re-married already, nor any help if I want to return home. I imagine, as he knew well enough when he gave me these impossible choices, that I am left with the single option of never more being a sister to him.

Little loss to me! When he left me here without a word, gave me an ambassador who was almost unpaid, failed to send adequate proof of the renunciation of the Lorraine betrothal, he was no good brother to me then. He is no good brother now. Least of all is he my good brother when the Duke of Norfolk and half the Privy Council come thundering down to Richmond in a rage, since they have, of course, picked up his letter almost from the moment it left his hand, copied it, translated it, and read it before it ever came to me, and now they want to know if I think my brother will incite the Holy Roman Emperor to war against England and Henry on my behalf?

As calmly as I can, I point out to them that the Holy Roman Emperor is not likely to make war at my brother's behest and that (emphatically) I do not ask my brother to make war at my behest.

'I warn the king that I cannot rule my brother,' I say, speaking slowly and directly to the Duke of Norfolk. 'William will do as he wishes. He does not take my advice.'

The duke looks doubtful. I turn to Richard Beard and speak in German. 'Please point out to His Grace that if I could make my brother obey me then I would have told him to send the document which showed that the betrothal to Lorraine was renounced,' I say.

He turns and translates and the duke's dark eyes gleam at my mistake. 'Except it was not renounced,' he reminds me.

I nod. 'I forgot.'

He shows me a wintry smile. 'I know you cannot command your brother,' he concedes.

I turn to Richard Beard again. 'Please point out to His Grace that this letter from my brother actually proves that I have honoured the king, since it makes clear that he has so little faith in me that he threatens me with being cut off from my family forever.' Richard Beard translates and the duke's cold smile widens slightly.

'What he thinks and what he does, how he blusters and threatens me, is clearly not of my choosing,' I conclude.

Thank God, they may be the king's council, but they do not share his unreasonable terrors, they do not see plots where there are none – except when it suits them, of course. Only when it suits them to be rid of an enemy like Thomas Cromwell, or a rival like poor Lord Lisle, do they exaggerate the king's fears and assure him that they are real. The king is in perpetual anxiety about one conspiracy or another and the council play on his fears like a master might tune a lute. Provided that I am neither threat nor rival to any one of them they will not alert any royal fears about me. So the frail peace between the king and I is not broken by my brother's intemperate speech. I wonder did he even stop for a moment to think if his letter would put me in such danger? Worse still, I wonder, did he intend to put me in such danger?

'Do you think your brother will make trouble for us?' Norfolk asks me simply.

I answer him in German. 'Not for my sake, sir. He would do nothing for me. He has never done anything for my benefit, except to let me go. He might use me as the excuse but I am not his cause. And even if he meant to make trouble, I doubt very much that the Holy Roman Emperor would go to war with the King of England over a fourth wife, when the king has already helped himself to his fifth.'

Richard Beard translates this and both he and Norfolk have to hide their amusement. 'I have your word then,' the duke says shortly.

I nod. 'You do. And I never break my word. I shall make no trouble for the king. I wish to live here alone, in peace.'

He looks around, he is something of a connoisseur of beautiful buildings. He has built his own great house and he has torn down some fine abbeys. 'You are happy here?'

'I am,' I say, and I am telling the truth. 'I am happy here.'

Jane Boleyn, Hampton Court,
October 1540

I should have warned Lady Margaret Douglas not to meddle with a man who was certain to land her in trouble, but I was so absorbed with trying to keep Katherine Howard steady in her first days of marriage that I did not watch the ladies as I should have done. Besides, Lady Margaret is the king's own niece, daughter of his sister. Who would have thought that his hard, suspicious gaze would fall on her? In the first days of his marriage? When he told us all that for the first time in his long life he had found happiness? Why, in those honeymoon weeks, should I have thought that he would plot his own niece's arrest?

Because this is Henry – that is why. Because I have been in his court for long enough to know that things he may overlook when he is chasing a woman will be reckoned up the moment that he has her. Nothing distracts the king from his suspicious terrors for very long. As soon as he was up and out of bed from his fever he was looking around the court to see who had misbehaved in his absence. I was so desperate that he should not suspect the queen and her silly friends that I forgot to look to her ladies. In any case, Lady Margaret Douglas would never have listened to me, given her complete inability to see any sense at all. All the Tudors follow their hearts and make up their reasons after, and Lady Margaret is just like her mother before her, Queen Margaret of Scotland who fell in love with a man with nothing to recommend him, and now her daughter has done the same. Only a few years ago Lady Margaret married Thomas Howard, my kinsman, in secret and had the pleasure of enjoying him for no more than days before the king discovered the couple and sent the young man to the Tower for his impertinence. He was dead within months and she was in disgrace. Of course! Of course! Where is the surprise in this? You cannot have the king's niece marrying where she pleases and her fancy lighting on a Howard! You cannot have one of the greatest families in England, close to the throne on their own account, coming closer yet because a girl likes a dark glance and a merry smile and a certain devil-may-care approach to life. The king swore he would teach her the respect her position deserves and for months she was a widow with a broken heart.

Well, it's mended now.

I knew that something was going on, and within weeks everyone knew of it too. When the king took to his bed with his fever the young couple gave up all attempt to conceal their love affair. Anyone with eyes could see that the king's niece was wholly in love with the queen's brother Charles.

Another Howard, of course, and a favourite; a member of the Privy Council and high in the family command. What did he think he would gain from such a betrothal? The Howards are ambitious, but even he must have considered that he might be over-reaching himself. Good God, did he think he might get Scotland by this girl? Did he fancy himself as King Consort? And she? Why would she not see her own danger? And what is it about these Howards that is a magnet for the Tudors? You would think it was some kind of alchemy, like jam for wasps.

But I should have warned her that she would be discovered. It was a certainty. We live in a house of glass, as if the Venetian glass blowers of Murano had devised a special torment for us. In this court there is not a secret that can be kept, there is not a curtain that can conceal, there is not a wall that is not transparent. Everything is always discovered. Sooner or later, everyone knows everything. And as soon as it is known, everything splinters into a million jagged shards.

I went to my lord duke and found his barge ready to sail and he himself on the pier. 'May I see you?'

'Trouble?' he asked. 'I have to catch the tide.'

'It is Lady Margaret Douglas,' I say shortly. 'She is in love with Charles Howard.'

'I know,' he says. 'Are they married?'

Even I am shocked. 'He is a dead man if they are.'

The thought of the queen's brother, his own nephew, dead for treason does not disturb him. But then, it is a familiar thought. 'Unless the king, in honeymoon mood, is minded to forgive young love.'

'He might,' I concede.

'If Katherine were to put it to him?'

'He has refused her nothing so far; but all she has asked for has been jewels and ribbons,' I say. 'Should she ask him if another member of her family can marry another of his? Won't he suspect?'

'Suspect what?' he asks blandly.

I look around us. The boatmen are too far away to hear, the servants are all in Norfolk livery. Even so, I step closer. 'The king will suspect that we are planning to take the throne,' I say. 'Look what happened to Henry Fitzroy when he was married to our Mary. Look what happened to our Thomas Howard when he was married to Lady Margaret. When these Tudor–Howard marriages take place a death follows thereafter.'

'But if he was in generous mood . . .' the duke starts.

'You have planned this,' I suddenly see.

He smiles. 'Surely not; but I can see an advantage if it happens to come about. We hold so much of northern England, it would be such a pleasure to see a Howard on the throne of Scotland. A Howard heir to the Scots throne, a Howard grandson on the English throne. Worth a little risk, don't you think? Worth a little gamble to see if our girl can pull it off?'

I am silenced by his ambition. 'The king will see this,' is reluctantly forced out of me by my own fear. 'He is in love but he is not blinded with love. And he is a most dangerous enemy, sir. You know this. He is at his worst when he thinks his inheritance is threatened.'

The duke nods. 'Fortunately we have other Howard children if dear Charles is snatched from us; and Lady Margaret is a fool who can be locked up at Syon Abbey for another year or two. At the very worst we do not lose much.'

'Is Katherine to try to save them?' I ask.

'Yes. It's worth a try,' he says carelessly. 'It's a great gamble for a great prize,' and he steps up the gangplank into the waiting barge. I watch them cast off the ropes and I see the barge swing into the current. The rowers' oars are held upwards, like lances, and at the command they lower them in one smooth sweep into the green water. The Norfolk standard at the stern ripples out and the barge leaps forwards as the oars bite. In a moment the duke has gone.

Katherine, Hampton Court, October 1540

Like a fool I am in the privy garden at half past nine. I cannot trust anybody with the secret that I am meeting Thomas Culpepper, so I send my ladies to my rooms ahead of me as soon as I hear the clock strike ten. Within a minute of them leaving, the door in the wall opens and he comes in.

He walks like a young man. He does not drag his fat leg like the king. He walks on the balls of his feet like a dancer, as if he were ready to run or to fight at a moment's notice. I find I am smiling in silence, and he comes to my side and looks at me, saying nothing. We look at each other for a long time and for once I am not thinking what I should say, nor even how I look. I just drink in the sight of him.

'Thomas,' I breathe, and his name is so sweet that my voice comes out all dreamy.

'Your Grace,' he says back.

Gently he takes my hand and raises it to his lips. At the last moment, as he touches his lips to my fingers, he looks at me with those piercing blue eyes and I can feel my knees go quite weak, just at this slight touch.

'Are you well?' he asks.

'Yes,' I say. 'Oh, yes. Are you?'

He nods. We stand, as if the music has just stopped in a dance, facing each other, looking into each other's eyes.

'The king?' I ask. For a moment I had forgotten all about him.

'Better this morning,' he says. 'The physician came and purged him last night and he laboured painfully for some hours but now he has passed a great motion and is better for it.'

I turn my head away at the very thought of it and Thomas gives a little laugh. 'I am sorry. I am too accustomed; all of us in his rooms are accustomed to talk in much detail about his health. I did not mean . . .'

'No,' I say. 'I have to know all about it too.'

'I suppose it is natural, once one reaches such a great age . . .'

'My grandmama is his age and she does not talk about purges all the time, nor does she smell of the privy.'

He laughs again. 'Well, I swear that if I ever get to forty I shall drown myself. I couldn't bear to grow old and flatulent.'

I laugh now, at the thought of this radiant young man growing old and flatulent. 'You will be as fat as the king,' I predict. 'And surrounded by adoring great-grandchildren and an old wife.'

'Oh I don't expect to marry.'

'Don't you?'

'I can't imagine it.'

'Why ever not?'

He looks at me intently. 'I am so much in love. I am too much in love. I can only think of one woman, and she is not free.'

I am breathless. 'Can you? Does she know?'

He smiles at me. 'I don't know. D'you think I should tell her?'

The door behind me opens and Lady Rochford is there. 'Your Grace?'

'Here is Thomas Culpepper come to tell me that the king has been purged and is better for it,' I say brightly, my voice high and thin. I turn back to him, I dare not meet his eyes. 'Will you ask His Grace if I may visit him today?'

He bows without looking at me. 'I will ask him at once,' he says, and goes quickly from the garden.

'What d'you know of Lady Margaret and your brother Charles?' Lady Rochford demands.

'Nothing,' I lie at once.

'Has she asked you to speak to the king for her?'

'Yes.'

'Are you going to?'

'Yes. I am hoping that he will be pleased.'

She shakes her head. 'Take care how you do it,' she warns me. 'It may be that he is not pleased.'

'Why should he not be pleased?' I ask. 'I think it is lovely. She is so pretty and a Tudor! It is such a high match for my brother!'

Lady Rochford looks at me. 'The king may think it a high match for your brother too,' she says. 'He may think it too high. You may need to use all your charm and all your skills to persuade him to allow them to marry. If you want to save your brother and advance your family, you had better manage him as well as you have ever done. You had better choose your time and be very persuasive. You must do this, your uncle would like it.'

I make a little face at her. 'I can do it,' I say confidently. 'I shall tell the king that it is my wish that they be happy and he will grant my wish. *Voilà!*'

'*Voilà* perhaps,' she says sourly, the old cat.

But then it all goes wrong. I think I shall tell the king when I see him that night, and Lady Margaret agrees to follow me in and beg for his forgiveness. Actually, we are both quite excited, certain that it will go well. I am going to plead and she is going to cry. But before dinner Thomas Culpepper comes to my rooms with a message to say that the king will see me on the morrow. I agree and go to my dinner – why should I care? The king has missed dinner so many times I don't think that it matters. Certainly he's not going to fade away in a hurry. But poor me! It does matter, for while I am at dinner, and dancing actually, someone pours poison in the king's ear about his niece and even about me and poor management of my rooms, and *voilà!*

Jane Boleyn, Hampton Court, October 1540

The king marches into her private rooms and jerks his head at the three of us ladies in waiting, and says, 'Outside', as if we were dogs for his ordering. We scuttle from the rooms like whipped hounds and linger at the half-closed door and hear the terrifying rumble of royal rage. The king, out of bed for only half a day, knows everything and is most displeased.

Perhaps Lady Margaret thought that Katherine would intercede for them before they were caught and that she could be persuasive enough. Perhaps the lovers thought that the king, rising out of his sickbed, returning to wallow in his own uxorious joy, would be forgiving to other lovers, to other Howard lovers. They are sadly mistaken. The king speaks his mind briefly and to the point and then strides out of her room. Katherine comes running after, white as her collar, flooded with tears, and says that the king is scenting plots and conspiracies and lush unchastity at the court of his rose, and he is blaming her.

'What shall I do?' she demands. 'He asks if I cannot keep control of my ladies. How should I know how to keep control of my ladies? How should I command his own niece? She is the daughter of the Queen of Scotland, she is royal and six years older than me. Why would she ever listen to me? What can I do? He says he is disappointed in me and that he will punish her, he says the two of them will face his extreme displeasure. What can I do?'

'Nothing,' I tell her. 'You can do nothing to save her.' What can be easier to understand than this?

'I cannot let my own brother be sent to the Tower!'

She says this, unthinking, to the woman, me, who saw her own husband go to the Tower. 'I've seen worse happen,' I say dryly.

'Oh then, yes.' She flaps her hand dismissively and twenty diamonds catch the light and dazzle away the ghosts of them, Anne and George, going to the Tower without a word to save them. 'Never mind then! What about now? This is Lady Margaret, my friend, and Charles, my own brother. They will expect me to save them.'

'If you so much as admit that you knew they were meddling with each other then it could be you in the Tower as well as them,' I warn her. 'He is against it now, you had better pretend you knew nothing of it. Why can you not understand this? Why should Lady Margaret be such a fool? The king's ward cannot bestow her favours where she wishes. And the king's wife cannot put her own brother into bed with a royal. We all know this. It was a gamble, a great and reckless gamble, and it has failed. Lady Margaret must be mad to risk her life for this. You would be mad to condone it.'

'But if she is in love?'

'Is love worth dying for?'

That stops her romantic little ballad. She gives a little shudder. 'No, never. Of course not. But the king cannot behead her for falling in love with a man of good family and marrying him?'

'No,' I say harshly. 'He will behead her lover; so you had better say farewell to your brother and make sure that you never speak with him again unless you want the king to think you are in a plot to supplant him with Howards.'

She blanches white at that. 'He would never send me to the Tower,' she whispers. 'You always think of that. You always harp on about that. It happened only once, to one wife. It will never happen again. He adores me.'

'He loves his niece and yet he will send her to Syon to imprisonment and heartbreak, and her lover to the Tower and death,' I predict. 'The king may love you, but he hates to think of others doing their own will. The king may love you, but he wants you like a little queen of ice. If there is any unchastity in your rooms he will blame you and punish you for it. The king may love you, but he would see you dead at his feet rather than set up a rival royal family. Think of the Pole family – in the Tower for life. Think of Margaret Pole spending year after year in there, innocent as a saint and as old as your grandmother, yet imprisoned for life. Would you see the Howards go that way too?'

'This is a nightmare for me!' she bursts out; poor little girl, white-faced in her diamonds. 'This is my own brother. I am queen. I must be able to save him. All he has done is fall in love. My uncle shall hear of this. He will save Charles.'

'Your uncle is away from court,' I say dryly. 'Surprisingly he has gone to Kenninghall. You can't reach him in time.'

'What does he know of this?'

'Nothing,' I say. 'You will find that he knows nothing about it. You will find that if the king asks him he will be shocked to his soul at the presumption. You will have to give up your brother. You cannot save him. If the king has turned his face away, then Charles is a dead man. I know this. Of all the people in the world: I know this.'

'You didn't let your own husband go to his death without a word. You didn't let the king order his death without praying for mercy for him!' she swears, knowing nothing, knowing nothing at all.

I do not say: 'Oh, but I did. I was so afraid then. I was so afraid for myself.' I do not say: 'Oh, but I did; and for darker reasons than you will ever be able to imagine.' Instead, I say: 'Never mind what I did or didn't do. You will have to say goodbye to your brother and hope that something distracts the king from the sentence of death, and if not, you will have to remember him only in your prayers.'

'What good is that?' she demands heretically. 'If God is always on the king's side? If the king's will is God's will? What good is praying to God when the king is God in England?'

'Hush,' I say instantly. 'You will have to learn to live without your brother, as I had to learn to live without my sister-in-law, without my husband. The king turned his face away and George went into the Tower and came out headless. And I had to learn to bear it. As you will have to do.'

'It isn't right,' she says mutinously.

I take her wrists and I hold her as I would a maid that I was about to beat for stupidity. 'Learn this,' I say harshly. 'It is the will of the king. And there is no man strong enough to stand against him. Not even your uncle, not the archbishop, not the Pope himself. The king will do what he wants to do. Your job is to make sure that he never turns his face from you, from us.'

Anne, Richmond Palace,
November 1540

So: I am to go to court for the Christmas feast. He holds true to his word that I shall be second only to little Kitty Howard (I must learn to say Queen Katherine before I get there). I have a letter from the Lord Chamberlain today, bidding my attendance and telling me I will be housed in the queen's rooms. No doubt I shall have one of the best bedrooms and the Princess Mary another, and I shall learn to see Kitty Howard (Queen Katherine) go to bed in my bed, and change her clothes in my rooms and receive her visitors in my chair.

If I am to do this at all, it has to be done gracefully. And I have no choice but to do this.

I can be sure that Kitty Howard will play her part. She will be rehearsing now, if I know her. She likes to practise her moves and her smiles. I imagine she will have a new, gracious smile prepared for my reception, and I must be gracious too.

I must buy gifts. The king loves gifts and of course little Kitty Howard (Queen Katherine) is an utter magpie. If I take some very fine things I will be able to attend with some confidence. I so need confidence. I have been a duchess and the Queen of England and now I am some sort of princess. I must learn courage to be myself, Anne of Cleves, and enter the court, and my new position in it, with grace. It will be Christmas. My first Christmas in England. I could laugh to think that I had thought that I would be merry, with a merry court, at the Christmas feast. I had thought I would be queen of that court; but, as it turns out, I shall only be a favoured guest. So it goes. So it goes in a woman's life. I am quite without fault and yet I am not in the position that I was called to. I am quite without fault and yet I am thrown down. What I must see if I can do, is to be a good Princess of England where once I planned to be a good queen.

Jane Boleyn, Hampton Court, Christmas 1540

The king has turned against his wife's family, against his own niece, and everyone stays quiet, keeps their heads low and hopes that his disfavour will not turn on them. Charles Howard, warned in advance by someone braver than the rest of us, has skipped downriver in a little fishing boat, begged a place on a coaster, and sailed for France. He will join the growing number of exiles who cannot live in Henry's England: Papists, reformers, men and women caught in the new treason laws, and men and women whose crime is nothing more than to be kin to someone the king has named as a traitor. The greater their numbers grow, the more suspicious and fearful is this king. His own father took England with a handful of disaffected men, in exile from King Richard. He knows, none better, that tyranny is hated, and that enough exiles, enough pretenders, can overthrow the throne.

So Charles is safe away in France, waiting for the king to die. In some ways his life is better than ours. He is exiled from his home and his family but he is free; we are here, but scarcely dare to breathe. Lady Margaret is back in her old prison of Syon Abbey. She cried very bitterly when she knew the king was imprisoning her again. She says she has three rooms to walk in, and a corner view of the river. She says she is only twenty-one and the days are dreary for her. She says the days pass very slowly and the nights go on forever.

She says all she wants is to be allowed to love a good man, to marry him, and to be happy.

We all know that the king will never allow this. Happiness has become the scarcest commodity of all in the kingdom this winter. No-one shall be happy but him.

Katherine, Hampton Court,
Christmas 1540

Now, let me see, what do I have now?

I have the Seymour inheritance, yes, all of it. All the castles, lordships and manors that were given to Jane Seymour are now given to me. Imagine how furious the Seymours are? One moment the greatest landholders in England; next, up jump I; and all of Jane's lands are mine.

I have most of the lands that belonged to Thomas Cromwell, now executed for treason, which is good riddance to bad rubbish, my uncle tells me. My uncle tells me that although he was a commoner, Thomas Cromwell kept his lands in very good heart and I can expect a handsome revenue from them. Me! A handsome revenue! As though I ever knew what a plough was for! I even have tenants, think of that!

I am to have the lands from Lord Hungerford who was condemned to death for witchcraft and buggery, and the lands of Lord Hugh, the Abbot of Reading. As usual with the king, it is not very pleasant to have lands that were owned by people now dead, and some of them dead to oblige me. But as Lady Rochford pointed out, and I do remember (though some people say that nothing stays in my head for longer than a moment), everything comes from dead people and there is no point in being too squeamish.

This is no doubt true, and yet I cannot help but think that she, for one, seems to inherit the goods of dead men with good cheer. She relishes her Boleyn inheritance of a title and wishes she had the house to go with it. I am sure if I were a widow I would be much more sad and reflective than she is; but she hardly mentions her husband at all. Not once. If ever I say to her, 'Is it not odd being in my rooms that were your sister-in-law's?' she looks at me almost sternly and says, 'Hush'. Now, is it likely that I would chatter all over the court that I am the second Howard girl to wear the crown? Of course not. But I would have thought that a widow would welcome a little thoughtful reflection on those she had lost. Especially if it is done sensitively, as I do it.

Not me, obviously, should I ever be widowed, for my case would be very different. No-one could expect me to be very sad. Since my husband is so very much older than me, it is only natural for him to die soon and then I shall be free to make my own life. Obviously, I should never be so impolite as to remark upon this, for one of the things I quickly learned as a courtier is that the king never needs a true portrait of himself, however he might demand true likenesses of others, like poor Queen Anne. He never wants to be reminded that he is old and he never wants to be told that he looks tired or that his limp is worse or his wound is stinking. Part of my task as his wife is to pretend that he is the same age as me, and is only not up and dancing with the rest of us because he prefers to sit and watch me. I never ever do anything, not by word or deed, to suggest that I am aware that he is old enough to be my father, and an injured, fat, weak, costive old father at that.

And I cannot help it if his daughter is older than me, and stricter than me, and better educated than me. She has arrived at court for the Christmas feast like an old ghost reminding everyone of her mother. I don't even complain of her; because I don't have to. Her very presence beside me, so serious, so much more grown-up, more like a mother to me than I could ever be to her, is enough to irritate the king. And he takes his irritation out on her, I am glad to say. It's enough to make a cat laugh. I have to do nothing. She makes him feel old and I make him feel young. So he dislikes her, and he adores me.

And though it is a certainty that he will die soon, I should be very sad for him if it were to be at once, say this year. But when it does happen, say next year, I would be Queen Regent and care for my stepson, Prince Edward. It would be very merry, I think. To be Queen Regent would be the best thing in all the world. For I would have all the pleasures and wealth of a queen but no old king to worry about. Indeed, everyone would have to worry about me and the greatest joke would be that in fifty years from now I could insist that they all behave as if I was not old and not tired but, on the contrary, as beautiful every morning as I am today.

The thought of him dying is something I never mention, not even in my prayers, for, amazingly, it is treason even to suggest that the king might die. Isn't he ridiculous? Fancy making it illegal to say something that is so obviously true! In any case, I take no chances with treason, and so never wish for his death and never even pray for it. But sometimes, when I am dancing with Thomas Culpepper and his hand is on my waist and I can feel his warm breath on my neck, I think that if the king were to die here and now I might have a young husband, I might know the touch of a young man again, the scent of fresh sweat in bed, the feel of a hard young body, the thrill of a kiss from a clean mouth. Sometimes, when Thomas catches me in a move in the dance and I feel him grip my waist, I ache for the touch of him. Whenever I think like this I whisper to him that I am tired, and I turn away from him and ignore the slight pressure of his fingers, and I go and sit down beside the king. Lady Margaret is a prisoner in Syon Abbey for loving a man against the king's will. There is no point in thinking like this. It is not very merry to think like this.

Jane Boleyn, Hampton Court, Christmas 1540

This is to be Katherine's Christmas, the happiest Christmas she has ever had. Her household is reformed around her, she is served by the greatest ladies of the land and befriended by the worst girls that ever romped in a dormitory. She has her lands in her own right, she has retainers by the thousand, she has jewels that would be the envy of the Moors, now she has to have the happiest Christmas of her life and we are ordered to make it so.

The king is rested and revived, excited at the thought of a dazzling celebration to show the world that he is the ardent husband of a young and pretty wife. The brief scandal of his niece's love affair is forgotten, she is locked up in Syon Abbey and her lover is run away. Kitty Howard has blamed everybody but herself for the laxity of her rooms and all is forgiven. Nothing shall spoil this first Christmas for the newly-weds.

But straight away there is a little pout on the pretty face. Princess Mary comes to court as she is bidden, and bends the knee to her new stepmother, but does not come up smiling. Princess Mary is clearly not impressed by a girl nine years her junior, and cannot seem to form her mouth to say the word 'Mother' to a silly, vain child, when that beloved title once belonged to the finest queen in Europe. Princess Mary, who has always been a girl of high scholarly ability and seriousness, a child of the church, a child of Spain, cannot stomach a girl younger than her, perched on her mother's throne like a tiny cuckoo chick and jumping down to dance the moment anyone asks her. Princess Mary first met Kitty Howard last spring when she was the vainest, silliest girl in service to the queen. How to believe that this little imp is now the queen herself? If it were the Feast of Misrule, Princess Mary would laugh. But this stunted version of royalty is not funny when it is played out every day. She does not laugh.

The court is grown merry, as some say, or wild, as others say. I say that if you put a young fool in command of her own household and bid her to please herself you will see an explosion of flirtation, adultery, posturing, misbehaviour, drunkenness, dishonesty and downright lechery. And so we see. Princess Mary walks among us like a woman of judgement through a market of fools. She sees nothing that she can like.

The little pout tells the king that his child-bride is discontented and so he takes his daughter to one side and tells her to mind her manners if she wants a place at court at all. Princess Mary, who has endured worse than this, bites her tongue and bides her time. She says nothing against the girl-queen, she merely watches her, as a thoughtful young woman would watch a dirty babbling stream. There is something about Mary's dark gaze that makes Katherine as insubstantial as a little laughing ghost.

Little Kitty Howard, alas, does not improve as a result of great position. But nobody, except her adoring husband, ever thought she would. Her uncle the duke keeps a strict eye on her public behaviour, and relies on me to watch her in private. More than once he has summoned her to his rooms for a fierce lecture on propriety and the behaviour expected of a queen. She breaks down into the penitent tears that are so easy for her. And he, relieved that – unlike Anne – she does not argue, or throw his own behaviour back at him, or cite the polite manners of the French court, or laugh in his face, thinks the deed is done. But the very next week there is a romp in the queen's rooms when the young courtiers chase the girls all around the queen's chambers, her own bedroom as well, smacking them with pillows and the queen is in the midst of it all, screaming and dancing on the bed and awarding points in the joust of the pillows. So what is to be done?

No power on earth can make a sensible woman out of Katherine Howard because there is nothing to work on. She is lacking in education or training or even common sense. God knows what the duchess thought she was doing with the young people in her house. She sent Katherine to music lessons – where she was kissed by the music master – but she never taught her to read or write or to reckon accounts. The child has no languages, she cannot read a score – despite the attentions of Henry Manox – she can sing with a thin little voice, she can dance like a whore, she is learning to ride. What else? No, nothing else. That is all.

She has wit enough to please a man, and some of her late-night foolery in Norfolk House has taught her a handful of whorish tricks. Thank God, she sets herself to please the king, and she succeeds beyond belief. He has taken it into his head that she is a perfect girl. In his eyes she has replaced the daughter he never loved, the virgin bride that his brother had first, the wife he was never sure of. For a man who has two daughters of his own, and wedded and bedded four women, he certainly has a lot of dreams unfulfilled. Katherine is to be the one who finally makes him happy, and he does everything to convince himself that she is the girl who can do it.

The duke summons me to his rooms every week, he leaves nothing to chance with this Howard girl, having lost control of the previous two Boleyns.

'Is she behaving herself?' he asks curtly.

I nod. 'She is wild with the girls of her chamber, but she says nothing and does nothing to which you could seriously object in public.'

He sniffs. 'Never mind if I object. Is there anything to which the king could object?'

I pause. Who knows what the king could object to? 'She has done nothing to dishonour herself or her high calling,' I say cautiously.

He glares at me under his fierce eyebrows. 'Don't mince words with me,' he says coldly. 'I don't keep you here for you to tell me riddles. Is she doing anything that would cause me concern?'

'She has a fancy for one of the king's chamber,' I say. 'Nothing has happened beyond them making cow's eyes at each other.'

He scowls. 'Has the king seen?'

'No. It's Thomas Culpepper, one of his favourites. He is blinded by his affection for them both. He orders them to dance together, he says they make a perfect pair.'

'I've seen them.' He nods. 'It's bound to happen. Watch her, and make sure she is never alone with him. But a girl of fifteen is going to fall in love, and never with a husband of forty-nine. We will have to watch her for years. Anything else?'

I hesitate. 'She is greedy,' I say frankly. 'Every time the king comes to dinner she asks him for something. He hates that. Everyone knows he hates that. He doesn't hate it in her, yet. But how long can she go on asking him for a place for this or that cousin, or this or that friend? Or asking for a gift?'

The duke makes a minute mark on the paper before him. 'I agree,' he says. 'She shall get the ambassadorship to France for William and then I shall tell her to ask for no more. Anything else?'

'The girls she has put in her chamber,' I say. 'The girls from Norfolk House and Horsham.'

'Yes?'

'They misbehave with her,' I say bluntly. 'And I cannot manage them. They are silly girls, there is always an affair going on with one young man or another, there is always one of them sneaking out or trying to sneak him in.'

'Sneak him in?' he demands, suddenly alert.

'Yes,' I say. 'No harm can be done to the queen's reputation when the king sleeps in her bed. But say that he is weary or sick and he misses a night, and her enemies find that a young man is creeping up the back stairs. Who is to say that he is coming to see Agnes Restwold and not the queen herself?'

'She has her enemies,' he says thoughtfully. 'There is not a reformist nor a Lutheran in the kingdom who would not be glad to see her disgraced. Already they are whispering against her.'

'You would know more than I.'

'And there are all our enemies. Every family in England would be glad to see her fall and us dragged down with her. It was ever thus. I would have given anything to see Jane Seymour shamed by a scandal. The king always fills his household with the friends of his wives. Now we are in the ascendancy again, and our enemies are gathering.'

'If we did not insist on having everything . . .'

'I shall have the Lord Lieutenancy of the North, cost me what it will,' he growls irritably.

'Yes, but after that?'

'Do you not see?' He suddenly rounds on me. 'The king is a man for favourites and for adversaries. When he has a Spanish wife we go to war with France. When he is married to a Boleyn he destroys the monasteries and the Pope with them. When he is married to a Seymour we Howards have to creep about and snatch up the crumbs under the table. When he has the Cleves woman we are all in thrall to Thomas Cromwell who made the match. Now it is our time again. Our girl is on the throne of England, everything that can be lifted is ours to carry away.'

'But if everyone is our enemy?' I suggest. 'If our greed makes us enemies of everyone else?'

He bares his yellow teeth in a smile at me. 'Everyone is always our enemy,' he says. 'But right now, we are winning.'

Anne, Hampton Court,
Christmas 1540

'If it is to be done at all, it must be done with grace.' This has become my motto, and as the barge comes upriver from Richmond, with the men on the wherries and the fishermen in their little boats doffing their caps when they see my standard and shouting out, 'God bless Queen Anne!' and sometimes other less polite encouragements, such as, 'I'd have kept yer, dearie!' and, 'Try a Thamesman, why don't yer?' and worse than that, I smile and wave, repeating to myself again: 'If it is to be done at all, it must be done with grace.'

The king cannot behave with grace; his selfishness and folly in this matter are too plain for everyone to see. The ambassadors of Spain and France must have laughed until they were sick over the excess of his wild vanity. Little Kitty Howard (Queen Katherine, I must, I will, remember to call her queen) cannot be expected to behave with grace. I might as well ask a puppy to be graceful. If he does not put her aside within the year, if she does not die in childbirth, then she may learn the grace of a queen . . . perhaps. But she doesn't have it now. In truth, she wasn't even a very good maid in waiting. Her manners were not fit for the queen's rooms then; how will she ever suit the throne?

It has to be me who shows a little grace, if the three of us are not to become a laughing stock of the entire country. I will have to enter my old rooms at this, my favourite palace, as an honoured guest. I will have to bend the knee to the girl who now sits in my chair, I will have to address her as Queen Katherine without laughing, or crying, either. I will have to be, as the king has said I may be: his sister and his dearest friend.

That this gives me no protection from arrest and accusation at the whim of the king is as obvious to me as anyone else. He has arrested his own niece and imprisoned her in the old abbey of Syon. Clearly, kinship with the king gives no immunity from fear, friendship with the king gives no safety; as the man who built this very palace, Thomas Wolsey, could prove. But I, rowed steadily upriver, dressed in my best, looking a hundred times happier since the denial of my marriage, can perhaps survive these dangerous times, endure this dangerous proximity, and make a life for myself as a single woman in Henry's kingdom which I plainly could not do as a wife.

It is strange, this journey in my own barge with the pennant of Cleves over my head. Travelling alone, without the court following behind in their barges, and without a great reception ahead of me, reminds me, as every day reminds me, that the king has indeed done what he wanted to do – and I can still hardly believe it is possible. I was his wife; and now I am his sister. Is there another king in Christendom who could perform such a transmutation such as that? I was Queen of England and now there is another queen, and she was my maid in waiting and now I am to be hers. This is the philosopher's stone, turning base metal to gold in the twinkling of an eye. The king has done what a thousand alchemists cannot do: turn base to gold. He has made that basest of maids, Katherine Howard, into a golden queen.

We are coming ashore. The rowers ship their oars in one practised motion and shoulder them, so the oars stand upright in rows like an avenue for me to walk through, down the barge from my warm seat, huddled in furs at the stern, to where the pages and servants are running out the gangplank and lining the sides.

And here's an honour! The Duke of Norfolk himself is on the

bank to greet me, and two or three from the Privy Council, most of them, I see, kinsmen or allies of the Howards. I am favoured by this reception, and I see by his ironic smile that he is as amused as me.

Just as I foretold, the Howards are everywhere; the kingdom will be out of balance by the summer. The duke is not a man to let an opportunity slip by him; he will take advantage, as any battle-hardened veteran would do. Now he has occupied the heights, soon he will win the war. Then we shall see how long it is before tempers fray in the Seymour camp, in the Percy camp, among the Parrs and Culpeppers and Nevilles, among the reformist churchmen around Cranmer who were accustomed to power and influence and wealth and will not tolerate being excluded for long.

I am handed ashore and the duke bows to me and says, 'Welcome to Hampton Court, Your Grace,' just as if I were still queen.

'I thank you,' I say. 'I am glad to be here.' Both of us will know that this is true for, God knows, there was a day, several days, when I never expected to see Hampton Court again. The watergate of the Tower of London where they bring in traitors by night – yes. But Hampton Court for the Christmas feast? No.

'You must have had a cold journey,' he remarks.

I take his arm and we walk together up the great path to the river frontage of the palace as if we were dear friends.

'I don't mind the cold,' I say.

'Queen Katherine is expecting you in her rooms.'

'Her Majesty is generous,' I say. There; the words are said. I have called the silliest of all my maids in waiting 'Her Majesty' as if she were a goddess; and that to her uncle.

'The queen is eager to see you,' he says. 'We have all missed you.'

I smile and look down. This is not modesty, it is to prevent me from laughing out loud. This man missed me so much that he was gathering evidence to prove that I had emasculated the king through witchcraft, an accusation that would have taken me to the scaffold before anyone could have saved me.

I look up. 'I am very grateful for your friendship,' I say dryly.

We go in through the garden door and there are half a dozen pages and young lords who used to be in my household loitering between the door and the queen's rooms to bow and greet me. I am more moved than I dare to show, but when one young page dashes up to me, kneels and kisses my hand, I have to swallow down the tears and keep my head up. I was their mistress for such a short time, just six months, it is touching to me to think that they care for me still, even though another girl lives in my rooms and takes their service.

The duke grimaces but says nothing. I am far too cautious to comment, so the two of us behave as if all the people on the stairs and in the halls and the whispered blessings are absolutely normal. He leads the way to the queen's rooms and the soldiers at the double doors throw them open at his nod and bellow, 'Her Grace, the Duchess of Cleves,' and I go in.

The throne is empty. This is my first bemused impression and I almost think, for one mad moment, that it has all been a joke, one of the famous English jokes, and the duke is about to turn to me and say, 'Of course you are queen, take your place again!' and we will all laugh and everything will be as it was.

But then I see that the throne is empty because the queen is on the floor playing with a ball of wool and a kitten, and her ladies are rising to their feet, very dignified and bowing, with immaculate care to the right depth for royalty, but only minor royalty, and at last that child Kitty Howard looks up and sees me and cries out, 'Your Grace!' and dashes towards me.

One glance from her uncle tells me how unwelcome would be any sign of intimacy or affection. Down I go into a curtsey as deep as I would show to the king himself.

'Queen Katherine,' I say firmly.

My tone steadies her, and my curtsey reminds her that we have to play this out before many spies, and she halts in her run and wavers into a small curtsey to me. 'Duchess,' she says faintly.

I rise up. I so want to tell her that it is all right, that we can be as we were, something like sisters, something like friends, but we have to wait until the chamber door is shut. It must be secret.

'I am honoured by your invitation, Your Grace,' I say solemnly. 'And I am very glad to share the Christmas feast with you and your husband, His Majesty the king, God bless him.'

She gives a little uncertain laugh and then, when I look promptingly at her, she glances at her uncle and replies: 'We are delighted to have you at our court. My husband the king embraces you as his sister and so do I.'

Then she steps towards me, as clearly she has been told to do only it had flown out of her head the moment she saw me, and offers me her royal cheek to kiss.

The duke observes this and announces: 'His Majesty the king tells me that he will dine here with you two ladies this evening.'

'Then we must make him welcome,' Katherine says. She turns to Lady Rochford and says: 'The duchess and I will sit in my privy chamber while the room is being readied for dinner. We will sit alone,' and then she sails towards my – her – privy chamber as if she had owned it all her life and I find myself following in her wake.

As soon as the door is shut behind us she rounds on me. 'I think that was all right, wasn't it?' she demands. 'Your curtsey was lovely, thank you.'

I smile. 'I think it was all right.'

'Sit down, sit down,' she urges me. 'You can sit in your chair, you'll feel more at home.'

I hesitate. 'No,' I say. 'It is not right so. You sit in the chair and I will sit beside you. In case someone comes in.'

'What if they do?'

'We will always be watched,' I say, finding the words. 'You will always be watched. You have to take care. All the time.'

She shakes her head. 'You don't know what he is like with me,' she assures me. 'You have never seen him like this. I can ask for anything, I can have anything I want. Anything in the world I think I could ask for and have. He will allow me anything, he will forgive me anything.'

'Good,' I say, smiling at her.

But her little face is not radiant as it was when she was playing with the kitten.

'I know it is good,' she says hesitantly. 'I should be the happiest woman in the world. Like Jane Seymour, you know? Her motto was: "the most happy".'

'You will have to become accustomed to life as a wife and Queen of England,' I say firmly. I really do not want to hear Katherine Howard's regrets.

'I will,' she says earnestly. She is such a child, she still tries to please anyone who scolds her. 'I really do try, Your Gr– er, Anne.'

Jane Boleyn, Hampton Court, January 1541

This is the court with two queens: nothing like it has ever been seen before. Those who had served Queen Anne, the now-duchess, were glad to see her again, and glad to serve her. The warmth of her welcome surprised everyone, even me. But she always had a charm about her that made her servants glad to do any little thing for her, she was ready with her thanks and quick to reward. Madame Kitty, on the other hand, is quick to order and quick to complain, and she has an endless number of demands. In short, we have put a child in charge of the nursery and she is making enemies of her little playmates as fast as she dishes out her favours.

The court was glad to see Queen Anne in her old place, and scandalised but fascinated that she should dance so merrily with Queen Katherine, that they should walk arm in arm, that they should ride out to hunt together, and dine with their husband in common. The king smiled on them as if they were two favourite daughters, his pleasure was so indulgent, his satisfaction in this happy resolution so apparent. The duchess who had been queen had prepared her own way with some skill, she had brought great gifts for the new husband and wife, beautiful matching horses dressed in purple velvet: a kingly gift. She has, as it turns out now, exquisite manners: queenly manners. Under the strain of being the former wife at the first Christmas of the new wife's court, Anne of Cleves is a model of tact and elegance. There is not a woman in the world that could have played the part with more discretion. And she is more remarkable for being the only woman, in the history of mankind, ever to do such a thing. Other women in the past may have stepped aside, or been forced out, the first queen of this very court for one – but no-one has ever stepped graciously to one side as if it were a choreographed move in a masque, and gone on to dance her part in another place.

There was more than one man who said that if the king were not utterly besotted by a precocious child, he would be regretting his choice to put a silly girl in the place of this thoughtful, charming woman. And there was more than one prediction which said that she would be well-married before the year was out; for who could resist a woman who could fall from being queen to commoner and yet still carry herself as if greatness was within?

I was not one of those, because I think ahead. She has signed an agreement which says that she was legally contracted to marry another man. Her marriage to the king was invalid, so would be her marriage to anyone else. He has tied her to spinsterhood for as long as the son of the Duke of Lorraine shall live. The king has cursed her with spinsterhood and infertility and I doubt he has even considered this. But she is no fool. She will have considered this. She must have considered it a bargain worth making. In which case she is a stranger woman than any we have ever seen at court. She is a charming and graceful woman of only twenty-five years old, in possession of a large personal fortune, of unstained reputation, in her fertile years, and she has determined never to marry again. What a curious queen this one from Cleves has turned out to be!

She is in good looks. We now see that the plainness in her face and the pallor in her cheeks when she was queen were caused by the draining anxiety of being the fourth wife. Now that the fifth has taken her place we can see the young woman bloom, freed of the danger of privilege. She has used the time of her exile to improve herself. Her command of the language is much greater and her voice, now she is not struggling with the words, is mellow and clear. She is merrier, now that she can understand a witty remark, and now that she is lighter of heart. She has learned to play cards and to dance. She has outgrown her Cleves Lutheran strictness both in behaviour and appearance. Her dress is beyond recognition! When I think how she came to this country dressed like a German peasant girl in layer after layer of heavy cloth, with a hood squashing her head and her body wrapped like a barrel of gunpowder, and now I see this fashionable beauty, I see a woman who has taken the freedom to re-make herself. She rides with the king and talks seriously and interestingly with him about the courts of Europe and what the future holds for England, and she laughs with Katherine like another silly girl. She plays cards with the courtiers and dances with the queen. She is Princess Mary's only true friend at court and they read and pray together for a private hour every morning. She is the Lady Elizabeth's only advocate and she keeps a touching correspondence with her former step-daughter and has been promised the role of guardian and beloved aunt. She is a regular visitor to Prince Edward's nursery and his little face lights up to see her. In short, Anne of Cleves behaves in every way as a beautiful and highly regarded royal sister should do, and everyone has to say that she is fit for the part. Indeed, many people say that she is most fit to be queen – but that is so much empty regret. At any rate, we are all now very glad that our evidence did not send her to the scaffold; though everyone praising her now would have sworn king's evidence against her just as eagerly, had they been asked, as I was asked.

The duke summons me to his rooms one evening. He talks firstly of Queen Anne and how pleasantly she behaves herself at court. He asks me how Catherine Carey, my niece, Mary's child, is serving as a maid in waiting to her cousin.

'She does her duty,' I say shortly. 'Her mother has taught her well, I have very little to do with her.'

He allows himself a smirk. 'And you and Mary Boleyn were never the best of friends.'

'We know each other well enough,' I say of my self-regarding sister-in-law.

'Of course she has the Boleyn inheritance,' he says as if to remind me, as if I ever forget. 'We could not save everything.'

I nod. Rochford Hall, my house, went to George's parents at his death and from them to Mary. They should have left it to me, he should have left it to me; but no. I faced all the danger and the horror of what had to be done and ended up saving only my title and earning only my pension.

'And little Catherine Carey? Is she another queen in the making?' he asks, just to tease me. 'Shall we have her schooled to please Prince Edward? Do you think we can put her in a king's bed?'

'I think you will find her mother has already forbidden it,' I say coldly. 'She will want a good marriage and a quiet life for her daughter. She has had enough of courts.'

The duke laughs, and lets it go. 'So what of our present passport to greatness, our queen: Katherine?'

'She is happy enough.'

'I don't really care if she is happy or not. Does she show any sign of being with child?'

'No, none,' I say.

'How did she mistake before, in the first month of marriage? She had us all in hopes.'

'She can barely count,' I say irritably. 'And she has no sense of how important it is. I watch her courses now, there will be no mistake again.'

He raises an eyebrow at me. 'Is the king even capable?' he asks very quietly.

I do not need to glance towards the door, I know it must be secure

357

or we would not be having this most dangerous conversation. 'He can do the act in the end, though he labours overlong on it, and it exhausts him.'

'Then is she fertile?' he demands.

'She has regular courses. And she seems healthy and strong.'

'If she does not get with child then he will look for a reason,' he warns me, as if there is anything I can do about the whims of a king. 'If she is not with child by Easter at the latest, he will be asking why.'

I shrug my shoulders. 'Sometimes these things take time.'

'The last wife who took time died on the scaffold,' he says sharply.

'You need not remind me.' I am fired into defiance. 'I do remember all of that, and what she did, and what she attempted, and the price she paid. And then the price we paid. And the price I had to pay.'

My outburst shocks him. I have shocked myself. I had promised myself I would never complain. I did my best. And so, in their terms, did they.

'All I am saying is that we should prevent the question coming into his mind,' he soothes me. 'Clearly, it would be better for us all, for the family, Jane, for us Howards, if Katherine were to conceive a child before he has to wonder. Before a question even enters his head. This would be the safest course for us.'

'Bricks without straw,' I say coldly. I am still irritated. 'If the king has no power to give her a child, then what can we do? He is an old man, he is a sick man. He has never been a fertile man and what potency he has must be soured by his rotting leg and his locked-up bowels. What can any of us do?'

'We can assist him,' he suggests.

'How can we do more?' I demand. 'Our girl already does every trick that a Smithfield whore might do. She works him as if he were a drunken captain in a brothel. She does everything a woman can do, and all he can do is lie on his back and moan: "Oh, Katherine, oh my rose!" There is no vigour left in him. I am not surprised there is no baby coming from him. What are we to do?'

'We could hire some,' he says, as sly as any pander.

'What?'

'We could hire some vigour,' he suggests.

'You mean?'

'I mean that if there were a young man, perhaps someone we know that we can trust, who would be glad of a discreet affair, we might allow him to meet her, we might encourage her to treat him kindly, they might give each other a little pleasure, and we might have a child to put into the Tudor cradle and no man any the wiser.'

I am horrified. 'You would never do this again,' I say flatly.

His look is as cold as winter. 'I have never done it before,' he specifies carefully. 'Not I.'

'It is to put her head on the block.'

'Not if it is carefully done.'

'She would never be safe.'

'If she were carefully guided, and chaperoned. If you were to be with her, every step of the way, if you were ready to swear to her honour. Who would disbelieve you, who have been such a reliable witness for the king so many times?'

'Exactly. I have always borne witness for the king,' I say, my throat dry with fear. 'I give evidence for the hangman. I am always on the winning side. I have never offered evidence for the defence.'

'You have always borne witness for our side,' he corrects me. 'And you would still be on the winning side, in safety. And you would be kinswoman to the next King of England. A Howard-Tudor boy.'

'But the man?' I am almost panting with fear. 'There is no-one we could trust with such a secret.'

He nods. 'Ah yes, the man. I think we would have to ensure that he was gone when he had done his duty, don't you? An accident of some sort, or a sword fight? Or set upon by thieves? Certainly he would have to be removed. We could not risk another . . .' The duke pauses for the word. 'Scandal.'

I close my eyes at the thought of it. For a moment, against the darkness of my eyelids I can see my husband's face turned towards me, his expression quite incredulous as he saw me come into court and take my seat before the panel of judges. A moment of hope as he thought I was coming to save him. Then slowly, his dawning horror at what I was prepared to say.

I shake my head. 'These are terrible thoughts,' I say. 'And terrible thoughts to be shared by you with me. We, who have already seen such things and done such things . . .' I break off. I cannot speak for terror at what he will bring me to do.

'It is because you have looked at horror without flinching that I talk with you,' he says, and for the first time this evening there is a warmth in his voice, I almost think I hear affection. 'Who would I trust better than you, with my ambitions for the family? Your courage and skill have brought us here. I don't doubt but that you will take us forwards. You must know a young man who would be glad of a chance at the queen. A young man who could easily meet with her, a dispensable young man who would be no loss later on. Perhaps one of the king's favourites that he encourages to hang around her.'

I am almost gagging with fear. 'You don't understand,' I say. 'Please, my lord, hear me. You don't understand. What I did then . . . I have put from my mind . . . I never speak of it, I never think of it. If anyone makes me think of it I shall go mad. I loved George . . . Truly, don't make me think of it, don't make me remember it.'

He rises to his feet. He comes round from his side of the table and he puts his hands on my shoulders. It would almost be a gentle gesture except that it feels as if he is holding me down in my chair. 'You shall decide, my dear Lady Jane. You shall think about these matters and tell me what you think, on reflection. I trust you implicitly. I am certain that you will want to do what is best for our family. I have faith that you will always do what is best for yourself.'

Anne, Richmond Palace,
February 1541

I am home, and it is such relief to be here, I could laugh at myself for being a dull old spinster, shying away from society. But it is not just the pleasure of coming home to my own rooms and my own view from my windows and my own cook – it is the pleasure of escaping from the court, that court of darkness. Good God, it is a poisonous place that they are making for themselves, I wonder that anyone can bear to be there. The king's mood is more unreliable than ever. In one moment he is passionate to Kitty Howard, fondling her like a lecher before everyone so that she blushes red and he laughs to see her embarrassment, then half an hour later he is raging against one of his councillors, flinging his cap to the ground, lashing out at a page, or silent and withdrawn, in a mood of quiet hatred and suspicion, his eyes darting round, seeking someone to blame for his unhappiness. His temper, always indulged, has become a danger. He cannot control it himself, he cannot control his own fears. He sees plots in every corner and assassins at every turn. The court is becoming adept at diverting him and confusing him, everyone fears the sudden turning of his moods into darkness.

Katherine runs to him when he wants her and she shies away when his temper is bad as if she were one of his pretty greyhounds; but the strain must tell on her in time. And she has surrounded herself with the silliest and most vulgar girls that were ever allowed in a gentleman's house. Their dress is incredibly ostentatious with as much bare flesh and jewels as they can afford; their manners are bad. They are sober enough when the king is awake and in the court, they parade before him and bow to him as if he were a brooding idol; but the moment he is gone they run wild like schoolgirls. Kitty does nothing to control them, indeed, when the doors of her rooms are shut, she is the ringleader. They have pages and young men of the court running in and out of her rooms all day, musicians playing, gambling, drinking, flirting. She herself is little more than a child and it is a great joy to her to have a water fight in a priceless gown and then change into another. But the people about her are older and less innocent and the court is becoming lax, perhaps worse. There is a great scurry into decorum when someone dashes in and says the king is coming, which Kitty adores, the schoolchild that she is; but this is now a court without discipline. It is becoming a court without morals.

It is hard to predict what will happen. She said she was with child in the first month of marriage, but she was mistaken; she seems to have no idea how grave a mistake this can be, and there have been no hopes since. As I came away the wound on the king's leg was giving him terrible pain and he had taken to his bed again, seeing nobody. Kitty tells me that she thinks he cannot give her a child, that he is with her as he was with me, incapable. She tells me that she works such tricks on him that he has some pleasure, and she assures him that he is potent and strong, but the reality of the matter is that he rarely manages the act.

'We pretend,' she told me miserably. 'I sigh and groan and say it is such bliss for me, and he tries to thrust, but, truth be told, he cannot move, it is a pathetic mime he does, not the real thing.'

I told her that she should not speak of this to me. But she asked me, very trustingly, who should advise her? I shook my head. 'You can trust no-one,' I said. 'They would have had me hanged for a witch if I had said half what you have told me. If you say the king

362

is impotent, or you predict his death, that is treason, Kitty. The sentence for treason is death. You must never speak of this to anyone, and if anyone asks me did you speak to me, I shall lie for you and say you did not.'

Her little face was white. 'But what shall I do?' she asked me. 'If I cannot ask for help, and I don't know what to do? If it is a crime even to tell someone what is wrong? What can I do? Who can I go to?'

I gave her no answer for I had none. When I was in the same trouble and danger, I never found anyone who would help me.

Poor child, perhaps my lord duke has a plan for her, perhaps Lady Rochford knows what can be done. But when the king is tired of her – and he must tire of her, for what can she do to create a lasting love? – when he is tired of her, if she does not have a child, then why would he keep her? And if he has a mind to be rid of her, will he make as generous a settlement on her as he did for me, given that I was a duchess with powerful friends and she is a light, slight-witted girl with no defence? Or will he find some easier, quicker and cheaper way to be rid of her?

Katherine, Hampton Court, March 1541

Let me see, what do I have?

My winter gowns are all completed, though I have some more for spring in the making but they are of no use, for the season of Lent is coming and I cannot wear them.

I have my Christmas gifts from the king, that is, amongst other things that I have already forgotten or given away to my women, I have two pendants made of twenty-six table diamonds and twenty-seven ordinary diamonds, so heavy that I can hardly hold up my head when they are round my neck. I have a rope of pearls with two hundred pearls as big as strawberries. I have the lovely horse from my dear Anne. I call her Anne now and she still calls me Kitty when we are alone. But the jewels make no difference for those too have to be put aside for Lent.

I have a choir of new singers and musicians but they cannot play merry music for me to dance when Lent comes. Also, I will not be allowed to eat anything worth having during Lent. I may not play cards or hunt, I may not dance or play games, it is too cold to go out on the river and even if it were not, it will be Lent soon. I will not even play jokes with my ladies or run around the apartments or play catch or bowls or bat and ball as soon as it is dreary, dreary Lent.

And the king, for some reason, is making Lent come early this year. Out of sheer ill humour he has taken to his rooms since February and now he doesn't even come out to dine, and never sees me, and is never kind to me, and has not given me anything nor called me pretty rose since Twelfth Night. They say he is ill, but since he is always lame and always costive and since his leg constantly rots from the wound, I can't see what difference it makes. And besides, he is so cross with everyone, and there is no pleasing him. He has all but closed up the court and everyone tiptoes around as if they were frightened to breathe. Indeed, half the families have gone home to their houses since the king is not here, and no business is being done by the Privy Council, and the king won't see anyone, so a lot of the young men have gone away and there is no amusement at all.

'He's missing Queen Anne,' Agnes Restwold says, because she is a spiteful cat.

'He is not,' I say flatly. 'Why should he? He put her aside by his own choice.'

'He is,' she insists. 'For see? As soon as she went away he went quiet, and then he became ill and now see, he has withdrawn from court to think about what he can do, and how he might get her back.'

'It's a lie,' I say. It is a terrible thing to say to me. Who should know better than me that you can love someone and then wake up and scarcely be troubled with them? I thought that was just me and my shallow heart, as my grandmother says. But what if the king has a shallow heart too? What if he thought – actually as I did, as obviously everyone did – that she had never looked better or appeared better? Everything about her that had been so foreign and stupid was somehow smoothed away and she was – I don't know the word – gracious. She was like a real queen and I was, like I always am, the prettiest girl in the room. I always am the prettiest girl in the room. But I am only that. I am never more than that. What if he now wants a woman with grace?

'Agnes, you do wrong to presume on your long friendship with Her Grace to distress her,' Lady Rochford says. I adore how she can say things like that. The words are as good as a play and her tone is like a shower of February rain down your neck. 'This is idle gossip about the king's ill health for which we should be praying.'

'I do pray,' I say quickly, for everyone says I go into chapel and spend all my time craning my head over the edge of the queen's box to see Thomas Culpepper, who glances up at me and smiles. His smile is the best thing in church, it lights up the chapel like a miracle. 'I do pray. And when it is Lent, God knows, I will have nothing to do but pray.'

Lady Rochford nods. 'Indeed, we shall all pray for the king's health.'

'But why? Is he so very ill?' I ask her quietly, so that Agnes and the rest of them can't hear. Sometimes I wish indeed that I had never allowed them all to join me. They were good enough for the maids' chamber at Lambeth but really, I don't think they always behave as proper ladies at the queen's court. I am sure Queen Anne never had a rowdy ladies' room like mine. Her ladies were better behaved by far. We would never have dared to speak to her as my ladies speak to me.

'The wound on his leg has closed up again,' Lady Rochford says. 'Surely you were listening when the physician explained it?'

'I didn't understand,' I say. 'I started listening; but then I didn't understand. I just stopped hearing the words.'

She frowns. 'Years ago the king took a dreadful injury in his leg. The wound has never healed. You know that much, at least.'

'Yes,' I say sulkily. 'Everyone knows that much.'

'The wound has gone bad and has to be drained, every day the pus from the flesh has to be drained away.'

'I know that,' I say. 'Don't talk about it.'

'Well, the wound has closed,' she says.

'That's a good thing, isn't it? It has healed? He is better.'

'The wound closes over the top, but it is still bad underneath,' she explains. 'The poison cannot get away, it mounts to his belly, to his heart.'

'No!' I am quite shocked.

'Last time this happened we feared that we might lose him,' she says most seriously. 'His face went black as a poisoned corpse, he lay like a dead man until they opened the wound again and drained off the poison.'

'How do they open it?' I ask. 'You know, this is really disgusting.'

'They cut into it and then they hold it open,' she says. 'They wedge it open with little chips of gold. They have to push the chips into the wound to keep it raw, otherwise it will close over. He has to bear the pain of an open wound all the time, and they will have to do it again. Cut into his leg and then cut again.'

'Then he will be well again?' I ask brightly, I really want her to stop telling me these things.

'No,' she says. 'Then he will be as he was, lame and in pain, and being poisoned by it. The pain makes him angry and, worse than that, it makes him feel old and weary. The lameness means he cannot be the man he was. You helped him to feel young again, but now the wound reminds him that he is an old man.'

'He can't really have thought he was young. He can't have thought he was young and handsome. Not even he can have thought that.'

She looks at me seriously. 'Oh, Katherine, he did think he was young and in love. He has to be made to think that again.'

'But what can I do?' I can feel myself pouting. 'I cannot put ideas in his head. Besides, he does not come to my bed while he is ill.'

'You will have to go to him,' she says. 'Go to him and make something up that will make him feel young and in love again. Make him feel like a young man, filled with lust.'

I frown. 'I don't know how.'

'What would you do if he were a young man?'

'I could tell him that one of the young men of the court is in love with me,' I suggest. 'I could make him jealous. There are young men here,' I am thinking of Thomas Culpepper, 'that I know I could really, truly desire.'

'Never,' she says urgently. 'Never do that. You don't know how dangerous it is to do that.'

'Yes, but you said . . .'

'Can you not think of a way that would make him feel in love again without putting your neck on the block?' she demands irritably.

'Really!' I exclaim. 'I only thought . . .'

'Think again,' she says, quite rudely.

I say nothing. I am not thinking, I am purposely not speaking to show her that she has been rude and I will not have it.

'Tell him that you are afraid he wants to go back to the Duchess of Cleves,' she says.

This is so surprising that I forget to sulk and I look at her in astonishment. 'But that is just what Agnes was saying and you told her not to distress me.'

'Exactly,' she says. 'That is why it is such a clever lie. Because it is all but true. Half the court is saying it behind their hands, Agnes Restwold says it to your face. If you ever thought for a moment about anything but yourself and your looks and your jewels, you would indeed be anxious and distressed. And, best of all, if you go to him and you behave anxiously and distressed then he will feel that two women have been fighting over him and he will feel filled with confidence in his own charm again. If you do it well it might get him back into your bed before Lent.'

I hesitate. 'I want him to be happy, of course,' I say carefully. 'But if he does not come to my bed before Lent then it does not much matter . . .'

'It does matter. This is not about your pleasure or even his,' she says gravely. 'He has to get a son on you. You seem to keep forgetting it is not about dancing or music or even jewels or land. You do not earn your place as queen by being the woman he dotes on, you earn your place as queen by being the mother of his son. Until you give him a son I don't think he will even have you crowned.'

'I must be crowned,' I protest.

'Then you must get him into your bed to give you a child,' she says. 'Anything else is too dangerous even to think about.'

'I'll go.' I sigh a great hard-done-by sigh, so she can see that I am not frightened by her threats, but on the contrary I am wearily going to do my duty. 'I'll go and tell him I am unhappy.'

By luck, when I get there the outer presence chamber is unusually empty, so many people have gone home. So Thomas Culpepper is almost alone, playing at dice, right hand against left, in the window-seat.

'Are you winning?' I ask him, trying to speak lightly.

He leaps to his feet as he sees me, and bows.

'I always win, Your Grace,' he says. His smile makes my heart skip a beat. It really does, it truly does, when he tosses his head like that and smiles I can hear my heart go: thud-thud.

'That is not a great skill if you are playing alone,' I say aloud, and to myself I say: and that's not very witty.

'I win at dice and I win at cards but I am hopeless at love,' he says very quietly.

I glance behind me, Katherine Tylney has stopped to talk to the Duke of Hertford's kinsman and is not listening, for once. Catherine Carey is at a discreet distance, looking out of the window.

'You are in love?' I ask.

'You must know it,' he says in a whisper.

I hardly dare think. He must mean me, he must be about to declare his love for me. But I swear if he is talking about someone else I shall just die. I can't bear him to want someone else. But I keep my voice light.

'Why should I know it?'

369

'You must know who I love,' he says. 'You, of all people in the world.'

This conversation is so delicious I can feel my toes curling up inside my new slippers. I feel hot, I am certain I am blushing and he will be able to see.

'Must I?'

'The king will see you now,' announces the idiot Dr Butt and I jump and start away from Thomas Culpepper, for I had utterly forgotten that I was there to see the king and to make him love me again. 'I'll come in a minute,' I say over my shoulder.

Thomas gives a little snort of laughter, and I have to clap my hand over my mouth to stop myself giggling too. 'No, you must go,' he reminds me quietly. 'You can't keep the king waiting. I'll be here when you come out.'

'Of course I am going at once,' I say, remembering that I have to seem upset at the king's neglect, and I turn away from him in a hurry and dash into the king's room, where he is lying on his bed like a great ship stranded in dry dock, his leg stuck up into the air on embroidered cushions and his big round face all wan and self-pitiful; and I walk slowly towards his big bed and try to look anxious for his love.

Jane Boleyn, Hampton Court,
March 1541

The king is sliding into some kind of melancholy, he insists on being alone, shut away like some old dying smelly dog, and Katherine's attempts to make him turn to her are doomed since she cannot sustain an interest in anyone but herself for more than half a day. She has gone to his room again but this time he would not even let her in, and instead of showing concern, she tossed her pretty head and said that if he would not let her in she would not visit again.

But she lingered long enough to meet Thomas Culpepper and he took her walking in the garden. I sent Catherine Carey after her with a shawl and another well-behaved maid to give them the appearance of decorum, but from the way the queen was holding his arm, and chattering and laughing, anybody could see that she was happy in his company and had forgotten all about her husband lying in silence in a darkened room.

My lord duke gives me a long, hard look at dinner but says nothing, and I know that he expects me to get our little bitch serviced and in pup. A son would raise the king from his melancholy, and secure the crown for the Howard family forever. We have to do it this time. We have to manage it. No other family in the world has had two attempts at such a prize. We cannot fail twice.

In her pique Katherine summons musicians to the ladies' chamber and dances with her women and the people of her household. It isn't very merry and two of the wilder girls, Joan and Agnes, run down to the dining hall and invite some men from the court. When I see they have done this I send a page for Thomas Culpepper to see if he will be fool enough to come. He is.

I see her face as he comes into the room, the rise of her colour, and then how quickly she turns away and speaks to little Catherine Carey at her side. Plainly, she is quite besotted with him and for a moment I remember that she is not just a pawn in our game, but a girl, a young girl, and she is falling in love for the first time in her life. To see little Kitty Howard at a loss, stumbling in her speech, blushing like a rose, thinking of someone else and not herself is to see a girl become a woman. It would be very endearing if she were not Queen of England and a Howard with work to do.

Thomas Culpepper joins the set of dancers and places himself so that he will partner the queen when the couples pair off. She looks down at the ground to hide her smile of pleasure and to affect modesty, but when the dance brings them together and she takes his hand her eyes come up to him and they gaze at each other with absolute longing.

I glance round, nobody else seems to have noticed, and indeed half the queen's ladies are making sheep's eyes at one young man or another. I glance across at Lady Rutland and raise my eyebrows, she nods and goes to the queen and speaks quietly in her ear. Katherine scowls like a disappointed child, and then turns to the musicians. 'This must be the last dance,' she says sulkily. But she turns and her hand goes out, almost without her volition, to Thomas Culpepper.

Katherine, Hampton Court, March 1541

Every day I see him and every day we are a little bolder with each other. The king still has not come out from his rooms, and his circle of physicians and doctors and the old men who advise him hardly ever come to my rooms so it is as if we are free in these days – just us young people together. The court is quiet with no dancing and no entertainment, since it is Lent. I cannot even have dancing privately in my rooms any more. We cannot hunt, nor boat on the river, nor play games, nor anything amusing. But we are allowed to walk in the gardens, or by the river after Mass, and when I am walking Thomas Culpepper walks beside me, and I would rather walk with him than dance dressed in my best with a prince.

'Are you cold?' he says.

Hardly, I am buried in my sables, but I look up at him and say: 'A little.'

'Let me warm your hand,' he says, and tucks it under his arm so that it is pressed against his jacket. I have such a longing to open the front of his jacket and put both my hands inside. His belly would be smooth and hard, I think. His chest may be covered with light hair. I don't know, it is so thrilling that I don't know. I know the scent of him, at least, I can recognise it now. He has a warm smell, like good-quality candles. It burns me up.

'Is that better?' he asks, pressing my hand to his side.

'Much better,' I say.

We are walking beside the river and a boatman goes past and shouts something at the two of us. With only a handful of ladies and courtiers before and behind us, nobody knows that I am the queen.

'I wish we were just a boy and a girl walking out together.'

'Do you wish you were not queen?'

'No, I like being queen – and of course I love His Majesty the king with all my heart and soul – but if we were just a girl and a boy we could be strolling to an inn for some dinner and dancing, and that would be fun.'

'If we were a girl and a boy I would take you to a special house I know,' he says.

'Would you? Why?' I can hear the entranced giggle in my own voice, but I cannot help myself.

'It has a private dining room and a very good cook. I would give you the finest of dinners and then I would court you,' he says.

I give a little gasp of pretend shock. 'Master Culpepper!'

'I would not stop till I had a kiss,' he says outrageously. 'And then I would go on.'

'My grandmother would box your ears,' I threaten him.

'It would be worth it.' He smiles and I can feel my heart thudding. I want to laugh out loud for the sheer joy of him.

'Perhaps I would kiss you back,' I whisper.

'I am quite sure you would,' he says, and ignores my delighted gasp. 'I have never in all my life kissed a girl and not had her kiss me back. I am quite sure you would kiss me and I think you would say, "Oh, Thomas!"'

'Then you are very sure of yourself indeed, Master Culpepper.'

'Call me Thomas.'

'I will not!'

'Call me Thomas when we are alone like this.'

'Oh, Thomas!'

'There you are, you said it, and I have not even kissed you yet.'

'You must not talk to me of kissing when anyone else is near.'

'I know that. I should never let any danger come to you. I shall guard you as my life itself.'

'The king knows everything,' I warn him. 'Everything we say, perhaps even everything we think. He has spies everywhere and he knows what is in people's very hearts.'

'My love is hidden deep,' he says.

'Your love?' I can hardly breathe for this.

'My love,' he repeats.

Lady Rochford comes up beside me. 'We have to go in,' she says. 'It is going to rain.'

At once Thomas Culpepper turns around and leads me back towards the palace. 'I don't want to go in,' I say stubbornly.

'Go in, and then say you want to change your gown, and slip down the garden stairs from your privy chamber and I will wait for you in the doorway,' he says very quietly.

'You didn't meet me last time we agreed.'

He chuckles. 'You must forgive me for that, it was months ago. I shall meet you without fail this time. There is something very special that I want to do.'

'And what is that?'

'I want to see if I can make you say, "Oh, Thomas," again.'

Anne, Richmond Palace,
March 1541

Ambassador Harst has come to tell me the news from court. He has placed a young man as a servant in the king's rooms and the boy says that the physicians attend the king every day and are struggling to keep the wound open so that the poison can drain from his leg. They are putting pellets of gold into the wound so that it cannot close, and tying the edges back with string, they are pulling at the poor man's living flesh as if they were making a pudding.

'He must be in agony,' I say.

Dr Harst nods. 'And he is in despair,' he says. 'He thinks he will never recover, he thinks his time is done, and he is sick with fear at leaving Prince Edward without a safe guardian. The Privy Council are thinking that they will have to form a regency.'

'Who will he trust to guard the prince in his minority?'

'He trusts nobody, and the prince's family, the Seymours, are declared enemies of the queen's family, the Howards. There is no doubt that they will tear the country apart between them. The Tudor peace will end as it began, in a war for the kingdom between the great families. The king fears for the people's faith as well. The Howards are determined on the old religion and will take the country back to Rome; but Cranmer has the church behind him and will fight for reform.'

I nibble my finger, thinking. 'Does the king still fear there is a plot to overthrow him?'

'There is news of a new uprising in the North, in support of the old religion. The king fears that the men will come out again, that it will spread, he believes there are Papists everywhere calling for a rebellion against him.'

'None of this endangers me? He will not turn against me?'

His tired face folds downwards into a grimace. 'He might. He fears the Lutherans as well.'

'But everybody knows I am a practising member of the king's church!' I protest. 'I do everything to show that I conform to the king's instructions.'

'You were brought in as a Protestant princess,' he says. 'And the man who brought you in paid with his life. I am fearful.'

'What can we do?' I ask.

'I shall keep watch on the king,' he says. 'While he acts against the Papists we are safe enough, but if he turns against the reformers we should make sure that we can get home, if we need to.'

I give a little shudder, thinking of the mad tyranny of my brother as opposed to the mad tyranny of this king. 'I have no home there.'

'You may have no home here.'

'The king has promised me my safety,' I say.

'He promised you the throne,' the ambassador says wryly. 'And who sits there now?'

'I don't envy her.' I am thinking of her husband brooding on his wrongs, trapped in his bed by his suppurating wound, counting his enemies and allocating blame, while his fever burns and his sense of injustice grows more mad.

'I should think no woman in the world would envy her,' the ambassador replies.

Jane Boleyn, Hampton Court, April 1541

'What actually happened to Anne Boleyn?' the child-queen horrifies me by asking as we walk back from Mass early one morning in April. The king was, as usual, absent from the royal box and for once she was not peering over the edge of the box to see Culpepper. She even closed her eyes during the prayers as if praying, and she seemed thoughtful. Now this.

'She was accused of treason,' I say coolly. 'Surely, you know that?'

'Yes, but why? Exactly why? What happened?'

'You should ask your grandmother, or the duke,' I say.

'Weren't you there?'

Was I not there? Was I not there for every agonising second of it all? 'Yes, I was at court,' I say.

'Don't you remember?'

As if it were engraved on my skin with a knife. 'Oh, I remember. But I don't like to talk of it. Why would you seek to know of the past? It means nothing now.'

'But it's not as if it were a secret,' she presses me. 'There is nothing to be ashamed of, is there?'

I swallow on a dry throat. 'No, nothing. But it cost me my sister-in-law and my husband and our good name.'

'Why did they execute your husband?'

'He was accused of treason with her, and the other men.'

'I thought that the other men were accused of adultery?'

'It's the same thing,' I say tersely. 'If the queen takes a lover that is treason to the king. D'you see? Now can we speak of something else?'

'Then why did they execute her brother, your husband?'

I grit my teeth. 'They were accused of being lovers,' I say grimly. 'Now do you see why I don't want to speak of it? Why no-one wants to speak of it? So can we say no more of it?'

She does not even hear my tone, she is so shocked. 'They accused her of taking her brother as a lover?' she demanded. 'How could they think she would do such a thing? How could they have evidence of such a thing?'

'Spies and liars,' I say bitterly. 'Be warned. Don't trust those stupid girls you have gathered around you.'

'Who accused them?' she asks, still puzzled. 'Who could give such evidence?'

'I don't know,' I say, I am desperate to get away from her, from her determined hunt after these old truths. 'It is too long ago, and I cannot remember, and if I could, I would not discuss it.'

I stride away from her, ignoring royal protocol, I cannot stand the dawning suspicion in her face. 'Who could know?' she repeats. But I have gone.

Katherine, Hampton Court,
April 1541

I am much reassured by all that I am learning, and I wish I had thought to ask before. I had always believed that my cousin Queen Anne had been caught with a lover and beheaded for that. Now I find that it was far more complicated than that, she was at the centre of a treasonous plot, too long ago for me to understand. I was afraid in case she and I were treading the same road to the same destination, I was afraid that I had inherited her wickedness. But it turns out that there was a great plot and even my Lady Rochford and her husband were tied up in it somehow. It will have been about religion, I daresay, for Anne was a furious Sacramentary, I think, whereas now everyone with any sense is for the old ways. So I think as long as I am very clever and very discreet that I can at least be friends with Thomas Culpepper, I can see him often, he can be my companion and my comforter, and nobody need know or think anything of it. And while he is a loyal servant of the king and while I am a good wife, then no harm will be done.

Cleverly, I call my cousin Catherine Carey to my side and tell her to sort embroidery silks into shades of colour for me, as if I am about to start sewing. If she had been longer at court she would know at once that this is a ruse since I have not touched a needle since I became queen, but she brings a stool and sits at my feet and puts one pink silk beside another, and we look at them together.

'Has your mother ever told you what happened to her sister, Queen Anne?' I ask quietly.

She looks up at me. She has hazel eyes, not as dark as the Boleyn shade. 'Oh, I was there,' she says simply.

'You were there!' I exclaim. 'But I didn't know anything about it!'

She smiles. 'You were in the country, weren't you? We are about the same age. But I was a child at court. My mother was lady in waiting to her sister Anne Boleyn, and I was maid in waiting.'

'So what happened?' I am almost choking with curiosity. 'Lady Rochford will never tell me a thing! And she gets so cross when I ask.'

'It is a bad story and not worth the telling,' she says.

'Not you as well! I will be told, Catherine. She is my aunt too, you know. I have a right to know.'

'Oh, I'll tell you. But it still won't make it a good story. The queen was accused of adultery with her own brother, my uncle.' Catherine speaks quietly, as if it is an everyday event. 'Also with other men. She was found guilty, he was found guilty, the men were found guilty. The queen and her brother George were both sentenced to death. I went into the Tower with her. I was her maid in the Tower. I was with her when they came for her, and she went out to die.'

I look at this girl, this cousin of mine, my own age, my own family. 'You were in the Tower?' I whisper.

She nods. 'As soon as it was over my stepfather came and took me away. My mother swore we would never go back to court.' She smiles, and shrugs. 'But here I am,' she says cheerfully. 'As my step-father says: where else can a girl go?'

'You were in the Tower?' I cannot get rid of the thought of it.

'I heard them build her scaffold,' she says seriously. 'I prayed with her. I saw her go out for the last time. It was terrible. It was truly terrible. I don't like to think of it, even now.' She turns her face away and briefly closes her eyes. 'It was terrible,' she repeats. 'It is a terrible death to die.'

'She was guilty of treason,' I whisper.

'She was found guilty by the king's court of treason,' she corrects me, but I don't quite see the difference.

'So she was guilty.'

She looks at me again. 'Well, anyway, it is a long time ago, and whether she was guilty or not, she was executed at the king's command, and she died in her faith, and she is dead now.'

'Then she must have been guilty of treason. The king would not execute an innocent woman.'

She bows her head to hide her face. 'As you say, the king is not capable of making a mistake.'

'Do you think she was innocent?' I whisper.

'I know she was not a witch, I know she was not guilty of treason, I am sure she was innocent of adultery with all those men,' she says firmly. 'But I do not argue with the king. His Grace must know best.'

'Was she very afraid?' I whisper.

'Yes.'

There seems nothing more to say. Lady Rochford comes into the room and takes in the sight of the two of us, head to head. 'What are you doing, Catherine?' she asks irritably.

Catherine looks up. 'Sorting embroidery silks for Her Grace.'

Lady Rochford gives me a long, hard look. She knows I am hardly likely to start sewing if there is no-one watching. 'Put them in the box carefully when you have finished,' she says, and goes out again.

'But she was not charged,' I whisper, nodding to the door where her ladyship has gone. 'And your mother was not charged. Just George.'

'My mother was newly come to court.' Catherine starts to gather up the silks. 'And an old favourite of the king. Lady Rochford was not charged for she gave evidence against her husband and the queen. They would not accuse her, she was their chief witness.'

'What?' I am so astounded I give a little scream, and Catherine glances at the door behind us as if she fears someone hearing us. 'She betrayed her own husband and sister-in-law?'

She nods. 'It was a long time ago,' she repeats. 'My mother says that there is no value in thinking of old scores and old wrongs.'

'How could she?' I am stammering with shock. 'How could she do such a thing? Send her husband to his death? Accuse him – of that? How can Lady Rochford be so trusted by my uncle? If she betrayed her own husband and her queen?'

My cousin Catherine rises from the floor and puts the silks in the box, as she was ordered. 'My mother commanded me to trust nobody at court,' she observes. 'She said, especially Lady Rochford.'

All this leaves me with something to think about. I cannot imagine what it was like, all that long time ago. I cannot imagine what the king must have been like when he was a young man, a healthy young man, perhaps as handsome and desirable as Thomas Culpepper is now. And what must it have been like for Queen Anne my cousin, admired as I am admired, surrounded by courtiers as I am surrounded, confiding in Jane Boleyn, just as I do.

I cannot think what this means. I cannot think what it means to me. As Catherine says, it was a long time ago, and everyone is different now. I cannot be haunted by these old, sad stories. Anne Boleyn has been a shameful secret in our family for so long it hardly matters whether she was innocent or not, since she died a traitor's death in the end. Surely, it does not matter to me? It is not as if I have to follow her footsteps, it is not as if there is a Boleyn inheritance of the scaffold and I am her heir. It is not as if any of this makes any difference to me. It is not as if I should learn from her.

I am the queen now, and I shall have to live my life as I please. I shall have to manage as well as I can with a king who is no husband to me at all. He has hardly been out of his rooms for a month, and he will not admit me even when I go to his door for a visit. And since he never sees me, he is never pleased with me and I have had nothing from him for months: not even a trinket. It is so rude of him and so selfish that I think it would quite serve him right if I were to fall in love with another man.

I would not do so, nor would I take a lover, not for anything. But it would undoubtedly be his fault if I did so. He is a poor husband to me, and it is all very well everyone wanting to know if I am in good health and if there is any sign of an heir, but if he will not let me into his rooms, how am I to get a child?

Tonight I am resolved to be a good wife and try again, and I have sent my pageboy with a request that I might dine with the king in his chamber. Thomas Culpepper sends back a message to say that the king is a little better today, and more cheerful. He has risen from his bed and sat in the window to hear the birds in the garden. Thomas comes to my rooms himself to tell me that the king looked down from the window and saw me playing with my little dog and that he smiled at the sight of me.

'Did he?' I ask. I was wearing one of my new gowns, it is a very pale rose pink to celebrate the end of Lent, at last, and I wore it with my Christmas pearls. To be honest, I must have looked quite enchanting, playing in the garden. If I had only known he was watching! 'Did you see me?'

He turns his head away as if he does not dare to confess. 'If I had been the king I would have run down the stairs to be with you, pain or no pain. If I were your husband I don't think I'd ever let you out of my sight.'

Two of my maids in waiting come in and glance curiously at us. I know that we are turned towards each other, almost as if we would kiss.

'Tell His Majesty that I shall dine with him this evening, if he will allow it, and I shall do my best to cheer him,' I say clearly, and Thomas bows and goes out.

'Cheer him?' Agnes remarks. 'How? Give him a new enema?' They all laugh together as if this is great wit.

'I shall try to cheer him if he is not determined to be miserable,' I say. 'And mind your manners.'

Nobody can say that I don't do every duty as a wife, even if he is disagreeable. And at least tonight I shall see Thomas, who will fetch me to and from the king's rooms, so we shall have moments together. If we can get somewhere where we cannot be seen he will kiss me, I know he will, and I melt like sugar in a sauce pot at the thought of it.

Jane Boleyn, Hampton Court, April 1541

'Very good,' says my uncle Howard to me. 'The king's wound is no better, but at least he is on speaking terms with the queen again. He has been to her bed?'

'Last night. She had to take the man's part on him, astride him, above him, working him up, she does not like it.'

'No matter. As long as the deed is done. And he likes it?'

'For certainty. What man does not?'

He nods with a grim smile.

'And she played your play to perfection? He is convinced that when he withdraws from court she breaks her heart at his absence and that she is always afraid that he will go back to the Cleves woman?'

'I think so.'

He gives a short laugh. 'Jane, my Jane, what a wonderful duke you would have made. You should have been head of our house, you are wasted as a woman. Your talents are all twisted and crushed into a woman's compass. If you had a kingdom to defend you would have been a great man.'

I cannot stop myself smiling. I have come a long, long way from disgrace when the head of the family tells me I should have been a duke like him.

'I have a request,' I say, while I am in such high favour.

'Oh, yes? I would almost say: "anything".'

'I know you cannot give me a dukedom,' I begin.

'You are Lady Rochford,' he reminds me. 'Our battle to keep your title was successful, you have that part of your Boleyn inheritance, whatever else we lost.'

I don't remark that the title is not much since the hall which carries my name is occupied by my husband's sister and her brats, rather than me. 'I was thinking I might seek another title,' I suggest.

'What title?'

'I was thinking I might marry again,' I say boldly now. 'Not to leave this family, but to make an alliance for us with another great house. To increase our greatness and our connections, to improve my own fortune, and to get a higher title.' I pause. 'For us, my lord. To advance us all. You like to position your women to their advantage, and I should like to be married again.'

The duke turns to the window so I cannot see his face. He pauses for a long while and then when he turns back there is nothing to see; his expression is like a painting, it is so still and unrevealing. 'Do you have a man in mind?' he asks. 'A favourite?'

I shake my head. 'I would not dream of it,' I say cleverly. 'I have merely brought the suggestion to you, so that you might think what alliance might suit us: us Howards.'

'And what rank would suit you?' he asks silkily.

'I should like to be a duchess,' I say honestly. 'I should like to wear ermine. I should like to be called Your Grace. And I should like lands to be settled on me, in my own right, not held for me by my husband.'

'And why should we consider such a great alliance for you?' he asks me, as if he already knows the answer.

'Because I am going to be the kinswoman to the next King of England,' I whisper.

'One way or another?' he asks, thinking of the sick king on his back with our slight girl working her hardest above him.

'One way or another,' I reply, thinking of young Culpepper, slowly making his way towards the queen's bed, thinking he is following his desires, not knowing he is following our plan.

'I will think about it,' he says.

'I should like to marry again,' I repeat. 'I should like a man in my bed.'

'You feel desire?' he asks, almost surprised to learn that I am not some kind of cold-blooded snake.

'Like any woman,' I say. 'I should like a husband and I should like to have another child.'

'But unlike most women, you would only want that husband if he is a duke,' he says with a small smile. 'And presumably wealthy.'

I smile back. 'Well, yes, my lord,' I say. 'I am not a fool to marry for love like some we know.'

Anne, Richmond Palace,
April 1541

Calculation and, to tell truth, a grain of vanity took me to court for Christmas, and I think it was wise to be there to remind the king that I am his new sister. But fear brought me home again swiftly enough to Richmond. Long after the festivities and the presents are forgotten, the fear remains. The king was merry at Christmas but was in a dark mood for Lent, and I was glad to be here, and happy to be forgotten by the court. I decided not to go to court for Easter; nor shall I go with them on the summer progress. I am afraid of the king, I see in him both my brother's tyranny and my father's madness. I look at his darting, suspicious eyes and think that I have seen this before. He is not a safe man, and I think the rest of the court will come to realise that their handsome boy has turned into a strong man, and now the man is slowly becoming beyond control.

The king speaks wildly against reformers, Protestants and Lutherans, and both my conscience and my sense of safety encourage me to attend the old church and observe the old ways. Princess Mary's faith is an example to me, but even without her I would be bending my knee to the sacrament and believing that wine is blood and bread is flesh. It is too dangerous to think otherwise in Henry's England, not even thoughts are safe.

Why should he, who has indulged his own desire in his power and prosperity, look round like some savage animal for others that he can threaten? If he were not the king, people would say that this must be a madman, who marries a young wife and, within months of the wedding, is hunting out martyrs to burn. A man who chose the very day of his wedding for the execution day of his greatest friend and advisor. This is a mad and dangerous man, and slowly everyone is coming to see it.

He has taken it into his head that there is a plot by reformers and Protestants to overthrow him. The Duke of Norfolk and Archbishop Gardiner are determined to keep the church as it is now, stripped of its wealth but basically Catholic. They want the reform to freeze where it is now. Little Kitty can say nothing to contradict them, for she knows nothing; in all truth, I doubt she knows what prayers are in her book. Obedient to their hints, the king has ordered the bishops and even the parish priests to hunt down men and women in the churches all over England who do not show proper respect at the raising of the host, charge them with heresy, and have them burned.

The butchers' market at Smithfield has become a place for human grief as well as beasts', it has become a great centre for burning martyrs, and there is a store of faggots and stakes kept for the men and women that Henry's churchmen can find to satisfy him. It is not yet called the Inquisition, but it is an Inquisition. Young people, ignorant people, stupid people and the very few with a passionate conviction are questioned and cross-questioned on little points of theology till they contradict themselves in their fear and confusion, and are declared guilty, and then the king, the man who should be father to his people, has them dragged out and burned to death.

People are still talking of Robert Barnes who asked the very sheriff who was tying him to the stake, what was the reason for his death? The sheriff himself did not know and could not name his crime. Nor could the watching crowd. Barnes himself did not know as they lit the flames around his feet. He had done nothing against the law, he had said nothing against the church. He was innocent of any crime. How can such things be? How can a king who was once the handsomest prince in Christendom, the Defender of the Faith, the light of his nation, have become such a – dare I name it? – such a monster?

It makes me shiver as if I were cold, even here in my warm privy chamber at Richmond. Why should the king have grown so spiteful in his happiness? How can he be so cruel to his people? Why is he so whimsical in his sudden rages? How does anyone dare to live at court?

Jane Boleyn, Hampton Court, April 1541

We have our candidate for the queen's favour and I have done next to nothing to hasten the courtship. Without any prompting but a girl's desire, she has fallen head over heels in love with Thomas Culpepper, and by all I can see, he with her. The king's leg is giving him less pain and he has come out from his private rooms since Easter and the court is back to normal again; but there are still many chances for the young couple to meet and, indeed, the king throws them together, telling Culpepper to dance with the queen, or advising her on her gambling when Culpepper is dealing. The king loves Culpepper as his favourite groom of the bedchamber, and takes him everywhere he goes, delighting in his charm and his wit and his good looks. Whenever he visits the queen, Culpepper is always in his train and the king likes to see the two young people together. If he were not blinded by his monstrous vanity he would see that he is throwing them into each other's arms; but instead he sees the three of them as a merry trio, and swears that Culpepper reminds him of his boyhood.

The girl-queen and the boy-courtier are playing pairs together, with the king overlooking both of their cards like an indulgent father with two handsome children, when the Duke of Norfolk makes his way around the room to talk to me.

'He is back in her rooms? She is bedding the king as she should?'

'Yes,' I say, hardly moving my lips, my face turned towards the handsome young pair and their doting elder. 'But to what effect, no-one can know.'

He nods. 'And Culpepper is willing to service her?'

I smile and glance up at him. 'As you see, she is hot for him, and he longs for her.'

He nods. 'I thought as much. And he is a great favourite with the king, that's to our advantage, the king likes to see her dance with his favourites. And he is a conscienceless bastard, that's to our advantage too. D'you think he is reckless enough to risk it?'

I take a moment to admire the way the duke can plot with his eyes on his victim, and anyone would think he was talking of nothing but the weather.

'I think he is in love with her, I think he would risk his life for her right now.'

'Sweet,' he says sourly. 'We'll have to watch him. He has a temper. There was some incident, wasn't there? He raped some gamekeeper's wife?'

I shake my head and turn away. 'I hadn't heard.'

He offers me his arm and together we stroll down the gallery. 'Raped her and killed her husband when he tried to defend her. The king issued him with a pardon for both offences.'

I am too old to be shocked. 'A favourite indeed,' I say dryly. 'What else might the king forgive him?'

'But why would Katherine fancy him, above all the others? There's no merit in him at all except youth and good looks and arrogance.'

I laugh. 'For a girl married to an ugly man old enough to be her grandfather, that is probably enough.'

'Well, she can have him, if she wishes, and I may find another youth to throw in her way as well. I have my eye on a former favourite of hers, just returned from Ireland and still carrying a torch. Can you encourage her, while we are on progress perhaps? She will be less watched, and if she were to conceive this summer she could be

393

crowned before Christmas. I would feel safer if she had the crown on her head and a baby in her belly, especially if the king falls sick again. His doctor says his bowels are bound up tight.'

'I can help the two of them,' I say. 'I can make it easy for them to meet. But I can hardly do more than that.'

The duke smiles. 'Culpepper is such a blackguard, and she is such a flirt, that I doubt you need do more than that, my dear Lady Rochford.'

He is so warm and so confiding that I dare to put my hand on his arm as he moves to go back to the inner circle. 'And my own affairs,' I remind him.

His smile does not waver for a moment. 'Ah, your hopes for marriage,' he says. 'I am pursuing something. I will tell you later.'

'Who is it?' I ask. Foolish, but I find I have caught my breath, like a girl. If I were to be married soon, it is not impossible but that I could have another child. If I were to be married to some great man I could lay down the foundation of a great family, build a big house, amass a fortune to hand down to my own heirs. I could do better than the Boleyns did. I could see my family rise. I could leave a fortune; and the shame and distress of my first marriage would be forgotten in the glamour of my second.

'You will have to be patient,' he says. 'Let's get this business with Katherine settled first.'

Katherine, Hampton Court, April 1541

It is springtime. I have never noticed a season so much in my life before; but this year the sun is so bright and the birdsong so loud that I wake at dawn and I lie awake with every inch of my skin like silk, and my lips moist, and my heart thudding with desire. I want to laugh without cause, I want to give my ladies little gifts to make them happy. I want to dance, I want to run down the long allées of the garden and twirl around at the bottom and fall on the grass and smell the pale scent of the primroses. I want to ride all day and dance all night and gamble the king's fortune away. I have an enormous appetite, I taste all the dishes that come to the royal table and then I send the best, the very best, to one table or another; but never, never to his.

I have a secret, it is a secret so great that some days I think I can hardly breathe for the way it burns on my tongue, hot for telling. Some days it is like a tickle that makes me want to laugh. Every day, every night and day, it is like the warm, insistent pulse of lust.

One person knows it, only one. He looks at me during Mass when I peer over the balcony of the queen's box and see him down below. Slowly, slowly his head turns as if he can feel my gaze on him, he looks up, he gives me that smile, the one that starts at his blue eyes and then moves to his kissable mouth, and then he gives me the cheekiest, quickest flash of a wink. Because he knows the secret.

When we are riding, his horse comes alongside mine in the hunt and his bare hand brushes my glove and it is as if I am scalded by his touch. I dare not even look at him then, he does no more than this, the gentlest touch, just to tell me that he knows the secret; he knows the secret too.

And when we are dancing and the steps bring us together and we are handclasped and we should, according to the rules of the dance, lock gazes as we go round, then we drop our eyes, or look away, or seem quite indifferent. Because we dare not be too close, I dare not have my face near his, I dare not look at his eyes, his warm mouth, the temptation of his smile.

When he kisses my hand to leave my rooms he does not touch my fingers with his lips, he breathes on them. It is the most extraordinary sensation, the most overwhelming feeling. All I can feel is the warmth of his breath. In his gentle grasp he must feel my fingers stir like a sweet meadow beneath a breeze, under that slightest touch.

And what is this secret, that wakes me at dawn and keeps me quivering like a hare until darkness when my fingers tremble at the warmth of his breath? It is such a secret that I never even name it to myself. It is a secret. It is a secret. I hug it to myself in the darkness of the night when King Henry is at last asleep and I can find a little patch of the bed that is not heated by his bulk nor stinking of his wound, then I form the words in my head but I do not even whisper them to myself: 'I have a secret.'

I pull my pillow down towards me, I stroke back a lock of hair from my face, I smooth my cheek against the pillow, I am ready for sleep, I close my eyes: 'I have a secret.'

Anne, Richmond Palace, May 1541

My ambassador Dr Harst brings me the most shocking, the most pitiful news that I think I shall ever hear. As he told me I started to shake at the very words. How could the king do such a thing? How could any man do such a thing? The king has executed Margaret Pole, the Countess of Salisbury. The king has ordered the death of an innocent, nearly seventy-year-old woman, for no reason in the world. Or at the very least, if he has a reason it is the one that governs so many of his actions: nothing but his own insane spite.

Good God, he is becoming a terrifying man. In my little court here at Richmond I hug my cloak around me, tell my ladies that they need not come, and that the ambassador and I are going to walk in the garden. I want to make sure that no-one can see the fear in my face. Now I know for sure how lucky I have been to escape so lightly, to escape so well. Thank God in his mercy that I was spared. There was every reason to fear the king as a murderous madman. They all warned me and although I was afraid, I did not know how vicious he could be. This wickedness, this mad malice against a woman old enough to be his own mother, the ward of his grandmother, the dearest friend of his wife, the godmother of his own daughter, a saintly woman, innocent of any crime – this proves to me once and for all that he is a most dangerous man.

That he should have a woman of nearly seventy years old dragged from her bed and beheaded – and for no reason! No reason at all except to break the heart of her son, her family, and those that love them. This king is a monster, for all that he smiles so sweetly on his little bride, for all that he is now so kind and generous to me, let me remember this: Henry of England is a monster and a tyrant, and no-one is safe in his realm. There can be no safety in the country when there is a man like this on the throne. He must be mad to behave so. That can be the only answer. He must be mad and I am living in a country ruled by a mad king and dependent on his favour for my safety.

Dr Harst lengthens his pace to keep up with me, I am striding along as if I could get away from this kingdom on foot. 'You are distressed,' he says.

'Who would not be?' I glance around, we are speaking in German and cannot be understood, my pageboy has fallen behind us. 'Why should the king have Lady Pole executed now? He has held her in the Tower for years. She could hardly be plotting against him! She has seen no-one but her jailers for years, he has already killed half her family and taken the rest into the Tower.'

'He does not think she was plotting,' he says quietly. 'But this new uprising in the North is to restore the old religion, they are calling for the Pole family to be kings again. The family are faithful Papists and much loved, they come from the North, they are the royal family of York, the Plantagenets. They are of the old faith. The king will not tolerate any rival. Even an innocent rival.'

I shudder. 'Then why does he not take a mission against the North?' I demand. 'He could lead an army to defeat the rebels. Why behead an old lady in London for their rebellion?'

'They say that he has hated her since she took Queen Katherine of Aragon's side against him,' he says quietly. 'When he was a young man he admired her and respected her, and she was the last Plantagenet princess, more royal than he is himself. But when he put the queen aside, Lady Pole took her side and declared for her.'

'That was years ago.'

'He does not forget an enemy.'

'Why not fight the rebels as he did before?'

He lowers his voice. 'They say he is afraid. Just as he was afraid before. He never fought them, he sent the duke, Thomas Howard, before. He will not go himself.'

I stride out and the ambassador keeps pace with me, my pageboy falls behind even more. 'I shall never be really safe,' I say, almost to myself. 'Not while he lives.'

He nods. 'You cannot trust his word,' he says shortly. 'And if you offend him, he never forgets it.'

'D'you think all this –' my gesture takes in the beautiful park, the river, the wonderful palace '– all this is just a sop? Something to keep me quiet, to keep my brother quiet, while the king makes his son on Katherine? And when she gives birth, and he crowns her queen, and he knows the deed is done, then he arrests me for treason or heresy or whatever offence he chooses to invent, and murders me too?'

The ambassador goes grey with fear at my suggestion. 'God knows, I pray not. But we cannot know for sure,' he says. 'At the time I thought he wanted a lasting settlement, and a lasting friendship with you. But we cannot know. With this king one can know nothing. Indeed, he could have intended friendship then, and he could change tomorrow. That is what they all say about him. That he is fearful and changeable, they never know who he will see as his enemy. We cannot trust him.'

'He is a nightmare!' I burst out. 'He will do anything he wishes, he can do anything he wishes. He is a danger. He is a terror.'

The sober ambassador does not correct me for exaggeration. Chillingly he nods. 'He is a terror,' he agrees. 'This man is the terror of his people. Thank God you are away from him. God help his young wife.'

Jane Boleyn, Hampton Court,
June 1541

The king, though he looks older and drawn, is at least returned to court and lives like a king instead of a sickly patient once more. His temper is a curse to his servants, and his rages can shake the court. The poison in his leg and in his bowels spills over into his nature. His Privy Council tiptoe in fear of offending him, as in the morning he will say one thing, and in the evening be a passionate advocate of the opposite course. He acts as if he cannot remember the morning and nobody dares to remind him. Whoever disagrees with him is disloyal, and the accusation of treason hangs in the air like the stink from his wound. This is a court of habitual change-coats but I have never before seen men fling away their opinions with such speed. The king contradicts himself every day and they fall into agreement with him, whatever he thinks.

His execution of the Countess of Salisbury has shaken us all, even the most hard-hearted. All of us knew her, all of us were proud to be her friend when she was the great friend and ally of Queen Katherine, and the last of our royal family of York. Easy enough to forget her when she fell from favour and was out of sight in the country. Harder to ignore her silent presence when she was in the Tower and everyone knew that she was ill-housed, and cold, and underfed, mourning her family, as even her little grandsons disappeared into the locked rooms of the Tower. Unbearable, when the king moves without warning against her, has her dragged from her bed without notice, and butchered on the block.

They say she ran from the axe, she did not make a dignified speech and lie down for him. She confessed nothing but insisted on her innocence. She fell on the scaffold and crawled to get away and the axeman had to run after her, raining down blows on her neck. It makes me shudder to hear it, it makes me sick to my soul to hear it. She crawled away from the same block that they brought out for Anne. How many women's heads will he put on it? Who will be next?

Katherine copes with this new irritable Henry better than one might hope. She has no interest in either religion or power so he does not speak to her of his policy and she does not know that his morning decisions are overturned by nightfall. Without an idea in her head she never argues with him. He treats her like a little pet, a lapdog, there for his caress, that can be sent away when it annoys him. She responds well to this and has the sense to hide her feelings for Culpepper under a veil of wifely devotion. Besides, what master would bother to ask a lapdog if she dreams of something better?

He pulls her about before the whole court, he is without embarrassment in his treatment of her. When they are at dinner, before everyone, he will reach over and tweak at her breast and watch the colour rise to her face. He asks her for a kiss and when she offers him her cheek he will suck on her mouth, and we can see his sly hand pat her rump. She never pulls away from him, she never steps back. When I look very carefully I can see her stiffen at his touch; but she never does anything that could enrage him. For a fifteen-year-old girl she does very well. For a girl passionately in love with another man she does very well indeed.

Whatever secret moments she manages to snatch with Culpepper between dinner and dancing, midnight finds her always in her bed, her gorgeous nightgown loosely tied, her white nightcap making her eyes look large and luminous: a sleepy angel, waiting for the king. If he is late coming to her bed she sometimes falls asleep. She sleeps like a child, and has a habit of smoothing her cheek across the pillow as she lies down her head, it is very endearing. He comes in his nightshirt with his thick robe around his broad shoulders, his bad leg heavily bandaged but the stain of the pus seeping through the white dressing. Most nights Thomas Culpepper is at his side, the heavy royal hand leaning heavily on the young man's shoulder for support. Culpepper and Katherine never exchange so much as one look when he brings her old husband to her bed. He gazes up at the bedhead behind her, where the king's initials are carved, entwined with hers, and she looks down at the silky embroidered sheets. He takes the king's cape from his fat shoulders, while a groom of the bedchamber raises the sheets. Two pages haul the king upwards to the bed and steady him as he balances on his only good leg. The stench of the suppurating wound fills the bedchamber and Katherine never flinches. Her smile is steady and welcoming and the king's groan as he gets into bed, and they gently thrust his legs under the covers, does not shake her composure. We all leave, reverently stepping backwards, and only when we have closed the door on them do I glance across to Thomas Culpepper and I see that his young face is twisted with a scowl.

'You want her,' I say quietly to him.

He glances at me with a denial on his lips, but then he shrugs and says nothing.

'She wants you,' I volunteer.

At once he snatches me by the elbow and draws me so that we are in the window bay, almost wrapped up in the thick curtain. 'She says this to you? She has told you this in so many words?'

'She has.'

'When has she said such a thing to you? What did she say?'

'She comes out of her bedroom when the king has fallen asleep most nights. I take off her nightcap, I brush her hair, sometimes she is almost crying.'

'He hurts her?' he asks, shocked.

'No,' I say. 'She is crying with lust. Night after night she labours over him to give him pleasure, and all she can do for herself is to wind herself up tighter and tighter, like a bowstring ready to snap.'

Culpepper's face is a picture, if I were not doing my work for my lord duke I would not be able to contain my laughter. 'She cries with lust?'

'She could scream with it,' I say. 'Some nights I give her a sleeping powder, other nights she takes mulled wine and spices. But even so, some nights she cannot sleep for hours. She paces round the chamber pulling at the ribbons of her nightgown, saying that she is burning up.'

'She always comes out after the king is asleep?'

'If you were to come back in an hour she would be coming out then,' I whisper.

He hesitates for a moment. 'I dare not,' he says.

'You could see her,' I tempt him. 'When she comes from his bed with her desire unslaked, longing for you.'

His face is a portrait of hunger.

'She wants you,' I remind him. 'I stroke her hair and she drops back her head and whispers, "Oh, Thomas".'

'She whispers my name?'

'She is mad for you.'

'If I were to be caught with her it would be her death, and mine,' he says.

'You could just come and talk to her,' I say. 'Soothe her. It would be a service to the king to keep her steady. How long can she go on like this? The king pulling her about every night, stripping her naked, running his eyes and then his hands all over her, touching every inch of her, and yet never giving her a moment of peace? She is wound up tight, I tell you, Master Culpepper, tight like a lute string overstrung.'

His throat contracts as he swallows at the picture. 'If I could just talk to her . . .'

'Come back in an hour and I will let you in,' I say. I am almost as breathless as him, as excited by my words as he is. 'You can talk to her in her privy chamber, the king will be asleep in the bedroom. I can be here with the two of you, all the time. What complaint could anyone make if I am there, with the two of you, all the time?'

Oddly, he is not reassured by my friendship; he pulls back and stares at me suspiciously. 'Why would you so serve me?' he demands. 'What benefit for you?'

'I serve the queen,' I say quickly. 'I always serve the queen. She wants your friendship, she wants to see you. All I do is make that safe for her.'

He must be mad with love if he thinks that anyone could make their meeting safe. 'In an hour,' he says.

I wait by the fire as it dies down. I am doing my duty for the duke but I find my mind straying all the time to my husband George, and to Anne. He used to wait for her to come from the king's bed, just as I am waiting now, just as Culpepper will wait for the queen. I shake my head, I have sworn not to think of them any more, I have sworn to put the thought of them away from me. I drove myself quite mad thinking about them before, now they are gone, I need not torment myself about them any more.

After a little while, the door to the bedchamber opens and Katherine comes out. There are dark shadows under her eyes, and her face is pale. 'Lady Rochford,' she says in a little whisper as she sees me. 'Do you have my wine ready?'

I am recalled to the present. 'It's ready.' I seat her in the chair nearest the fire.

She puts her bare feet up on the fender. She shudders. 'He disgusts me,' she says inconsequentially. 'Dear God, I disgust myself.'

'It is your duty.'

'I can't do it,' she says. She closes her eyes and tips back her head. A tear creeps out from under her closed eyelids and runs down her pale cheek. 'Not even for the jewels. I can't go on doing it.'

I pause for a moment and then I whisper: 'You will have a visitor tonight.'

At once she sits up, alert. 'Who?'

'Someone you will want to see,' I say. 'Someone you have longed for, for months, perhaps even years. Who would you most want to see?'

The colour floods into her cheeks. 'You cannot mean . . .' she starts. 'Is he coming?'

'Thomas Culpepper.'

She gives a little gasp at his name and she leaps up. 'I have to dress,' she says. 'You must do my hair.'

'You cannot,' I say. 'Let me turn the key in the bedroom door.'

'And lock the king inside?'

'Better that, than he wakes and comes out. We can always find an excuse.'

'I want my perfume!'

'Leave it.'

'I can't see him like this.'

'Shall I stop him at the door and tell him to go away again?'

'No!'

There is a little tap on the door, so soft that I could not have heard it if I had not the ears of a spy. 'There he is now.'

'Don't let him in!' She puts a hand on my arm. 'It's too dangerous. Dear God, I shan't lead him into danger.'

'He only wants to talk,' I soothe her. 'There can be no harm in that.' Quietly, I open the door to him. 'It is all right,' I say to the

405

sentry. 'The king wants Master Culpepper.' I open the door wide and Culpepper steps into the room.

At the fireside, Katherine rises to her feet. The glow of the fire illuminates her face, gilds her gown. Her hair, tumbled about her face, glints in the light, her lips part to whisper his name, her colour rises. The ribbons of her gown tremble at her throat where her pulse thuds.

Culpepper walks towards her like a man in a dream. He stretches out a hand to her and she takes it and puts his palm at once to her cheek. He holds a handful of her hair, his other hand blindly finds her waist, they slide towards each other as if they have been waiting for months to touch like this; indeed they have. Her hands go to his shoulders, he draws her closer, without a word being said, she gives him her mouth, and he bows his head and takes her.

I turn the key on the outer door so the sentry cannot come in. Then I go back to the bedroom door, I stand with my back to it, my ears pricked for any noise from the king. I can hear the stertorous sound of his wheezy breath, and a loud wet belch. In the firelight before me, Thomas Culpepper slides his hand inside the throat of her gown, I see her head drop back, resistless, as he touches her breast, she lets him caress her, and she runs her fingers through his curly brown hair, pulling his face down to her bared neck.

I cannot tear my gaze away. It is as I always imagined it, when I used to think of George with his mistress. A pleasure like a knife, desire as pain. He sits on the high-backed chair, and draws her to him. I can see little more than the back of the chair and their silhouettes, dark against the glow of the fire. It is like a dance of desire as he takes her hips and pulls her astride him. I see her fumble with his hose, as he pulls at the ribbons at the front of her gown. They are about to do it as I watch them. They are shameless: me in the same room, and her husband behind the door. They are so wanton and so helpless with their desire that they are about to do it here and now, in front of me.

I hardly dare breathe; I must see everything. The sleeping king's heavy breathing is matched by their quiet panting, they are moving together, then I see the gleam of her pale thigh as she pulls her nightgown aside, and I hear him groan and I know that she has straddled him and taken him in. I hear a little sigh of desire and it is me, aroused with stolen lust. The chair creaks as she clings to the back and rocks forwards and back on him, her breath is coming fast, he is thrusting up inside her, I hear her start to moan as her pleasure mounts and I am afraid that they will wake the king, but nothing could stop them, not even if he were to wake and shout, not even if he were to try the door and come out; they are tied together by lust, they cannot break free. I feel my own legs weaken with mirrored desire as Katherine's little cries mount, and I slide down to the floor, to my knees, watching them but seeing George's desirous face, and his mistress astride him, until Katherine suddenly lets out a gasp and falls to Thomas' shoulder, at the same moment he groans and grips her, then they both subside.

It feels like a long time before she gives a little murmur and stirs. Culpepper lets her go and she rises from the seat, dropping the hem of her nightgown and smiling back at him as she goes to the fire. He rises from the chair and ties his laces again, then he reaches for her, wraps his arms around her from behind, nuzzles at her neck, her hair. Like a young girl in love for the first time, she turns in his arms and gives him her mouth, she kisses him as if she adores him, she kisses him as if this is a love that will last forever.

In the morning I go to find my lord duke. The court is preparing to go hunting and the queen is being lifted into the saddle by one of the king's friends. The king himself, hauled to the back of his hunter, is in a merry mood, laughing at Culpepper's new bridle of red leather, and calling up his hounds. The duke is not riding today, he stands at the doorway, watching the horses and the hounds in the cool of the morning. I pause beside him as I go to my horse.

'It is done,' I say. 'Last night.'

He nods as if I am telling him of the cost of the blacksmith. 'Culpepper?' he asks.

'Yes.'

'Will she have him again?'

'As often as she can. She is besotted.'

'Keep her discreet,' he says. 'And tell me the moment she is with child.'

I nod. 'And my own affair?' I ask boldly.

'Your affair?' he repeats, pretending he has forgotten.

'My marriage,' I say. 'I . . . I need to be married.'

He raises his eyebrow. 'Better to be married than to burn, my dear Lady Rochford?' he asks. 'But your marriage to George did not prevent you from burning up.'

'That was not my fault,' I say quickly. 'It was her.'

He smiles, he does not have to ask whose shadow fell on my marriage and set the fire that burned us all up.

'What news of my new marriage?' I press him.

'I am exchanging letters now,' he says. 'When you tell me that the queen is with child, I shall confirm it.'

'And the nobleman?' I ask urgently. 'Who is he?'

'Monsignor le Compte?' he asks. 'Wait and see, my dear Lady Rochford. But believe me, he is wealthy, and he is young, handsome and – let me think – no more than three, perhaps four, steps from the throne of France. Will that satisfy you?'

'Completely.' I can hardly speak for excitement. 'I shall not fail you, my lord.'

Anne, Richmond Palace,
June 1541

I have a letter from the Lord Chamberlain to invite me to go on progress with the court this summer. The king is to go to his northern lands, which were so recently in revolt against him for his attack on the old religion. He is going to punish and reward, he has sent the hangman ahead of him and he will follow safely behind. I sit for a long time with this letter in my hand.

I am trying to weigh up the dangers. If I am at court with the king and he enjoys my company and I am high in his favour then I secure my safety for perhaps another year. But equally, the hard-faced men of his court will see that he likes me again and they will put their minds to how to keep me from him. Katherine's uncle, the Duke of Norfolk, will be anxious to keep his niece in high favour, and he will not like any comparison that is made between her and me. He will have kept the documents that prove that I was part of a Papist plot to destroy the king. He may have created evidence of worse: adultery or witchcraft, heresy or treason. Who knows what solemnly sworn statements he gathered when they thought they would put me to death? He will not have thrown them away when the king decided to divorce me. He will have kept them. He will keep them forever in case one day he wants to destroy me.

But if I do not go, then I am not there to defend myself. If anyone says anything against me, links me with the northern conspirators, or with poor Margaret Pole the countess, with the disgraced Thomas Cromwell, with anything my brother may do or say, then there is no-one to speak in my favour.

I tuck the letter in the pocket of my gown and walk to the window to look out at the bobbing branches in the orchards beyond the garden. I like it here, I like being my own mistress, I like being in command of my own fortune. The thought of going into the bear pit which is the English court and having to face the monstrous old terror which is the king is too much for me to dare. I think, pray God I am right, that I shall not go on progress with the king, I shall stay here and take the risk that they may speak against me. Better that, than travel with him in constant danger of attracting envy. Better anything than travel with him and see those piggy eyes turn on me and realise that by some act – nothing I even know that I have done – I have fired his enmity and I am in danger.

He is a danger, he is a danger, he is a danger to everyone who is near him. I shall stay at Richmond and hope that the danger that is Henry passes me by and that I can live here in safety and peace.

I shall stay free of the frightened flock that is the court, I shall be alone like a gyrfalcon, solitary in the arching silence of the sky. I have reason to be fearful but I will not live in fear. I shall take my chance. I shall have this summer to myself.

Jane Boleyn, Hampton Court, July 1541

The duke has come to pay a visit to his niece before the start of the summer progress, and realises, very quickly, that he could not have chosen a worse time. The queen's rooms are in chaos. Not even the most experienced servants, not even the queen's sister and stepmother, can make any sense of the orders, as Katherine swears she cannot go without her new gowns, and then remembers that she has had them packed and sent ahead, demands to see her jewel box, accuses a maid of stealing a silver ring, and then finds it again, almost bursts into tears at the quandary of whether or not to take her sables to York, and then finally pitches face down on her bed and swears she will not go at all since the king hardly pays any attention to her anyway, and what pleasure will she have at York when her life is hardly worth living?

'What the devil is going on?' the duke hisses at me, as if it were my fault.

'It has been like this all day,' I say wearily. 'But yesterday was worse.'

'Why do her servants not take care of all this?'

'Because she interrupts them, and orders one thing and then another. We have had her chest of gowns packed and corded and ready for the wagon twice already. Her wardrobe mistress cannot be blamed, it is Katherine who pulls everything out for a pair of gloves that she cannot do without.'

'It is impossible that the queen's rooms should be so disorderly,' he exclaims, and I see that for once he is genuinely disturbed. 'These are the queen's rooms,' he repeats. 'They should be gracious. She should have dignity. Queen Katherine of Aragon would never –'

'She was born and bred a queen, but these are a girl's rooms,' I say. 'And a spoiled, wilful girl at that. She doesn't behave like a queen, she behaves like a girl. And if she wants to turn the place upside down for a ribbon, she will do so, and no-one can tell her to behave.'

'You should command her.'

I raise my eyebrows. 'Your Grace, she is the queen. You made this child Queen of England. Between her upbringing in your houses and the king's indulgence she has been taught no sense whatsoever. I shall wait until she goes to dinner and then I shall have everything set to rights, and tomorrow all this will be forgotten and she will go on progress and everything she needs will be packed, and anything she has left behind she will buy new.'

The duke shrugs and turns from the room. 'Anyway, it's you I wanted to see,' he says. 'Come out into the hall. I cannot stand this women's noise.'

He takes my hand and leads me out of the room. The sentry stands to one side of the door and we move away so he cannot listen.

'She is discreet with Culpepper at least,' he says bluntly. 'No-one has any idea. How many times has he bedded her?'

'Half a dozen,' I say. 'And I am glad that there is no talk of her in the court. But here in her rooms at least two of her women know that she loves him. She looks for him, her face lights up when she sees him. She has gone missing at least once in the last week. But the king comes to her rooms at night and in the day there is someone always with her. Nobody could prove anything against them.'

'You will have to find a way for them when they are on progress,' he says. 'Travelling from one house to another, there must be oppor-

412

tunities. It is no good for us if they can meet only seldom. We need a son from this girl, she has to be serviced until she is in pup.'

I raise my eyebrows at his vulgarity but I nod in agreement. 'I will help her,' I say. 'She can plan no better than a kitten.'

'Let her plan like a bitch in heat,' he says. 'As long as he beds her.'

'And my affair?' I remind him. 'You said that you were thinking of a husband for me?'

The duke smiles. 'I have written to the French count. How would you like to be Madame la Comtesse?'

'Oh,' I breathe. 'He has replied?'

'He has indicated an interest. There will be your dowry to be considered and any settlement on your children. But I can promise you this, if you can get that girl with child by the end of the summer then I shall kiss your hand as Madame la Comtesse by winter.'

I am almost panting in my eagerness. 'And is he a young man?'

'He is about your age, and with a good fortune. But he would not insist on you living in France, I have already asked. He would be happy that you remain as lady in waiting to the queen and would only ask that you have a house in both England and France.'

'He has a chateau?'

'All but a palace.'

'Have I met him? Do I know him? Oh, who is he?'

He pats my hand. 'Be patient, my most useful of all the Boleyn girls. Do your work and you shall have your reward. We have an agreement, do we not?'

'Yes,' I say. 'We do. I shall keep my side of the bargain.' I look at him expectantly.

'And I shall keep mine, of course.'

Katherine, Lincoln Castle,
August 1541

I had feared it would be terribly dull, travelling round the country while people turn out to stare and offer us loyal addresses at every market cross, and the king sits in state in every town hall in the country and I grit my teeth to stop myself yawning while fat aldermen in gowns address him in Latin – at least I suppose it's Latin, Thomas is very naughty and swears it is Ethiopian because we have got lost and are in Africa – but actually, it's tremendous fun. The speeches are very dull indeed, but as soon as they are over there's a masque or a dance or an entertainment or a picnic or something of the sort, and it is much more fun being the queen on progress than being the queen at court because every few days we move to another castle or house, and I have no time to get bored.

Here at Lincoln the king commanded that I and all my ladies should dress in Lincoln green and it was like a masque when we entered the town. The king himself was in dark green with a bow and quiver of arrows over his shoulder and a rakish bonnet with a feather.

'Is he Robin Hood, or is he Sherwood Forest?' Thomas Culpepper whispered to me and I had to put my gloves to my mouth to smother a laugh.

Everywhere we have gone there has been Tom Culpepper, catching my eye and making me giggle so even the most tedious loyal address is a moment when I can feel his eyes on me. And the king is much better in both health and temper, which is a relief for all of us. He was very irritated by the rebellion in the North, but that seems to be defeated now, and of course he beheaded the poor Countess of Salisbury, which upset me very much at the time, but now all the wicked people are defeated or dead and we can sleep easily in our beds again, he tells me. He has made an alliance with the emperor against the King of France that will defend us from France, he tells me – they are our enemies now, *voilà!* – and this is a good thing too.

I should not waste my time grieving for the countess for she was very old, after all, as old as my grandmother. But best of all, when we get to York we are going to meet with the Scots court and with the king's nephew King James of Scotland. The king is looking forward to this, and I am too, for there will be a great meeting of the two countries and jousting and tournaments and the English knights are certain to win for we have the bravest men and the best fighters. Tom Culpepper will wear his new suit of armour and I will be Queen of the Joust, with my new curtains on the royal box, and I cannot wait to see it.

I have practised everything. I have practised walking down the steps into the box and looking round to smile. I have practised sitting in the box and I have practised my gracious queen face, one that I shall put on when people cheer for me. And I have practised how I shall lean over the box and hand out the prizes.

'You might as well practise how to breathe,' Joan Bulmer says rudely.

'I like to get things right,' I say. 'Everyone will be looking at me. I like to do it right.'

There will be more than a hundred English knights jousting and I believe every single one of them has asked to carry my favour. Thomas Culpepper took the opportunity to come to my presence chamber at Lincoln Castle, and kneel to me and ask if he could be my knight.

'Has the king ordered you to ask me?' I say, knowing very well that he has not.

He has the grace to look down, as if embarrassed. 'This is my own suit from my own beating heart,' he says.

'You are not always so humble,' I say. I am thinking of a very hard kiss and his hand clutching at my buttocks as if he would lift me on to his cock then and there in the gallery before we left Hampton Court.

He glances up at me, one quick, dark glance, and I know that he is thinking of that too. 'Sometimes I dare to hope.'

'You certainly act like a hopeful man,' I say.

He giggles and ducks his head. I put my gloves to my lips to bite them so I don't laugh aloud.

'I know my mistress and my queen,' he says seriously. 'My heart beats faster when she just walks past me.'

'Oh, Thomas,' I whisper.

This is so delightful that I wish it could go on all day. One of my ladies comes towards us and I think she is going to interrupt but Lady Rochford says something to her and she is distracted, and pauses.

'I always have to walk past,' I say. 'I can never pause for as long as I would wish.'

'I know,' he says, and under the caressing, flirtatious tone there is real regret. I can hear it. 'I know. But I have to see you tonight, I have to touch you.'

I really don't dare to reply to this, it is too passionate, and though there are only the ladies of my chamber around us, I know that my desire for him must just blaze out of my face.

'Ask Lady Rochford,' I whisper. 'She will find a way.' Aloud, I say: 'Anyway, I cannot give you my favour. I shall have to ask the king who he favours.'

'You can keep your favour if you will only give me a smile as I ride out,' he says. 'They say the Scots are formidable fighters, big

416

men with strong horses. Say you will be watching me and hoping that I don't fall beneath a Scots lance.'

This is so poignant I could almost cry. 'I always watch you, you know I do. I have always watched you joust, and I have always prayed for your safety.'

'And I watch you,' he says, so quietly that I can hardly hear him. 'I watch you with such desire, Katherine, my love.'

I can see that they are all looking at me. I rise, a little unsteadily, to my feet and he gets to his. 'You can ride with me tomorrow,' I say, as if I don't much care either way. 'We are going hunting in the morning before Mass.'

He bows and steps back, and as he turns away I give a little gasp of shock for there in the doorway, like a ghost, so like a ghost that for a moment I almost think he is a ghost – is Francis Dereham. My Francis, my first love, turned up on my doorstep in a smart cloak and a good jacket and a handsome hat, as if he were doing very well indeed, and as handsome as he was all those days ago when we played at husband and wife in my bed at Lambeth.

'Mr Dereham,' I say very clearly, so that he shall make no mistake that we are not on first name terms any more.

He understands it well enough for he drops to one knee. 'Your Grace,' he says. He has a letter in his hand and he holds it out. 'Your respected grandmother, the duchess, bid me to come to you and bring you this letter.'

I nod to my page and I let Francis see that I don't bestir myself to go three paces for my own letters. The lad takes it from Francis and hands it to me, for I am far too important to lean. Without looking towards him I can see Thomas Culpepper, as stiff as a heron, standing by and glaring at Francis.

I open the duchess's letter. It is a terrible scrawl for she can hardly write, and since I can barely read we are very poor correspondents. I look for Lady Rochford and she is at my side in a moment. 'What does she say?' I pass it over.

She reads it quickly and since I am watching her face and not the page I see an expression flicker across her eyes. It is as if she is playing cards and she has just seen a very good suit come up in her partner's hand, she is almost amused.

'She writes to remind you of this gentleman, Francis Dereham, who served in her household when you were there.'

I have to admire the mask of her face, which is now absolutely without expression, given that she knows what Francis was to me and I to him, for I told her all about him when I was nothing more than a maid in waiting and she a far grander lady in waiting to Queen Anne. And, now I come to think of it, since half my ladies in waiting were my friends and companions in those days too they all know that Francis and I, facing each other so politely, used to be naked bedmates on every night he could sneak into the girls' bedchamber. Agnes Restwold gives a smothered little giggle and I shoot her a look which tells her to keep her stupid mouth shut. Joan Bulmer, who had him before I did, is utterly transfixed.

'Oh, yes,' I say, taking my cue from Lady Rochford, and I turn and smile at Francis as if we were long-standing acquaintances. I can feel Thomas Culpepper's eyes flicking on me and around at the others and I think that I'm going to have to explain this to him later, and he won't like it.

'She recommends him to your service and asks you to take him as a private secretary.'

'Yes,' I say, I can't think what to do. 'Of course.'

I turn to Francis. 'My lady grandmother recommends you to me.' I really cannot think why she would interest herself in putting him into my household. And I can't understand why she would put him in a position so close to me, when she herself boxed my ears and called me a lustful slut for letting him into the bedchamber when I was a girl in her household. 'You are indebted to her.'

'I am,' he says.

I lean towards Lady Rochford. 'Appoint him,' she says briefly in my ear. 'Your grandmother says so.'

'So to oblige my grandmother, I am pleased to welcome you to my court,' I finish.

He rises to his feet. He is such a handsome young man. I really cannot blame myself for loving him when I was a girl. He turns his head and smiles at me as if he were shy of me now. 'I thank you, Your Grace,' he says. 'I will serve you loyally. Heart and soul.'

I give him my hand to kiss and when he comes close I can smell the scent of his skin, that familiar, sexy smell that I once knew so well. That was the scent of my first lover, he meant everything to me. Why, I kept his shirt under my pillow so that I could bury my face in it when I went to sleep and dream of him. I adored Francis Dereham then, I only wish to God I didn't have to meet him again now.

He bends over my hand and his lips on my fingertips are as soft and as yielding as I remember them on my mouth. I lean forwards. 'You will have to be very discreet in my service,' I say. 'I am the queen now and there must be no gossip about me, not about now, and not about the old days.'

'I am yours heart and soul,' he says, and I feel that disloyal, betraying, irresistible flicker of desire. He loves me still, he must love me still, otherwise why would he come to serve me? And though we parted on bad terms, I remember his touch and the utter breath-taking excitement of his kisses, and the slide of his naked thigh between mine when he first came to my bed, and the insistent pressing of his lust, which was never resisted.

'Take heed what words you speak,' I say, and he smiles at me as if he knows as well as I do what I am thinking.

'Take heed what you remember,' he says.

Jane Boleyn, Pontefract Castle,
August 1541

The two young men, and half a dozen others, each of them with good reason to believe that they are the queen's favourites, circle her every day and the court has all the tension of a whorehouse before a brawl. The queen, excited by the attention she gets at every corner, at every hunt and breakfast and masque, is like a child who has stayed up too late; she is feverish with arousal. On the one hand she has Thomas Culpepper, holding her when she dismounts from her horse, at her side for dancing, whispering in her ear when she plays cards, first to greet her in the morning, and last to leave her rooms at night. On the other she has young Dereham, appointed to wait for her orders, at her right hand with his little writing desk, as if she ever dictated a letter to anyone, constantly whispering to her, stepping forwards to advise, ever present where he need not be. And then, how many others? A dozen? Twenty? Not even Anne Boleyn at her most capricious had so many young men circling her, like dogs slavering at a butcher's door. But Anne, even at her most flirtatious, never appeared to be a girl who might bestow her favours for a smile, who might be seduced by a song, by a poem, by a word. The whole court begins to see that the queen's joy, which has made the king so happy, is not that of an innocent girl whom he so fondly believes adores only him, it is that of a flirt who revels in constant male attention.

Of course there is trouble, there is almost a fight. One of the senior men at court tells Dereham that he should have risen from the dinner table and gone, since he is not of the queen's council and only they are sitting over their wine. Dereham, loose-mouthed, says that he was in the queen's counsels long before the rest of us knew her, and will be familiar with her long after the rest of us are dismissed. Of course: uproar. The terror is that it might get to the king's ears and so Dereham is summoned to the queen's rooms and she sees him, with me standing by.

'I cannot have you causing trouble in my household,' she says stiffly to him.

He bows but his eyes are bright with confidence. 'I meant to cause no trouble, I am yours: heart and soul.'

'It is all very well to say that,' she says irritably. 'But I don't want people asking what I was to you, and you were to me.'

'We were in love,' he maintains staunchly.

'This should never be said,' I interpose. 'She is the queen. Her previous life must be as if it had never been.'

He looks at her, ignoring me. 'I will never deny it.'

'It is over,' she says determinedly, I am proud of her. 'And I will not have gossip about the past, Francis. I cannot have people talking about me. I shall have to send you away if you cannot keep silent.'

He pauses for a moment. 'We were husband and wife before God,' he says quietly. 'You cannot deny that.'

She makes a little gesture with her hand. 'I don't know,' she says helplessly. 'At any rate, it is over now. You can have a place at court only if you never speak of it. Can't he, Lady Rochford?'

'Can you keep your mouth shut?' I ask. 'Never mind all this never denying it nonsense. You can stay if you can keep your mouth shut. If you are a braggart you will have to go.'

He looks at me without warmth, there is no love between us. 'I can keep my mouth shut,' he says.

Anne, Richmond Palace,
September 1541

It has been a good summer for me, my first as a free woman in England. The farms attached to my palace are in good heart and I have ridden out and watched the crops ripen, and in the fruit orchards the trees are growing heavy with fruit. This is a rich country, we have built great stacks of hay to feed the animals through the winter, and in the barns we are piling up great mountains of grain to go to the miller for flour. If the country was ruled by a man who wanted peace, and who would share the wealth, then it would be a peaceful and prosperous land.

The king's hatred of both Papists and Protestants sours the life of his country. In the church when they raise the Host even the smallest children are trained to keep their eyes on it, and bob their heads and cross themselves by rote, and are threatened by their parents that if they do not do as the king demands, then they will be taken away and burned. There is no understanding of the sanctity of the act among the poor people, they just know that it is the king's desire now that they should bob and bow and bless themselves, just as before they had to hear the Mass in English, not Latin, and they had a Bible put in the church for anyone to read, and now it has been taken away again. The king commands the church just as the king commands more and more unjust taxation: because he can, because no-one can dare to stop him, because now it is treason even to question him.

There are quiet murmurs that the rebellion in the North was led by brave men, courageous men who thought that they could fight for their God against the king. But the older men of the little town point out that they are all dead now, and the king's progress to the North this year is to march over their graves and insult their widows.

I don't interfere with anything that anyone says, if there is anything spoken in my hearing which could amount to treason I go quickly away, and make sure that I tell one of my ladies or one of my household that something was said, but I did not understand it. I hide in my stupidity, I think it will be my salvation. I put on my dull, uncomprehending face and trust that my reputation for ugliness and stolidity will save me. In general, people say nothing before me but treat me with a sort of puzzled kindness, as if I have survived some terrible illness and should still be treated with care. In a way, I have. I am the first woman to survive marriage with the king. That is a more remarkable feat than surviving the plague. The plague will go through a town and in the worst summer, in the poorest areas, perhaps one in ten women will die. But of the king's four wives only one has emerged with her health intact: me.

Dr Harst's spy reports that the king's spirits are much improved and his temper lifted by his travels north. The man was not ordered to go with the court but has stayed behind to clean the king's rooms in the general sweetening of Hampton Court Palace. So I cannot know how their progress is going. I had a brief letter from Lady Rochford and she told me that the king's health is better and that he and Katherine are merry. If that poor child does not conceive a baby soon, I do not think she will be merry for much longer.

I write also to the Princess Mary. She is much relieved that the question of her marriage to a French prince has been utterly put to one side as Spain and France are to go to war and King Henry will side with Spain. His great fear is of an invasion from France and some of the hated taxation is being well spent on forts all along the south coast. From Princess Mary's point of view, only one thing matters: if her father is aligned with Spain then she will not be married off to a French prince. She is such a passionate daughter of her Spanish mother that I think she would rather live and die a virgin than be married to a Frenchman. She hopes the king will allow me to visit her before autumn. When he returns from his progress I shall write to the king and ask him if I may invite the Princess Mary to stay with me. I should like to spend time with her. She laughs at me and calls us the royal spinsters, and so we are. Two women who are of no use. Nobody knows whether I am a duchess or a queen or a nothing. Nobody knows if she is a princess or a bastard. The royal spinsters. I wonder what will become of us?

Katherine, King's Manor, York, September 1541

Well, it is as I could have predicted, an utter disappointment. King James of Scotland is not coming and there is to be no jousting and no rival courts, and I am queen only of the little English court and nothing special is happening at all. I shall not see my darling Thomas joust, and he will not see me in the royal box with my new curtains. The king swears that James is too afraid to show his face this far south of the border, and if that is true, then it can only be because he does not trust the king's own honourable word of truce. And, though nobody dare say it, he is quite right to be cautious. For the king promised a truce to the leaders of the northern revolt and his friendship, and all manner of changes that they wanted, he swore it on his royal name; and then, when they trusted him, he caught them and hanged them. Their dead heads are still stuck on the walls all around York, and I must say it is most disagreeable. I remark to Henry that perhaps James fears being hanged too and he laughs a lot and says that I am a clever little kitten and that James might well be afraid. But actually, I don't think it's very good if people can't trust you. Because if James had been able to trust the king's word then he would have come and we would all have had a merry time.

Also, this is a very fine house and newly done for us, and yet I can't help but notice that it was a beautiful abbey before it was the King's Manor, and I should think that since the people of York are great sympathisers for the old faith (if not secret Papists) that they would very much resent us dancing about where the monks used to pray. I don't say this of course, I am not quite an idiot. But I can imagine how I might feel if I had come here for help and prayer and now find the place quite changed and a great fat greedy king sitting in the middle of it all, and calling for his dinner.

Anyway, what matters most is that the king is happy, and even I, amazingly enough, don't mind about missing the joust nearly as much as I should. I am a little disappointed by the lack of handsome Scotsmen, and being so far from the London goldsmiths; but I cannot really be troubled about it. Astoundingly, it doesn't even seem that important. For I am in love. For the first time in my life, utterly and completely, I have fallen in love, and I cannot believe it myself.

Thomas Culpepper is my lover, he is my heart's desire, he is the only man I have ever loved, he is the only man I ever will love. I am his and he is mine, heart and soul. All the complaints I have ever made about having to bed a man old enough to be my father are now forgotten. I do my duty by the king as a form of tax, a fine I have to pay; and then the moment he is asleep I am free to be with my love. Better even than that, and far less risky, is that the king is so wearied by the celebrations on this progress that he often does not come to my rooms at all. I wait until the court is quiet and then Lady Rochford creeps down the stairs, or opens the side door, or unlocks a hidden door to the gallery and in steps my Thomas and we can have hours together.

We have to be careful, we have to be as careful as if our very lives depended on it. But every time we move to a new place Lady Rochford finds a private way to my rooms, and tells Thomas how it is to be done. Without fail he comes to me, he loves me as I love him. We go to my room and Lady Rochford guards the door for us, and all night I lie in his arms and we kiss and whisper and make promises of love that will last forever. At dawn she makes a little scratch on the door and I get up and we kiss, and he slips away like a ghost. Nobody sees him. Nobody sees him come, and nobody sees him go, it is a wonderful secret.

Of course the girls talk, this is a most unruly crowd. I cannot believe that they would dare to chatter such gossip and scandal if Queen Anne were still on the throne. But because it is only me and most of them are older than me, and so many are from the old days at Lambeth, they have no respect at all, and they laugh at me, and they tease me about Francis Dereham, and I am afraid that they watch what time I go to bed and wonder that my only companion is Lady Rochford, and that the door to my bedroom is locked and no-one can come in.

'They know nothing,' she assures me. 'And they would tell nobody, anyway.'

'They should not be gossiping at all,' I say. 'Can you not tell them to keep their tongues off my business?'

'How can I, when it was you laughing about Francis Dereham with Joan Bulmer, yourself?'

'Well, I never laugh about Thomas,' I say. 'I never mention his name. I don't even say his name in the confessional. I don't even say his name to myself.'

'That is wise,' she says. 'Keep it a secret. Keep it a complete secret.'

She is brushing my hair and she gives a little pause and looks at me in the mirror. 'When is your course due?' she asks.

'I can't remember.' I never keep count. 'Was it last week? Anyway, it hasn't come.'

There is a sort of bright alertness in her face. 'It has not come?'

'No. Brush at the back, Jane, Thomas likes it smooth at the back.'

Her hand moves but she does not do it very carefully. 'Do you feel at all sick?' she asks. 'Are your breasts any bigger?'

'No,' I say. Then I realise what is in her mind. 'Oh! Are you thinking I might be with child?'

'Yes,' she whispers. 'Please God.'

'But that would be dreadful!' I exclaim. 'Because, don't you see? Don't you think? Lady Rochford, it might not be the king's child!'

She puts down the brush and shakes her head. 'It is God's will,' she says slowly, as if she wants me to learn something. 'If you are married to the king and you conceive a child then that is God's will. It is God's will that the king has a child. So it *is* the king's child, as far as you are concerned, it is the king's own child, whatever has happened between you and another.'

I feel a little muddled by this. 'But what if it is Thomas's child?' At once I have a picture of Thomas's little son, a brown-haired, blue-eyed rascal like his father, a strong boy from a young father.

She sees my face and she guesses what I am thinking. 'You are the queen,' she says firmly. 'Any child you bear will be the king's child, as God wishes. You cannot think for one moment anything different.'

'But ... '

'No,' she says. 'And you should tell the king that you have hopes of being with his child.'

'Is it not too early?'

'It's never too early to give him cause for hope,' she says. 'The last thing we want is to have him discontented.'

'I will tell him,' I say. 'He is coming to my room tonight. You will have to fetch Thomas to me later. Then I will tell him too.'

'No,' she says. 'You won't tell Thomas Culpepper.'

'But I want to!'

'It would spoil everything.' She speaks very fast, persuasively. 'If he thinks you are with child he will not lie with you. He will find you disgusting. He wants a mistress, not a mother of his children. You say nothing to Thomas Culpepper, but you can give the king hope. That's the way to handle this.'

'He would be pleased . . .'

'No.' She shakes her head. 'He would be kind, I am sure, but he would not come to your bed again. He would take a mistress. I have seen him talking to Catherine Carey. He would take a mistress until your time was over.'

'I couldn't bear that!'

'So tell him nothing. Tell the king you have hopes, but tell Thomas nothing.'

'Thank you, Lady Rochford,' I say humbly. If it were not for her advice I don't know what I would do.

That night the king comes to my rooms and they help him into my bed. I stand by the fire while they labour to heave him in and they leave him tucked up with the sheets under his chin like an enormous baby.

'Husband,' I say sweetly.

'Come to bed, my rose,' he says. 'Henry wants his rose.'

I grit my teeth on the stupidity of him calling himself Henry. 'I want to tell you something,' I say. 'I have some happy news.'

He heaves himself up, so that his head with the nightcap askew bobs up a little.

'Yes?'

'I have missed my course,' I say. 'I may be with child.'

'Oh, rose! My sweetest rose!'

'It is early days,' I warn him. 'But I thought you would want to know at once.'

'Before anything else!' he assures me. 'Dearest, as soon as you tell me it is true, I shall have you crowned queen.'

'But Edward will still be your heir,' I query.

'Yes, yes, but it would be such a weight off my mind if I knew that Edward had a brother. A family cannot be safe with only one son: a dynasty needs boys. One small accident and everything is finished, but if you have two boys you are safe.'

'And I will have a grand coronation,' I specify, thinking of the crown and the jewels and the gown and the feasting and the thousands of people who will come out to cheer me, the new Queen of England.

429

'You will have the greatest coronation that England has ever seen, for you are the greatest queen,' he promises me. 'And as soon as we get back to London I shall declare a day of national celebration for you.'

'Oh?' This sounds rather wonderful, a day to celebrate my existence! Kitty Howard: *voilà* indeed! 'A whole day for me?'

'A day when everyone will go to church and say prayers of thanksgiving that God has given you to me.'

Just church, after all. I give a faint, disappointed smile.

'And the master of the revels will prepare a great feast and celebration at court,' he says. 'And everyone will give you presents.'

I beam. 'That sounds lovely,' I say with satisfaction.

'You are my sweetest rose,' he says. 'My rose without a thorn. Come to bed with me now, Katherine.'

'Yes.' I make sure I do not think of my Thomas as I go to the bloated figure in the big bed. I have a wide, happy smile on my face and I close my eyes so I need not look at him. I cannot avoid the smell of him or the feel of him, but I can make sure that I do not think of him at all while I do what I have to do, and then lie beside him and wait for the little snuffles of satisfaction to turn to wheezy snores as he goes to sleep.

Jane Boleyn, Ampthill,
October 1541

Her course started something like a week late; but I was not too disheartened. The mere thought of it had been enough to make the king more in love with her than ever, and she had at least agreed that though the sun rises and shines only on Thomas Culpepper, he does not have to be privy to every little secret.

She has behaved very prettily with the people that she has met on this progress, even when she has been bored and inattentive she has kept a pleasant smile on her face, and she has learned to follow a little behind the king and to maintain an appearance of demure obedience. She serves him in bed like a paid whore, and she sits next to him at dinner and never shows by a flicker of expression that he has broken wind. She is a selfish, stupid girl but she might, given time, make quite a good queen. If she conceives a child and gives England a son she might live long enough to learn to be a queen that is admired.

The king, at any rate, is mad about her. His indulgence makes our task of getting Culpepper in and out of her bedchamber so much easier. We had a bad night in Pontefract when he sent Sir Anthony Denny to her room without announcement, and she was locked in with Culpepper. Denny tried the door and went away without saying anything. There was another night when the king stirred in her bed while they were at their business only on the other side of the door, and she had to go flying back in to the old man, still damp with sweat and kisses. If the air had not been heavy with the stink of his wind he would have smelled the scent of lust for certain. At Grafton Regis the lovers coupled in the jakes – Culpepper crept up the stairs to the stone-walled chamber which overhangs the moat, and she told her ladies that she was sick as a dog and spent the afternoon with him in there, frantically humping while the rest of us made possets. If it were not so dangerous it would be funny. As it is, it still makes me breathless with a mixture of fear and lust when I hear them together.

I never laugh. I think of my husband and his sister and any laughter dies in my mouth. I think of him promising to be her man through any trouble. I think of her, desperate to conceive a son, sure that Henry could not give her one. I think of the unholy pact they must have made. Then, with a little moan, I think that all this is my fear, my fantasy, and perhaps it never happened. The worst thing about the two of them being dead is that now I will never know what happened. The only way I have borne the thought of what they did, and the part I played, in all these years has been to put the thought far from me. I never think of it, I never speak of it, and no-one ever speaks of them in my hearing. It is as if they never were. That is the only way I can bear the fact that I am alive and they are gone: to pretend that they never were.

'So when Queen Anne Boleyn was accused of treason did they really mean adultery?' Katherine asks me.

The question, so sharp on the point of my own thinking, is like a stab. 'What d'you mean?' I ask.

We are riding from Collyweston to Ampthill on a bright, cold morning in October. The king is ahead, galloping with the young men of his court, thinking he is winning a race as they hold their horses back, Thomas Culpepper among them. Katherine is ambling along on her grey mare, and I am at her side on one of the Howard hunters. Everyone else has dropped back to gossip and there is no-one to shield me from her curiosity.

'You said earlier that she and the other men were accused of adultery,' she pursues.

'That was months ago.'

'I know, I have been thinking about it.'

'You think very slowly,' I say nastily.

'I know I do,' she says, quite unabashed. 'And I have been thinking that they accused Anne Boleyn, my cousin, of treason only because she was unfaithful to the king, and they beheaded her.' She glances around her. 'And I have been thinking that I am in the same situation,' she says. 'That if anyone knew – they would say that I am unfaithful to the king. Perhaps they would call it treason too. Then what would happen to me?'

'That is why we never say anything,' I reply. 'That is why we take care. Remember? I have warned you from the beginning to take care.'

'But why did you help me meet Thomas? Knowing as you do what a danger it is? After your own sister-in-law was killed for just the same thing?'

I am lost for an answer. I never thought that she would ask me this question. But her stupidity is such that she does, sometimes, go straight to the most obvious. I turn my head as if I am looking over the cold meadows where the river, swollen with the recent rains, shines like a sword, a French sword.

'Because you asked me to help you,' I say. 'I am your friend.'

'Did you help Anne Boleyn?'

'No!' I exclaim. 'She would have no help of mine!'

'You were not her friend?'

'I was her sister-in-law.'

'Did she not like you?'

'I doubt she ever saw me from start to finish. She had no eyes for me.'

This does not halt her speculation, as I intended, but feeds it. I can almost hear the slow revolving of her thoughts.

'She didn't like you?' Katherine asks. 'She and her husband and her sister, they were always together. But they left you out.'

I laugh but it doesn't come out well. 'You make it sound like children in the schoolyard.'

She nods. 'That is just how it is in a royal court. And did you hate them for not letting you join them?'

'I was a Boleyn,' I say. 'I was a Boleyn as much as they. I was a Boleyn by marriage, their uncle the duke is my uncle. My interests are in the family as theirs were.'

'So why did you give evidence against them?' she asks.

I am so shocked at her directly accusing me, I can hardly speak. I look at her. 'Where did you hear of this? Why would you speak of this?'

'Catherine Carey told me,' she says, as if it is unremarkable that the two girls, all but children, should share confidences about treason and incest and death. 'She said that you bore witness against your husband and his sister. You gave evidence to show that they were lovers and traitors.'

'I did not,' I whisper. 'I did not.' I cannot bear her naming this, I never think of it. I will not think of it today. 'It wasn't like that,' I say. 'You don't understand because you are only a girl. You were a child when all this happened. I tried to save him, I tried to save her. It was a great plan of your uncle's devising. It failed, but it should have succeeded. I thought that I would save him if I gave evidence, but it all went wrong.'

'Is that how it was?'

'It was heartbreaking!' I cry out in my pain. 'I tried to save him, I loved him, I would have done anything for him.'

Her pretty young face is filled with sympathy. 'You meant to save him?'

I dash the tears from my eyes with the back of my glove. 'I would have died for him,' I say. 'I thought I would save him. I was going to save him. I would have done anything to save him.'

'Why did it go wrong?' she whispers.

'Your uncle and I thought that if they pleaded guilty that she would be divorced and would be sent away, to a convent. We thought that he would be stripped of his title and his honours and banished. The men who were named with her were never guilty, everyone knew that. They were George's friends and her courtiers, not lovers. We thought they would all be forgiven, as Thomas Wyatt was forgiven.'

'So what happened?'

It is like a dream, this re-telling. It is the dream that comes to me often, that wakes me in the night like sickness, that sends me from my bed to walk and walk in the dark room until the first grey light comes into the sky and I know my ordeal is over.

'They denied their guilt. That was not part of the plan. They should have confessed but they denied everything except saying some words against the king, George had said that the king was impotent.' Even on this bright autumn day, five years after the trial, I still lower my voice and glance around me to make sure that no-one can hear. 'Their courage failed them, they denied their guilt and did not ask for mercy. I stayed with the plan, as your uncle said I should. I saved the title, I saved the lands, I saved the Boleyn inheritance, I saved their fortune.'

Katherine is waiting for more. She does not understand that this is the end of the story. This is my great act and my triumph: I saved the title and the lands. She even looks puzzled.

'I did what I had to do to save the Boleyn inheritance,' I repeat. 'My father-in-law, George and Anne's father, had built a fortune over his lifetime. George had added to it. Anne's wealth had gone into it. I saved it. I saved Rochford Hall for us, I kept the title. I am Lady Rochford still.'

'You saved the inheritance, but they didn't inherit it,' Katherine says, uncomprehending. 'Your husband died, and he must have thought you were giving evidence against him. He must have thought that while he was pleading not guilty, you were accusing him. You were a witness for his prosecution.' Slowly she thinks, slowly she speaks, slowly she says the worst thing of all. 'He must have thought that you let him go to his death so that you could keep the title and the lands, even though you had killed him.'

I could scream at her for saying this, for putting words to this nightmare. I rub my face with the back of my glove as if I would scrub my scowl away. 'No. Not so! Not so! He won't have thought that,' I say desperately. 'He knew that I loved him, that I was trying to save him. As he went to his death he would have known that I was on my knees before the king, asking him to spare my husband. When she went to her death she will have known that at the very last moment I was before the king, asking him to spare her.'

She nods. 'Well, I hope you never bear witness to save me,' she says. It is a miserable attempt at humour; I do not even accord it a smile.

'It was the end of my life,' I say simply. 'It was not just the end of their lives, it was death to me too.'

We ride in silence for a while, and then two or three of Katherine's friends kick their horses forward to ride beside her and chatter to her about Ampthill and the greeting we are certain to have, and whether Katherine has finished with her yellow gown and will give it to Katherine Tylney. In a moment there is a quarrel breaking out because Katherine had promised it to Joan but Margaret is insisting that it should go to her.

'You can both hold your peace,' I rule, dragging myself back to the present moment. 'For the queen has worn that gown not more than three times and it will stay in her wardrobe until she has had more use out of it.'

'I don't care,' Katherine says. 'I can always order another.'

Anne, Richmond Palace,
November 1541

At church I enter, cross myself, curtsey to the altar, and take my place in my high-walled pew. Thank God that no-one can see me in here; the high door closes behind me, the walls guarantee my privacy, and even the front of the pew is panelled with a lattice so I can see but not be observed. Only the priest, if he is standing high up in the choir stalls, can look down on me. If I glance away from the Host, or fail to cross myself at the right time, or use the wrong hand or do it the wrong way round, I will not be reported for heresy. There are thousands in this country who now guard their every movement because they do not have my privacy. There are hundreds who will die because they got it wrong.

I stand, and bow, and kneel, and sit, as I am bidden by the order of the service; but I can take little pleasure today from the liturgy. This is the king's order of service, and in every rolling phrase I hear the power of Henry, not the power of God. In the past I have known God in many places; in small Lutheran chapels at home, in the great soaring majesty of St Paul's in London, and in the quiet of the royal chapel at Hampton Court when I once knelt beside the Princess Mary and felt the peace of heaven descend around us; but it seems that the king has soured his church for me and for so many others. I find God now in silence: when I walk in the park, or beside the river, when I hear a blackbird calling at midday, when I see a flight of geese arrowing overhead, when the falconer releases a bird and I see her mount up high and soar. God no longer speaks to me when Henry allows it, in the words that Henry prefers. I am in hiding from the king and I am deaf to his God.

We are on our knees praying for the health and safety of the royal family when to my surprise there is a new prayer inserted without warning into the familiar words. Without a flicker of shame, the priest bids my court, my ladies and myself to give thanks for the king's wife Katherine.

'We render thanks to thee, oh Lord, that after so many strange accidents that have befallen the king's marriages, that Thou hast been pleased to give him a wife so entirely conformed to his inclinations as her, he now has.'

I cannot help myself, my head bobs up from reverent submission and I meet the surprised gaze of the Richmond priest in the choir stalls. He is reading the celebration of the king's wife from an official document, he has been ordered to read this as he might be ordered to read a new law. Henry, in his madness, has commanded every church in England to thank God that after the many 'strange accidents' of his previous marriages, he now has a wife who conforms to his inclinations. I am so outraged by the language of this, by the sentiment of it, and by the fact that I have to be on my knees listening to this insult, that I half-rise to my feet in protest.

At once an insistent hand grabs the back of my gown and pulls me down, I stumble for a moment and fall back to my knees again. Lotte, my translator, gives me a small smile, puts her hands together in a portrait of devotion and closes her eyes. Her gesture steadies me. This is indeed an insult, most gross and thoughtless; but to respond to it is to charge into danger. If the king requires me to go on my knees and describe myself to the kingdom as a strange accident, then it is not for me to point out that our marriage was no accident but a well-planned and thoughtfully considered contract which he broke for the simple and sufficient reason that he preferred someone else. It is not my place to point out that since our marriage was real and valid he is now either an adulterer, or a bigamist, living in sin with a second wife. It is not my place to point out that if little Kitty Howard, a light-hearted, light-mannered child, is the only woman he has ever found who conforms to his inclinations then either she must be the greatest actor that ever lived, or he must be the most deluded fool that ever married a girl young enough to be his own daughter.

Henry is a madman now, doting on a girl like a senile fool, and he has just ordered the whole of his country to thank God for his folly. In churches up and down the land people will be biting their lips to contain their smiles, honest men will be cursing the luck that puts them in Henry's church with this nonsense included in their prayers. 'Amen,' I say loudly, and when we rise to our feet for the blessing I show the priest a serene and devout face. My only thought, as we leave the church, is that poor Princess Mary at Hunsden will be choking with indignation at the insult to her mother, at the blasphemy of having to pray for Kitty Howard, and the idiocy of her father. Please God she has the sense to say nothing. It seems whatever the king likes to do, we must all say nothing.

On Tuesday, one of my ladies gazing out of the window remarks: 'Here is the ambassador, running up the garden from a river boat. What can have happened?'

I rise to my feet. Dr Harst never visits me without first sending notice that he is coming. Something must have happened at court. My first thought is for Elizabeth or Mary, my first fear is that something has happened to them. If only Mary has not been driven by her father to defy him! 'Stay here,' I say shortly to my women, and I throw a shawl around my shoulders, and go down to greet him.

He is entering the hall as I come down the stairs and at once I know that something serious has happened.

'What is it?' I ask him in German.

He shakes his head at me, and I have to wait until the servants have come and gone, served him with wine and biscuits, and I can send them all from the room. 'What is it?'

'I came at once, without the full story, because I want you to be forewarned,' he says.

'Forewarned of what? It is not the Princess Mary?'

'No. It is the queen.'

'She is with child?'

He shakes his head. 'I don't know exactly. But she has been confined to her chambers since yesterday. And the king will not see her.'

'She is ill? He is terrified of taking the plague.'

'No. There are no physicians called.'

'She is not accused of plotting against him?' I name the greatest fear.

'I will tell you all I know, and it is mostly gathered from the servant we have in the king's rooms. The king and queen attended Mass on the Sunday, and the priest gave thanks for the king's marriage, as you know.'

'I know.'

'Sunday evening the king was quiet and dined alone, as if he was sinking into his old illness. He didn't go to her rooms. Monday he locked himself in his rooms and the queen was locked in hers. Today Archbishop Cranmer went in to talk with her, and came out in silence.'

I look at him. 'She was locked in? And the king locked himself away?'

Silently he nods.

'What d'you think it means?'

'I think the queen has been accused. But we cannot yet know the accusation. What we must consider is whether she will implicate you.'

'Me?'

'If she is accused of a Papist plot, or of bewitching the king into impotence, people will remember that you were accused of a Papist plot, and that he was impotent with you. People will remember your friendship with her. People will remember that you danced with her at court at Christmas and he was ill by Lent, as soon as you left. People may think that the two of you have made a plot against him. They may even say the two of you have ill-wished him.'

I put out my hand as if I would stop him. 'No, no.'

'I know it is not true. But we have to consider the worst that could be said. And try to guard against it. Shall I write to your brother?'

'He won't help me,' I say sullenly. 'I am alone.'

'Then we must prepare,' he says. 'You have good horses in your stables?'

I nod.

'Then give me some money and I shall have other horses ready all the way down the road to Dover,' he says decisively. 'The moment I think that it is going against you, we can leave the country.'

'He will close the ports,' I warn. 'He did the last time.'

'We won't be trapped again. I shall hire a fishing boat to serve us,' he says. 'We know now what he can do. We know what lengths he will go to. We will get away before they have even decided to arrest you.'

I look at the closed door. 'There will be someone in my service who will know that you have come to warn me,' I say. 'Just as we have a man in his service, he will have put a spy here. I am watched.'

'I know the man,' Dr Harst says with quiet pleasure. 'And he will report my visit today but he will say nothing more. He is my man now. I think we are safe.'

'Safe as mice under the scaffold,' I say bitterly.

He nods. 'As long as the axe falls on others.'

I shudder. 'Who deserves it? Not me, but not little Kitty Howard either! What did she and I ever do but marry where we were bid?'

'As long as you escape it, my job is done,' he says. 'The queen must look to her own friends for help.'

Katherine, Hampton Court,
November 1541

Now, let me see, what do I have now?

Surprise, surprise! I have no friends and I thought I had dozens.

I have no lovers, and I thought I was pestered by them.

I don't even have a family, as it turns out, they are all gone.

I have no husband for he won't see me, and I don't even have a confessor for the archbishop himself has become my inquisitor. Everyone is so mean to me and it is so unfair, I don't know what to think or say. They came to me when I was dancing with my ladies, and said that it was the king's orders that I was not to leave my rooms.

For a moment – I am such a fool, grandmother was right when she said that there never was a greater fool than me – I thought it was a masque and that someone would come in costume and capture me, and then someone would come in costume and rescue me and there would be a joust or a mock battle on the river or something amusing. The whole country had said prayers on the Sunday to thank God for me, so I was expecting some kind of celebration on the day after. So I waited in my room, behind the locked doors, looking forward to a knight errant coming, perhaps even a tower coming to my window, or a mock siege, perhaps a cavalcade riding into the garden, and I said to my ladies: 'Here's a good joke, I expect!' But we waited all day in my room and even though I rushed and changed my dress to be ready, no-one came and I called for music and to make merry and then Archbishop Cranmer came and said that the time for dancing was over.

Oh, he can be so unkind! He looks so serious, as if there is something very wrong. And then he asks me about Francis Dereham! Francis Dereham of all people, only in my service at the request of my own respectable grandmother! As if it is my fault! And all because some pathetic tittle-tattle tale-bearer has told the archbishop that there was a flirtation at Lambeth, as though anyone should care about that now! And I must say, if I were archbishop I would try to be a better person than one who listens to such gossip.

So I say that all this is most untrue, and if I can see the king I will easily persuade him not to hear a word against me. And then my lord Cranmer gives me a real fright for he says in a most awful voice: 'That, Madam, is why you will not see His Grace until your name has been utterly cleared. We will inquire into every circumstance until we have utterly scotched every slur against you.'

Well, I don't reply because I know that my slur cannot be utterly scotched, or anything like it; but surely, all that at Lambeth was a matter between a maid and a young man, and now I am married to the king, who should trouble themselves about what happened all that long time ago? Why, it is a lifetime ago, it is all of two years ago! Who should care one way or another now?

Perhaps it will all blow over in the morning. The king has his funny whims sometimes, he takes against one man or another and has them beheaded and often he is sorry afterwards. He took against poor Queen Anne of Cleves, and she got away with Richmond Palace and being his best sister. So we go to bed quite cheerful, and I ask Lady Rochford what she thinks, and she looks rather queer and says that she thinks I may get through it if I keep my nerve and deny everything. This is rather cold comfort from her, who saw her own husband go to the gallows denying everything. But I don't tell her so, for fear of making her angry.

444

Katherine Tylney sleeps with me, and she laughs as she gets into bed and says that she bets I wish she were Tom Culpepper. I say nothing, for I do wish it. I wish it so much that I could cry for him. Long after she is snoring I lie awake and wish that everything had been different for me, and Tom had come to the house at Lambeth and perhaps fought with Francis and perhaps killed him, and then taken me away and married me. If he had come for me then I would never have been queen and never had my necklace of table diamonds. But I should have slept the whole night in his arms and sometimes that seems a better choice. It seems a better choice tonight, for sure.

I sleep so badly that I am awake at dawn, and I lie in the quiet with the grey light shining through the shutters and I think that I would give all my jewels to see Tom Culpepper and hear his laugh. I would give my fortune to be in his arms. Please God he knows that I am kept in my rooms and does not think that I am keeping away from him. It would be too awful, if, when I come out, he has taken offence at my neglect, and is courting someone else. I would die if he were to take a fancy to another girl. I really think my heart would break.

I would send him a note if I dared, but no-one is to leave my rooms and I dare not trust one of the servants with a message. They come with breakfast to my rooms, I am not even allowed to go out to eat. I am not even to go to chapel, a confessor is to come to my rooms to pray with me before the archbishop comes to talk with me again.

I really do begin to think this is not right, I should perhaps protest against it. I am Queen of England, I cannot be kept in my rooms as if I were a naughty girl. I am fully grown, I am a lady, I am a Howard. I am wife to the king. Who do they think I am? I am Queen of England, after all. I think I shall speak to the archbishop and tell him that he cannot treat me so. I think about this until I become quite indignant and resolve that I shall insist to the archbishop that he treats me with proper respect.

And then he doesn't come! We spent the whole morning sitting around, trying to sew things, trying to appear seriously employed in case the door suddenly opens and my lord the archbishop walks in. But no! It is not till the end of the afternoon, and a dreary afternoon at that, that the door opens and he enters, his kindly face all grave.

My ladies all flutter up as if they were themselves as innocent as a flock of butterflies, imprisoned with a mouldy slug. I remain seated, after all, I am queen. I just wish I could look like Queen Anne did when they came for her. She really did look innocent, she really did look unjustly accused. I am sorry now that I signed a piece of paper to bear witness against her. I realise now how very unpleasant it is to be doubted. But how was I to know that one day I would be in the same case?

The archbishop walks up to me as if he were terribly sorry for something. He has his sad face on, as if he were struggling with an argument inside his own head. For a moment I am certain that he is going to apologise for being so unkind to me yesterday, and beg my pardon and release me.

'Your Grace,' he says very quietly. 'I am so much grieved to discover that you have employed the man Francis Dereham in your household.'

For a moment I am so amazed that I don't say anything. Everyone knows this. Good God, Francis has caused enough trouble at court for everyone to know it. He has hardly been discreet. How should the archbishop discover it? As well as claim to discover Hull! 'Well, yes,' I say. 'As everyone knows.'

Down go his eyes again, clasp go his hands together over his cassocked tummy. 'We know that you had relations with Dereham when you were at your grandmother's house,' he says. 'He has confessed it.'

Oh! The fool. Now I cannot deny it. Why would he say such a thing? Why would he be such a slack-mouthed braggart?

'What are we to suppose, but that you put your paramour in a position close to you for a bad purpose?' he asks. 'Where you could meet every day? Where he could come to you without your ladies being present? Even unannounced?'

'Well, suppose nothing,' I say pertly enough. 'And he isn't my paramour anyway. Where is the king? I want to see him.'

'You were Dereham's lover at Lambeth, you were not a virgin when you married the king, and you were his lover after your marriage,' he says. 'You are an adulteress.'

'No!' I say again. The truth is all muddled up with a lie, and besides, I don't know what they know for sure. If only Francis had been born with the sense to shut up. 'Where is the king? I insist that I see him!'

'It is the king himself who has ordered me to inquire into your conduct,' he says. 'You cannot see him until you have answered my questions and your name is cleared without blemish.'

'I shall see him!' I jump to my feet. 'You shan't keep me from my husband. It has to be against the law!'

'Anyway, he has gone.'

'Gone?' For a moment it feels as if the floor has rocked under my quick feet as if I were dancing on a barge. 'Gone? Where has he gone? He can't have gone. We're staying here until we go to Whitehall for Christmas. There is nowhere else to go to, he wouldn't just leave me here. Where has he gone?'

'He has gone to Oatlands Palace.'

'To Oatlands?' This is the house where we were married. He would never go there without me. 'That is a lie! When did he go? This cannot be true!'

'I had to tell him, it was the greatest sadness of my life, that you had been Dereham's lover and that I fear you are his lover still,' Cranmer says. 'God knows I would have spared him that news. I thought he would lose his mind for grief, you have broken his heart, I think. He left for Oatlands at once, taking only the smallest household. He will see no-one, you have broken his heart and ruined yourself.'

'Gracious no,' I say feebly. 'Oh, gracious, no.' This is very bad indeed but if he has taken Thomas with him then at least my dearest love is safe, and we are not suspected. 'He will be lonely without me,' I say, hoping that the archbishop will name his companions.

'He is like to go mad of grief,' he says flatly.

'Oh, dear.' Well, what can I say? The king was mad as a March hare before any of this, and that in fairness cannot be laid at my door.

'Has he no companions?' I ask cleverly. Pray God that Thomas is safe.

'The groom of his chamber,' he replies. So thank God Thomas is in no danger. 'All you can do now is confess.'

'But I have done nothing!' I exclaim.

'You took Dereham into your household.'

'At my grandmother's request. And he has not been alone with me, nor so much as touched my hand.' I draw a little strength from my true innocence. 'Archbishop, you have done very wrong to upset the king. You don't know what he's like when he is upset.'

'All you can do is confess. All you can do is confess.'

This is so like being some poor soul trudging towards Smithfield with a faggot of wood to be burned to death that I stop, and giggle, from sheer terror. 'Really, Archbishop, I have done nothing. And I confess every day, you know I do, and I have never done anything.'

'You laugh?' he says, horrified.

'Oh, only from the shock!' I say impatiently. 'You must let me go to Oatlands, Archbishop. Indeed you must. I have to see the king and explain.'

'No, you have to explain to me, my child,' he says earnestly. 'You have to tell me what you did at Lambeth, and what you did thereafter. You have to make a full and honest confession and perhaps then I can save you from the scaffold.'

'The scaffold?' I shriek the word as if I have never heard it before. 'What do you mean, the scaffold?'

'If you have betrayed the king then this is an act of treason,' he says slowly and clearly, as if I am a child. 'The punishment for treason is death. You must know that.'

'But I have not betrayed him,' I gabble at him. 'The scaffold! I could swear it on the Bible. I could swear it on my life. I've never committed treason, I've never committed anything! Ask anyone! Ask anyone! I am a good girl, you know I am, the king calls me his rose, his rose without a thorn. I have no other will than his . . .'

'Indeed, you will have to swear to all of this on the Bible. And so you should make very sure that there is not a word of a lie. Now, tell me about what took place between you and the young man at Lambeth. And remember, God hears every word you say, and besides, we already have his confession, he has told us everything.'

'What has he confessed?' I ask.

'Never you mind. You tell me. What did you do?'

'I was very young,' I say. I peep up at him in case he is disposed to be sorry for me. He is! He is! His eyes are actually filled with tears. This is such a good sign that I feel much more confident. 'I was very young and all the girls in the ladies' chamber were badly behaved, I am afraid. They were not good friends and advisors to me.'

He nods. 'They allowed the young men of the household to come in to the girls' chamber?'

'They did. And Francis came in at night to court another girl; but then he took a fancy to me.' I pause. 'She wasn't half as pretty as me, and I didn't even have my lovely clothes then.'

The archbishop sighs for some reason. 'This is vanity. You are supposed to be confessing your sin with the young man.'

'I am! I am confessing. I am very distressed. He was very pressing. He insisted. He swore he was in love with me, and I believed him. I was very young. He promised me marriage, I thought we were married. He insisted.'

'He came to your bed?'

I want to say, 'No.' But if that fool Dereham has told them every-thing, then all I can do is make it seem better. 'He did. I did not invite him, but he insisted. He forced me.'

'He raped you?'

'Yes, almost.'

'Did you not cry out? You were in the room with all the other young ladies? They would have heard you.'

'I let him do it. But I did not want it.'

'So he lay with you.'

'Yes. But he was never naked.'

'He was fully dressed?'

'I mean he was never naked except for when he took his hose down. And then he was.'

'He was, what?'

'He was naked then.' Even to me this sounds weak.

'And he took your virginity.'

I cannot see a way to avoid this. 'Er . . .'

'He was your lover.'

'I don't think . . .'

He rises from his feet as if he would go. 'This does you no good at all. I cannot save you if you lie to me.'

I am so afraid of him walking away that I cry out, and run after him and catch his arm. 'Please, Archbishop. I will tell you. I am just so ashamed, and so sorry . . .' I am sobbing now, he looks so stern and if he does not take my side then how shall I explain all this to the king? And I am afraid of the archbishop; but I am utterly terri-fied of the king.

'Tell me. You lay with him. You were as husband and wife to each other.'

'Yes,' I say, driven to honesty. 'Yes, we were.'

He lifts my hand from his arm as if I have some infection of the skin and he does not want to touch me. As if I am a

450

leper. I, who only two days ago was so precious that the whole country thanked God that the king had found me! It is not possible. It is not possible that everything could have gone so wrong so quickly.

'I shall consider your confession,' he says. 'I shall take it to God in prayer. I have to tell the king. We will consider what charges you will have to face.'

'Can't we just forget that it all happened?' I whisper, my hands twisting together, the rings heavy on my fingers. 'It was so long ago. It was years ago. Nobody can even remember it. The king doesn't need to know, you said yourself, it will break his heart. Just tell him that nothing important happened, and can't everything be as it was?'

He looks at me as if I am quite mad. 'Queen Katherine,' he says gently. 'You have betrayed the King of England. The punishment is death. Can you not understand that?'

'But this was all long before I was married,' I whimper. 'It wasn't betraying the king. I hadn't even met him. Surely the king will forgive me for my errors as a girl?' I can feel the sobs coming up into my throat, and I can't hold them back. 'Surely he won't cruelly judge me for my childhood errors when I was nothing but a little girl with poor guardians?' I gulp. 'Surely, His Grace will be kind to me? He has loved me and I have made him so happy. He thanked God for me, and this, this is nothing.' The tears are pouring down my face, I am not pretending to be sorry, I am absolutely appalled to be here, facing this awful man, having to twist myself up in lies to make things look better. 'Please, sir, please forgive me. Please tell the king that I have done nothing that matters.'

The archbishop pulls away from me. 'Calm yourself. Calm yourself. We will say no more now.'

'Say you will forgive me, say that the king will forgive me.'

'I hope he will, I hope he can. I hope you can be saved.'

I grab on to him, sobbing without control. 'You cannot go until you promise me I will be safe.'

He drags himself to the door though I am clinging to him like a wailing child. 'Madam, you must be calm.'

'How can I be calm when you tell me that the king is angry with me? When you tell me that the punishment is death? How can I be calm? How can I be calm? I'm only sixteen, I can't be accused, I can't be . . .'

'Let me go, madam, this behaviour does not serve you.'

'You shan't go without blessing me.'

He pushes me from him and then crosses the air rapidly above my head. 'There. There you are, *in nomine . . . filii . . .* there, now be quiet.'

I throw myself down on the floor to sob but I hear the door close behind him, and even though he is not there to see me, I cannot stop crying. Even when the inner door opens and my ladies come in, I am still crying. Even when they flutter round me and pat me on the head I do not sit up and cheer up. I am so afraid now, I am so afraid.

Jane Boleyn, Hampton Court, November 1541

That devil the archbishop has terrified the girl half out of her wits and now she does not know whether to lie or confess. My lord the duke has come with him for another visit and while they try to pull the sobbing queen from her bed he pauses beside me. 'Will she confess to Culpepper?' he whispers, so low that I have to lean against him to hear it.

'If you let the archbishop work on her she will confess to anything,' I warn him in a hurried whisper. 'I cannot keep her quiet. He torments her with hope and then he threatens her with damnation. She is only a silly girl, and he seems determined to break her. He will drive her mad if he keeps threatening her.'

He gives a short laugh, almost like a groan. 'She had better pray for madness, it could be the only thing that saves her,' he says. 'Good God. Two nieces as Queens of England and both of them end on the scaffold!'

'What could save her?'

'They can't execute her if she is mad,' he says absently. 'You can't stand trial for treason if you are mad. They would have to send her away to a convent. Good God, is that her screaming now?'

The eerie cries of Kitty Howard begging to be spared are echoing through her rooms as the women try to pull her in to face the archbishop.

'What will you do?' I demand. 'This can't go on.'

'I'll try to keep clear of this,' he says bleakly. 'I hoped to see her with her wits about her today. I was going to advise her to plead guilty to Dereham and deny Culpepper, then she has done nothing worse than marry with a pre-contract in place, as Anne of Cleves. She might have got away with that. He might even have taken her back. But at this rate she will kill herself before the axeman gets her.'

'Keep clear?' I demand. 'And what about me?'

His face is like a flint. 'What about you?'

'I'll take the French count,' I say to him rapidly. 'Whatever the contract is, I'll take him. I'll live with him in France for a few years, wherever he likes. I'll lie low until the king has recovered from this, I can't go back into exile, I can't go back to Blickling. I can't stand it. I can't go through it all again. I really can't. I'll take the French count even without a good settlement. Even if he is old and ugly, even if he's deformed. I'll take the French count.'

The duke shouts with sudden laughter like a baited bear, bellowing in my face. I recoil; but his amusement is horribly sincere. In these terrible rooms filled with women crying to Katherine to compose herself and her awful, high-pitched wailing, and the archbishop praying loudly over the noise, the duke roars out his merriment. 'A French count!' he bellows. 'A French count! Are you mad? Are you run as mad as my niece?'

'What?' I demand, quite baffled. 'What are you laughing at? Hush, my lord. Hush. There's nothing to laugh at.'

'Nothing to laugh at?' He cannot contain himself. 'There never was a French count. There never could have been a French count. There never would be a French count or an English earl or an English baron. There would never be a Spanish don, or an Italian prince. No man in the world would ever have you. Are you such a fool that you don't know that?'

'But you said . . .'

'I said anything to keep you at work for me, as you would say

454

anything to suit your own cause. But I never thought you really believed me. Don't you know what men think of you?'

I can feel my legs starting to tremble, it is like the time before, when I knew that I would have to betray them. When I knew that I would have to hide my falseness from my own face. 'I don't know,' I say. 'I don't want to know.'

His hard hands come down on my shoulders and he drags me to one of the queen's expensive gilt-edged looking-glasses. In the soft silver reflection I see my own wide eyes looking back at me, and his face as hard as the face of Death himself. 'Look,' he says. 'Look at yourself and know what you are: you liar, you false wife. There is not a man in the world who would marry you. You are known the length and breadth of Europe as the woman who sent her husband and her sister-in-law to the axeman. You are known in every court in Europe as a woman so vile that she sent her husband to be hanged . . .' he gives me a shake '. . . to be cut down while still living, in his piss-wet breeches,' he shakes me again, 'to be slit from cock to throat, to see his belly and his liver and his lights pulled out and shown to him, to bleed to death while they burned his liver and his heart and his belly and his lungs before his face,' he shakes me again, 'and then finally to be sliced up like a beast on the butcher's block, the head, the arms, the legs.'

'They didn't do that to him,' I whisper, but my lips barely move in the reflection.

'No thanks to you,' he says. 'That's what people remember. The king, his worst enemy, spared him the torture that you had sent him to. The king let him be beheaded, but you sent him to be disem-bowelled. You, on the witness stand, swearing that he and Anne had been lovers, that he had mounted his own sister, that he was a sodomite, a bugger, with half the court, swearing that they had plotted the king's death, swearing his life away, sending him to a death that you would not give to a dog.'

'It was your plan.' In the mirror my face is green with sickness at the truth being spoken out loud at last, my dark eyes bulging with horror. 'It was your plan, not mine. I shall not be blamed for it. You said that we would save them. They would be pardoned if we gave evidence and they pleaded guilty.'

'You knew that was a lie.' He shakes me like a terrier shakes a rat. 'You knew, you liar. You never took the stand to save him. You took the stand to save your title and your fortune, you called it your inheritance, the Boleyn inheritance. You knew that if you turned evidence against your own husband then the king would leave you with your title and your lands. That's all you wanted in the end. That's all you cared for. You sent that young man and that beauty, his sister, to the gallows so that you could save your own yellow skin and your paltry title. You sent them to their deaths, a savage death, for being beautiful and merry and happy in each other's company and for excluding you. You are a byword for malice, jealousy and twisted lust. D'you think any man would trust you with a title again? D'you think any man would risk calling you wife? After that?'

'I was going to save him.' I bare my teeth at the two of us in the mirror. 'I accused him so that he could confess and be pardoned. I would have saved him.'

'You are a killer worse than the king,' he says brutally, and throws me to one side. I rebound off the wall and grab at the tapestry to steady myself. 'You testified against your own sister-in-law and husband, you stood by the sickbed while Jane Seymour died, you testified against Anne of Cleves and would have seen her beheaded, and now, without a doubt, you will see another cousin go to the gallows, and I confidently expect you to bear witness against her.'

'I loved him,' I say stubbornly, going to the only charge that I cannot bear to hear. 'You shall not deny that I loved George. I loved him with all my heart.'

'Then you are worse than a liar and a false friend,' he says coldly. 'For your love brought the man you love to a most pitiable death. Your love is worse than hatred. Dozens hated George Boleyn but it was your loving word that took him to his death. Don't you see how evil you are?'

'If he had stood by me, if he had cleaved to me, I would have saved him,' I cry out from my own pain. 'If he had loved me as he loved her, if he had let me into his life, if I had been as dear to him as she was . . .'

'He would never have stood by you,' the duke says with contempt like poison in his voice. 'He would never have loved you. Your father bought him for you with a fortune, but nobody and no fortune could make you lovable. George despised you, and Anne and Mary laughed at you. That's why you accused them, none of this high-flying, self-sacrificing lie has a shred of truth. You accused them, because if you could not have George you would rather have seen him dead than loving his sister.'

'She came between us,' I gasp.

'His hounds came between you. His horses. He loved the horses in his stable, he loved his hawks in his mews more than he loved you. And you would have killed every one of them, horse, hound and hawk, from sheer jealousy. You are an evil woman, Jane, and I have used you as I would use a piece of filth. But now I am finished with that foolish girl Katherine and I am finished with you. You can advise her to save herself as best she can. You can bear witness for her, you can bear witness against her. I don't care for either of you.'

I feel the wall behind me and I push myself forwards to glare into his face. 'You will not treat me so,' I say. 'I am no piece of filth, I am your ally. If you turn against me you will regret it. I know all the secrets. Enough to send her to the gallows, enough to send you there too. I will destroy her, and you with her.' I am panting now, flushed with rage. 'I will bring her to the scaffold and every Howard with her. Even if I die myself this time!'

He laughs again but now he is quiet, his anger spent. 'She is a lost cause,' he says. 'The king has finished with her. I have finished with her. I can save myself and I will. You will go down with the slut. You cannot get off twice.'

'I shall tell the archbishop about Culpepper,' I threaten. 'I shall tell him that you meant them to be lovers. That you told me to throw them together.'

'You can say what you like,' he replies easily. 'You will have no proof. There is only one person who was seen carrying messages and letting him into her rooms. That would be you. Everything you say to incriminate me will point to your guilt. You will die for it, and God knows, I don't care one way or another.'

I scream then, I scream and fall to my knees and clasp him around the legs. 'Don't say that, I have served you, I have served you for years, I have been your most faithful servant and I have had next to no reward. Get me out of here and she can die and Culpepper can die but I shall be safe with you.'

Slowly the duke leans down and detaches my hands as if I were some kind of sticky weed that has tangled unpleasantly around his legs. 'No, no,' he says, as if he has lost all interest in the conversation. 'No. She cannot be saved and I wouldn't lift a finger to save you. The world will be a better place when you are dead, Jane Boleyn. You will not be missed.'

'I am yours.' I look up at him, but I dare not grab him again, and so he walks away from me, to tap on the door to the outside world, where the sentries, who used to stand on the outside to keep everyone out, are now keeping us locked in. 'I am yours,' I shout. 'Heart and soul. I love you.'

'I don't want you,' he remarks. 'Nobody wants you. And the last man you promised to love died because of your testament. You are a foul thing, Jane Boleyn, the axeman can finish what the devil has started for all I care.' He pauses with his hand on the door, as a thought strikes him. 'I should think you will be beheaded on Tower Green, where they killed Anne,' he says. 'There's an irony for you. I should think she and her brother are laughing in hell, waiting for you.'

Anne, Richmond Palace,
November 1541

They have moved Kitty Howard to Syon Abbey and she is kept as a prisoner, with only a few of her ladies. They have arrested two young men from her grandmother's household and they will be tortured until they confess what they know, and then they will be tortured until they confess what they are required to say. Her ladies who were in her confidence are taken to the Tower for questioning too. His Grace the king has returned from his private musing at Oatlands Palace and has come back to Hampton Court. He is said to be very quiet, very grieved, but not angry. We must thank God that he is not angry. If he does not fly into one of his vindictive rages then he might sink into self-pity and banish her. He is going to annul his marriage to the queen on the grounds of her abominable behaviour – those are the very words he has put to parliament. Please God that they will agree with him that she is not fit to be queen, and the poor child can be released, and her friends go home.

She could go to France, she would be a delight to that court, who would find her vanity and her prettiness a pleasure to watch. Or perhaps she could be persuaded to live in the country as I do, and call herself another sister to the king. She might even come and live with me and we could be friends as we used to be in the old days when I was the queen he did not want, and she was the maid that he did. She could be sent away to a thousand different places where she could do the king no harm and where her folly might make people laugh, and where she might grow into a sensible woman. Surely, everyone agrees that she cannot be executed. She is simply too young to be executed. This is not an Anne Boleyn, who schemed and contrived her way to the throne over six years of striving, and was then thrown down by her own ambition. This is a girl with no more judgement than one of her kittens. Nobody could be so harsh as to send a child like this to the block. Thank God, the king is sad and not angry. Please God, the parliament will advise him that the marriage can be annulled, and pray heaven that Archbishop Cranmer is satisfied with the disgrace of the queen on the basis of her child-hood amours, and does not start to investigate her follies since her marriage.

I don't know what goes on at court these days, but I saw her at Christmas and the New Year, and I thought then that she was ready for a lover, and hoping for love. And how could she stop herself? She is a girl coming into womanhood with a man old enough to be her father as her husband, a sickly man, an impotent man, perhaps even a madman. Even a sensible young woman in those circum-stances would turn for friendship and comfort to one of the young men who gather round her. And Katherine is a flirt.

Dr Harst comes riding out from London to see me, and the moment that he arrives, he sends my ladies away so that we can talk alone. I know from this that it is grave news from the court.

'What news of the queen?' I ask him as soon as they have gone from the room and we are seated, side by side, like conspirators before the fire.

'She is still being questioned,' he says. 'If there is any more to be had they will get it out of her. She is kept close in her apartments at Syon, she is allowed to see no-one. She is not even allowed out to walk in the garden. Her uncle has abandoned her and she has no friends. Four of her ladies are locked up with her, they would leave if they could. Her closest friends are under arrest and being questioned in the Tower. They say she cries all the time and begs them to forgive her. She is too distressed to eat or sleep. She is said to be starving herself to death.'

'God help her, poor little Kitty,' I say. 'God help her. But surely they have evidence for the annulment of her marriage to the king? He has enough to divorce her and let her go?'

'No, now they are seeking evidence for worse,' he says shortly.

We are both silent. We both know what he means by that, and we both fear that there may be worse to discover.

'I have come to see you for something even more grave than this,' he says.

'Good God, what worse could there be?'

'I hear that the king is thinking of taking you back as his wife.'

For a moment I am so stunned that I cannot say anything, then I grip the carved arms of my chair and watch my fingertips go white. 'You cannot mean this.'

'I do. King Francis of France is keen that the two of you shall remarry and that your brother and the king join with him in a war against Spain.'

'The king wants another alliance with my brother?'

'Against Spain.'

'They can do that without me! They can make an alliance without me!'

'The King of France and your brother want you restored and the king wants to rid himself of the memory of Katherine. It is to be just as it was. It is to be as if she never existed. As if you have just arrived in England, and everything can go as planned.'

'He is Henry of England; but not even he can turn back the clock!' I cry out and I push myself up from my chair and stride across the room. 'I won't do it. I daren't do it. He will have me killed within a year. He is a wife-killer. He takes a woman and destroys her. It has become his habit. This will be my death!'

'If he were to deal with you honourably . . .'

'Dr Harst, I have escaped him once, I am the only wife of his to come out from the marriage alive! I can't go back to put my head on the block.'

'I am advised that he would offer you guarantees . . .'

'This is Henry of England!' I round on the ambassador. 'This is a man who has been the death of three wives and is now building the scaffold for his fourth! There are no guarantees. He is a murderer. If you put me in his bed I am a dead woman.'

'He will divorce Queen Katherine, I am certain of it. He has laid it before parliament. They know that she was no virgin when she married him. The news of her scandalous behaviour has been released to the ambassadors at the European courts for them to announce. She is publicly named as a whore. He will put her aside. He will not kill her.'

'How can you be so sure?'

'There is no reason for him to kill her,' he says gently. 'You are overwrought, you are not thinking clearly. She married him under false pretences, that is a sin and she is wrong. He has announced that. But since they were not married, she has not cuckolded him, he has no reason to do anything other than let her go.'

'Then why is he seeking more evidence against her?' I ask. 'Since he has enough against her to name her as a whore, since he has enough against her to bring her into shame and divorce her? Why does he need more evidence?'

'To punish the men,' he replies.

Our eyes meet, neither of us knows what we dare to believe.

'I fear him,' I say miserably.

'And so you should, he is a fearsome king. But he divorced you, and he kept his word to you. He made a fair settlement on you and he has kept you in peace and prosperity. Perhaps he will divorce her and make a settlement on her, perhaps this is his way now. Then he may want to marry you again.'

'I cannot,' I say quietly. 'Believe me, Dr Harst, even if you are right and he treats Katherine with forgiveness, even with generosity, I would not dare to marry him. I cannot bear to be married to him again. I still thank God on my knees every morning for my good fortune in escaping last time. When the councillors ask you, or my brother asks you, or the French ambassador asks you, then you must tell them that I am settled to the single state, I believe myself to be pre-contracted as the king himself said. Just as he said: I am not free to marry. Persuade them that it cannot be done. I swear I cannot do it. I will not put my head back on the block and wait to hear the whistle of the falling axe.'

Katherine, Syon Abbey, November 1541

Now, let me see, what do I have now?

I have to say, I'm not doing very well at all.

I have six French hoods edged with gold. I have six pairs of sleeves, I have six plain kirtles, I have six gowns, they are in navy blue, black, dark green and grey. I have no jewels, I have no toys. I don't even have my kitten. Everything that the king gave me has been taken from my rooms by Sir Thomas Seymour – a Seymour! taking a Howard's goods! Think how we shall resent that! – to be returned to the king. So, as it turns out, all the things I counted before were never really mine. They were loans and not gifts at all.

I have three rooms with very poor tapestries. My servants live in one and I live in the other two with my half-sister Isabel, Lady Baynton and two other ladies. None of them speaks to me for resentment at the position they find themselves in through my wickedness, except Isabel, who has been told to bring me to a sense of my sin. I have to say that this makes for very poor company in a confined space. My confessor is ready for my call should I be such a fool as to wish to hang myself by confessing to him what I have denied to everyone else and twice a day Isabel scolds me as if I were her servant. I have some books of prayers and the Bible. I have some sewing to do, shirts for the poor; but surely they must have enough shirts by now? I have no pageboys, or courtiers, or jesters or musicians or singers. Even my little dogs have been taken away and I know they will pine for me.

My friends are all gone. My uncle has disappeared like the mist in the morning, and they tell me that most of my household, Lady Rochford, and Francis Dereham, Katherine Tylney, and Joan Bulmer, Margaret Morton and Agnes Restwold, are in the Tower being questioned about me.

But even worse than all of this, I heard today that they have taken Thomas Culpepper to the Tower also. My poor, beautiful Thomas! The thought of him being arrested by some ugly man at arms is a horror, but the thought of my Thomas being questioned makes me fall to my knees and lie my face against the rough cloth of my bed and weep. If only we had run away when we first knew that we were in love. If only he had come for me before I even went to court, when I was still a girl at Lambeth. If only I had told him that I was his, only his when I first came to court, before all of this went wrong.

'Do you want your confessor?' Lady Baynton says coldly as she finds me weeping. They will have told her to say this, they are eager for me to break down and tell everything.

'No,' I say quickly. 'I have nothing to confess.'

And what is so horrid is that these rooms are Lady Margaret Douglas's rooms, where she was kept on her own in silence for the crime of falling in love. Fancy that! She was here, just like me, wandering from one room to the other and back again, under arrest for loving a man, not knowing what the charge could be, nor what the sentence could be, nor when the blow would fall. She was here all on her own, in disgrace for thirteen months, hoping that the king would forgive her, wondering what was going to happen. She was taken away just a few days ago to make room for me – I can't believe it! – they took her to Kenninghall, where she will be imprisoned again until the king forgives her, if he ever forgives her.

I think of her, a young woman only a little older than me, locked up and alone just like me, imprisoned for the crime of loving a man who loved her back, and I wish now that I had gone down on my knees to the king and begged him to be kind to her. But how was I to know that one day I should be in just the same state? In the very same rooms? Suspected of being a young woman in love, just as she is? I wish I had told him that she is only young and perhaps silly and she should be guided; not arrested and punished. But I didn't speak up for her, nor did I speak for poor Margaret Pole, nor for all the men and women at Smithfield. I didn't speak up for the men of the North who rose up against him. I didn't say a word for Thomas Cromwell but I got married on the day he died without even a moment of pity. I didn't speak up for the king's daughter Princess Mary, but worse: I complained of her. I didn't even speak up for my own mistress and queen, Anne, who I loved. I promised her my loyalty and friendship and yet when they asked me I signed a paper against her without bothering to read it. And now there is nobody who will go down on their knees and ask for mercy for me.

Of course, I don't know what is going on. If they have arrested Henry Manox along with Francis Dereham then he will tell them whatever they want to hear. We did not part on good terms and he has no love for Francis. He will tell them that he and I were all but lovers, and then he is certain to tell them that I dropped him and went on to Francis Dereham. My name will be quite sullied, and my grandmother will be furious.

I suppose they will ask the Lambeth girls all about me. Agnes Restwold and Joan Bulmer are no great friends of mine in their hearts. They liked me well enough when I was queen with favours to give but they won't defend me or lie for me. And if they dig up half a dozen of the others from whatever little lives they are living, they will say anything for a trip to London. If they ask Joan Bulmer anything about Francis she will tell them everything, I don't doubt. Every single one of the girls at Norfolk House knows that Francis called me wife, and I answered to it. That he bedded me as if we were husband and wife, and I didn't know – to be honest – whether we were married or not. I never really thought about it. Katherine Tylney will tell them all about Lambeth, quick enough; I just hope that they don't ask her about Lincoln, or Pontefract, or Hull. If she starts telling them about the nights I was missing from my room then that will lead them to Thomas. Oh, God, if only I had never laid eyes on him. He would be safe now and so would I.

If they talk to Margaret Morton she will tell them that I had words with her when she tried the door of my bedroom and found it locked. I had Thomas, darling Thomas, in bed with me, and I had to fly across the room and shout at her to show more respect, with the door half-closed to keep him hidden. She laughed in my face, she knew that someone was inside. Oh, God, if only I had not quarrelled with them all so often. If I had kept them sweet with bribes and dresses then perhaps now they would be lying for me.

And, now I think of it, Margaret was outside in the presence chamber when Thomas was with me in my privy chamber, one day at Hampton Court. We spent the whole afternoon by the fire, kissing and touching, laughing at the courtiers just outside the door. I was excited by our daring then; now I pinch my own palms till my skin is red and swollen at the thought of what a fool I was. But even now, I can't regret it. Even if I were to die for that afternoon, I would not regret having had his mouth on mine and his touch on me. Thank God we had that time, at least. I won't wish it away.

They will bring me another tray of food in a moment. I shan't touch it. I can't eat, I can't sleep, I can't do anything but walk around these two rooms and think that Lady Margaret Douglas walked here too, missing the man she loved. She didn't have half her friends telling the world about her. She didn't have every enemy of the Howards turning the king against her. She is the most unfortunate woman I know and she is lucky compared to me.

I know Lady Rochford will stay my friend, I know she will. She knows what Thomas is to me, and I to him. She will keep her head, she's been in danger before, she knows how to answer questions. She is an older woman, a person of experience. Before we parted she said to me, 'Deny everything', and I shall. She knows what should be done. I know she will keep herself safe, and me with her.

She knows everything, of course, that's the worst of it. She knows when I fell in love with Thomas and she managed all the secret meetings and the letters and the times we could steal together. She hid him for me behind wall hangings, and once in the shadows on the stairs at York. She smuggled me to him down winding corridors in strange houses. He had a room of his own at Pontefract and we met there after hunting one afternoon. She told me where we might meet and one night when the king himself tried the outer door, thinking he would come to my bed, she kept her nerve and called out that I was ill and was asleep and sent him away. She did that! She sent the King of England away and her voice did not quaver for one second. She has such courage, she will not be crying and confessing. I daresay even if they rack her she will just look at them with her cold face and say nothing. I am not afraid of her betraying me. I can trust her to deny everything they ask. I know I can trust her to defend me.

Except . . . except I keep wondering now that she could not save her husband when he was accused. She never likes to talk about him and that makes me wonder too. I always thought it was because she was so very sad about him, but now I wonder if it was something worse than that. Catherine Carey was certain that she had not given evidence for them but against them. How could that be? And she said that she had saved their inheritance, and not them. Yet how could they die and she get off scot-free if she had not made some kind of agreement with the king? And if she betrayed one queen – and that her own sister-in-law – and condemned her own husband, why should she save me?

Oh, I get these fearful thoughts because of the situation I am in, which is not an easy one. I know that. Poor Margaret Douglas must have gone half-mad walking from one room to another and not knowing what would become of her. Fancy spending a year here, walking from one room to another and not knowing if you will ever be released. I can't bear the waiting, and at least, unlike her, I am sure to be released soon. I am sure everything will come out right but I do worry about things, about everything really. And one of the things I worry about is how come Anne Boleyn was killed, and George Boleyn was killed, and Jane his wife just walked away? And how come nobody ever said anything about it? And how come she could save his inheritance; but her evidence couldn't save him?

Now I must stop this, for I start to think that she might give evidence for me and it might take me to the same place as Anne Boleyn, and that is ridiculous for Lady Anne was an adulteress and a witch and guilty of treason. And all I have done is go a bit too far with Henry Manox and Francis Dereham when I was a girl. And since then, nobody knows what I have done, and I will deny everything.

Dear God, if they take Thomas for questioning I know he will lie to protect me, but if they rack him . . .

This is no good. The thought of Thomas on the rack makes me howl out like a baited bear as it goes down before the dogs. Thomas in pain! Thomas crying out as I am crying out! But I won't think of it. It cannot happen. He is the king's beloved boy, the king calls him that: the beloved boy. The king would never hurt Thomas, and he would never hurt me. He has no reason to suspect him. And I daresay, if he did know that Thomas loves me and I him, he would understand. If you love someone, you understand how they feel. He might even laugh and say that after my marriage to him is ended we can be married. He may give us his blessing. He does forgive people, especially his favourites. It's not as if I were Margaret Douglas and married without his permission. It's not as if I defied him. I would never do that.

Dear God, she must have thought she would die in here. It has only been a few days and already I feel like carving my name on the stone walls. The rooms face down over the long gardens, I can see the sunlight on the pale grass. This was an abbey and the nuns who lived here were the pride of England for the strictness of their order and the beauty of their singing. Or so Lady Baynton says. But the king drove the nuns away and took the building into his own keeping so now it is like trying to live in a church, and I swear the place is haunted with their sadness. It is not a fit place for me, at all. After all I am Queen of England, and if not Queen of England then I am Katherine Howard, and a member of one of the greatest families in the kingdom. To be a Howard is to be one of the first, after all.

Now, let me see, I must cheer myself somehow. So, what do I have? But, oh, it's not very cheering. Really, not very cheering at all. Six gowns, which is not much, and in very dull colours, old lady colours. Two rooms for my own use and a small household to serve me. So to see the best of it, I am really in a better case than when I was little Mistress Katherine Howard at Lambeth. I have a man who loves me and who I love with my whole heart, and a very good chance of being released to marry him, I should think. I have a faithful friend in Lady Rochford who will give evidence in my favour, Tom would die to save me so all I have to do when the archbishop comes again is go on confessing to Francis Dereham and Henry Manox and never say a word about Tom. I can do that. Even a fool like me can do that. And then everything will come out right and when I next count I shall have many lovely things again. I don't doubt it. I don't doubt it at all.

But all the while I am reassuring myself of this, the tears are just pouring out of my eyes and I am sobbing and sobbing. I can't seem to stop crying though I know I am in a most hopeful state. Really, things are quite all right for me, I have always been lucky; I just can't seem to stop crying,

Jane Boleyn, the Tower of London, November 1541

I am in such terror I think I shall go mad in truth. They keep asking me about Katherine and that fool Dereham, and I thought at first that I could deny everything. I was not there at Lambeth when they were lovers, and for sure they were never lovers after that. I could tell them all I know and with a clear conscience. But when that great wooden gate banged shut behind me, and the shadow of the Tower fell cold on me, I felt a terror that I had never known before.

The ghosts that have haunted me since that day in May will take me for their own now. I am where they walked, I feel the chill of the same walls, I know the same terror, I am living their deaths.

Dear God, it must have been like this for him, for George, my beloved George. He must have heard that gate bang, he must have seen the stone bulk of the Tower block out the sky, he must have known that his friends and his enemies were somewhere inside these walls, lying their heads off to save themselves and to condemn him. And now I am here walking where he walked, and now I know what he felt, and now I know fear, as he knew it.

If Cranmer and his inquisitors look no further than Katherine's life when she was a girl, before she came to court, they have enough to destroy her; and what more do they need than that? If they rest on her affairs with Manox and Dereham, then they need nothing from me. I did not even know her then. It is nothing to do with me. So I should have nothing to fear. But if that is the case, then why am I here?

The room is cramped, with stone-paved floors and damp stone walls. The walls are pocked with the carved initials of people who have been held here before me. I will not look for GB, 'George Boleyn'; I think I should go mad if I saw his name. I will sit quietly by the window, and look out to the courtyard below. I will not go over the walls for his name, fingering the cold stone looking for 'Boleyn', and touch where he carved. I will sit quietly here and look out of the window.

No, this is no good. The window looks out on to Tower Green, my prison chamber looks down on the very spot where Anne was beheaded on my evidence. I cannot look at that place, I cannot look at the bright greenness of the grass – surely it is more verdant than any autumn grass should be? – if I look at the green I will surely lose my mind. It must have been like this for her when she was waiting, and she would have known that I knew enough to have her beheaded. And she must have known that I would choose to have her beheaded. She knew that she had tormented me and teased me and laughed at me until I was beside myself with jealousy, she must have wondered how far I would follow my evil rage, even to seek her death? Then she knew. She knew I gave witness against the two of them, that I spoke out in a clear voice and condemned them without remorse. Well, I feel remorse now; God knows that I do.

I feel as if I have been hiding myself from the truth for all these years, but it took that hard man the Duke of Norfolk to spell it out to me, and it took these cold walls to make it real for me. I was jealous of Anne and her love for George and his devotion to her, and I bore witness not from what I knew to be a fact, but from what would harm them the most. God forgive me. I took his tenderness and his care and his kindness for his sister and I made it into something dirty and dark and bad because I could not bear that he was not tender nor careful nor kind to me. I brought him to his death to punish him for neglecting me. And now, like some old play in which the gods are furious, I am still neglected. I have never been more alone. I have committed the greatest sin a wife could do, and still I have no satisfaction.

The duke has withdrawn to the country, neither Katherine nor I will ever see him again. I know him well enough to know that his sole care will be to protect his own old skin and guard his well-loved fortune. And the king needs a Howard to march and fight and execute for him. The king may hate him for this second adultery but he will not make the mistake of losing a commander as well as a wife. Katherine's step-grandmother, the duchess, may lose her life for this. If they can prove that she knew that Katherine, in her care, was little more than a slut, then they will accuse her of treason: for failing to warn the king. She will be tearing open documents, and swearing servants to secrecy, sacking old retainers, and cleaning out her rooms, if I know her. She may be able to hide enough to save herself.

But what about me?

My way is clear. I shall say nothing of Thomas Culpepper and the evidence I can give of Francis Dereham is that he was secretary to the queen at the request of her step-grandmother, and nothing passed between them under my eye. If they discover about Thomas Culpepper (and if they look only a little, they are certain to discover all about Thomas Culpepper), then they will see it all. If they see it all I shall tell them that she lay with him at Hampton Court, when the king first was ill, all through the royal progress when she thought she was with child, till the very day that we all went down on our knees and thanked God for her. That I knew she was a slut from that first day, but that she ordered me, and the duke ordered me, and I was not free to do what I thought right.

This is what I shall say. She shall die for it, and the duke may die for it; but I will not.

This is all I should consider.

My room faces east, the sun rises in the morning at seven, and I am always awake to see it rise. The Tower throws a long shadow across the bright grass of the green where she died, as if it is pointing a dark finger to my window. If I think of Anne, in her beauty and her allure, in her cleverness and her wit, then I think I shall go mad. She was in these rooms, and she went down those stairs, and she went out to that piece of grass (which I could see if I went to the window; but I never go to the window) and put her head down on the block and died a brave death, knowing that she was betrayed by everyone who had benefited from her rise. Knowing that her brother and his friends, the little circle who loved her so well, had died the day before, knowing that I gave the fatal evidence, her uncle gave the death sentence and the king celebrated it. I cannot think of this. I must take good care of myself and not think of this.

Dear God, she knew that I betrayed her. Dear God, he went to a traitor's death on the scaffold knowing that I betrayed him. He perhaps did not realise that it was from love. That's the worst thing. He will never have known that it was from love. It was such a murderous thing to do, it was such a gesture from hatred that he will never have known that I loved him and I couldn't bear that he should look at another woman. Let alone Anne. Let alone what he was to her.

I sit and face the wall. I cannot bear to look out of the window, I cannot bear to trace the writings on the walls of the cell for fear of finding his initials. I sit and fold my hands in my lap. To anyone watching me I am composed. I am an innocent woman. I am as innocent and composed as – say – Lady Margaret Pole, who was also beheaded outside my window. I never said one word for her, either. Dear God, how can I even breathe the air of this place?

I can hear the shuffle of many feet on the stairs. How many do they think they need? The key grates in the lock, the door swings open. I am irritated by the slowness. Do they think they can frighten me with this theatre of threat? Then they come in. Two men and the guards. I recognise Sir Thomas Wriothsley, but not the clerk. They fuss about, setting up the table, putting out a chair for me. I stand and try to look unmoved, my hands clasped. Then I realise I am wringing my hands and I make myself be still.

'We wish to ask you about the queen's behaviour at Lambeth when she was a girl,' he says. He nods at the clerk to indicate that he should write.

'I know nothing about it,' I say. 'As you will see from your own records I was in the country, at Blickling Hall, and then in service with Queen Anne, to whom I gave good and honourable service. I did not know Katherine Howard until she came to serve Queen Anne.'

The clerk makes one mark, only one. I see it. It is a tick. This means that they knew what I would say, it is not worth writing down. They have prepared for this interview, I should not trust a word they say. They know what they want to say and what they want me to reply. I have to be ready. I have to be armed against them. I wish I could think clearly, I wish my thoughts were not such a whirl. I must be calm, I must be clever.

'When the queen took on Francis Dereham as her secretary, did you know that he was her old friend and previous lover?'

'No, I knew nothing of her life before,' I say.

The clerk puts down a tick. This too is expected.

'When the queen asked you to fetch Thomas Culpepper to her room, did you know what were her intentions?'

I am stunned. How do we go from Francis Dereham to Thomas Culpepper in one leap? How do they know of Thomas Culpepper? What do they know of Thomas Culpepper? What has he told them? Is he on the rack vomiting in pain and sicking up the truth?

'She never asked me,' I say.

The clerk puts down a dash.

'We know that she asked you to fetch him, and we know that he came. Now, to save your life, will you tell us what took place between Thomas Culpepper and Katherine Howard?'

The clerk's pen is poised, I can feel the words in my dry mouth. It is over. She is ruined, he is a dead man, I am on the brink of betrayal: again.

Anne, Richmond Palace,
December 1541

The Dowager Duchess of Norfolk has been questioned on her sickbed as to the behaviour of her granddaughter. She will be tried for letting the girl go to the king without warning him that she was no virgin. This is now called treason. She will be accused of treason because her granddaughter took a lover. If she is found guilty that will be another old lady's head on Henry's block.

Dereham is accused with Culpepper of presumptive treason. The cause is that they both had intercourse with the queen. Dereham is accused even though there is no evidence against him and most believe that he laid with her long before she was queen, before even I was queen. Nonetheless this is to be called treason. The king has named Katherine Howard as a 'common harlot' – oh, Kitty, that anyone should speak like that of you! Both young men plead guilty to presumptive treason in the hopes of forgiveness. Both deny having lain with the queen. Their judge – unbelievable though it is to anyone but a subject of King Henry's – is the Duke of Norfolk, who knows more of this than any man can say. His Grace the duke has returned from the country to hear the evidence of his niece Katherine promising to marry Dereham, admitting him to her bedroom and to her bed. He has heard the evidence of Dereham coming into her household when she was queen and that is apparently enough to prove the young couple guilty. For why, the inquisitors indignantly demand, would Dereham come to work for the queen if not to seduce her? The idea that he would hope to profit from her success as all the rest of them have done, her uncle among them, is not mentioned.

Culpepper started by denying everything, but once the queen's ladies had given their statements, Lady Rochford among them, he could see that he was finished and he is now pleading guilty. Both young men are to be half-hanged and then their bellies slit open, their guts pulled out, and then butchered as they bleed to death, for the crime of loving the pretty girl who married the king.

This foreshadows Katherine's fate. I know it and I am on my knees for her every day. If the men accused of loving her are to be killed in the cruellest way that England can devise, then the chances of her being forgiven and released are slight indeed. I am afraid she will spend the rest of her life in the Tower. Dear God, she is only sixteen now. Do they not think that two years ago she was too young to judge? Did her own uncle not think that a girl of fourteen is not likely to resist temptation when she is constantly encouraged to indulge her whims in everything? I don't even consider what Henry thought, Henry is a madman. He thought of nothing but his own pleasure in her, and his own belief that she adored him. That is what she will pay for: for disappointing the vain dreams of a madman. As I did.

When I turned away from him in disgust at Rochester he hated me for it, and he punished me for it as soon as he could, calling me ugly and fat with slack breasts and belly, no virgin, full of noisome airs, stinking in fact. When Kitty chooses a young handsome man over his bloated, rotting body he calls her a scandal and a whore. He punishes me with shame and exile from the court, and then takes pleasure in showing his generosity. I don't think she will get off so lightly.

I am on my knees in my privy chamber at my prie-dieu when I hear the door behind me open quietly. I am so afraid of my shadow in these dangerous days that I spin around. It is Lotte, my lady secretary, and her face is white.

'What is it?' I am on my feet at once. Stumbling as my heel catches the hem of my gown, I nearly fall and have to catch on to the little altar to save myself. The cross wobbles and crashes down to the floor.

'They have arrested your maid Frances, and they have taken your squire Richard Taverner too.'

I gasp in terror, and then I wait until I can breathe out again. She mistakes my blank face for incomprehension and she repeats the awful thing she has just said in German: 'They have arrested your lady in waiting Frances, and they have taken Richard Taverner too.'

'On what charges?' I whisper.

'They don't say. The inquisitors are in the house now. We are all to be questioned.'

'They must have said something.'

'Just that we are all to be questioned. Even you.'

I am icy with fear. 'Quick,' I say. 'Go to the stables at once and get a boy to take a boat downriver to Dr Harst in London. Tell him that I am in grave danger. Go at once. Go by the garden stairs and make sure no-one sees you.'

She nods and goes to the little private door to the garden as the other door to my presence chamber is thrown open and five men walk in.

'Stop right there,' one of them orders, seeing the open door. Lotte stops, she does not even look towards me.

'I was just going to the garden,' she says in English. 'I need to take the air. I am unwell.'

'You are under arrest,' he replies.

I step forwards. 'On what grounds? What is alleged against her?'

The senior man, one I don't know, steps towards me and bows slightly. 'Lady Anne,' he says. 'There are reports circulating in London that there has been grave wrongdoing in your household. The king has commanded that we investigate. Anyone attempting to hide anything or failing to assist our investigation will be regarded as an enemy to the king, and guilty of treason.'

'We are all good subjects of our lord the king,' I say quickly. I can hear the fear in my own voice. He will hear it too. 'But there is no wrongdoing in my household, I am innocent of any wrongdoing.'

He nods. Presumably Kitty Howard said the same; as did Culpepper and Dereham.

'These are trying times and we have to root out sin,' he says simply. 'If you please you will stay in this room, with this lady as companion if you wish, while we question your household. Then we will come to speak with you.'

'My ambassador should be informed,' I say. 'I am not to be treated as an ordinary woman. My ambassador will need to know of your inquiry.'

The man gives me a smile. 'He is being questioned at his house right now,' he says. 'Or rather, I should say, at the inn where he stays. If I had not known that he was an ambassador for a great duke I should have thought him an unsuccessful merchant. He does not keep a great estate, does he?'

I flush with embarrassment. This again is my brother's doing. Dr Harst has never had a proper fee, he has never had a proper establishment. Now I am being taunted for my brother's meanness.

'You may question who you like,' I say as bravely as I can. 'I have nothing to hide. I live as the king bid me when we made our agreement. I live on my own, I entertain no more than is right and proper, my rents are collected and my bills are paid. As far as I can tell my servants are under good and sober discipline and we attend church and pray according to the king's rule.'

'Then you have nothing to fear,' he says. He looks at my white face and smiles. 'Please, do not be fearful. Only the guilty should show fear.'

I crack my lips into a smile and I go to my chair and sit down. His eye turns to the fallen crucifix and the cloth pulled down from the prie-dieu and he raises an eyebrow, shocked.

'You have thrown down the cross of Our Lord?' he whispers in horror.

'I had an accident.' Even to myself it sounds feeble. 'Pick it up, Lotte.'

He exchanges a glance with one of the other men as if this is evidence to be noted; then he goes from the room.

Katherine, Syon Abbey,
Christmas 1541

Let me see, what do I have now?

I have my six gowns still, and my six hoods. I have two rooms with a view over the garden, which runs down to the river where I can now walk if I wish; but I don't wish as it is freezing cold and rains all the time. I have a handsome fireplace of stone and a good store of wood is kept in for me as the walls are cold and when the wind blows from the east it is damp. I pity the nuns who had to live here for all their lives, and I pray God that I shall be released soon. I have a copy of the Bible and the prayer book. I have a crucifix (very plain, no jewels) and a kneeler. I have the reluctant attendance of a pair of maids to help me dress and Lady Baynton and two others to sit with me in the afternoon. None of them are very merry.

I think that is all I have now.

What makes it worse is that it is Christmastime, and I so love Christmas. Last year I was dancing with Queen Anne at court and the king was smiling at me and I had my pendant with the twenty-six table diamonds and my rope of pearls and Queen Anne brought me my horse with violet velvet trappings. I danced with Thomas every evening and Henry said we were the prettiest couple in all of the world. Thomas held my hand at midnight on Christmas Eve and when he gave me a kiss on the cheek he whispered in my ear: 'You are beautiful.'

I can still hear it, I can still hear his whisper: 'You are beautiful.' Now he is dead, they cut his sweet head from his body, and I may be still beautiful but I have not even a looking-glass to comfort me with that.

It may be a stupid thing to say, but more than anything else I am so surprised how much things have changed in such a short time. The Christmas feast when I was newly married and the most beautiful queen in the world was only last year, just this time last year, and now here am I in the worst state that I have ever known, and perhaps the worst state that anyone could be in. I think now that I am learning great wisdom that comes from suffering. I have been a very foolish girl but now I am grown to a woman. Indeed, I think I would be a good woman if I had a chance to be queen again. I really think I would be a good queen this time. And since my love, Thomas, is dead, I expect I would be faithful to the king.

When I think of Thomas dying for my sake I can hardly bear it. When I think he is no longer here, he is just gone, I cannot understand it. I never thought of death before, I never realised that it is so very, very final. I cannot believe that I will never see him again in this world. It quite makes me believe in heaven and I hope I will meet him there, and we will be in love again; only this time I won't be married.

I am sure that when they release me everyone will see that I am a better person now. I have not been tried as poor Thomas was tried, nor tortured as they tortured him. But I have still suffered, in my own foolish way. I have suffered thinking about him, and about the love we had, which has cost him his life. I have suffered thinking of him trying to keep our secret and fearing for me. And I miss him. I am still in love with him even though he is not in the world and cannot be in love with me. I am still in love with him even if he is dead, and I miss him like any young woman would miss her lover in the first few months of their love affair. I keep hoping to see him and then remembering that I will never see him again. This is more painful than I had thought possible.

Anyway, the only good thing to come out of this is that now there is no-one to give evidence against me since Thomas and Francis are both dead. They were the only ones who knew what took place and they cannot bear witness against me. This must mean that the king intends to release me. Perhaps in the New Year he will release me and I shall have to go and live somewhere terribly dreary. Or perhaps the king will forgive me now that Thomas is dead and he will let me be his sister like Queen Anne, and then at least I could come to court for the summer and for the Christmas feast. Maybe next Christmas I shall be happy again. Maybe I shall have wonderful presents next year and I shall look back on this sorrowful Christmas and laugh at myself for being so silly as to think my life was over.

The days are terribly long, even though it gets light so late and dark so early. I am glad that I am being ennobled by suffering because otherwise it would seem such a waste of time. I am throwing away my youth in this dull place. I will be seventeen next birthday, practically an old woman. It is shocking that I should have to wait for week after week in this place, as my youth drags away. I have kept a little counter of the days on the wall by the window and when I look at the scratched marks they seem to march onwards forever. Some days I miss a day and don't put it on, so that the time does not seem so long. But that makes the count wrong, which is a nuisance. It is so stupid not to be able even to keep count of the days. But I'm not sure that I really want to know. What if he keeps me here for years? No, that can't happen. I expect the king will spend Christmas at Whitehall and after Twelfth Night he will order them to release me. But I won't even know when that is, because I have muddled up my own counting. Sometimes I think my grandmother was right and I am a fool and that is very dispiriting.

I am afraid the king will still be very displeased with me, though I am sure he will not blame me for everything as Archbishop Cranmer seems to do. But when I see him, I am sure he will forgive me. He is like the duchess's old steward who would tell us all that we should be punished for some naughtiness like jumping in the hay or breaking the boughs of the apple trees, and he would beat one or two of the boys but when it came to me and I would look up at him with tears in my eyes, he would pat my cheek and tell me that I must not cry and it was all the fault of the older children. I expect the king will be like that when I actually get to see him. Surely, since he knows everything, he knows that I was always a silly girl and always very easily led astray? And surely, in his wisdom, he will understand that I fell in love and couldn't help myself? Someone as old as he is must understand that a girl can fall in love and quite forget right and wrong? A girl can fall in love and think of nothing but when she can next see the boy she loves. And now that poor Thomas has been taken from me and I will never see him again, surely I have been punished enough?

Jane Boleyn, the Tower of London, January 1542

And so we wait.

The king must be minded to forgive the whore his queen, since he waits for so long. And if he forgives her, he forgives me, and I escape the axe again.

Ha ha! What a joke my life has become that I should end up here in the Tower where my husband was kept, awaiting the fate that met him, when I could have walked away from court and the court life, when I could have been safe and snug in Norfolk. I had escaped once, escaped with my title and a pension. Why ever did I rush to come back?

I did truly think I would set him free. I did think that if I confessed everything on his behalf then they would see that she was a witch, as they called her, and an adulteress, as they called her, and they would see he was ensnared and enslaved and they would release him to be with me, and I should have taken him home to our house, Rochford Hall, and made him well again, and we could have had our children and we could have been happy.

That was my plan, that was what should have happened. I did think that she would go to the block and he would be spared. I did think I would see her lovely neck hacked in two but that I would have my husband safe in my own bed at last. I thought I would comfort him for the loss of her and that he would come to see that she was no great loss.

Not really.

No, not really.

I suppose sometimes I thought that she would be killed and it would be her deserts for the scheming whore she was, and that he would die too and it would be her fault, and he would realise on the gallows that he should have left her and loved me. That I had always been his true wife and she was always a bad sister. I suppose I thought that if it took him to get to the very steps of the gallows to see what a false friend she was, then it was worth doing. I never really believed that they would die and I would never see them again. I never really believed that they could disappear from my life, from this life, and I would never see them again. How could one think that? That there could be a day when they would never stroll through the door, arm in arm, laughing at some private joke, her hood as high as his dark curly head, her hand on his arm, equally assured, equally beautiful, equally regal. The cleverest, wittiest, most glamorous couple at court. What woman, married to him, and looking at her, would not wish them both dead rather than walking forever, arm in arm, in their beauty and their pride?

Oh, God, I hope that spring comes early this year, the dark afternoons are like a nightmare that goes on forever in this little room. It is dark till eight in the morning and then dusk by three. Sometimes they forget to replace the candles and I have to sit by the fire for light. I am cold all the time. If spring comes early and I can see the morning light coming up golden over the stone windowsill then I will have lived through these dark days, and I can be sure that I will live to see others. By my reckoning – and who knows the king better than I? – if he does not have her beheaded by Easter, then he will not have it done at all.

If he does not have her beheaded by Easter then I will escape, because why would he spare her and kill me who is accused with her? If she keeps her wits about her and denies everything then she could live. I hope that someone has told her that if she denies

Culpepper but says that she was married in the sight of God to Dereham then she can live. If she declares herself Dereham's wife then she has not then cuckolded the king but only Dereham; and since his head is on London Bridge he is in no position to complain. I could laugh, it is such an obvious escape for her, but if no-one tells her of it then she might die for the lack of wit.

Dear God, why would I, who was sister to Anne Boleyn, ever plot with such a half-wit as that slut Katherine?

I was wrong to put my faith in the Duke of Norfolk. I thought that we were working together, I thought that he would find me a husband and that I would have a great match. I know now that he is not to be trusted. I should have known that before. He used me to keep Katherine in check, and then he used me again to put her in the way of Culpepper. And now he has gone to the country and his own stepmother, her son, and his wife are here in the Tower somewhere, and they will all die for their parts in entrapping the king. He will not lift a finger to save his stepmother, he will not lift a finger to save his little niece; God knows, he will not lift a finger to save me.

If I survive this, if I am spared this, I shall find some way to report him for treason and I shall see him confined to one room, living in daily terror, waiting for the sound of them building the scaffold below the window, waiting for the keeper of the Tower to come and say that tomorrow is the day, and tomorrow he will die. If I survive this I shall make him pay for what he said to me, for what he called me, for what he did to them. He will suffer in this little room as I am suffering now.

When I think of this happening to me, I could go mad with terror. My only comfort, my only safety, is that if I go mad with terror, they will not be able to execute me. A madman cannot be beheaded. I could laugh if I were not afraid of the sound of my laughter echoing off the walls. A madman cannot be executed, so at the very end of this, if it goes as badly as it might, I shall escape the block where

Katherine dies. I shall pretend to be mad and they will send me back to Blickling with a keeper, and slowly I shall recover my wits.

Some days I rave a little so that they can see I have the tendency. Some days I cry out that it is raining, and I let them find me sobbing because the slates outside my window are shining with the wet. Some nights I cry out that the moon is whispering happy dreams to me. I frighten myself, to tell the truth. For some days, when I am not acting mad, I think that I must be mad, I must have been mad, quite mad, perhaps since my childhood. Mad to marry George who never loved me, mad to love and hate him with such a passion, mad to find such intense pleasure in thinking of him with a lover, mad to bear witness against him, maddest of all to love him with such jealousy that I could send him to the gallows . . .

Stop, I must stop. I can't think about this now. I cannot have this before me now. I am to act mad. I am not to drive myself mad. I am to pretend to madness, not feel it. I shall remember that everything I could do to save George, I did do. Anything anyone says against that is a lie. I was a good and faithful wife and I tried to save my husband and my sister-in-law. And I tried to save Katherine too. I cannot be blamed if the three of them were all as bad as each other. Indeed I should be pitied for having such ill luck in my life.

Anne, Richmond Palace,
February 1542

I am seated in a chair in my room, my hands clasped in my lap, three lords from the Privy Council before me, their faces grave. They have sent for Dr Harst at last, so this must be the moment of judgement after weeks of questioning my household, seeing my household accounts, and even talking to my stable boys about where I ride out, and who goes with me.

Clearly, they have been inquiring as to whether I have secret meetings but whether they suspect me of plotting with the emperor, with Spain, with France or the Pope, I cannot know. They may suspect me of taking a lover, they may accuse me of joining a coven of witches. They have asked everyone where I have been and who regularly visits me. It is the company I keep that is the focus of their inquiry but I cannot know what is their suspicion.

Since I am innocent of plotting, lust or witchcraft, I should be able to hold my head up and declare my conscience clear, but there is a girl far younger than me on trial for her life and there are men and women of absolute purity burned to death in this country merely for disagreeing with the king about the raising of the Host. Innocence is not enough any more.

I hold up my head anyway, for I know that when a power far greater comes against me, whether it be my brother in his wanton cruelty, or the King of England in his vain madness, it is always

490

better to keep my head up and my courage high and wait for the worst that can come. Dr Harst, by contrast, is sweating, there are beads on his forehead and every now and then he mops his face with a grubby handkerchief.

'There has been an allegation,' says Wriothsley pompously.

I look at him coolly. I have never liked him nor he me, but by God, he serves Henry. Whatever Henry wants this man will deliver to him with a veneer of legality. We shall see what Henry wants now.

'The king has heard that you have given birth to a child,' he says. 'We were told that a boy was born to you this summer and has been hidden away by your confederates.'

Dr Harst's jaw drops almost to his chest. 'What is this?' he asks.

I keep my own face completely serene. 'It is a lie,' I say. 'I have known no man since I parted from His Grace the king. And as you yourself proved then: I did not know him. The king himself swore I was a virgin then, I am a virgin still. You may ask my maids that I have not borne a child.'

'We have asked your maids,' he replies, he is enjoying this. 'We have questioned every one of them and we have received very different answers. You have some enemies in your household.'

'I am sorry to hear it,' I say. 'And I am at fault for not keeping them in better order. Sometimes maids lie. But that is my only fault.'

'They tell us worse than this,' he says.

Dr Harst has flushed scarlet, he is gulping for air. He is wondering, as I am, what could be worse than a secret birth? If this is the preparation for a show trial and an accusation of treason then the case is being carefully built against me. I doubt that I can defend myself against sworn witnesses, and someone's newborn baby.

'What could be worse?' I ask.

'They say that there was no child, but that you pretended to give birth to a son, a boy, and that you have assured your confederates that this is the king's child and heir to the throne of England. You plan with treasonous Papists to put him on the throne of England and usurp the Tudors. What do you say to this, madam?'

My throat is very dry, I can feel myself searching for words, hunting for a persuasive reply, but nothing comes. If they want to, they can arrest me now, on this allegation alone. If they have a witness to say that I pretended to give birth, that I claimed it was the king's child, then they have a witness to prove that I am guilty of treason and I shall join Katherine at Syon and we will die together, two disgraced queens on one scaffold.

'I say it is untrue,' I reply simply. 'Whoever has told you this is a liar and a false witness. I know of no plot against the king, and I would be party to nothing against him. I am his sister and his faithful subject as he bid me to be.'

'You deny that you have horses waiting to take you to France?' he says in a sudden rush.

'I deny it.' As soon as the words are out of my mouth I realise this is a mistake, for they will know that we have horses waiting.

Sir Thomas smiles at me, he knows he has caught me. 'You deny it?' he asks again.

'They are waiting for me,' Dr Harst says, his voice trembling. 'I have debts, as you know, I am ashamed to say that I have many debts. I thought if my debtors became too pressing that I should go quickly to Cleves and speak to my master for more money. I have had the horses waiting in case my debtors came for me.'

I look at him in absolute incredulity. I am amazed at the quickness of his lie; but they cannot know that. He bows. 'I beg your pardon, Lady Anne. I should have told you. But I was ashamed.'

Sir Thomas glances at the two other councillors, they nod to him. It is an explanation, if not the one they would have preferred.

'So,' he says briskly. 'Your two servants who made up this story against you have been arrested for slander and will be taken to the Tower. The king is determined that your reputation shall be unsullied.'

The shift is almost too much for me. It sounds as if I am to be released from suspicion, and at once I think it is a trick. 'I am grateful to His Majesty for his fraternal care,' I say carefully. 'I count myself his most loyal subject.'

He nods. 'Good. We will go now. The council will want to know that your name has been cleared.'

'You are leaving?' I ask. I know that they hope to catch me in a moment of relief. They do not know how deeply afraid I am. I don't think I will ever celebrate my escape, for I will never trust it.

In a dream I rise from my chair and walk with him from the room, we go down the great stairs to the front door where his escort is waiting, mounted with the royal standard before them. 'I trust the king is well,' I say.

'His heart is broken,' Sir Thomas says frankly. 'It is a bad business, a bad business indeed. His leg is giving him much pain and Katherine Howard's behaviour has caused him great unhappiness. The whole court has been in mourning this Christmastide, almost as if she were dead.'

'Will she be released?' I ask.

He shoots me a quick, guarded look. 'What do you think?'

I shake my head, I am not such a fool to speak my thoughts, especially not when I have just been on trial myself.

If I ever did tell the truth I would say that I have thought for some months that the king is out of his wits and that no-one has the courage to challenge him. He could release her and take her back as his wife, he could call her his sister or he could behead her, as the mood takes him. He could summon me for marriage or he could behead me for treason. He is a monstrous madman and nobody but me seems to know it.

'The king will be judge,' he says, confirming my silent thoughts. 'He alone is guided by God.'

I laugh, I skip about, sometimes I look out of the window and talk to the seagulls. There is to be no trial, no questioning, no chance to clear my name, so there is no advantage to having my wits about me. They do not dare put that idiot Katherine before a court, or she has refused to go, I don't know which and I don't care. All I know is what they tell me. They speak very loudly to me, as if I were deaf or old, rather than mad. They say that parliament has passed an act of attainder against Katherine and against me for treason and conspiracy. We have been judged and found guilty without trial, without judge or jury or defence. This is Henry's justice. I look blank and giggle, I sing a little song and ask when we shall go hunting. It can't be long now. In a few days I expect them to fetch Katherine from Syon and then they will behead her.

They send the king's own doctor, Dr Butt, to see me. He comes every day and sits in a chair in the centre of my room and watches me from under thick eyebrows as if I were one of the beasts. He is to judge if I am mad. This makes me laugh out loud without pretence. If this doctor knew when someone was mad he would have locked up the king six years ago, before he murdered my husband. I curtsey to the good doctor, and dance around him, and laugh at his questioning when he asks me for my name and for my family. I am absolutely convincing, I can see it in his pitying gaze. Undoubtedly he will report to the king that I am out of my wits and they will have to release me.

Listen! Listen! I hear it! The noise of saws and hammers. I peep out of the window and I clap my hands as if delighted to see the workmen building the scaffold: Katherine's scaffold. They will behead her under my window. If I dare, I can watch it all happen. I shall have the best view of everyone. When she is dead they will send me away, probably to my family at Blickling, and then I can quietly and secretly grow sane again. I shall take my time, I want no-one inquiring after me. I shall dance about for a year or two, singing songs and talking to clouds, and at the end of it, when the new king, King Edward, is on the throne and the old scores forgotten I shall return to court and serve the new queen as well as I can.

Oh! There's a plank gone down with a clatter and a young man cuffed for carelessness. I shall set up a cushion on the window-ledge and watch them all day, it is as good as a masque at court to see them measuring and sawing and building. What a fuss to make about building such a stage when the show will last for only a few minutes! When they bring me my dinner I clap my hands and point and the warders shake their heads and put down the dishes and go quietly away.

Katherine, Syon Abbey,
February 1542

It is a morning like every other morning, quiet, nothing to do, no entertainment, no amusement, no company. I am so bored with everything and with myself that when I hear the tramp of feet on the path outside my window, I am absolutely delighted at the thought of something happening – I am beyond caring what. I run like a child to the tall window and I look out, and there is a royal escort marching up the path through the garden from the river. They have come by barge, and there is my uncle the duke's standard, and there are the men in his livery, and there he is himself, looking powerful and bad tempered as always, at the head of them, and half a dozen Privy Councillors with him.

At last! At last! I am so relieved that I could weep to see them. It is my uncle returned to me! My uncle come back to tell me what to do. At last I am to be freed. At last he has come for me and I am to be released. I should think I shall be taken by my uncle to one of his houses in the country, which will not be very amusing, but better than here. Or perhaps I shall have to go far away, perhaps France. France would be wonderful, except I cannot speak French or at any rate only *'voilà!'* but surely they must mostly all speak English? And if not, then they can learn?

The door opens and the warden of my household comes in. His eyes are filled with tears. 'Madam,' he says. 'They have come for you.'

'I know!' I say jubilantly. 'And you needn't pack my gowns either for I don't care if I ever see them again, I shall order new. Where am I going?'

The door opens a little wider and there is my uncle himself, looking stern as he must, for this is obviously to be a very solemn scene.

'Your Grace!' I say. I can hardly stop myself giving him a wink. So we have got through, have we? Here we are again. Him, looking stern; and me, waiting for my orders. He will have some plan to have me back on the throne and forgiven within a month. I thought I was in grave trouble and that he had deserted me; but here he is, and wherever he goes, prosperity always follows. I take a good look at his face as I come up smiling out of my curtsey and I see he is looking terribly solemn, so I look serious too. I cast my eyes down and I look wonderfully penitent. I am quite pale from being indoors all the time and I really think that with my eyes down and my lips slightly pouting I must look utterly saintly.

'Your Grace,' I say in a soft, mournful tone.

'I bring you news of your sentence,' he says.

I wait.

'The king's parliament has consulted and has passed a Bill of Attainder against you.'

If I knew what this is, I would know better how to respond. As it is, I think it best just to widen my eyes and look agreeable. I suppose that a Bill of Attainder is some kind of official forgiveness.

'The king has given his assent.'

Yes, yes, but so what? What does this mean for me?

'You will be taken to the Tower and you will be executed in private on Tower Green as soon as may be. Your lands and goods are forfeit to the Crown.'

I really have no idea what he is talking about. Besides, thanks to his poor protection of my royal fortune, I now have no lands and goods to speak of anyway. I haven't forgotten Thomas Seymour

497

taking my own jewels away from me as if they were still belonging to his sister.

The duke looks a bit surprised at my silence. 'Do you understand?'

I say nothing but still look saintly.

'Katherine! Do you understand?'

'I don't know what attainted means,' I confess. It sounds like a joint of meat that has gone off.

He looks at me as if I am a half-wit. 'Attainder,' he corrects me. 'Not attainted. Attainder.'

I shrug. Who cares how it is said? Does it mean that I go back to court?

'It means that parliament has sentenced you to death and the king has given his assent,' he says quietly. 'It is to be done without trial. You are to die, Katherine. You will be beheaded on the green in the Tower.'

'Die?'

'Yes.'

'Me?'

'Yes.'

I look at him. He must have a plan. 'What should I do?' I ask him in a whisper.

'You should acknowledge your sins, and ask for forgiveness,' he says promptly.

I am so relieved I could almost weep. Of course I will be forgiven if I say I am sorry. 'What should I say?' I demand. 'Tell me exactly what I must say.'

He produces a rolled sheet of paper from the pocket of his jacket. He always has a plan. Thank God for him, he always has a plan. I unroll it and look at him. It is dreadfully long. He nods to me, apparently I have to read it all. I start to read out loud.

The first paragraph is me acknowledging my very great crime against the king, against the most high God and the whole English nation, which I think is rather an exaggeration since all I did was what hundreds of other young women do every day, especially when they are married to old, disagreeable men; and in my case I had been very unkindly treated. Anyway, I read the words on the paper and the duke nods and the councillors with him nod too, so it is obviously the right thing to say, and everyone is pleased with me, which is always the best way to be. I wish he had given me a copy of this earlier to practise with. I like to do things right when people are watching. I unroll the scroll to the next section and I say that I implore His Majesty not to impute my crime to my kindred and family but to extend his unbounded mercy and benevolence to them all so that they don't suffer for my faults.

I give my uncle a hard look at this, for it is clear to me that he is making sure that he does not suffer for my troubles. His expression is perfectly bland. Then I ask the king to give my clothing to my maids after my death as I have nothing else to give them. This is so sad that I find I can hardly read it aloud. Fancy that! Me, with all I have owned, with nothing to give! Fancy me giving my clothes away because I will never wear them again! And how ridiculous to think that I would care a groat about what happens to those vile six gowns, six pairs of sleeves, six kirtles and six French hoods without a single jewel, in the most miserable colours I can imagine. They can burn them on a bonfire for all I care.

But despite the gowns and my uncle saving his own skin, by the time I have finished my speech I am weeping at the sadness of it, and all of the councillors look very grieved and it is a poignant scene that they can report to the king, and I have no doubt but that he will be moved at the thought of me begging pardon for others and giving away my little wardrobe. It is so sad that it makes me cry, although I know that it's all make-believe. If I thought it was true I would break down altogether.

My uncle nods. I have done what he wants and now it is up to him to persuade the king that I am utterly penitent and ready for death. That should be all anyone can ask for, I should think. They all troop off the way they came and I have to sit myself down in my one chair, in my dull gown, and wait for them to come back and tell me that since I am so very sorry I am quite forgiven.

I am waiting for the barge this time, I am up at the window from terribly early in the morning. Usually, with nothing to get up for and nothing to do, I try to sleep through breakfast all the way till dinner, but today I am certain that they will come with my royal pardon and I want to look my best. As soon as it is light I ring for my maid to come and lay out my dresses. Hmm, such a choice I have before me! I have a gown of black, two of very dark blue, almost black, a gown of dark green that it is almost black, a gown of grey, and just in case I need two, another gown of black. So what shall I wear? However shall I choose? I take the gown of black but I wear it with the dark green sleeves and a dark green hood that will symbolise my penitence and my love of Tudor green to those who take an interest in these things. It makes my eyes look beautiful as well, which is always a good thing.

I don't know how this will be done, and I always rather like to be prepared for these ceremonies. My master of the household always used to tell me where I should stand and how I should look, and I like to practise. It comes from being made queen while still quite young, and not really brought up to it. But as far as I know, no queen has ever been forgiven for adultery and treason and all the rest of it, so I suppose we shall just have to make it up as we go along. At any rate, that old wolf my uncle will no doubt guide me through it all.

I am dressed and waiting by nine in the morning but nobody comes. I hear Mass and take breakfast in sulky silence and still nothing. But then, just before noon, I hear the welcome tramp of feet on the stones of the path and I dash to the window, see my uncle's black square hat bobbing along, the staves of office in the hands of the other councillors, the royal standard before them, and I rush back to my seat and sit down, put my feet together, my hands in my lap, and cast down my eyes in great penitence.

They open the double doors and everyone comes trooping in, dressed in their best. I rise to my feet and curtsey to my uncle as I should, since he is head of my house, but he no longer bows to me as his queen. I stand and wait. I am surprised he doesn't look more relieved that this is all over.

'We have come to take you to the Tower,' he says.

I nod. I had thought we would go to Kenninghall but perhaps this is even better, the king often uses the Tower as his London palace, perhaps I am to meet him there. 'As you wish, my lord duke,' I say sweetly.

He looks a little surprised at my demure tone. I have to try very hard not to giggle.

'Katherine, you are to be executed,' he says. 'You will go to the Tower as a condemned traitor.'

'Traitor?' I repeat.

'I told you last time,' he says impatiently. 'You were convicted by a Bill of Attainder. I told you. You are not required to stand trial, you understood that. You confessed your sins. That confession has been entered against your name. Now the time has come for the sentence.'

'I confessed so that I would be forgiven,' I point out.

He looks at me quite exasperated. 'But you have not been forgiven,' he says. 'All that was left to agree was the sentence.'

'And?' I say a little pertly.

He takes a deep breath as if to dispel his irritation. 'His Grace has agreed that you shall be put to death.'

'He will forgive me when I get to the Tower?' I suggest.

To my increasing anxiety he shakes his head. 'For God's sake, girl, don't be such an idiot! You cannot hope for that. There is no reason to hope for it. When he first heard what you had done, he drew his sword and said he would kill you himself. It is over, Katherine. You must prepare yourself for death.'

'That can't happen,' I say. 'I'm only sixteen. Nobody could put me to death when I'm only sixteen.'

'They can,' he says bleakly. 'Believe me, they will.'

'The king will stop them.'

'It is his own wish.'

'You will stop them.'

His eyes are as cold as a fish on a marble slab. 'I will not.'

'Well, somebody must stop them!'

He turns his head. 'Take her,' he says.

Half a dozen men march into the room, the royal guard who used to parade so handsomely for me.

'I shan't go,' I say. I am really afraid now. I stand to my tallest height and I scowl at them. 'I shan't go. You can't make me.'

They hesitate a little, and look at my uncle. He makes a quick chopping gesture with his hand. 'Take her,' he says again.

I turn and run into my privy chamber, swinging the door behind me, but it delays them for only a moment, they catch it before it bangs, they are after me so quickly. I lay hold of one of the posts of the bed and I latch my fingers around it. 'I shan't go!' I shout. 'You can't make me. You can't touch me! I am Queen of England! Nobody can touch me!'

One of the men grabs me around the waist. The other reaches forwards and unlaces my hands, as soon as my hands are free I slap the first one round the face as hard as I can and he lets me go, but a third man grabs me again and the second has my hands this time so though I struggle, he forces them behind my back and I hear one of the sleeves tear. 'Let me go!' I scream. 'You can't hold me. I am Katherine, Queen of England. You can't touch me, my person is sacred. Let me go!'

My uncle stands in the doorway, his face as dark as the devil. He nods to a man standing beside me, who bends down and grabs at my feet. I try to kick him but he takes me as if I were a little bucking foal and the three of them shuffle out of the room with me held between them. My ladies are in tears, the warden of my household is white with horror.

'Don't let them take me!' I scream. Mutely, he shakes his head. I see he is clinging to the door to support himself. 'Help me!' I scream. 'Send for –' I break off then, for there is no-one to send for. My uncle, guardian and mentor is standing by, this is being done under his orders. My grandmother and sisters and stepmother are all under arrest, the rest of the family are frantically insisting that they hardly knew me. There is no-one who will defend me, and no-one has ever loved me but Francis Dereham and Tom Culpepper and they are dead.

'I can't go to the Tower!' I am sobbing now, the breath shaken out of me by their big, bouncy strides with me slung between them like a sack. 'Don't take me to the Tower, I beg you. Take me to the king, let me plead with him. Please. If he is determined I'll go to the Tower then, I'll make a good death then, but I'm not ready yet. I'm only sixteen. I can't die yet.'

They don't say anything, they march up the gangplank to the barge and I give a little wriggle thinking I might throw myself into the water and get away, but they have huge hands and they hold me tightly. They sling me on to the dais at the back of the barge and they all but sit on me to keep me still. They have hold of my hands and my feet, and I am crying now and begging them to take me to the king, and they look away, out over the river, as if they are deaf.

My uncle and the councillors come on board, looking like men going to their own funeral. 'My lord duke, hear me!' I shout, and he shakes his head at me and goes to the front of the barge where he can't hear or see me.

I am so afraid now that I can't stop crying, the tears are pouring down my face and my nose is running and that brute has hold of my hands and I can't even wipe my face. It is cold where my tears are wet on my cheeks and the disgusting taste of snot is on my lips, and they won't even let me wipe my nose. 'Please,' I say. 'Please.' But nobody listens at all.

The barge goes quickly downriver, they have caught the tide just right, and the oarsmen feather their blades so they catch the safest part of the current at London Bridge. I glance up, I wish I hadn't, at once I see the two new heads, two fresh severed heads, Tom Culpepper and Francis Dereham, like damp, soft gargoyles, their eyes wide open and their teeth bared, a seagull struggling to find its footing on Dereham's dark hair. They have set their heads on the spikes beside the horrible rotting shapes of so many others, and the birds will peck out their eyes and tongues, and poke sharp beaks in their ears to winkle out their brains.

'Please,' I whisper. I don't even know what I am begging for now. I just hope that this will stop. I just want it not to be happening. 'Please, good sirs . . . please.'

We go in by the watergate, it rolls up silently as soon as the guards see us coming, and the oarsmen ship their oars and our boat glides into the dock inside the dark shadow of the wall. The Lieutenant of the Tower, Sir Edmund Walsingham, is standing at the steps, waiting to greet me as if I were arriving to stay in the royal apartments, as if I were still queen and a pretty new queen at that. The portcullis splashes down behind us as the chains roll it down, and they lift me out of the barge and take both my arms and heave me up the steps, my feet stumbling.

'Good day, Lady Katherine,' he says, as polite as ever. But I say nothing because I cannot stop sobbing, little gasping sobs that come and go with every breath. I look back and my uncle is standing on the barge, waiting to see me go. He will be out of the watergate like a wherry shooting the rapids the moment his duty is done. He will be desperate that the shadow of the Tower does not fall on him. He will be rushing back to the king to assure him that the Howard family has given up their bad girl. It is me who is going to pay the price for the Howard ambition; not him.

I scream, 'Uncle!' but he just gives a gesture of his hand as if to say, 'take her away', and they do. They lead me up the stairs, past the White Tower, and across the green. The workmen are building a platform on the lawn, a little wooden stage standing about three foot high, with broad steps going up to it. Others are fencing off the paths. The men on either side of me walk a little faster and look away, and this makes me absolutely certain that this is my scaffold, and the fence is to hold back the crowd who will come to see me die.

'How many people will come?' I ask, the little coughing sobs make it hard for me to breathe.

'A couple of hundred,' the warden says uncomfortably. 'It is not open to the public. Just to the court. As a favour to you. The king's own orders.'

I nod, it is not much of a favour, I think. Ahead the door of the tower opens before us and I go up the narrow stone stairs with one man slightly ahead of me hauling me up and the other pushing from behind. 'I can walk,' I say and they let go of my arms but stay close beside me. My room is on the first floor, the large glazed window overlooks the green. There is a fire in the grate, there is a stool by the fire and a table with a Bible, and beyond that there is a bed.

The men let me go and stand by the door. The warden and I look at each other. 'Shall you be wanting anything?' he asks.

I laugh out loud at this most ridiculous question. 'Like what?' I ask.

He shrugs. 'Some delicacy, or some spiritual comfort?'

I shake my head. I don't even know if there is a God any more, for if Henry is special in the sight of God and he knows God's will then I suppose God wants me to die, but in private as a special favour. 'I should like to have the block,' I say.

'The block, my lady?'

505

'Yes, the executioner's block. Can I have it here in my room?'

'If you wish . . . but . . . what do you want it for?'

'To practise,' I say impatiently. I go across to the window and I look down. The green will be filled with people who were proud to be at my court, people who were desperate to be my friend. Now they will be watching me die. If I am to do it, I had better do it properly.

He gulps. Of course he doesn't understand what I mean, he is an old man, he will die in his bed with his friends watching his last breath. But I shall be watched by hundreds of critical eyes. I want to do it gracefully if I have to do it.

'I shall have them bring it at once,' he says. 'And will you see your confessor now?'

I nod. Though if God knows everything already, and already has decided that I am so bad that I should die before my seventeenth birthday, it is hard to know what the point of confession might be.

He bows and goes from the room. The soldiers bow and close the door. The key turns in the lock with a great clunk. I go and look out of the window at the workmen and the scaffold below. It looks as if they will be finished by tonight. Perhaps they will be ready tomorrow.

It takes two of them to bring in the block with much huffing and puffing as if it were heavy, and many sideways glances at me as if I am rather peculiar in needing to practise. Really, if they had been Queen of England like me, when I was still a girl, then they would know what a comfort it is to get the ceremonies right. There is nothing worse in the whole world than not knowing what you are supposed to do and looking foolish.

I kneel before the great thing and put my head down on it. I can't say it's very comfortable. I try it with my head turned one way and then the other. There's no vast improvement in either direction, and no change of view anyway as I will be blindfolded, and underneath the blindfold I shall have my eyes tight shut, hoping

506

like a child that it isn't happening. The wood is smooth, cool under my hot cheek.

I suppose I really do have to do this.

I sit back on my heels and look at the damned thing. Really, if it were not so dreadful, I could laugh. All along I thought I had the Boleyn inheritance of grace and beauty and charm, and it turns out that all I have inherited is this: her block. This is the Boleyn inheritance for me. *Voilà*: the executioner's block.

Jane Boleyn, the Tower of London,
13 February 1542

She is to be beheaded today, already the crowd is gathering on the green. Looking from the window I can see so many faces I know. These are friends and rivals who go back years and years with me, we were children together when Henry VII was on the throne, and some of us were ladies at the court of Queen Katherine of Aragon. I wave merrily and a couple of them see me, and point, and stare.

Here comes the block now! They have had it tucked away somewhere and two of the workmen heave it up to the scaffold and spread the sawdust around it. That's to catch her blood. Beneath the scaffold is a basket filled with straw to catch her head. I know all of this, for I have seen it before, more than once. Henry has been a king who has used the headsman very often. I was there at the beheading of Anne Boleyn, I saw her walk up those shallow steps to the scaffold, and stand before the crowd, and confess her sins and pray for her soul. She looked over our heads to the Tower gate, as if she were waiting for the pardon that she had been promised. It never came and she had to kneel down and put her head on the block and stretch out her arms as a signal that the sword could come down. I've often wondered what it must be like, to fling your arms out as if you were flying, and the next moment hear that swish and feel the hair on the back of your neck lift with the wind of the passing blade and then . . .

Well, Katherine will know soon enough. The door behind me opens and a priest comes in, very grave-looking in his vestments, with a Bible and a prayer book hugged to his chest.

'My child,' he says. 'Are you prepared for the hour of your death?'

I laugh out loud, and then it sounds so convincingly mad that I laugh again. I cannot tell him that he is mistaken and that I cannot be sentenced to die, because I am insane, but I point at him and say, 'Hello! Hello! Hello!' very loudly.

He sighs and kneels down on the floor before me, folds his hands together and closes his eyes. I skip away from him to the far side of the room and say, 'Hello?' But he starts the prayers of confession and penitence and pays no attention to me at all. Some fool has told him that I am to be prepared for death, and I suppose I shall have to go along with it since I can hardly argue with him. I suppose at the last moment they will come and commute the sentence to imprisonment. 'Hello!' I say again and climb up to the window-ledge.

There is a stir in the crowd, and everyone is craning to look at the door at the foot of the tower. I stand up on my toes and push my face against the cold glass so that I can see what they are all looking at. It is her: little Kitty Howard, staggering to the scaffold. Her legs seem to have given way, she is being carried between a guard and a woman in waiting, and they half drag her to the steps and then her little wavering feet wander about and they have to bodily lift her and push her up to the stage. I laugh at the incongruity of this, then I catch myself at the horror of laughing at a girl, almost a child, on the way to her death. Then I realise it sounds as if I am mad, and I laugh again for the benefit of the priest, praying for my soul in the room behind me.

She looks as if she has fainted, they are slapping her face and pinching her cheeks, poor little mite. She stumbles to the front of the stage and clutches the rail and tries to speak. I can't hear what she says, I doubt anybody can hear much. I can see her lips, it looks as if she is saying: 'Please'.

She falls back and they catch her and push her into kneeling before the block, she clings to it, as if it might save her. Even from here I can see she is weeping. Then gently, just as she does at bedtime, as if she were a little girl settling down to sleep, she strokes a lock of her hair away from her face with her hand, and puts her head down on the smooth wood. She turns her little head and lays her cheek on the wood. Tentatively – as if she wishes she didn't have to do it – she stretches out her trembling hands and the headsman is in a hurry and his axe flashes down like a bolt of lightning.

I scream at the great gout of blood and the way her head bounces on the platform. The priest behind me falls silent, and I remember that I must not forget my part, not for a moment, and so I call out: 'Kitty, is that you? Is that you, Kitty? Is it a game?'

'Poor woman,' the priest says, and gets to his feet. 'Give me a sign that you have confessed your sins and die in faith, poor witless thing.'

I jump down from the windowsill for I hear the grate of the key in the lock and now they will come to take me home. They will take me out of the back door and hurry me to the watergate and then, I guess, by unmarked barge, probably to Greenwich and then perhaps by boat to Norwich. 'Time to go,' I say merrily.

'God bless her and forgive her,' the priest says. He holds out his Bible for me to kiss.

'Time to go,' I say again. I kiss it, since he is so urgent that I should, and I laugh at his sad face.

The guards stand either side of me and we go quickly down the stairs. But when I expect them to turn away to the back of the tower they guide me to the front entrance, to the green. I check at once, I don't want to see Katherine Howard's body being wrapped up like old laundry, then I remember I have to appear mad, right up to the last moment when they put me on the boat, I have to appear so witless that I cannot be beheaded.

'Quick, quick!' I say. 'Trot, trot!'

The guards in reply take my arms and the door is swung open.

The court is still assembled, almost as if they are waiting for another show on the bloodstained stage. I don't like to be taken through them, past my friends who were honoured to know me. In the front row I see my kinsman, the Earl of Surrey, looking a little queasy at the sawdust drenched in his cousin's blood, but laughing it all off. I laugh too and look from one guard to the other. 'Trot! Trot!' I say.

They grimace as if this is disagreeable and they tighten their grip and we walk towards the scaffold. I hesitate. 'Not me,' I say.

'Come along now, Lady Rochford,' the man on my right says. 'Come up the steps.'

'No!' I protest, I dig my heels in, but they are too strong for me. They move me on.

'Come on now, there's a good girl.'

'You can't execute me,' I say. 'I am a madwoman. You can't execute a madwoman.'

'We can,' the man says.

I twist in their grip, when they march me to the steps I get my feet against the first tread and push off from it, and they have to wrestle to get me up one step. 'You can't,' I say. 'I am mad. The doctors say I am mad. The king sent his own doctors, his own doctors every day to see that I am mad.'

'Had the law changed, didn't he?' one of the guards puffs. Another fellow joins them and is pushing me from behind. His hard hands in my back propel me up the steps to the stage. They are lifting the wrapped body of Katherine off at the front, and her head is in the basket, her beautiful golden-brown hair spilling over the side.

'Not me!' I insist. 'I am mad.'

'He changed the law,' the guard shouts at me over the laughter of the crowd, which has cheered up at this battle to get me up the steps. 'Changed the law so that anyone convicted of treason could be beheaded, whether mad or not.'

'The doctor, the king's own doctor, says I'm mad.'

'Makes no difference, you're still going to die.'

They hold me at the front of the stage. I look out at the laughing, avid faces. Nobody has ever loved me in this court, nobody will shed a tear for me. Nobody will protest against this new injustice.

'I am not mad,' I shout. 'But I am completely innocent. Good people, I beg you to implore the king for mercy. I have done nothing wrong but one terrible thing, one terrible thing. And I was punished for that, you know I was punished for it. Nobody blamed me for it but it was the worst thing a wife could do . . . I loved him . . .' There is a roll of drums which drowns out everything but my own crying. 'I am sorry, I am sorry for it . . .'

They drag me back from the rail at the front of the stage and they force me down into the stained sawdust. They force my hands on to the block, which is wet with her blood. When I look at my hands they are as red with blood as if I am a killer. I will die with innocent blood on my hands.

'I am innocent,' I shout. They wrestle the blindfold on me so I can see nothing. 'I am innocent of everything. I have always been innocent of everything. The only thing I ever did, the only sin ever, was against George, for love of George, my husband George, God forgive me for that – I want to confess . . .'

'On the count of three,' the guard says. 'One-two-three.'

Five years later

Anne, Hever Castle,
January 1547

So, he is dead at last, my husband who denied me, the man who failed the promise of his youth, the king who turned tyrant, the scholar who went mad, the beloved boy who became a monster. It was only his death that saved his last wife, Katherine Parr, who was to be arrested for treason and heresy; but death, which had been his ally, his partner and his pander for so long, finally came for him.

How many did the king kill? We can start to count now that death has stilled his murderous will. Thousands. No-one will ever know. Up and down the land the burnings in the market place for heresy, the hanging at the gallows for treason. Thousands and thousands of men and women whose only crime was that they disagreed with him. Papists who held to the religion of their fathers, reformers who wanted the new ways. Little Kitty Howard among the dead, whose only crime was that she loved a boy of her own age and not a man old enough to be her father, and rotting from the leg upwards. This is the man they call a great king, the greatest king that we have ever had in England. Does it not teach us that we should have no king? That a people should be free? That a tyrant is still a tyrant even when he has a handsome face under a crown?

I think of the Boleyn inheritance that meant so much to Lady

Rochford. She was the heir, in the end. She inherited the death of her sister-in-law, of her husband. Her inheritance and poor Kitty's, was death on the scaffold, just like them. I have a share of the Boleyn inheritance too, this pretty little castle set in the Kent countryside, my favourite home.

So it is over. I shall wear mourning for the king, and then I shall attend the coronation of the prince, the little boy I loved, now to be King Edward. I have become what I promised myself I would be, if I was spared Henry's axe. I promised myself that I would live my own life, by my own lights, that I would play my part in the world as a woman in my own right; and I have done this.

I am a free woman now, free from him and finally free from fear. If there is a knock on my door in the night I will not start up from my bed, my heart hammering, thinking that my luck has run out and that he has sent his soldiers for me. If a stranger comes to my house I will not suspect a spy. If someone asks me for news of the court I will not fear entrapment.

I will own a cat and not fear being called a witch, I will dance and not fear being named a whore. I shall ride my horse and go where I please. I shall soar like a gyrfalcon. I shall live my own life and please myself. I shall be a free woman.

It is no small thing, this, for a woman: freedom.

Author's Note

Anne of Cleves and Katherine Howard are the two wives of Henry VIII that we know least; as is so often the case, we think we know them well. In this fictional account of the real facts I have tried to get past the convention that one wife was ugly and the other stupid, to consider the lives and circumstances of these two very young women who were, so briefly, the most important women of England, successive wives to a man on the brink of madness.

The main historical facts of the characters are as I describe them here. I could discover little detail about Anne of Cleves' childhood; but I thought the illness of her father and the dominance of her brother were interesting in the light of her later decision to take her chance on staying in England. Her prettiness and her charm were widely reported at the time and are shown in the painting by Holbein. I believe it was the disastrous meeting at Rochester that caused Henry to reject her out of grievously wounded vanity. The conspiracy to accuse her of witchcraft, or treason, as an alternative to divorce is well documented, especially by the historian Retha Warnicke, and was clearly as much of a lie as other evidence about her marriage given to the inquiry.

Katherine Howard's childhood is better known, but drawn almost wholly from evidence given against her. My fictional account explores the historical facts and my bias is towards understanding Katherine as a young girl at a court of far older and more sophisticated people. Her surviving letter to Thomas Culpepper shows, I believe, a very young girl sincerely in love.

The character of Jane Boleyn, Lady Rochford, is drawn from history – few novelists would dare to invent such a horror as she seems to have been. She did indeed give the crucial evidence that led to the beheading of her husband and sister-in-law, and there seems to be no explanation for this but jealousy and a determination to preserve her inheritance. She was at the deathbed of Jane Seymour, and gave evidence that could have been used to send Anne of Cleves to the scaffold (as I describe). The evidence against her and her own confession clearly show that she encouraged Katherine Howard's adultery, fully understanding the fatal danger to the young queen. The suggestion that she did this with the purpose of getting the queen pregnant is my own. I suggest that she pretended madness in the hope of escaping the scaffold, but I hope I show, both in this book and in *The Other Boleyn Girl*, that Jane Boleyn was never wholly sane.

On my website philippagregory.com there is a family tree and more background information about the writing of this novel.

The following works have been invaluable in the research for this book:

Baldwin Smith, Lacey, *A Tudor Tragedy, The Life and Times of Catherine Howard*, Jonathan Cape, 1961

Bindoff, S. T., *Pelican History of England: Tudor England*, Penguin, 1993

Bruce, Marie Louise, *Anne Boleyn*, Collins, 1972

Cressy, David, *Birth, Marriage and Death: Ritual Religions and the Life-cycle in Tudor and Stuart England*, OUP, 1977

Darby, H. C., *A New Historical Geography of England before 1600*, CUP, 1976

Denny, Joanna, *Katherine Howard, A Tudor Conspiracy*, Portrait, 2005

Elton, G. R., *England under the Tudors*, Methuen, 1955

Fletcher, Anthony, *Tudor Rebellions*, Longman, 1968

Guy, John, *Tudor England*, OUP, 1988

Haynes, Alan, *Sex in Elizabethan England*, Sutton, 1997

Hutchinson, Robert, *The Last Days of Henry VIII*, Weidenfeld and Nicolson, 2005

Lindsey, Karen, *Divorced, Beheaded, Survived, A Feminist Reinterpretation of the Wives of Henry VIII*, Perseus Publishing, 1995

Loades, David, *The Tudor Court*, Batsford, 1986

Loades, David, *Henry VIII and His Queens*, Sutton, 2000

Mackie, J. D., *Oxford History of England: The Earlier Tudors*, OUP, 1952

Mumby, Frank Arthur, *The Youth of Henry VIII*, Constable and Co., 1913

Plowden, Alison, *The House of Tudor*, Weidenfeld and Nicolson, 1976

Plowden, Alison, *Tudor Women: Queens and Commoners*, Sutton, 1998

Randall, Keith, *Henry VIII and the Reformation in England*, Hodder, 1993

Robinson, John Martin, *The Dukes of Norfolk*, OUP, 1982

Routh, C.R.N., *Who's Who in Tudor England*, Shepheard-Walwyn, 1990

Scarisbrick, J. J., *Yale English Monarchs: Henry VIII*, YUP, 1997

Starkey, David, *Henry VIII: A European Court in England*, Collins & Brown, 1991

Starkey, David, *The Reign of Henry VIII: Personalities and Politics*, G. Philip, 1985

Starkey, David, *Six Wives: The Queens of Henry VIII*, Vintage, 2003

Tillyard, E. M. W., *The Elizabethan World Picture*, Pimlico, 1943

Turner, Robert, *Elizabethan Magic*, Element, 1989

Warnicke, Retha M., *The Marrying of Anne of Cleves*, CUP, 2000

Warnicke, Retha M., *The Rise and Fall of Anne Boleyn*, CUP, 1991

Weir, Alison, *Henry VIII: King and Court*, Pimlico, 2002

Weir, Alison, *The Six Wives of Henry VIII*, Pimlico, 1997

Youings, Joyce, *Sixteenth-Century England*, Penguin, 1991

The Other Boleyn Girl
Philippa Gregory

Two sisters competing for the greatest prize . . . the love of a king.

Mary Boleyn catches the eye of Henry VIII when she comes to court as a girl of fourteen. Dazzled by the golden prince, Mary's joy is cut short when she discovers that she is a pawn in the dynastic plots of her family. When the capricious king's interest wanes, Mary is ordered to pass on her knowledge to her friend and rival: her sister, Anne.

Anne soon becomes irresistible to Henry, and Mary can do nothing but watch her sister's rise. Anne stops at nothing to achieve her own ambition. From now on, Mary will be no more than the other Boleyn girl. But beyond the court is a man who dares to challenge the power of her family to offer Mary a life of freedom and passion. If only she has the courage to break away – before the Boleyn enemies turn on the Boleyn girls . . .

'This compulsively readable novel is a wonderful account of the Tudor court. This is the finest historical novel of the year.'
Daily Mail

'The very believable dialogue and detail takes you all the way into the claustrophobic privy chambers of the royal palaces.'
The Times

ISBN 0-00-651400-6